THE FIRST BOOMERANG

A Spiritual Odyssey

———

PAUL BRYDEN

ETT IMPRINT
Exile Bay

This edition published by ETT Imprint, Exile Bay 2021

First published by ETT Imprint in 2018. Reprinted 2018

ETT IMPRINT
PO Box R1906
Royal Exchange NSW 1225
Australia

Copyright © Paul Bryden 2018

ISBN 978-1-925706-48-2 (ebook)
ISBN 978-1-925706-49-9 (paper)

Design by Hanna Gotlieb
Cover photograph by Paul Bryden

AUTHOR'S NOTE

In 1976 I made and threw my first boomerangs and a 'window' into Australia's Aboriginal culture opened. In that year I travelled to Alice Springs and met a local Aboriginal watercolour artist. Then in 1983 I visited Cairns to meet a Mornington Island artist known for bark paintings, and later flew to Broome and shared special days with two highly respected elders. Since then I've had the privilege of meeting custodians and boomerang craftsmen from various regions, some of whom I'm still in touch with. I gained valuable information from them about traditional subjects and enjoyed many good times, but *The First Boomerang* is a work of fiction, except for historical details, created from my thoughts, intuition and experiences.

Traditionally, Aboriginal peoples had no written languages, their cultures maintained by oral tradition. "Language" words therefore are usually interpretations made by linguists after interacting with native speakers. In the text I've written English names first, followed by language names. For example Ayers Rock *(Uluru)*, which is well known, and Anzac Hill *(Atnelkentyarliweke)* that's hardly known at all. As well as difficult pronunciation, spellings change. For example *Arunta, Aranda, Arrarnta and Arrernte* have been, or still are, used to name

Aboriginal clans in and around Alice Springs. For the story I prefer *Aranda,* as does the Elder, because it is easier to pronounce at first attempt than *Arrernte,* the most recent version. Unfortunately, my use of "language" words is not consistent because spellings vary, but I urge the reader's indulgence! Also, because of respect for Aboriginal culture and the complexity of skin names and kinship systems, I gave the Elder a European name only.

Dreaming Track, a translation of *"Tywerrenge impatye,"* also has alternate spellings and describes pathways made by Ancestral Beings in Aboriginal country along which ceremonies are performed. Its widely used name is Songline, and the Elder and Rob Noble use it most often. The idea that Rob, a caucasian Australian, was Aboriginal in a passed life may surprise some readers. However, reincarnation was well known to many clans. I spoke with a traditional owner about this subject and he told me: *"When a child was born they used to look for marks (birthmarks) which may suggest a spear wound from the last life."*

Synchronicity played its part while I was writing. One example occurred when Rob was in Alice Springs after beginning his quest and the Araluen Arts Centre was hosting *The Yuendumu Doors* exhibition. On one painted door he saw a Dreamtime story that featured "comeback" boomerangs. This surprising discovery added real intrigue because returning boomerangs were never used by Aboriginal clans in Central Australia!

In Chapter 3 Rob travels with Rock Art researchers to Ewaninga *(Napwerte)* Conservation Reserve and they take photos and record video of the rock engravings. Even though a fictional trip, it occurred several years before the site's custodians stopped allowing filming or photography.

Finally, most of the action, apart from earlier historical events, is set in the year 2000. This means that some names and other references may have changed since then, however they do not detract from the plot, themes and characters of the story.

Paul Bryden, March 2018

I lovingly dedicate this book to my late parents
Les and Daphne Bryden

ACKNOWLEDGEMENTS

I wrote this story on and off over many years, so it is next to impossible to thank by name everyone who contributed. This includes friends and professionals who read sections or the entire text, edited a page or a chapter, enhanced it by formatting, guided my searches in libraries, encouraged me by asking "how's the book," confirmed information, especially about Central Australia, made original suggestions, and offered to buy a copy well before its publication.

My warm-hearted thanks to each of you who helped in those and all other ways, and to the great people I met during my research trips, as well as the Elders in spirit.

Many thanks also to writers of the numerous books and periodicals - published over the last 200 years or so - which I browsed or read completely for background.

Books I've quoted from are *Moon and Rainbow* by Dick Roughsey (A.H. & A.W. Reed, 1971), *Flinders Ranges Dreaming* by Dorothy Tunbridge (Aboriginal Studies Press, 1988) and *Lardil – Keepers of the Dreamtime* by D. McKnight (Chronicle Books, 1995), their words much appreciated.

I've also quoted from the "Dreamtime" books by Charles P. Mountford & Ainslie Roberts, and from *Dreamtime Heritage* by Melva Jean

Roberts (ETT Imprint 2021). Special thanks to Rhys Roberts, Ainslie Robert's son, who graciously gave his permission and made this possible.

And finally I wish to acknowledge the author who wrote: *"If the letter 'h' is taken off the end of the word 'earth' and placed in front, the word 'heart' is formed."* You'll see it on page 68, however, I cannot remember where or when I found it, so I offer my apologies, but please get in touch after reading this! I can be contacted at www. thefirstboomerang.com

CONTENTS

PART ONE

Return to Country

Part One — Return to Country

1

Rob was soaking lazily in the spa bath after a busy day working in a native art gallery on East 57th Street. Indulging like this was rare so he stretched out his long legs and relaxed completely. Suddenly a ringtone broke the silence, jolting him out of his watery bliss. Easing himself up he stepped out, dripping suds onto the marble tiles and picked up the phone.

"Hello?"

"G'day there. Is that you Rob? This is Hugo catching up from Sydney."

"Yes, Hugo. What a surprise. Great to hear your voice."

"I'm really pleased you're there Rob, and great to hear yours too. I did get your last email, but apologies, it's been a while."

"Yeah, for sure. But I understand. We all get busy."

Rob Noble had been overseas for three years including the last four months in New York. The big city was fascinating but overwhelming, a total contrast to the vast emptiness of Patagonia and rugged terrain of Tierra del Fuego where he had recently been hiking. Rob and Hugo Ableford met in Australia five years earlier while bushwalking in the Blue Mountains west of Sydney. Although not best friends they had a good personal rapport and shared a profound interest in Australia's Aboriginal culture which transcended their age difference. Rob was thirty one and Hugo was sixty three.

"I've finally got that big trip to tell you about," Hugo continued. "I'm taking a small group up the Tanami Track and into the Kimberley, then across to the Victoria River District in the Territory. We'll record Rock Art, meet traditional owners, and be out bush for about a month. Are you still interested?"

A surge of adrenaline instantly transported Rob to the Outback's rich red soil, endless wide horizons, and the vivid orange sunsets he loved so much. The spirit of that country meant everything to him. Painted and engraved figures on remote sandstone overhangs also flashed into mind, and he saw himself in the picture, reconnecting with Aboriginal culture.

"Yes! fantastic! Count me in!" Rob exclaimed. He was not going to miss this opportunity. "Give me the time and place and I'll be there."

"That's great Rob, I knew you'd jump at the chance. We're leaving from Alice Springs in sixteen days – that's June 27th. I know it's short notice, but I'll email all details including where we're staying in town. How's that sound?"

"Perfect Hugo, absolutely perfect. Thanks a million. See ya later. Bye."

Rob was ecstatic. He felt like running around the apartment, but sat on the edge of the spa trying to gather his racing thoughts. He had been dreaming about this for a long, long time. Now the desire to be there felt urgent. His love for Australia and Aboriginal culture lay deep in his bones and a rare chance to see Rock Art 'face to face' ignited both heart and soul.

Rob was well aware that a trip like this was not for the faint-hearted and home comforts would be left behind. The expedition would go far beyond the remotest towns on the map, on rugged dirt tracks or no tracks at all. But that was mere detail. He loved the bush. He was used to roughing it like he had just done in southern Chile and Argentina.

But it wasn't really roughing it. He enjoyed sleeping under the stars, much more than sleeping for too long in a big city apartment.

The Australian adventurer often day-dreamed about the Outback, especially when late Winter winds chilled Manhattan to its architectural bones and the snow in street gutters was crunched and blackened by constant traffic. Those were the times when Rob floated over vast red-brown landscapes in the 'hot-air balloon' of his imagination, marvelling at Ayers Rock (*Uluru*) and The Olgas (*Kata Tjuta*), two of the earth's most compelling natural cathedrals. Still thinking non-stop, he wrapped a thick white towel around his waist and hurried to the bedroom to get dressed.

Rob was living with Clara Beaumont whom he'd met in Miami, Florida after arriving from South America and accepting her invitation to "come visit". His feelings for Clara had developed quickly and he wanted to explain why the trip was so important without feeling guilty. Leaving her for a while would be hard, but he could not possibly miss this journey.

Clara was 5 feet 8 inches tall with dark eyes and long, straight black hair. Her good looks and warm heart typified her part-Chilean heritage, she had just turned thirty, and worked as a graphic designer in an advertising agency. Clara also freelanced her skills, completing projects for private clients, and rented the fifth floor apartment with the spa bath in midtown Manhattan.

Rob picked up the phone again and pressed a well-used contact.

"Hello sweetheart. Hope your work's going well."

"Yes honey, I'm busy but it sure is," Clara replied.

"Listen, I've just had a call from Hugo, an old friend, and he's invited me back home to join an Aboriginal Rock Art expedition."

Rob heard Clara catch her breath as he continued. "I've got to meet them in Alice Springs in two weeks." Sensing Clara's anxiety he quickly added, "The expedition's for four weeks and I'll take a few days to catch up with old mates. I'll be back in five weeks. It'll go really fast."

On the other end of the phone Clara was not convinced, but knew this was what Rob had been hoping for. "I've been dreading this call and I'll miss you the whole time, but I know this is important to you. I can't talk now honey. Let's talk about it properly tonight," she added affectionately.

"Okay, let's do that. See you later. Love you." Rob ended the call and took a deep breath, relieved that he had contacted Clara. He felt she did understand his desire to go, and would reluctantly give her blessing, and he admired her for that.

* * *

The thrilling long-distance call from Hugo reinvigorated Rob's spirit. Years of imagining himself back in the Outback must have resonated in the Cosmos, and now the Universe had delivered.

Born in coastal Wollongong south of Sydney, Rob's curious spirit compelled him to travel after completing a Bachelor of Arts degree in which he majored in Oceania Anthropology. During 1991 he made the epic 3,000km train journey from Sydney to Perth on the "Indian-Pacific", and explored Central Australia on a coach camping trip, his first in-depth experience of the Outback. Rob was inspired by the landscape's raw, diverse beauty and the beliefs and stories of Aboriginal people. He felt connected spiritually to those worlds and knew he would return one day.

Rob was 6 feet 3 inches tall with broad shoulders and sandy-coloured hair, the product of an English-Scandinavian heritage. At university he won medals in Athletics and his stamina was a bonus when hiking in challenging conditions. His fascination with different cultures, customs and languages had taken him to many parts of the world.

He made London home for a couple of years, working in various jobs and visiting regional museums, including the Pitt Rivers Museum in Oxford, to view Aboriginal collections. It was surprising to him that so much material from Australia was hidden away in institutions, most not even having enough staff to catalogue the stored artefacts. Why don't they send some of these precious items back to Australian Museums and Aboriginal Cultural Centres, he thought to himself at the time.

* * *

Aboriginal culture and its expressions in art, ceremony and daily life embrace the entire natural world, including stars and planets. Hundreds of clans speaking their own traditional languages occupied diverse climatic regions throughout Australia and adapted success-fully. Across the Outback, where Winter temperatures can range from below freezing to 30 degrees Celsius in the same day, Rob would feel at home again. He had a keen interest in the links between Aboriginal life and the Cosmos, a perfect theme to pursue under Australia's dia-mond-studded skies.

Rob could now give his imagination wings and explore canvasses of sky and earth called *home* by Aboriginal clans. He would walk the same country and feel the vibrations of Ancestors peering out from their resting places in the landscape. He would learn about Songlines, see where the Rainbow Serpent travelled, and watch stars and constel-lations sparkle into life as day turned into night.

Rob was totally thrilled. He had been offered a once-in-a-lifetime opportunity to help record the oldest art in the world, and as a result learn more about culture from local Aboriginal people he would meet in remote communities. The Universe had heard his heart calling.

* * *

Over the next week Rob prioritised his list of tasks. He first com-pleted his bookings on American Airlines to Los Angeles and Qantas to Sydney, Ayers Rock Resort and Alice Springs.

Rob then turned his attention to clothing and equipment. He knew how to travel light, and unless going to extreme locations, the same range of gear suited most conditions in most places. The key was to dress in layers, adding or taking off when wind and temperatures changed. The gear he used in the southern Andes in late Summer and early Autumn would be similar for Australia's Outback Winter. He packed his favourite pair of charcoal-coloured hiking shorts, two pairs of khaki long pants that zippered off at the knees to convert to shorts, one pair of running tights for extra cold days, and high quality walking boots with vibram soles and leather uppers for easy cleaning. Also, two vests and tee-shirts, two long-sleeved shirts, a rainproof, waist-length red and green jacket, and a thin but tough orange plastic poncho to cover body and backpack if caught in the rain, was all he needed.

Rob's other gear was just as important, especially because he would be recording at Rock Art sites. He made sure his still camera and camcorder were clean and ready to shoot vast and varied landscapes, sunsets and sunrises, time-lapse star trails and engraved and painted images on stone surfaces. He checked all batteries, made sure he had the correct adaptors for Australia's 240 volt electricity supply, finally double-checking his laptop which he used for emailing and storing files of research notes.

Clara had projects on the go but arranged some time off so they could be together before departure day. Rob particularly wanted to see the Hayden Planetarium again and because it was close to Central Park they planned to combine the two venues.

Occupying a part of the American Museum of Natural History the Hayden Planetarium is a beacon for lovers of the Cosmos. Rob and Clara hailed a yellow taxi outside her apartment building, and after a direct but lengthy drive uptown, enjoyed two virtual hours beyond earth, marvelling at nebulae, galaxies and constellations that dwarf our blue planet.

They followed these spectacular journeys in the cosmic wonderland with a walk in Central Park, holding hands playfully and admiring trees and gardens that provide oxygen to a hectic and non-stop Manhattan metropolis.

At the end of the day they returned to the apartment a little tired but happy and sat together sipping a favourite wine and talking about Rob's plans and hopes for his trip. He was excited by the prospects, yet also feeling very relaxed at this stage of the day and shared a personal story with Clara.

"I've had a recurring dream for years now, even once down in Tierra del Fuego. It always involves an Aboriginal elder handing me a sacred object called a tjurunga or churinga, as part of my initiation into manhood. I've never told anyone. You're the first to know."

"Thanks honey, that's real special," Clara said, squeezing his arm as they snuggled closer on a cosy, fashionable lounge.

"The other part is quite gruesome because the elder and other men use sharp pieces of quartz to cut lines into my chest and upper arms. It hurts like hell, but I'm not allowed to scream, and blood flows everywhere. I usually wake up when the pain really bites. But overall it's positive, because I feel I belong."

"That's so powerful Rob. Is it the same elder each time?"

"His face is never clear, but I think so because his voice is always the same."

"That helps me understand why you've talked so much about Aboriginal culture. You're so deeply connected. Now I really get your excitement for the trip."

Rob was happy and relieved that Clara fully realised how important the trip was to him. They hugged and kissed the long kiss of lovers who have just reached a new level of understanding. Clara had learned more about Rob, and he felt more deeply appreciated. Their last night together was a beautiful, intimate expression of how much closer they had become.

* * *

The next morning arrived too quickly and Clara was trying to keep the mood light-hearted as they said their farewells at John F. Kennedy International Airport.

"Does the water really flow down the plug hole the opposite way Down Under?" She asked without any enthusiasm. They had both been quiet during the taxi ride out to the airport and Rob knew that Clara was close to tears.

"As long as I've got enough water to drink on the expedition, I don't care which way it goes!" Rob chuckled weakly.

They kissed and held each other tightly. Rob responded warmly but his mind was already speeding through visions of Outback landscapes, his anticipation beginning to burn inside as he added, "You know, I might even find that Aboriginal elder! Wouldn't that be fantastic. See you later sweetheart."

"Bye honey, take care," Clara replied, tears now visible on her cheeks. She clung to his outstretched hand and brought it up to her lips for a final kiss.

Then he was gone. Through the main entrance of the customs section, on his way to Australia with mixed feelings about leaving Clara behind, but barely containing his excitement about the adventure that lay ahead.

2

Rob was flying from Sydney to Uluru and drifting off amidst the constant engine noise of a Qantas Boeing 737-400 cruising at 38,000 feet. After more than half the trip, endless expanses of red-brown landscape veined by network after network of dry, black watercourses dominated the view far below. Rob tried to focus on the horizon in the hazy blue distance, but his eyes closed and he slipped into another time and place.

Overnight dew had dampened the red soil that lay on the unmarked track to the sacred cave, until the first bare foot of the first man pushed gently into it. The earth was fresh and alive. He was leading a group of five fully initiated elders who had left camp early to go and prepare the sacred objects that were hidden and stored safely in a distant corner of their country. There was no well-worn track to follow because the cave was only visited about three times each year, yet these men walked as if signposts guided them. Knowing the correct direction is what western man might call "second nature". Yet in the Aboriginal men's reality it was "first nature", because they and the trees, the rocks and the tracks, seen and unseen, were all One. They also lived in the Now, or Present, a challenging concept for most modern urbanised people.

The custodians' walk to the cave coincided with the coming Full Moon, a common indicator for certain ceremonies including some initiations. They had names for a dull moon, a bright moon, a crescent moon, and the Full Moon was called 'Taye impanke' by the Western Aranda people. The moon and the planets, in fact the entire Cosmos had always offered them rich worlds of story and creation.

The traditional countries of the Aranda clans were defined in the most ancient days, in the Dreamtime or Beginning when Ancestral Beings created whole worlds of nature, people, and the laws by which they lived. From an enormous black sky bursting with galaxies and legends, including the starry campfires of departed brothers and sisters, traditional men, women and children were given meaning for daily life. They upheld their Ancestral laws, passing them on to each successive generation by spoken word and rhythmical dance.

The senior men were getting closer to the secret location. Even though it was early morning the heat was rising fast, and the temperature was already well above half of the maximum it would climb to later. They kept to the shade of the trees where possible and moved quietly and purposefully. Nearing the cave the five men stopped without any signal from the leader. He then held up both hands with palms upturned and spoke aloud, alerting the Ancestor Spirits that they were approaching...

Rob opened his eyes as if he had just woken from a dreamy sleep. The landscape below looked the same and there was no change either in the constant engine sound. The dream-like vision had seemed so real, and his mouth was dry as if he had been walking to the cave. He pressed the flight attendant button, and soon after a neatly uniformed and smiling lady delivered a small plastic glass of water and ice. As he sipped the cold drink he tried to gather his thoughts and emotions about the vision and what may lie ahead.

Nearly ten years had passed since he visited 'the Red Centre' as Australians often call it. Rob always wanted to return and this trip was a rare opportunity to explore Aboriginal Rock Art under the biggest star-filled skies. He also hoped to talk to local Aborigines and hear their stories of the constellations. In Rob's research he had discovered connections between the night skies and timeless legends. Now he wanted to sit and talk to the elders who knew traditional ways and ask his questions.

* * *

Before Europeans arrived and had devastating impacts on Aboriginal people's lives, clans throughout the continent maintained cultural laws through storytelling and ceremony. Rob had been fortunate to find some early contact references to Aboriginal Cosmology while at university, even though little had been recorded. He was surprised by the detail and originality with which they described stars and constellations. Fascinating connections existed between these stories and daily life, and in some areas even kinship groups were directly linked to specific stars.

This valuable information helped Rob professionally when he was working at an auction house in Sydney. He introduced Cosmology and other aspects of culture when they were featured in artworks, including bark paintings. The most well-known character was the Rainbow Serpent whose story and illustrated image vary throughout Australia, but which is recognised universally as the world's oldest religious symbol.

Naturally, many birds and animals are linked in story to the land and sea, and some are linked to the stars. For example *Otjout* the cod fish made the winding Murray River which forms the border between Victoria and New South Wales, and is linked to Constellation Delphinus. Another tells of *Gallerlek* the rose-crested cockatoo which is a symbol of Alderbaran, a binary star in Constellation Taurus. He played a major role in the legend of the Seven Sisters. Variations of this story occur throughout Australia, but it mainly tells the tale of beautiful young women chased by lustful men on earth and into the sky back to Constellation Pleiades, their home.

Rob was always surprised by the unimaginable scale of these stories. How did the old Aboriginal people know so much about the Sky-World? He discovered that some legends contained astronomical mysteries, and he was very keen to discuss them with traditional men. And yet, the knowledge he may gain would not be complete because he was a whitefella from a different culture and could never find out everything.

Rob also had questions about the intriguing tjurunga he examined in the Royal Albert Memorial Museum in Exeter, England. He definitely wanted to talk about them, but there was no guarantee anyone would discuss 'sacred business' with a stranger. Even so, Rob was quietly confident he would learn a lot because he was sincere and respectful. He was not trying to exploit Aboriginal people, but wanted to form friendly associations which he sensed would deepen throughout his trip.

* * *

After three hours of flying through endless blue skies and hovering white clouds, Rob caught his first glimpse of Uluru sitting majestically alone on the flat landscape. The huge, mystical monolith captivated him and he was compelled to stare, drawn in by unseen energies. These were special moments for Rob because Uluru was the spirit of his country, his Australia. He had not been back for a decade, yet when he travelled and experienced different cultures, this sacred, awe-inspiring site was ever-present in his heart. Known locally as *"The Rock,"* ancient Uluru was his old friend, and its magnetic attraction had released him to take other journeys, until today. But unfortunately he could only make a brief stopover, so an in-depth encounter would have to wait.

As the Qantas jet came in to land at Ayers Rock Airport unexpected sprinkles of rain streaked across its small passenger windows, and Rob strained his eyes and neck to keep Uluru in sight. Every drop of rain was welcome in this arid country, and the light sun shower continued as he and other passengers walked briskly across the tarmac and into the terminal. They only had time for a quick look around because in about twenty minutes they would board their connecting flight to Alice Springs.

Rob always knew he would return to Central Australia. The call of its unique landscape and timeless spirituality resonated strongly within wherever he lived in the world. Now, today, he really was back. Seeing Uluru again confirmed his return. Rob was home. His feelings were as simple and as comfortable as that.

The few spots of rain that had fallen out of nothing disappeared before Rob and the others walked out to board their flight. While waiting in the terminal he told several passengers that Alice Springs was about 450kms away by road, and they were very surprised. Most said they were pleased to be flying, although Rob assured them the drive was a fascinating close-up experience of the Outback. But today, like them, he just wanted to get there.

Rob had flown from the Big Apple, New York City, to the Big Rock, Central Australia, and in a few minutes would take-off on the last leg of his journey, a short flight of fifty minutes.

* * *

Alice Springs is an oasis of the Outback with an indefinable mystique that attracts people from all over the world. Bold geological forms and the rich, changeable colours of Dreamtime landscapes entice visitors to explore. Many locals lead the way by jumping into their 4WDs and going 'out bush' on camping trips, the wide land and big sky engendering a sense of freedom and adventure.

A fresh water spring in the famously dry Todd River (*Lhere Mparntwe*) gave rise to the European settlement called Stuart until 1933 when the name was changed to Alice Springs. The town sits in the middle of arid country yet is surprisingly abundant with trees, sports fields and recreational parks. Surrounded by large pastoral properties, Aboriginal communities on vast traditional lands, and immense orange-red country alive with stories, the Alice is the heart of a continent.

In local Aranda language it is Mparntwe or Mbantua meaning "meeting place" which it has been for thousands of years. And this tradition is ongoing because tracks of different kinds and from many different places still converge there today.

* * *

Rob's flight was on descent and only minutes away from the town's airport when he saw the magnificent MacDonnell Ranges (*Tyurretye*), unmistakable backbone of geologically ancient Central Australia. In traditional Aranda lore these ranges were created by three Caterpillar Ancestors, and this Aboriginal Dreaming and the Wild Dog Dreaming are perennial signatures of Alice Springs, as well as its oldest stories.

Flying in on wings of Winter sunshine, bright afternoon light created such clarity that the rock faces of the MacDonnells seemed touchable from Rob's seat. He could almost taste the invigorating fresh air outside. As feelings of 'coming home' bubbled up inside, Rob was filled with nostalgia. He did not fully understand these feelings, but his longing for this special region was only matched by his anticipation about the coming days.

3

Along Todd Mall Aboriginal Art galleries overflow with bright, multi-coloured dot-style paintings. They represent the world's latest art movement which only began in the 1970s, and first-time visitors stare at the exquisite designs on canvas and ponder their meanings. Few know that these captivating artworks symbolically depict Central Australian landscapes they have flown over or driven through. Or that others tell personal stories or Dreamings of traditional custodians, men and women they may walk past in the street.

Rob visited five galleries in the Mall before leaving its southern end and crossing Gregory Terrace. Continuing on Todd Street for almost a block he passed Desert Oak Tours, Outback Camping Safaris and Arunta Art Gallery & Book Shop, before discovering the Aboriginal Red Ochre Gallery. Displayed on its front brick wall was a sign advertising daily cultural tours and didgeridoo lessons.

"Hello there..." Rob offered in a friendly manner as he walked in.

Inside the stone-floored gallery, an older Aboriginal man was showing paintings to a young woman at the tile-topped counter.

"Morning, howya going," the manager replied, as both she and the artist greeted him with a smile and nod of the head.

The Aboriginal artist was talking about his works and they caught Rob's eye. The major local contemporary style was dot painting, but these were different. They were landscapes of Central Australia, true-to-life watercolours with ghost gums, distant purple hills and rugged rocky outcrops, evoking the Outback perfectly. Rob was familiar with this classic style because he owned several similar paintings, so he walked closer and commented.

"I love those colours, that clarity of light, the aura around the gum trees. They're beautiful. I feel at home just looking at them."

Rob felt comfortable in saying this to the Aboriginal artist and the older man turned to him and warmly acknowledged the compliment.

"Thanks. Thanks brother. I'm happy you've come."

Rob sensed something deeper about the greeting and also responded warmly.

"My name's Rob, I hope we can talk about your paintings while I'm in town."

"I'm Lindsay, but most call me 'Uncle' or 'the Elder.' Have you come far?"

"Yeah, from New York, but I'm Aussie."

"Good. Welcome. Let's catch up after I finish."

As well as dark jeans, leather riding boots and a long-sleeved flannelette shirt, patterned with small red and blue squares, the artist wore a fawn-coloured Akubra hat. The hand-made band was decorated with very small painted dots, and a solid silver heart about the size of a thumb nail was attached to its left side. Like any good hat, it became the man, and because of contrast, his grey sideburns looked even more distinguished.

The Elder and manager continued their discussion while Rob started to explore the Gallery, but after only fifteen minutes the Elder approached Rob and caught his eye.

"Thanks for waiting. Let's go if you're ready..."

They walked out of the Aboriginal Red Ochre Gallery, crossed Todd Street and sat down on short green grass in the shade of a tall, white-trunked eucalyptus tree. Taking off his hat and placing it on the ground, the Elder said...

"Welcome to Mparntwe or Mbantua, the Arrernte or Aranda name for Alice Springs. My full name's Lindsay Williams and I was born in Western Aranda country. Do you know Albert Namatjira? He was a Western Aranda man."

"Yeah, of course," Rob smiled confidently. "The first Aboriginal person to paint Outback landscapes with watercolours back in the 1930s, 40s and 50s."

"Uncle Albert was gifted," the Elder added. "He showed city people our country's real heart and spirit for the first time. And even met the Queen."

"Yeah, he was the best." Rob continued. "Isn't there a permanent exhibition of his paintings in town?"

"It's up at Araluen. Try and see it if you can."

"I will for sure," Rob confirmed, then asked, "What about your art?"

"I've been doing watercolours on and off for forty years. Started by myself with an uncle's help, but now there's a mob of us who love the style and want to keep the tradition going. Like Albert I'm from out near Hermannsburg, the old Lutheran Church Mission. We call it *Ntaria* and it's about 125kms west on a good bitumen road. Do you know that country?"

"Yeah, in a way. Central Australia always feels familiar," Rob replied.

"Albert's also honoured by Namatjira Drive. It branches off Larapinta Drive heading west and provides access to the superb gorges of the West Macs. You'd love it."

"Maybe I can get out there," Rob said, adding: "Do you do other work?"

"I'm a senior lecturer at the Faculty of Aboriginal Development, or FAD, so I live in town these days. It's connected to the Northern Territory University in Darwin. Have you heard of it?"

"No, but it sounds interesting," Rob replied.

"I've got to get back to the office soon, but we must talk again while you're in town. I can meet late tomorrow afternoon on Anzac Hill (*Atnelkentyarliweke*) – there's a great view of country in all directions."

"I'd love to," Rob said. "But I'll have to say 'Anzac Hill' because your name's too hard!"

"I know what you mean. Our languages are very difficult. I'm an old timer and I still prefer the spelling *Aranda* because people can pronounce it when they see it."

"Okay, I'll do the same. And thanks so much for the invite. I'll be there."

They got to their feet and shook hands, and Rob walked away quickly to the Heart of Australia Resort across a road bridge over the Todd River, shaking his head happily. He knew instinctively that Lindsay from Western Aranda country was the Aboriginal elder he'd been hoping to find for years. And suddenly it had happened.

The meeting was inspiring for the Elder too. As he walked steadily back to his faculty office he acknowledged within that Rob had come at precisely the right time. With insight as clear as the blue skies of his watercolours he knew Rob would gain important knowledge and be guided on a journey of discovery.

* * *

Earlier that morning at the Resort Rob picked up a message from Dr Hugo Ableford, leader of the Rock Art group, expressing his wish to discuss the expedition. The plan was to meet at a restaurant in an arcade off Todd Mall, so Rob wrote a quick note saying *"See you there"* and left it at Reception. Both men were looking forward to catching up in person because they had not seen each other since Rob flew to London three years earlier.

"Great to see you. How's New York?" Hugo asked, raising his eyebrows in anticipation as they warmly shook hands.

"Wonderful. So much energy in one corner of the planet. Who knows how it all keeps going." Rob replied. "Now I'm back, I'd much rather be here. The Centre does something for me." He added with understatement.

The two men had met for lunch at The Desert Oak which offered more international cuisine than local bush tucker, but all was homemade and delicious. Rob ordered Thai fish cakes, rice balls with cheese in the middle and green salad, while Hugo selected a wholesome chicken and vegetable soup served with hot multi-grain bread rolls and butter.

They took it in turns to catch up with each other's activities of the past few years, and after finishing their tasty food, Hugo told Rob the Rock Art group's plans.

"In the morning we're going out on a good dirt road to the Ewaninga site. Do you know it? There's hundreds of well-preserved petroglyphs in a protected area, and we'll be back by one or two o'clock. There's ten in the group and most want to go shopping and have a look around town. You're welcome to come."

"I'd like to, I've never been there." Rob said.

"Then in two and a half days we're off. As you know, it's to Yuendumu first up the Tanami Track, on to Halls Creek and Fitzroy Crossing, then across to Broome. After the old pearling town we take on the Gibb River Road and eventually reach Kununurra and Timber Creek. Then we'll head south into the VRD. Our co-leader actually re-discovered a lot of the art, and we'll be the first group to see it."

"That's epic," Rob interrupted. "How many people get that opportunity. I know it's taken a lot of organising."

"A couple of years Rob, so it's very good that you were able to come back," Hugo said genuinely. "You got the last seat, too!"

"Thanks to you. Your phone call really got me going. You must've known I've been talking to the Outback stars!" Rob winked and continued. "The Outback's always felt close since I first came through in the '90s. I don't think I need the big cities now. Oh, and I met an Aboriginal artist, we're meeting tomorrow afternoon. I'll tell you about it later."

They finished their coffee, agreed to 'go dutch' with the bill for old time's sake, then as they stood up Hugo added...

"I'm so pleased you've made it, and you're looking well too. We're all in the same Resort, so that makes it easy. Let's talk tomorrow, but if you're coming to Ewaninga we're meeting for breakfast at eight in the dining room and departing about nine."

"Sounds good. It's fantastic to be here," Rob smiled, shaking Hugo's hand. "Seeya later." He was so happy to link up with Hugo and the Rock Art group after so much anticipation and his long flight.

* * *

Rob planned to watch sunset from a rocky hill near the Resort, but as the afternoon unfolded, the western sky turned dark blue. Threatening storm clouds built up and rapidly approached Alice Springs. Jagged shafts of bolt lightning struck the countryside and thunder rumbled loud and long. This type of storm usually occurred in Summer so its abrupt arrival on a Winter's day was surprising. Suddenly an unusual thought popped into Rob's mind. Could its spectacular show be a *sign* from the Universe that meeting the Elder was an auspicious event? Rob had read enough about traditional Aboriginal life to know that unexplained things happened, but he was not sure if this was one of them.

* * *

On the following morning Hugo, Rob and the group drove to Ewaninga Conservation Reserve on a rusty red dirt road, firm and dust-free after the previous night's heavy showers. At the site they found hundreds of symbols pecked into large slabs of tan-brown sandstone, and the marked walking track presented opportunities for close-up viewing and photography. The atmosphere was still, there was no one else around and everything seemed straight forward until Hugo gestured to the group to come close, saying precisely and without introduction.

"This site embodies a mystery!"

Everyone standing around him eagerly focused on his next words.

"Even though Ewaninga's been studied for years, the petroglyphs have never been explained publicly. Senior custodians hold the knowledge of these rock carvings but will not reveal their meaning because it would be too dangerous!"

An instant buzz of conversation swept around the group, but Hugo, not wanting to answer any questions, said with a chuckle.

"Let's talk about it later, around a campfire under the stars somewhere."

This site visit was just a warm-up for the big Rock Art trip ahead, but already the group had been confronted with a puzzle. For Rob it came soon after his unusual thoughts about the Universe and the unseasonal storm, so he made a written note then finished his video recording and photography. Then he and the group returned to the Resort with an ancient, yet modern-day mystery fresh in their minds.

A brisk morning of about six degrees Celsius had become 24 degrees after lunch, as group members set out on foot to explore the famous town. Some walked through the sandy Todd River bed, others took the road bridge, all eventually meeting at Ghost Gums Bar & Grill for dinner. Later that afternoon was also the time when Rob and the Elder were to meet on Anzac Hill, and the natural atmosphere was changing.

* * *

The stormy, windy weather of the previous day had flung up a sky of long, wispy clouds, and thin beams of sunlight caught and coloured their tails a rich, burnt orange. The men had not arranged a time to meet but despite neither of them wearing a watch, they arrived at the bottom of Anzac Hill on Wills Terrace at the same time. As they walked up the track the elongated clouds brightened into a deep, desert red, becoming light-hearted scarves on a fading blue sky. Such colour promised another warm day in Central Australia. Sunset would not linger this afternoon because of Winter, so as soon as they made it to the top and were sitting on a wide seat facing the MacDonnell Ranges, the Elder asked an unexpected question.

"Do you know what tjurunga or churinga are?"

A little surprised by the subject matter, because he did know, Rob answered.

"They're sacred objects that link individuals to their Ancestors in spirit, and are only brought out at special times, like initiation ceremonies."

The Western Aranda elder nodded approvingly and seemed to confirm by the dancing light in his eyes that the right man had come. The Universe as usual was on course and on time!

Rob was encouraged by the comfortable energy and continued.

"I've been interested in sacred tjurunga for years without telling anyone. In England I visited a Museum and was shown small, wooden tjurunga and bullroarers with similar markings. I was in the basement wearing white gloves so the physical condition of each artefact wouldn't be damaged. Yet I was holding an object representing the spiritual link of a traditional man to the source of his life! What a privilege, but I didn't fully realise it. I couldn't interpret the incised designs, but I've been researching tjurunga quietly ever since."

Rob paused as he reflected on that episode, and the Elder commented straight away.

"Your intentions had integrity and Ancestor Spirits were watching. Handling the objects respectfully opened a deeper window to culture."

Rob nodded thoughtfully as the Elder added historical perspective.

"In early contact times some whitefellas who stole, or *collected* sacred objects as they called it, didn't know what they were handling. But others did and removed our objects like conquerors. They weren't interested in the ceremonial life of *"primitive natives"*. They only wanted curios of their adventures in the new British colonies in the South Seas."

Yet despite blatant disregard for Aboriginal cultures and the violence perpetrated against them for generations, the Elder believed positive changes in attitudes were growing across the world.

"Many more are becoming aware and learning that Aboriginal groups have the spiritual connections to the land, sea and sky that they want to experience. They realise that traditional cultures offer valuable perspectives about life and nature."

Then the Elder turned and looked directly at Rob.

"You've travelled conscious spiritual paths for many lifetimes and returned to an old home. You've come back to receive information because the Ancestors know you can help reveal it to an awakening world. That's why we've met. That's why I said in the Gallery, 'Thanks brother. I'm happy you've come.' I knew you were the right man."

A natural break in the Elder's wise words gave Rob the chance to venture his thoughts.

"I didn't expect you to be so universal in outlook. People usually think particular groups hold particular knowledge, so they'd expect you to share Aboriginal knowledge only, and not other philosophies. How long have you thought like this?"

The sinking sun was colouring orange the few elongated clouds that hovered beyond Mount Gillen (*Alhekulyele*), its distinctive, familiar outline bathed in dark blue shadow as the Elder answered.

"The spiritual journey's similar whatever tradition we're born into. Race, colour, and language make things seem different, but the wisdom of all cultures belongs to everyone. That's my belief. I belong to my Aboriginal heritage and went through some of the Law, but I also respect other cultures. I've read about them for years. Everything from Buddhism and Taoism to the Mayans and Aztecs, Ancient Egypt, Christianity and more – you'd be fascinated by my library. My sense of peoples' Oneness is strong. Around the earth the same themes appear in legends and so-called mythology, so it's natural to feel part of the whole world."

"That's a wonderful outlook," Rob acknowledged.

Now much clearer about the Elder's philosophy, he knew he would gain much greater understandings if they spent more time together.

"Yeah, I suspected there were connections between Aboriginal cultures, but I was touched most when I realised that all Humanity is spiritually One. We're all brothers and sisters in heart and spirit. But not enough of us recognize it."

The Elder was nodding slowly in agreement, at peace with himself and the world, as Rob continued.

"It's so good to be sitting here. I'd forgotten how much I need this level of conversation. Life floods my soul when I share like this. But I've got a problem. I'm booked to go on a Rock Art Expedition in thirty six hours, but I want more of this!"

"Listen to your inner truth, the answer's already there," the Elder suggested.

4

A couple of days later the two men are many kilometres west of Alice Springs in the Elder's traditional country, crouching in the shade of a hardy mulga tree. Rob had rented a 4WD Toyota Landcruiser to travel to Western Aranda country whenever the Elder wanted to go. The vehicle was about five years old, white in colour, diesel-fuelled and a reliable workhorse. Similar vehicles are used all over the Northern Territory and Rob had negotiated a good deal with Outback Oz Rent-a-Car. He and the Elder had not yet driven on any dirt roads but they were sure to in the near future.

The Elder began to speak in his sincere and positive manner, as if there had been no interruption in their previous conversation.

"Returning to country was destiny. You came to join a Rock Art group but universal energy flows around us and within us and things happen that match where we're up to spiritually. A sign comes and the next step's possible. We don't always see signs, but you've wanted more knowledge since holding those tjurunga in England. I'm an instrument of the Universe and Ancestor Spirits to help guide your path."

Rob was comfortably tuning into the Elder's spiritual wavelength.

"Yeah, I wanted to find an elder with traditional knowledge, a senior man in tune with the big planetary picture. That's been my consistent, positive vision, so I'm not surprised we've met. Cosmic Timing's a fundamental part of the Universe and we're all affected by it, but it's challenging to be aware of every day."

The Elder nodded in agreement then changed the conversation's direction.

"If you talk about tjurunga and old knowledge people will react. Anthropologists, Museum academics, Aboriginal leaders, and even some of my mob will criticize you. They'll say you misrepresent culture and offend Aboriginal people. You'll be attacked for interfering with sacred objects, and be accused of trying to make a name for yourself."

Rob nodded knowingly because he had anticipated negative reactions, even though his motives had integrity.

"It's a sensitive subject, that's why I didn't tell anyone. I had to meet the right man and discuss tjurunga so I'd know how much I could say. By clear intention I've helped bring you into the picture to gain traditional and universal knowledge. That's how the Universe flows. We co-create the worlds we live in, and the people we meet. And you knew I was coming?"

"Yes Rob. You're here to discover and share knowledge, but," the Elder emphasised, "it won't be about tjurunga."

* * *

They noticed the tree's shade move silently toward other colonies of insects and small animals hidden nearby in the spinifex clumps and other native grasses.

As they stood to move, the Elder spoke.

"My mob had a lot of totems, and the mulga tree was a totem that belonged to certain people who were accountable for it. It represented personal strengths and weaknesses, was connected to the Ancestors and was important in daily life. The seeds were roasted then ground into paste for damper or 'johnny cakes', and it was high energy tucker. It's about the best wood for making women's digging sticks and men's hunting boomerangs because it's very strong, dense and good to work."

This mention of trees reminded Rob of special times he had experienced years earlier, so he added with a smiling voice.

"Up in Broome I met Bill and Jacky, two highly respected elders. I visited them every day and we yarned about life and artwork, just like brothers who'd found each other after a long, long time. One day I went with Bill into the backyard and we walked under a tree. Suddenly he said: *"That tree ... he's my father."* I didn't know what he meant, but since then I've thought the tree was possibly his totem, and he respected it like a *'father'* or Ancestor. Or maybe it was an example of the Oneness of all things, as a spiritual message for me."

The Elder took in what Rob said quietly and knowingly, then began to explain.

"Those old fellas were my brothers. Before Europeans came the north-west mobs sent pearl shell pendants on a trade route, passing them from clan to clan over huge distances. We called them Lonka Lonka and they had engraved designs in-filled with red ochre. But they were hard to get and we used them in rain-making ceremonies. We also 'talked' with the coastal mobs on other wavelengths. This big land wasn't as big when we 'spoke' with thoughts!"

Rob wanted to comment on this incredible last statement, but the Elder continued without a break.

"It's a good day to talk about legends, out here where you walked in another lifetime. A lot of my mob and thousands more around this continent lost personal connection with the Ancestors because of whitefellas. There's plenty written about that, but white people suffered too. They still are, but they don't realise it."

Rob was moved deeply and wanted to comment, but the Elder's insights kept coming.

"That's also why you returned to country: to help non-Aboriginals connect to stories. That's what they're missing. Wait till they hear that Caterpillar Ancestors made the MacDonnell Ranges. Find out that our old people have campfires in the Milky Way. Discover that Uluru has a big boomerang story," enthused the Elder, finally pausing to give Rob a chance to speak.

"They'll love the Dreamtime characters coming to life. Be amazed that land, sea and sky have other dimensions. Realise the Cosmos is more than darkness and diamonds. Wonder how the old people could see so far with the naked eye. We've got books and the internet now, but traditional clans didn't have telescopes. Yet the details are so realistic. Your worlds are richer and more multi-layered than the 'same' ones I see through Western eyes."

The sun had moved slightly again and without speaking they got up and walked towards the shade of another mulga tree nearby, while drinking fresh water from their thick plastic bottles. It wasn't hot, they were just being careful because of ultra-violet (UV) radiation. The rhythm of the conversation moved to the Elder, one of the last speakers of old Aranda.

"Some of our knowledge puzzles anthropologists. How did my elders know certain stars existed? Some Aboriginal paintings show facts about the Cosmos that Europeans didn't know until telescopes were invented! Academics scratch their heads too, but we keep some knowledge to ourselves and don't share everything."

The Elder concluded his explanation, and although both men were comfortable amongst the spirits of the trees, they stood up, stretched, walked to the vehicle and drove back to sunny, late afternoon Alice Springs.

* * *

The Rock Art group had left town and most members understood Rob's predicament. Having flown from New York City to join them and explore Outback sites, he met the Elder during his first morning in town. Although he knew he must grab the opportunity to spend time with the Elder, it was difficult to explain this to Hugo Ableford who invited him. Rob had travelled overseas, had been yearning to return to the Outback, and the Rock Art expedition provided the perfect solution.

However, because of what he regarded as Cosmic Timing he could not go with the group. He sensed he would learn a lot with the Elder's guidance, and knew he had mentally co-created this outcome. His long-held vision was to meet an Aboriginal elder and begin a journey, and suddenly it had happened.

While discussing the disappointing change of plan, Hugo showed Rob the expedition's itinerary and suggested they could meet up in Broome five days later. The enthusiastic leader knew Rob would be captivated by the Rock Art sites, the vast, silent landscapes, and the seemingly reachable stars at night. For Rob, these possibilities were exciting to contemplate. There was no question about that. He made a photocopy of the itinerary, wrote contact details, and arranged to pay the expenses Hugo had incurred on his behalf. Then on a cold, clear morning at 6.30 he waved off the four-vehicle 4WD convoy as it headed north.

* * *

The Elder was born west of Alice Springs in about 1930 on a large cattle station which had been established without Aboriginal consent in the 1880s. His father was a white stockman and his mother a young Western Aranda woman, and even though the cattle station had been superimposed on traditional country, various rites and ceremonies continued.

Through dance and storytelling he was introduced to traditional ways and learned about his Dreamtime heritage. As a boy he was deeply connected spiritually to his mother's father who was an invaluable source of stories and language, much of which the Elder retained throughout his life. This learning occurred despite the Hermansburg Mission in the area which was established by German Lutherans in 1877. Originally called Finke River Mission, its missionaries and families endured countless hardships, but irreversibly affected the lives of Western Aranda and Luritja people. Some children from those clans, including Lindsay Williams attended the mission school.

The Elder's young life was affected by the second World War which caused upheaval throughout the Northern Territory, particularly after the bombing of Darwin in 1942. Although a child, he and others moved to Adelaide, a move which changed his life.

He was raised from about the age of thirteen by a white foster family and went to High School. Having a good memory as a student assisted him in the white world because he passed his High School exams, initially working for a local council in Adelaide and later at the Department of Aboriginal Affairs in Canberra.

The valuable traditional knowledge gained by the Elder as a boy gave him a profound sense of personal identity, a feeling of self-confidence he drew upon whenever life's challenges confronted him. Unfortunately this was far too often in twentieth century Australia because of anti-Aboriginal attitudes. But the journey of his younger and middle years had steeled him to negative criticism, specifically because he saw a wider world and recognised the spiritual Oneness of Humanity. He was able to forgive people for their ignorance and past deeds, even though his personal growth was hard won.

Now in his senior years the Elder celebrated life's multi-dimensional nature, accessed spiritual levels and dimensions of time and space, and utilised the teachings of the world's many faiths and cultures. To people who did not understand higher levels, and they were the majority, he was an ancient seer in a modern world. He knew things which they did not, so they called him wise and wanted to hear his wisdom. However, for now he was being guided by the Ancestors and the Universe to reintroduce Rob to country.

* * *

There was still much for the Elder to reveal so once again the two men left the dark, early morning streets of Alice Springs as resident pink and grey galahs woke each other with soft, muffled calls. They drove south for an hour and a half arriving at the wide and sandy Finke River *(Lhere Pirnte)* crossing as the sun began to rise. Rob slowed down and eased to the side of the road.

Ripples of cloud sat above the eastern horizon, highlighted by mauves and soft pinks as first sunlight soundlessly touched the landscape. The wide countryside was changing into day and the stillness of pre-dawn was disappearing.

After a few minutes of silent appreciation they calmly drove off, the Elder directing Rob to a dusty track beyond the bitumen. The 4WD rolled effortlessly over corrugations in the red dirt, a welcome consequence of Rob reducing air pressure in the tyres. They drove on until the Elder signalled to stop and Rob pulled off the track. Walking into the bush, their food and water bottles in small daypacks, they were well prepared to explore.

On this particular morning the men were heading towards a cave storehouse where tjurunga stones and boards had been kept for generations. Each traditional clan kept its sacred and secret objects in special places and severe punishment was inflicted if uninitiated clansmen went near them. Caves were often used because they afforded both security and dry shelter. They had gone about two kilometres when the Elder stopped and turned to Rob.

"No-one has walked here for decades, but the Ancestors are guiding me so we'll reach the cave safely. You can't go in because you're not initiated into our Law. When we're close I'll show respect by announcing our approach and ask permission to go forward. I'll speak in old Aranda." Then he added with emphasis. "The old language was kept alive in initiation ceremonies and secret men's business and came from the forefathers before the forefathers. A time before the Dreamtime, before the physical world we now walk and talk in."

Rob inhaled suddenly, the Elder's last two sentences figuratively grabbing him by the throat. What the Elder had expressed was incredible. It represented other times and dimensions of life unknown to science and history! But what was the full story? Would he hear more 'other-worldly' information?

The Elder asked Rob to wait as he walked forward, chanting in the old language and fulfilling his obligation, before moving out of sight. About twenty minutes later he returned, his body language passive, his face in pain.

"There's nothing in the cave, all the tjurunga are gone...."

His voice faded as feelings of sadness and disappointment overtook him. Rob did not respond in words but communicated sincere support with his eyes when they met the Elder's troubled stare.

"They probably went years ago, like all the others. This theft still hurts our culture deeply. But I think some of those tjurunga will return one day."

The Elder's remark was very surprising after finding the cave storehouse empty, but he placed his right hand over his heart.

"I'm confident that three tjurunga can be found. They belong to a Dreaming Track (*Tywerrenge impatye*) or Songline, but went missing decades ago! As a custodian it's my job to find them. Once they're back 'home' we'll perform ceremonies on the Songline's sacred sites. Dancing and chanting will energise people and country again."

Rob could see in the Elder's expressive eyes how much the return of the sacred objects meant to him.

"It's so important isn't it. Your connection to country's so deep, and I understand why they have to be returned. People need to know you're looking for them, so the word has to go out. What about a website, would that help? I'll show you a few ideas when we get back to Alice."

The Elder smiled gratefully as he barely took in what Rob said. His thoughts were taken up by the loss of so many sacred objects over the years and his fresh determination to bring three of them home.

* * *

They sat down on large, smooth rocks and opened their water bottles, as an image flashed into Rob's mind, surprising him because it was sudden as well as strangely familiar. After a few moments he began to describe it out loud.

"Five Aboriginal men are walking, one behind the other, through identical country to this. They're moving along at a good pace, it's early morning and they look like men of importance. That's it!" Rob exclaimed into the quietness. "I had the same vision on the plane flying out to Uluru, but what did I see? Was I one of the senior men walking towards the cave?"

The Elder heard every word, and apparently others between them. "That's when you were here before. Your vision enabled you to re-enter the dimension of a previous life! That gift came back clearly and quickly in just a few days!"

What more could Rob say? He went quiet, but was agitated within, the sound of his breath almost audible over the slight breeze. He was processing this huge realisation mentally and emotionally, and was not ready to get up. With eyes closed and his mind replaying the vision, his breaths now balanced, he gently shook his head from side to side in awe. After a lengthy pause and another mouthful of water he was ready to keep going.

Rob was comfortable that the Elder always knew which way to go, but the peculiar thing was he definitely felt this walk was familiar. Did his feeling confirm he had walked here many years ago as a traditional man? The Elder said he had, and the indications were becoming stronger and stronger. For now he would allow his feelings and the Elder's words to resonate within and keep walking the familiar track.

After half an hour they stopped for a drink, and Rob, who had internalised the incredible idea that he was a Western Aranda man in a previous life, had the urge to mention a favourite subject.

"I've collected a few legends about the Cosmos including one about Constellation Scorpius. It's by Mountford and Roberts who introduced a lot of Aussies to Aboriginal legends. It's fantastic how your culture tells stories about gigantic constellations. They're vivid, spectacular journeys. Much more colourful than big bang theories about stars and planets. Here's a taste," Rob said, taking a folded piece of paper out of his shirt pocket.

The guilty boy initiate, his indiscreet lover and the elders who chased them into the sky, became stars in and near the Constellation. Hunting boomerangs thrown by angry elders formed part of its tail, and they're still there in that starry scorpion rising above the eastern horizon on Winter nights.

"How's that. What a fantastic way to bring the stars to life!"

"Yes, it's beautiful. I know that story because it heralds the start of Winter. And it's very entertaining, but the young law breakers had to be punished, so it's a lesson for later generations," the Elder added.

Rob looked into a brightening blue sky and marvelled at the setting moon, clearly defined just above distant purple hills. That night he expected to see the beauty of the Cosmos in all its splendour, lavishly decorated with precious gems.

The Elder caught Rob's buoyant mood.

"Visitors come here and can't believe how close the stars are. Imagine if they knew our stories, like you said earlier. The whole sky would come to life and they'd have a bigger idea of the Cosmos and the culture. They'd want to tell the world."

Rob loved the Elder's enthusiasm for his culture, and sensed his next words would relate to him.

"When the elder in Broome said to you...*"that tree ... he's my father"* he spoke on many levels. He was song man and medicine man - high honours in traditional culture - and he knew life's energies and dimensions. His reality is impossible to comprehend. Rare men like him were always consciously connected to the Spiritual Source."

"That's amazing," Rob said, "He was a remarkable artist too. He'd sit and use lead pencils to sketch his stories into notebooks, then delicately paint them with watercolours. Bill was an encyclopedia of traditional knowledge and he'd chant all night with his boomerang clapsticks."

"Yes Rob. I can see it," the Elder added. "His knowledge is precious, but we're losing those old law men, and that's a loss for the whole nation."

Rob wholeheartedly agreed and understood how privileged he was to be learning from the Elder. His appreciation reinforced how important it was to consciously live in the present. There was no time to waste. Western Aranda country was calling again.

5

The days Rob and the Elder spent together evolved their own easy rhythm. Sunrise and sunset varied the vibrations of each day without completely interrupting them. Around the men was a quiet, wise energy interwoven with daily activities and they sometimes lost track of time, the linear time measured by man-made clocks.

Another early morning saw them loading up the 4WD with enough supplies for a few days and heading out of town as the first birds acknowledged first light. The Elder felt alive in the fresh flush of morning and started their first conversation while tying a pair of mulga wood hunting boomerangs (*ulperrenye*) together with thick string.

"We're going to a very special area, a hidden gorge hardly ever visited even in the old days. You'll be the first whitefella to see it!"

The Elder emphasised his last sentence like he rarely had before, and Rob was stunned.

"What?" He almost shouted, as much to the Universe as the Elder, sensing that this day and the next couple were going to be profoundly memorable.

"You know the importance of sites, so you're ready for deeper information. In life we have blood family and interact with many other people, but each person lives a unique spiritual journey. You and I have special roles this lifetime because we were connected before, but I'll talk more later. There's a lot in front of us today."

They turned off the bitumen road on to a dirt and gravel track and the desert oaks and mulga trees began thinning out. After reaching a rocky outcrop at the end of a ridge that angled off the West MacDonnells, the track narrowed. Rob eased the 4WD over increasingly sandy country, negotiating sections of bull dust, the powder-fine soil that can bog a vehicle, while the Elder rested the hunting boomerangs across his thighs and said...

"The hidden gorge can't be seen from local roads or tracks. It's even hard for helicopters to find. About thirty minutes further along we'll park then walk for about an hour. There's fresh water, plenty of overhangs to camp under, and we've got swags and enough tucker. You'll see what the boomerangs are for later."

Rob was intrigued about going into the unknown and as his excitement increased, the Elder continued.

"The gorge was created by the Ancestors and it has a cave gallery of paintings that materialised long, long ago. Only two people alive know they're here - you and I. We'll stay for three days and nights to receive the full cosmic vibrations that make it sacred.

Our individual frequencies pick up vibrations from people and places - positive and negative - but in the hidden gorge our frequency will rise because the energies are highly spiritual. As we walk, feel at One with all things, and we'll stop a couple of times for a rest. Don't feel obliged to speak, just absorb the energies of nature where no white man has ever been before!"

No one had ever said that to Rob because adventurers have been everywhere: crossing the driest deserts, climbing the highest mountains, even trekking the freezing snowscapes of the North and South Poles. To be the first white man to see any part of the planet first would be incredible, and Rob was bursting with anticipation.

As the men walked along in happy silence the bush aromas became sweeter, the sun's warmth evaporating the last pockets of morning dew. The bird life was plentiful and in excellent song, and although there was no track, the tireless Western Aranda elder knew exactly where he was going.

At the first short break neither of them spoke, but at the second, just forty minutes after leaving the vehicle, numerous thoughts and feelings had built up in Rob.

"It's such a privilege to be here. It's hard in New York and other cities to keep grounded. My thoughts and spirit just keep flying everywhere. But here, I'm balanced. I'm at home in the Dreamtime landscape. Why's it taken me so long to come back?"

Rob had not asked a direct question for a while, but the Elder was not surprised. Clarity on all levels was vital.

"We've got to be ready for our next step and reach certain spiritual levels before rising to higher ones. You've lived a lot and developed a lot of awareness. You wrote about the Outback while overseas and created a thought-pathway. Because your connection started in the mind, you've been here many times before arriving physically! So it's not long in terms of spiritual readiness. You're actually right on time."

"Yeah. That feels right," Rob agreed.

"Remember you mentioned Cosmic Timing?" the Elder continued. "This is it in practice. Your inner cosmos is on time because it's part of the larger cosmos. That's why you're sitting under a tree in the middle of Australia. Your journey's already partly written in the stars and partly etched in life's landscapes. You're the co-author, and the Universe, Ancestors and I are guiding you to fulfil this part of it."

Rob was not surprised by the profound and beautifully balanced explanation. This was the wise way of his guide and mentor. Now it was obvious he was destined to learn about much more than sacred tjurunga, although he would definitely help the Elder try and find the old, stolen ones.

Their second stop had been long enough for bananas, mixed nuts and refreshing drinks of water, and then, according to the Elder, they only had about twenty minutes to go.

"The sun will be at a certain angle when we get there, that's why the day's unfolding like it is," the Elder explained. "We must find a particular rectangular rock face when the sun's shining precisely onto it. We'll thank the Ancestors in advance for the opportunity to see the paintings, and be grateful for the information received. These affirmations will form thought-connections to the paintings before we locate them. We'll create a positive future, by creating a positive now."

Feeling invigorated after their break and snack both men stood up, ready for the last part of the hike. With rolled swags and full daypacks of supplies and cameras slung over rested shoulders, and the Elder carrying the two hunting boomerangs, they set off. Soon after, they came to a dry, sandy watercourse flanked by lush vegetation. For the first time they saw palm trees and another plant with strong, green fronds sprouting near the orange-red rocks.

"They're palms aren't they?" Rob wondered out loud.

"They're Red Cabbage Palm, and we call them *Rrankweye*," the Elder replied. "And that other fella is dinosaur tucker."

"What?" Rob cut in.

"It's the cycad. We call it *Tywekekwerle.*"

"But what do you mean by 'dinosaur tucker'?"

"Botanists call it a 'living fossil' because it survived the Ice Ages."

Rob heard what the Elder said but realised there must be a local story.

"They're Dreamtime Ancestors that became plants. Meaning, spirit lives beyond the limiting beliefs of science. Time's not a long line from start to finish. It's inter-dimensional and embodies past, present and future. The palms and cycads are in three *time* dimensions *at the same time.*"

The Elder paused for a few mouthfuls of cool water.

"That's the essence of the Dreamtime and it's a challenging concept. Yet more and more will understand as personal awareness grows and consciousness develops."

"As you say it's step by step, and everyone's steps are always on time." Rob added as he stood beside a palm tree whose age was incomprehensible to him. The explanation that it was in the *past* and the *present* "at the same time" resonated positively. He was open to higher levels of understanding as they came closer to the hidden gorge.

The sandy watercourse that sometimes ran as a creek, actually led from the gorge and only flowed after storms drenched the area, but the palms and cycads were fed by permanent underground water and replenished by fresh run-off. This dry watercourse was the men's route into the gorge, and after turning a slight bend they saw a pile of large rocks, moulded by the spirit hands of the Ancestors.

Now the destination was close and their intention had to be communicated.

"Like before, near the empty cave storehouse I'll speak in old Aranda so the spirits of the hidden gorge and the paintings know we're coming. The old language is purer and opens up channels of communication much faster than later dialects. After I've finished you can speak from your truth."

The Elder cupped a hand on either side of his mouth and spoke fluently to the sky. His words and phrases like music on the breeze, seemingly penetrating the leaves and branches of the guardian trees and palms. His language was in harmony with nature, vibrating in all dimensions of life.

In this reverent atmosphere, Rob then offered his words.

"Great Ancestors and Universe, I come respectfully and acknowledge the traditional creators of the Law. To be guided to this sacred place is a rare and unforgettable privilege. I come with honour and gratitude in my heart, and am open to greater spiritual understanding."

Knowing the spirits had been alerted, both men walked faster, more eager than ever. Around another bend a grove of cycads and tall palms blocked the watercourse, but the men pushed through the ancient beings, only temporarily slowing down. Within minutes they found their way through them and walked into the gorge.

Rising on each side of the bone dry creek bed, tan-brown walls of time-weathered quartzite confirmed they had found it. Just ahead of where Rob was standing the gorge opened out to about fifty metres wide, but he could not see far enough to estimate its length. However, he definitely felt that the temperature was higher.

The Elder made a quick mental survey and found that his memory of the area was surprisingly clear.

"There's an old rock fall we need to find first. It's not far along so let's get moving. I've been waiting a long time to come back. I was only twelve or thirteen when I was here before. My first initiation was over, and the elders allowed me to see the sacred paintings. I strongly remember the men chanting and chanting and clack, clack, clacking their boomerangs together. It was a big experience for a young boy."

He was *there*. Rob could feel the Elder was *there*. He was in the vivid depths of his memories and imagination, and already *with* the paintings. But imagination would not be needed for much longer.

They reached the fallen rock and the Elder looked for a certain boulder to indicate how close they were to their goal. Midday had just passed and the sun's rays beamed downward at a slight angle, hitting the heaped rocks. Several had angular sides, some were tall and wide, yet one showed a complete rectangle to the sun, and the Elder pointed excitedly.

"That's it. That's the rock. The light's nearly there!"

Only partial shadow remained on it and they stared intently, wanting the sun to speed up. But it only took about three minutes for the big rock's rectangular face to be completely covered with sunlight.

"It's there. Push the rock. Push the rock," the Elder urgently instructed. "Go within Rob, focus your energy. Push hard."

Taking a balanced stance and using his hands and right shoulder, Rob pushed, easing the rock forward until it over-balanced, falling sideways and sliding out of the way. Dust exploded into the air, then as it cleared and to Rob's amazement, several rock steps appeared.

"There," he said, sucking in a quick breath.

"We've found it!" Exclaimed the Elder.

Both men knew they were being shown the way, but there was no need to say so. Rob gestured to the Elder to go first and they descended into an underground cave, walking carefully and expectantly without speaking. At first it was semi dark, but as they gradually turned left and walked on for about twenty metres, the cave became lighter and larger.

Suddenly, images began taking shape before their re-focussing eyes. On the cave wall in front of them a gallery of painted figures appeared. Was the Dreamtime staring them in the face?

"Wow. Wow," Rob repeated, instantly overcome. He fell silent, allowing his eyes and other senses to perceive the ancient art. Mesmerised and speechless, he eased down onto the stone floor. Words could not describe what he was feeling.

The Elder was immediately affected and tears moistened his eyes.

"I remember paintings here from childhood, but I'm not sure about these images. Yet the energies are empowering and I'm filling with love. My inner being is opening up and I'm at One with all life. I belong to the whole Universe."

The Elder's eyes closed as he flowed with his spiritual recharge. After waiting for most of his life to return, and despite feeling puzzled by the paintings, he understood why he felt completely at One. He was being profoundly renewed on all levels because he was connecting to the Spiritual Source.

Rob was in bliss, flooded by loving energy radiating from the sacred art. Fortunately, the Elder had prepared him for a spiritual leap because he was barely coping with the higher vibrational frequency. However, he continued sitting and absorbing the immense personal experience until gradually drifting back into the conscious present.

* * *

Other levels may have absorbed Rob a few immeasurable moments earlier, but now totally revitalised he felt moved to describe the surprising discovery. His voice was purposeful, like the proud leader of a successful archaeological dig making an announcement to the world.

"In a sacred cave in the heart of Australia we've discovered paintings of Krishna, Jesus, Buddha and Sathya Sai Baba with black afro hair and an orange robe. Impossible. Unprecedented. What are paintings of great spiritual masters doing in the Outback? Who created them? Why are they here in the hidden gorge?"

Rob's mind raced through possibility after possibility. Then he noticed something else. Just near the orange-robed figure where the high cave wall angled away to the right, he could see part of a symbol. Quickly stepping forward he made another 'impossible' discovery, staring in disbelief.

"It's the star of David and a crescent moon and star, side by side, plus other symbols, one I've seen before, it's the Om sign - and next to them's a brown-skinned man with a black beard in a white robe! He's painted smaller than the large figures on the main wall, and I have a memory of his image too."

The Elder could almost hear Rob's mind over-working in the confines of the cave and before he could respond further, had to comment.

"I'm astonished. I thought I knew what was here! They're different than I remember, but we're meant to see them now. I don't have all the answers but the Universe and the Ancestors will guide us, I know that."

The Elder was not as confident as usual, because he was very, very surprised by the subjects of the paintings. Were they the same ones he saw as a boy? Had his mind played tricks on him over the years?

* * *

Later, both men were sitting under an overhang with dry twigs and branches piled together for their campfire. Dusk was settling on the day and with it the tangible quietness only found in remote places. For the next couple of days the hidden gorge would be their sanctuary.

After darkness fell they stared into the orange flames, comfortable in each other's presence, yet neither man had spoken a word since leaving the cave. On this momentous day the Ancestors provided a perfect, still evening for them to reflect upon the paintings and their feelings. But their minds were not fully relaxed under the sparkling night sky, and as the fire burned Rob simply said, "Totally unbelievable!"

The Elder nodded in agreement, then introduced the next morning.

"We'll sit near the painted images before sunrise to experience first light awakening the spirits. I'll build a small fire for warmth, and we'll simply Be. Be in the moment. Be our Spiritual or Higher selves. I'll perform a ceremony with the boomerangs which I know you've been wondering about."

He did not say anything about the paintings, apparently needing more inner space to reconcile what he believed he had seen as a boy.

* * *

Crisp, fresh air greeted both men as they rolled out of their swags. The early morning was cold because Winter temperatures drop markedly overnight in the Outback. They did not eat but only drank cool water, both feeling it was best to be empty of food to fully receive the potent spiritual energies in the cave.

After walking to the uncovered stone steps they descended carefully, passing through the left-turning part of the cave before arriving at the paintings. Instantly, a sense of awe and wonder engulfed Rob and the Elder again, filling their hearts and souls as they stared at the figures. Without a word they sat down a few metres away. The Elder had carried the boomerangs, Rob the water bottles, and they were on

53

time because the sun was yet to rise. It was cold, but referring to his words the night before, the Elder said.

"I won't make the fire because smoke could damage the paintings. Let's keep warm by breathing deeply and rubbing our hands together briskly. Take full conscious breaths. Visualise oxygen reaching every cell in your arms, hands, legs, feet, toes and fingers. That will help you feel warmer."

Questions about the paintings began to rise again, also distracting their thoughts from the cold. The Elder was leader and mentor, but he too was hearing the obvious questions. The biggest being 'why?' Why were portraits of spiritual masters and symbols of religions painted in a hidden gorge in the Outback? Neither Rob or the Elder had speculated aloud. Shared silence was a direct response to the shock of seeing figures far beyond their cultural and geographical origins. But the images were in the cave and the Elder was first to speak.

"I'm feeling at One, and the paintings are about Oneness. Major faiths of the world share the walls of a cave in Aboriginal country and no-one else knows they're here! It's totally amazing. I thought they were my Ancestors! The elders must have thought they were important when they showed me. But did they change over the years? I don't remember the exact figures and symbols, but what's here is here. They're spiritual beacons for all of us."

Rob inhaled audibly, fully realising what they were seeing.

"This is real spirituality, the unity of all people, faiths and religions. I feel it deeply and feel so blessed to see them."

"Yes, me too Rob," the Elder responded, before standing up and stepping closer to the paintings. He stretched his arms wide to confirm one figure's width, then held his right hand close to its hands to compare size. The spiritual masters had been shown great respect. Their painted hands on the sacred cave wall were twice as large as his!

Rob got up, equally impressed by their size and height. He was over six feet tall, but they towered above him. Painted in deep red and orange-red ochre, white pipe clay and charcoal black, the artwork was pristine, life-like, compelling. The artists had known their subjects well! Rob stared even harder as he went closer, seeing details he had not noticed the day before.

Questions flooded his mind. Were the paintings connected to the original people of the area? Were they painted by man's hand? Why had they been re-discovered now? Rob knew intuition was needed to find the answers, but his busy brain was overworking.

* * *

As Rob refocused his thoughts the Elder indicated with hand gestures, similar to traditional Aranda sign language, to sit and face the paintings again. Each man was experiencing a deeper spiritual reality in his own personal way, but the Elder wanted to change the energy.

"These *ulperrenye* hunting boomerangs embody spirit that came in the Dreamtime according to the old storytellers. Spirit lives on in the boomerang, and to keep both strong I'll perform a ceremony to honour them."

He made a similar introduction in old Aranda, one of the earth's first languages. Rob could not understand the fast moving sentences, but he felt totally comfortable with their sounds and rhythms.

The Elder tuned into his intuition, finding the words and melody of the chant he had not heard for sixty years. Holding the boomerangs vertically he began tapping a steady background rhythm, their clacking sound echoing around the cave. By changing angles different sounds leapt from the boomerang clapsticks, captivating Rob with variations in tempo and volume. Now flowing, the Elder started chanting the sacred words of his elders, singing the boomerang and enlivening the spirits. Drawn in by the repeated chanting and clacking Rob's whole being resonated with the vibrations. Clapping the boomerangs faster and faster, the Elder increased the intensity, the side of his right foot tapping in time on the rock floor, the huge painted figures looking down as if they could hear.

Suddenly, tapping sounds beyond the Elder's tapping beats echoed in the cave. He stopped abruptly, yet the echo continued! But was it echo? Rob heard it too, and they looked straight at each other.

"Hear that?" Rob asked, looking confused.

"Definitely," the surprised Elder confirmed.

Speculation flooded Rob's mind as the rhythmical tapping flowed on and on. But after a long two minutes the Elder was smiling.

"Ceremony re-empowers places and people so they reconnect with the Source. The cave's pure spiritual energy accelerated the process, and I performed enough of the boomerang ceremony to honour them! The Universe and Ancestors enabled us to hear the boomerang percussion continue and sound exactly the same, on a level of spirit!" The Elder explained.

"Like another dimension?" Rob queried.

"Exactly," the Elder confirmed.

Both men were profoundly moved. The Elder's eyes filled with delight, Rob's face flushed with awe. Still seated, Rob adjusted his cross-legged posture and the Elder placed the now silent boomerangs on the sandstone floor. On personal inner levels they absorbed the unexpected experience. They were being re-empowered by Universal Love Energy.

After a while they got up and walked back to the steps and out of the cave. The sun was directly overhead and they were surprised in one way, but not in another, because the life of spirit is timeless. Back at their camp the Elder lit twigs and broken branches, waited for them to burn well, then placed a billy of water on to boil. Rob reflected on the morning's events and half-asked, half-stated to the Elder.

"It's going to be interesting telling people that traditional hunting boomerangs are alive!" He suggested, raising his eyebrows. Then with a quick *look* into the future he reinforced his words. "Imagine the reactions, back in the urban never, never!"

Rob seemed to have some doubt, so as the Elder threw loose black tea leaves into the billy, he offered insightful words.

"You know I regard all things as One, and believe all things are interconnected. Most of our mobs say all objects and beings embody the same spirit, and that's common knowledge in other cultures and spiritual groups world-wide. But what does it mean? Who understands what's really being said?"

"I'm on that sort of wavelength," Rob responded.

"You are, but many aren't," the Elder said.

Rob sensed there was more to come and waited attentively as the Elder stirred the boiling tea in the billy with a long, thin eucalyptus stick. There was an art to making this traditional whitefella brew and the Elder was good at it.

"More will *get it* when they know our beliefs. See those mulga trees across the gorge? If we go closer we'll see which part of the slender trunk would make a good boomerang. In terms of spirit the boomerang's already there, and has been since the tree was a sacred seed. After we cut a section and make the boomerang it becomes another entity, physically separate from the tree. But it's still part of the whole, in spirit. Some may call the tree inanimate, but to us it's a living being. Same applies to the boomerang. He runs, he walks, he flies: why wouldn't he be alive!"

There was a twinkle in the Elder's eye as he described the *living* boomerang. His voice was animated as his mind filled with images of boomerangs in flight, spinning fast through the air. He was reliving youthful, more energetic days. The Elder had performed the ceremony and given clear explanations so Rob could speak about the spirit of the boomerang.

* * *

The Elder poured the hot, black tea into thick plastic mugs and sat down.

"Let me show you something." He placed his right thumb and index finger on one of his top, front teeth and applied pressure. Suddenly he was holding a partial denture with one tooth. "My original tooth was knocked out during first initiation..."

"Ouch, sounds bloody painful." Rob sympathised.

"It sure was, and I've had different part-plates ever since."

"Yeah? I hadn't even noticed," Rob responded.

"That's right," the Elder confirmed. "It was uncomfortable in the early days, but it's been good for years now."

"And it's a better look professionally," Rob said.

"Exactly," the Elder agreed as he replaced it. Then Rob introduced a new topic.

"Do you think the Ancestors show us signs, back in what seems like the spiritually starved world?"

Sipping his tea then placing the three quarter-full mug on a rock, the Elder picked up one of the clapstick boomerangs.

"Let's not think too much," he replied with conviction. "Thinking blocks our connection to Ancestors, Spiritual Masters and the Source. It's over-used. But the world's not spiritually starved. If it was, we wouldn't be here! Positive vibes keep the world more than half in the light."

"Yeah. Agreed. I see your point," Rob acknowledged.

"And universal signs are always available. If we're ready spiritually we see them. First recognise, then interpret correctly. Interpretation is tricky, but when they're obvious it's simple and everything flows.

Intuition interprets signs quickest and truest. Then the battle between intuition and intellect rises because mind wants to dominate. But as we grow spiritually it's easier to recognise signs and messages because our connection to the Source becomes deeper."

As soon as he finished his last word the Elder put the boomerang down, emptied the remains of his now cool tea in the sand, stood up, and beckoned Rob to follow.

"Let's go, there's another stand of palms further along, and I want to show you some rare bush tucker."

6

The two men walked in firm brown sand for about two hundred metres, passing a small rock pool of water just deep enough to reflect flashes of sunlight as their eyes caught the right angles. Upon seeing the red cabbage palms about fifty metres away the Elder held up his hand to stop. They both stood still and he alerted the spirits that they were approaching. Then as Rob concluded his silent words he wondered whether thought-messages would be acceptable on some occasions, and would ask the Elder about it later.

They reached the palms and the Elder selected a young plant, telling Rob to hold the slim trunk and bend it towards him a little. Choosing a frond the Elder carefully peeled off the outer layers with his fingers to reach the softer inner layers. He then took a small pocket-knife out of his trousers, unfolded the blade and cut small sections, handing one to Rob.

"This food is a gift from the Ancestors. Hope you like it."

Rob put it onto his tongue and began chewing slowly.

"Be perfect in a salad," he said, savouring the smooth, slightly tart flavour. The Elder also had a piece and chewed it until it was watery in his mouth. He had not tasted this rare bush tucker for many years, and after doing so had the look of a contented man.

"I remember grandfather letting me taste it, but our people stopped eating it years ago. Why? Because this palm will probably die now.''

"Oh,'' Rob uttered, surprised.

"Yes, but my actions should be okay because I'm explaining culture, and the Ancestors understand what we're doing...''

"Well, that's good. And thanks for the huge privilege.'' Rob responded, happy that he was gaining information about the old ways.

The mid-afternoon sun hit their hats at about 30 degrees Celsius, but they were comfortable enough. Rob called it honest heat because it was dry with no humidity. The gorge was hotter than Alice Springs because sunlight reflected into it from high rocky walls on both sides, and there was no breeze. They had become used to it because the temperatures had been higher ever since they arrived. Even so they began walking back on the shaded side and did not have far to go, or so Rob thought.

Large rocks stood around, water-worn and sun-baked after millennia in the elements. Rob walked ahead and after passing a larger rock suddenly stopped. On the other side was a circular-shaped depression in the ground at least twenty metres across. Compelled to walk down into it, he found a dark, round stone with shiny flecks about the size of a marble at the bottom. It was surprisingly heavy for its size and unlike any others Rob had seen in the gorge. He made a quick mental note that it looked out of place, then called out to the Elder who was several metres behind.

"What's this?" Rob asked, his voice brightened by the joy of discovery as he held the small stone above his head. The Elder caught up, and leaned against one of the taller shaded rocks.

"There's a big story about this fella. That's no ordinary stone! You know we've got stories about stars and planets. And we discovered asteroids and meteors before Europeans arrived. I'm using English names so what I say has more significance. This ancient burnt stone is a tektite, part of a meteorite!"

"What? That must be so rare," Rob responded as he glanced up into blue, expansive Central Australian sky, before refocusing on the stone.

"They are. But we found them from time to time," the Elder confirmed as he looked closely at the tektite.

"I know the stars and earth are connected in traditional culture, but are you saying your elders knew this little, heavy stone came from outer space?"

Rob could not have asked his question more precisely or succinctly. The Elder was expecting it and suggested they walk the hundred metres or so back to camp and the refreshing shade, before he answered.

The water in their bottles was not very cool but both men drank and replenished themselves. Rob, now sitting on his rolled-up swag had an expectant expression as the Elder began.

"Ancestors have always lived in the Sky-World and they're still up there as stars and constellations. They gave us stories about meteors and asteroids, but our elders also knew these dark, round stones came from beyond earth. There was no other possibility because they knew how stones behaved. Stones are living objects, but they didn't jump around making holes in the ground!"

"That's fantastic," Rob enthused. "I've never thought of them knowing the connection between a stone on earth and its cosmic origin."

But there it was staring him in the face. Proof that the old people knew exactly what happened in their country.

* * *

They had brought sufficient supplies for their stay, the morning had been eventful, and it was mid-afternoon so food was the next priority. The fire soon burned down and Rob removed the tops from cans of braised steak and onions, placing them in the coals to heat. Their spirits were being deeply nourished in this sanctuary of pure, loving energy, and the Elder mentioned another visit to the cave.

"We'll go in about an hour before dusk in time for last daylight. The paintings vibrate beauty and spirituality, and maybe we'll receive information about their origin and whether human hands were involved. You asked about that earlier, remember?"

Rob was feeling very excited as he stood up.

"Yeah, I've had a lot of thoughts about it. Either highly evolved artists, aligned to the Spiritual Source painted the images, or they miraculously appeared overnight. Like those out-of-this-world crop circle designs in England. I can't even guess when it happened. But if it was local artists how did they receive information way beyond their experience and cultural traditions? It's a magnificent mystery."

The Elder did not comment directly on Rob's ideas, but acknowledged him with warm eye contact, knowing they would be in the presence of the superb art very soon.

After a couple of hours relaxing at their shaded campsite they set out for the paintings. The rock steps they walked down for the third time were well defined, although definitely not made by human hands. The cave was long, formed by an overhang that arched towards the ground. At the bottom of the steps it was attached to the rock floor, but near the paintings it did not quite touch the earth, hence the variation in light along its length. It was a formation that only a higher hand could have created, something to be expected in this spiritual gorge.

The Elder carried a hunting boomerang in each hand and like Rob, stood in silence when they reached the sacred art. They wanted to know as much as possible. But what more would they be given or perceive this time?

* * *

Throughout Australia there are many outstanding styles of painted Aboriginal Rock Art. The most distinctive include the Wandjina in the Kimberley of Western Australia, the Quinkans and other Spirit Figures of Cape York Peninsular in Queensland, and the Lightning Brothers of the Northern Territory. These paintings represent stories, Ancestors and records of significant events, and are located in the country of specific traditional groups. When people who do not know the Aboriginal stories and interpretations view the paintings, they see examples of fine artwork comprising both familiar and unfamiliar images. Yet researchers who specialise in Rock Art speculate about the meaning and purpose of the paintings. They try and discover the 'why' and 'when' of the art, and many different theories have evolved. Aboriginal custodians are not always available to interpret, and sadly, because of forced removal from their land some sites may never be understood from a traditional perspective.

During the 1980s a tall, lone enthusiast discovered hundreds of previously unrecorded sites of Rock Art in the Victoria River District of the Northern Territory. Most are located in extremely remote areas, some only accessible on foot, and they contain outstanding examples of figures, symbols, and animals, known and unknown. These recent recordings suggest an obvious conclusion, particularly when the vastness of Australia is considered. There must be many more Rock Art sites awaiting re-discovery across the Dreamtime continent.

* * *

The eager explorers wanted to examine the unrivalled artwork more closely than before, and looked with expectant eyes.

"They're almost alive," Rob said, his hands instinctively clasped together with respect in front of his chest. The huge life-like figures astounded him, and he knew that anyone who saw them would feel the same!

Yet no-one would ever expect to find such paintings in Central Australia. Billions would recognise them, but the deeper significance was not their names or forms. It was the spirituality they represented. Rob believed that Universal Love Energy connected all people everywhere, including all faiths and religions, and he knew this was the paintings' vital message. It aligned with the Elder's words about Oneness and he spoke with conviction.

"According to your recollections these paintings of Krishna, Jesus, Buddha, Sathya Sai Baba plus other figures and symbols materialised in the Dreamtime. This suggests that future events were known in the beginning. That's absolutely incredible." Rob said, shaking his head from side to side. "The people or creative energy responsible knew about man's spiritual development on earth! These paintings whose age we don't know, represent the history of Humanity's spirituality, past, present *and* future! Totally mind boggling. I can hardly believe what I just said!"

Rob slowed for a deep breath and sat down on the cave floor, his thoughts overflowing with the revelations of the afternoon, especially the words he had just spoken. The Elder had been listening carefully.

"I still don't remember these exact paintings, but when I was twelve I presumed they were from the Dreamtime! They'll upset most academics and teachers. Images like these don't fit their world view or reference books. It's a hoax, they'll say! And they won't give your spiritual theories the time of day because for them the intellect is God, even though many don't use the word. Anthropologists and Aboriginal leaders will dismiss your ideas. They'll claim you're mocking traditional culture for your own ends. And they'll have a go at me too."

Rob listened closely, but he'd been around long enough to know there will always be critics, as the Elder continued.

"They'll write you off as an amateur, badly affected by the Outback sun. They'll challenge you to reveal your so-called spiritual paintings. One or two religious leaders may be sympathetic, but others will strongly disagree with your big picture. You'll have to handle a lot of criticism."

"Yeah, I see that. Sure there'll be noses out of joint, but awareness is growing and many people will be open to this discovery and what it represents," Rob said confidently.

"I agree," the Elder said, then his face lit up. "There's a growing pathway on the planet: a wide, colourful Songline awakening people and nations to the Spiritual Source. It's a multi-level journey and many will support the vision because now it's time to link hearts and souls."

Rob was still sitting on the rock floor as the Elder finished describing his inspired idea. The vision of a "wide, colourful Songline" appealed greatly to Rob and he could imagine people all over the world embracing it.

"It'll be a privilege to be involved," Rob said, his heart filled with positive feelings, even though he knew real challenges lay ahead when news of the paintings went public.

* * *

The Elder squatted down and introduced another puzzling artwork to Rob, far away in the north-west of Western Australia.

"Up in the west Kimberley near the coast there's a mysterious painting that European explorers found in a cave in the 1830s. It's a large human-like figure wearing a long, deep red robe. Maybe there's a link. The robe is similar to these, there's a halo around the head, but it's been lost for over a hundred and sixty five years. The explorers wrote about it, but local mobs kept people away for generations by saying they didn't know where it was. You might see it one day. The Elders up there know you've returned to country."

The Elder looked knowingly at Rob during the last two sentences. Did he have some insight about a future trip into the Kimberley for Rob? It certainly sounded like it. Or was he simply acknowledging that events unfolded when people and circumstances were ready?

The afternoon light had faded into semi-darkness since both men had been inside the cave, but they barely noticed. Rob got up effortlessly, the Elder picked up the boomerangs, and they walked out across the gorge towards their camp. A campfire was soon alight and dancing in the cool evening air as they sat and watched the billy boil.

"As a boy I thought the paintings were traditional Ancestors. But they're not. They're different and the concept's much broader. The spiritual masters of all faiths are our teachers, not just our own Ancestors. However these paintings manifested, they're for everyone." The Elder paused, allowing his words to hover.

"Over the last hundred years or so Aboriginal brothers and sisters adopted the Christianity imposed by missionaries. Jesus became a type of Ancestor, a father figure with strict laws to live by, and he was the son of the ultimate Ancestor. Now it's normal for our people to attend church services and maintain some traditional beliefs, although too many old ways have disappeared."

Rob suddenly remembered a painting with a similar theme, so with an urgent look on his face he spoke up.

"About ten years ago I bought a painting from a *Koori* Aboriginal artist in Sydney. He re-interpreted Christ's birth by setting it near Uluru! He used Outback colours, animal characters, the dot art technique and called it "Dreamtime Jesus." So he was definitely influenced by Christianity."

Nodding acknowledgement the Elder responded. "Be good to see it one day Rob." Then kept sharing his insights.

"Many Christian Aboriginals won't see a link between their faith and the paintings. They won't know all the figures. The challenge is to recognise that all great spiritual masters represent Universal Love Energy. And, there's only one God. We're all connected spiritually, that's what the paintings say. But most of us don't look beyond form because we're physical beings. It's hard to imagine friends and family as 'spiritual beings' in bodies."

* * *

Both men knew it was absolutely amazing to have seen the incredible art, and fully realised that mentioning it beyond the hidden gorge would be controversial. So they would talk about it only when the time was right. Only when personal timing and Cosmic Timing aligned. Also, the remote location was totally mystifying. These superbly painted images would be naturally at home in India or the Middle East. Why were they so far from their cultural and geographical origins?

Would Rob and the Elder find the answer? And other answers? They may not, but they did know how exceptional this discovery was and what it may lead to.

"I sometimes wonder how awareness will increase around the world. It takes a crisis to wake most of us up. It could take natural disasters, an oil shortage, computer collapse or financial crash to shock us into it." Rob suggested and continued.

"But maybe we can change without disasters. People will be astonished to hear that these paintings exist in Central Australia. The story will race around the world. Obvious questions will be asked. People will demand to see them. The superficial reactions will gradually decrease and be surpassed by the larger truth: all great teachers came to guide Humanity back to the Spiritual Source."

While listening to Rob the Elder placed a couple of large pieces of river red gum on the fire. The flames danced as if to welcome them and a few sparks shot off into the desert darkness as the fire took hold. This, their last night in the sacred gorge would become colder, and there was a good chance they would keep on talking. The Elder brushed a few grains of sand off his hands.

"The paintings are a gift for the whole world because they symbolise spiritual Oneness. They're a divine sign. We're being bathed in powerful vibrations and our heart chakras are receiving more Universal Love Energy. We're glowing inside and when we get back to Alice people will sense a difference. Our positive vibes will radiate and touch others."

"Our spirits are filling up," Rob offered.

"Yes. Yes," the Elder replied. "Vibrations of love and truth create personal change. We can help friends spread the energy with words, music and pictures so it can be shared. A lot of people are aware enough to be receptive."

"Yeah. There's growing awareness, but there's a fair way to go."

"But it's happening," the Elder agreed. "Across the planet people see signs every day confirming they're on their correct path. More and more will wake up and find the earth is really our Earth Mother, just like Aboriginal groups all over the world have known since time began. And have you heard this? If the letter 'h' is taken off the end of the word *earth* and placed in front, the word *heart* is formed!"

"What?" Rob exclaimed with a chuckle. He felt like asking the Elder to repeat the beautiful word play.

Rob was never surprised by the depth of the Elder's wisdom, and was delighted by the poetic interpretation of *earth* becoming *heart* so poignantly. What a wonderful way to impart a profound message. Rob was accustomed to him expressing complex concepts simply. It was the way of all world traditions, and the way in which his culture had survived longer than any other on the planet. No wonder our Aboriginal brothers and sisters have so much to share, he thought enthusiastically.

The fire needed a couple of small branches. What a magical thing. Colours and characters leaping all around the burning timber, warming the soul as well as the front of the body. The wood supply would not last for much more talking time, and the men were becoming quieter anyway.

Their relaxed reactions were the sign that it was time to climb into swags and go to sleep on another remarkable day. The last couple of branches burned quickly and the campfire's glow faded. Another type of dreaming would soon take over the men's consciousness and they would die to the world of supposed reality.

* * *

Sunlight tipped the higher fronds of the taller palms as both men woke up and stepped out of their swags. They shared almost an audible feeling of contentment in the peace-filled, invigorating air of morning as they packed up their simple camp, collecting empty cans to dispose of in town. Although it was cold they did not boil the billy, but had cool drinks of water before setting off down the gorge.

About an hour after leaving their sanctuary and walking through palms and cycads and the sandy creek bed, they were driving along the dirt and gravel track that would lead to the sealed road and later to Alice Springs.

After Rob turned onto the main road and accelerated, the Elder remarked. "It's good to be back on the black."

"What? Haven't heard that before," Rob quickly responded.

"That's what we call being on bitumen road," The Elder confirmed, holding the hunting boomerangs he had sung in the cave.

"Wondering what to do first? Who to tell? Where to go? Don't be side-tracked by your mind. The inner voice is key. Once you've heard it, trust it. Intuition's the connection to your higher self, and part of Universal Love Energy. The steps will unfold on time. That's what's been happening since we met. You know how it works."

"Yeah. And I'm ready," Rob smiled.

"When we get back to town we've got a lot to talk about, especially the lost tjurunga. It's very important business. For whitefellas too. And that website idea sounds good."

Rob was already excited about what was ahead, his eyes bright and wide open, his voice buoyant with happiness.

"It's absolutely fantastic. Everything happened so quickly. I had to meet an Elder but I didn't know I'd experience so much, so soon. The hidden gorge was life-changing and Humanity's spiritual future is already here. We've all got a part to play because every soul's important in the Divine plan."

7

Alice Springs looked the same as when they left a few days earlier, and Rob drove the Elder to his home on Bradshaw Drive near the southern end of town. He lived there with family members because he could see the MacDonnell Ranges or Caterpillar Dreaming, and he drew strength from this Aranda history.

The men needed time apart for space and reflection and agreed to meet on the following morning at the bottom of Anzac Hill and walk up to the lookout. Again they would see Dreamtime country spreading to the horizon as sunrise woke the ancient rhythms of the land.

Rob arrived back at the Resort, picked up a message in an envelope at Reception and walked to his room before opening it. It was a fax from Clara in New York directing him to an email. He opened his laptop, made sure the cord was plugged into the wall socket and turned on the power. With a couple of well-aimed clicks the message sprang to electronic life on the screen:

Hi-G'day Rob, I miss you... I know you'll be enjoying yourself in the outback, you always talked so much about it. I've decided to come down and see it for myself, if you want me to? I'd like to see you, I miss you a whole lot. I thought work would keep me busy but you're in my thoughts all the time. And I'd like to see how your research is going. Have you found an elder? Have you seen any rock art? Is it too hot?

Clara's caring message continued for a full page and highlighted some of their great times in Manhattan. She loved their togetherness and reminded Rob of special intimate moments, country and classical music they enjoyed, and of how they met in Miami. Rob read it through then bunched up two pillows at the head of the queen-sized bed, lying back on them to read it again.

For more than a week he had been completely absorbed by his time with the Elder. Other worlds and people including his lady friend had rarely been in the picture. But her message warmed his heart and put him on the spot at the same time. Was it appropriate for her to come? How would this affect his time with the Elder? Rob was experiencing the most profound moments of his life. It was a privilege being with the Elder, and he knew the paintings in the hidden gorge would fascinate people all over the world.

Recent discoveries and talks with the Elder resonated deeply within Rob's spirit and felt more substantial than any personal relationship he had experienced. Nevertheless, he missed the support and nurturing of a loving partner, someone to share his travels and possibly a home one day. But he always wondered if he could have both. To solve the issue Rob would tune in to his higher self, and also ask the Elder.

The afternoon was clear and sunny so he decided to have a swim in the Resort's pool. He would let the possibility of Clara's presence in Alice Springs play gently in his thoughts, like the water would play over his body. Fortunately, and especially for Winter, the Resort was taking part in a local initiative to use clean, sustainable energy by implementing the trial of a new solar-powered system to heat the pool.

Rob shallow-dived in, stroking under water for the full length of the short pool, something he loved doing on the first dive. After a couple of breaststroke laps Clara's possible visit invaded his relaxing mind. Rob was a giving and trusting type of man, and needed what he called "space" to think and just *be*. His positive attitude and adaptability were ideal qualities as he travelled by himself around the world. Not one to follow the crowd or pursue goals because of peer or community expectations, Rob would make his mark in his own time as it aligned with Cosmic Timing.

He pulled himself out of the pool, briskly towelled himself dry, and deposited his long frame in a plastic chair in the sunshine, out of the slight breeze and away from the shade of the palm trees. His busy mind was overwhelming any possibility of an intuitive response, yet he reasoned he still had to observe the thoughts that were coming up. But he was thinking too much, so he slowed his thinking and gave voice to snippets of his thoughts quietly to himself.

"I'd love to have Clara here. Go driving near the West Macs and explore the bush. She'd love Namatjira's landscapes. We'd imagine driving through one of his paintings, and at night try and count the stars. She'd love seeing the Outback first-hand, but it can't distract me from time with the Elder. I'll have to make sure of that."

Rob's last comment brought in to focus his need to speak with the Elder. They were due to meet early in the morning and Rob would make sure to seek his opinion.

* * *

Early morning before sunrise has a different aroma than daytime or night time in Central Australia, and in many rural and other Outback areas. Natural rhythms and cycles are more obvious than in cities, and the senses are usually more heightened. For some, the sense of smell develops and becomes a trusted indicator. One can smell the dew as dusk falls, many smell rain before it arrives, and some say you can even smell starlight with a bit of practice! The aroma that greeted Rob at the bottom of Anzac Hill was of a light frost, the first he had experienced since arriving. Deserts and arid lands have ranges in temperature that surprise first-time visitors. Hot afternoons can follow freezing conditions on the same day!

* * *

Before daybreak the Elder arrived at the base of Anzac Hill. A family member had driven him along Wills Terrace and Rob was already there. They greeted each other warmly with a handshake, before starting to walk up the hill on the marked track where strategically placed and cemented stones ensured it was solid underfoot. The Elder suggested they would appreciate the hill, a registered sacred site, and the spirit-filled landscape more after reaching the top, adding light-heartedly:

"The exercise will warm up our spirits too!"

"Hope so, it's cool enough," Rob added with understatement.

They could not see any frost from Anzac Hill lookout because it had not been heavy enough, but colder mornings could come at any time. Rob was first to speak, the tempo of his voice faster than usual in the pristine air.

"I got an email from Clara in New York and she wants to come to Central Australia. I miss her company, but I don't want to jeopardise anything we're doing. Everything you and I have shared is life-enhancing for me, and I feel I've got an ongoing role, but what do you reckon about her visiting?"

Rob's last sentence was delivered with a question mark, and with hardly any delay the Elder inhaled invigorating air and replied.

"She'd enjoy herself and feel relieved to be out of the city. Outback energies would help balance her, mind, body and spirit even without your presence, although *you* are why she's coming! Be good to know whether you two resonate in this environment, and if she relates to your research. We also have important 'men's business' to discuss, and naturally she can't be with us then."

"Yeah, of course. I understand that," Rob agreed.

"It could be a very valuable experience, more than you realise. Does that help? A few words that didn't say "yes," or "no"? You'll decide exactly the right thing," the Elder confirmed.

Rob half-smiled because he had hoped for a definite answer, one way or the other. However, he was also thankful because the decision was rightfully his and the reasons why were clear.

* * *

First light lit up the scattered high cloud with a gentle orange tone, matching the colour of the soil. Soon the MacDonnell Ranges would be touched by the same light that was bringing life to a new day. Both men absorbed the view and freshness as if it was their first experience of the Outback. It had that effect on them, and would continue to touch their souls for as long as they were blessed with breath. There was absolutely no need for words in this moment. In the quietness Rob would let thoughts of Clara simply flow with the vibrations of the day, and decide about her visit without pushing the proverbial river.

After a comfortable period without speaking, during which time the sun had risen and fully coloured the landscape, the Elder, now sitting with Rob on a wooden bench seat started to light the morning with his own words.

"That Sun Woman's like our Ancestor. She provides for our needs and her essence of light flows in us deeper than blood. She's so important that we'd die without her. That's why I'm up early to say welcome. She travels across the land faster than anything, and is everywhere at the same time. The Sun Woman sees and hears everything, even in the shade because she creates that too."

The beauty of the Elder's words fell gently and wisely on the morning. Throughout history people in their lust and greed to conquer had taken such simplicity to be weakness and ignorance. How misguided those prevailing voices had been. But in the years to come people will become aware of the real truths of living that Aboriginal cultures of the world have always known.

* * *

The horizon that Rob could see from Anzac Hill, formed in most directions by lines of hills, was not a boundary or a limit. It was the first circle of many concentric circles of energy and knowledge that would radiate from Central Australia. How this would commence was already established in other dimensions because the context was time-lessness, when past, present and future were one - when *now* was life's truest moment. Yet Rob wondered how the first step would manifest in practical terms. Fortunately he was confident about silently asking his higher self for guidance because he knew his increasingly finely-tuned intuition would provide the answers.

* * *

Still sitting quietly the Elder listened to his inner voice and Ancestors, his personal connections to Universal Love Energy. There was warmth and brightness in his eyes, a reflection of the awakening Winter's day. He leaned down and picked up his two hunting boomerangs.

"Surprised to see these?" He said, turning his head toward Rob. "They hold the essence of the ages because they're living beings. They've been sung dozens of times in just my lifetime. But the knowledge is on levels unknown to most people. They're usually seen as wooden tools or artefacts with multi-purpose uses. But it's their inner levels that people need to hear about and try to understand. The true spirit of the boomerang will be known again."

Rob was completely surprised and fell silent for a moment, but could not hold back his probing mind.

"Wow. How did they get here? I didn't see you carrying them. I understand what you're saying about other levels, but I can't explain how they got here!"

Anticipating Rob's response, the Elder passed one of the long mulga wood boomerangs to him.

"As you see that's one of the boomerangs I had at the gorge, and you know I brought it back to town. I wanted to talk about boomerangs this morning so I tuned in and asked the Ancestors and the Universe for guidance. The boomerangs manifested to illustrate the principle that there are realities beyond the logical, measurable world. Realities the god of science can't define or measure. How they materialised is simple. They moved from an unseen dimension into an observable one, the physical one we're in."

For the first time an explanation by the Elder did not completely satisfy Rob who suddenly thought of another possibility.

"Are you a clever-man?" He asked, speculating that his Western Aranda friend and mentor may be much more than he seemed.

In traditional culture the clever-men were highly respected, sometimes feared. Some were healers, teachers and visionaries, and all seemed to have magical powers. Very well known was the Kadaitcha man of Aranda country who administered punishment, justice, and sometimes death by pointing the bone.

"I've seen a lot and received much from the Universe and the Ancestors, even though I wasn't initiated into the highest levels. What just happened surprised me too, but it flowed and felt perfect in the moment. I'm not a clever-man, but I respond to the energies that come through."

"Yeah. I get what you mean. But isn't it mind boggling?" Rob asked, without needing an answer.

"I'll talk about materialisation if I'm guided to, but other levels are important, whether we know it or not. The hunting boomerangs were introduced in a magical way and they're tangible objects we can focus on. But for more impact and recognition I want you to have *this* boomerang."

Moments before finishing the sentence, the Elder leaned over and picked up another boomerang, an implement much more curved than the two longer, hunting ones. Rob had not noticed it before. "Unbeliev-able," he exclaimed then stared, shaking his head. But before he could say anything else, the Elder quickly asked a question.

"Ready for a huge challenge?"

"I'm ready for anything after seeing boomerangs appear out of thin air!" Rob answered eagerly.

Then the Elder's tone became formal.

"You are extremely privileged and have an incredible quest to undertake. You are going to search for *The First Boomerang*, the one that came in the Dreamtime!"

The Elder spoke with great weight and clarity, the words so tangible that Rob could have cupped them in his hands. Amazed and speechless, he hung on the Elder's next sentence.

"This curved boomerang is shaped like the one you're going to search for. The original artefact could be anywhere in Australia. Listen to your inner voice and your intuitive intelligence will flow. You'll be guided by it, and it will help more than logic. Take this traditional root returner and learn about it. How it was made. How it flies. How to throw it. Why it returns. If it's a sacred object. Your discoveries will inspire others. But this quest has to be totally confidential." The Elder emphasised. "A complete secret from *everyone*."

Rob held the boomerang reverently, totally astounded by his incomparable quest. He turned it over several times, felt the smooth, hard wood, instinctively balancing it on his right index finger on the lower curve of the bend. He knew something about boomerangs, but not enough. Discovering and communicating the true, complete story would be a privilege. There must be so many qualities embodied in this deceptively simple-looking flying implement, he thought, and before more thoughts came responded.

"Thank's Uncle. What an honour. There must be a lot of Australia's soul in the boomerang, but I don't think people know about it. I've got a long way to go too, but ideas and questions are coming in fast. It's amazing. About ten years ago I researched in the Mitchell Library in Sydney, but I haven't been back to it. Actually, the boomerang opened my window to Aboriginal culture."

The Elder responded with a knowing twinkle in his eye.

"Being ready is vital for progress. The research you did was groundwork that prepared the way for a bigger boomerang journey. Back then wasn't the time. It's often like that. We can't see the future, but think positively and we create a positive one."

"I'll bet throwing's a lot of fun. I can't wait." Rob added happily.

The Elder knew Rob would be thrilled and challenged, but there was a little more background to relate before he planned his search.

"German missionaries and adventurers took an active interest in Aboriginal culture for more than a hundred and fifty years. That was throughout Australia, including Hermannsburg of course, and a lot of papers, diaries and books are still in the German language. Get some early material translated if you need to. Anyway, you'll be guided to the correct books, but I'll give you a clue. One of the best ones is about my mob."

"Okay. Thanks so much. This is huge," Rob replied, his thoughts already transporting him across the continent searching for stories of the boomerang. He mentally flew over blue-green coastlines, orange-brown deserts and densely forested mountains, wondering where the search would lead him. Renewed enthusiasm and imagination were Rob's lively companions.

* * *

The sun was not casting shadows because it was noon in Alice Springs and both men, still sitting on a bench on Anzac Hill, were slightly surprised when they noticed. Several hours had vanished. Picking up on this theme, Rob ventured his thoughts.

"Isn't *time* a puzzle? You can't hold it in your hands. It goes fast, it goes slow. We whitefellas want to measure and manage it. But that hasn't helped us understand it any better. It's still a linear concept to most. Some even experience time moving about like jelly, yet invisible and outside the range of clocks and watches. Right now I'm surprised the morning's gone so quickly. Aren't you?"

This was suddenly an important topic for Rob, and seemed to spring up with its own force. As well as hearing the words, the Elder observed the energy around Rob and noticed something when he spoke. He was going to comment on it even before Rob aired his opinion, but waited.

"There's a special place we'll go on the next full moon to talk about the timelessness of time. That's better than starting the conversation now. When you were speaking the energy around your head had an edge of anxiety. Maybe you're not consciously aware of it, but it may be blocking your understanding of time, and yourself."

"Well, possibly. I'd say it's a mixture of anxiety and excitement plus emotion because of the quest." Rob explained.

"You're probably right," the Elder concluded.

After their cold, early morning start, the amazing announcement of Rob's quest, and the warming midday sun, both men were ready for food. Neither had arranged to be picked up but by the time they zigzagged back down the hill on the walking track, one of the Elder's relatives was waiting in his car. Much earlier Rob had walked from the Resort in the semi-darkness so he was pleased to get a ride.

They pulled away from the kerb and headed for the Heart of Australia Resort across the Todd River, still dry and sandy, its beautiful white-trunked river red gums the dominant trees. Rob had heard that visitors rushed down to watch the river flow after heavy rain upstream, and locals joined in too because it was so unusual. Understandable in such a dry region because it may only happen once every few years.

"Guess you've gotta be lucky to see water in the Todd?" Rob enquired.

"Yes. And there's an old local saying," the Elder began. "If you see the Todd flow three times you'll never leave."

"Love the sound of that. Thanks for the lift. We'll catch up soon," Rob responded.

Occasionally, a big flood would cause problems for local shop owners and residents, when swirling, muddy brown waters would affect property in low lying areas. But fortunately, those times were very rare.

Rob wondered whether he would see the Todd flowing, not necessarily on this trip, just one day. No doubt it played a role in the lives and stories of the Aranda, whether it was wet or dry. It was probably a Songline he reasoned, created by an Ancestral Being who travelled over this country in the Dreamtime. Was the Todd River a Songline? He would love to find out, but that research would have to wait.

He had arrived back a little sweaty so he went to his room and showered, then walked to the heated pool for a refreshing dip. As he frog-kicked under water, a message flashed into his mind. Popping his head out he said quickly and quietly.

"Clara should visit. I'll email her straight away."

That was it. A clear and concise message that answered Rob's pressing question. There was no effort, no lengthy deliberation or over use of the mind. The answer came easily. The solution had arrived and he felt much lighter.

Now comfortable in fresh clothes back in his room, Rob started planning his search for *The First Boomerang*.

In the middle of a large sheet of white paper he wrote *BOOMER-ANG* and circled it with a blue pen. Radiating from the central circle he drew short straight lines that linked with other circles in which he wrote sub-headings. They included themes to pursue, places to visit, resources to locate, and people to talk to. He also added "Intuition" in its own circle. For Rob this mind-map was a good way to get an idea moving, except perhaps for one other aspect. Did the project need a Mission Statement?

As far as Rob understood, Mission Statements enabled people to focus their energies on the same goals and be guided by agreed values and philosophy. They provided a format for people to express their visions in words for others and themselves. However, the quest to find *The First Boomerang* had been presented to Rob by the Elder. It was inspired by the Ancestors and the Universe, and was already imbued with sacred and positive energy.

This knowledge, plus the fact that the search must be kept secret, confirmed for Rob that no written mission was needed. Of most importance were an open mind, an open heart and an expanding intuition.

* * *

According to Rob's diary the moon would be full in thirteen days time. This was the evening when the Elder said they would go to a special place and watch it rise. It was also very close to the time Clara would probably arrive if she spent another week at work in New York City.

8

A perfect blue sky promised a reliably sunny Outback day and Rob woke with a clear purpose in mind. Before his meeting with the Elder that afternoon he wanted to complete his action plan for *The First Boomerang* quest.

After a brisk walk from the Resort he arrived at the Alice Springs Library at opening time, eager to find relevant books and to start writing detailed notes.

He was directed by friendly staff to the Alice Springs Collection housed in a reading room at the southern end of the building. The majority of books, maps and photographs recorded the life and lore of Central and Top End regions of the Northern Territory, and featured numerous works about Aboriginal art and culture as well as many others of European exploration and settlement.

Rob started browsing the shelves and found *A Straight-Out Man*, the life story of missionary F.W. Albrecht. It included personal accounts of the interactions between traditional Aranda and Luritja clans and the staff of the Lutheran Mission at Hermannsburg. This area was part of the Elder's country. Reports of the hardships of daily life including water shortages and the conversion of Aborigines to Christianity, were informative and fascinating.

Another valuable find was two illustrated books by Charles P. Mountford and Ainslie Roberts. Featuring Aboriginal legends from the Dreamtime and Robert's ink sketches and original oils, the stories transported Rob to ancient days and other dimensions.

The reference librarian mentioned other important works, directing Rob to a glass-doored cabinet which she opened with a key. The first volume that caught his eye was thick and looked old. It was the classic *Native Tribes of Central Australia* by Spencer and Gillen which presented highly detailed accounts of traditional Aranda life. Published in 1899 it contained superb black and white photographs never seen by Europeans before. After browsing illustrated pages of ceremonies and first-hand descriptions of daily activities, Rob noted it was one of several volumes by the same authors. Their names were familiar because on a map Rob had noticed Spencer Hill on the Old East Side of town, and he had admired distinctive Mt Gillen from Anzac Hill.

There was a wealth of material in the Collection and some of the volumes seemed to have been waiting for Rob to arrive! The appropriate books were finding him, as the Elder said they would.

* * *

About an hour before sunset Rob and the Elder overlooked the town and terrain from Anzac Hill. They had witnessed one beautiful sunset from this location but the colours, breezes and atmosphere changed often. There was always purpose in the Elder's decision to visit a place and Rob arrived expectantly, carrying the curved returning boomerang the Elder had given to him. International and local visitors marvelled at the panorama, eager to experience the Outback tones of sky and landscape that sunset brings, but they did not distract the two men. Pointing into the distance the Elder spoke.

"The clouds on that south-west horizon roll in from Pitjantjatjara and Yankunytjatjara country. Those mobs call themselves Anangu, meaning 'person' or 'people.' Uluru is there and so are Kata Tjuta's thirty six domes. Those sites are potent as you know, and hold big stories. The Anangu have their own language word for Dreamtime. They call it Tjukurpa or Chukurpa. Maybe we'll go over one day and listen to the old people's stories. They live in Multitjulu community close to Uluru."

Changing direction, the Elder drew Rob's attention to the Outback's most precious resource.

"Good drinking water was everything. It was a daily challenge and another reason I pointed out the far-off clouds. Even when they brought rain to that country they may not bring it to ours. We needed reliable soaks and waterholes. They were here, the Ancestors made sure of that. But too many droughts dried them up and we had to call on the Ancestors. You've heard of rain-making ceremonies?"

"Yeah. I know clans did rain dances," Rob answered straight away.

"My mob was one of them. Some elders were qualified to perform rain-making ceremonies. It was a special role and they belonged to the water totem. Water was one of their Dreamings."

Rob's curiosity had been aroused.

"Do you know much about it, how it worked?"

"In the old days magic was used in some circumstances including rain-making. It's very complex. I didn't go through all the Law so I don't know the full story. But the old people had profound belief in it. If results weren't positive, clan members knew failure was caused by incorrect behaviour in the ceremony. Or for neglecting a taboo. They had complete faith in the Ancestors, so it was the performers' fault if it didn't rain.

But what about now? There's water problems in Australia and across the world because of waste, theft and bad management. This is mainly because water isn't regarded as sacred. Do you regard it as sacred?" he asked Rob.

"I never waste it, that's my level of respect."

"That's a good start," he replied and continued. "The spiritual level has to be recognised so water is valued properly. But not with money.

Water is life. Life is priceless. Water *has* to be seen as sacred, and when more people get the message they'll respect it and use it better. But the situation's critical."

The need for sufficient water in the Outback is obvious, and the fact that both men were looking out over thousands of square kilometres of arid landscape gave the Elder's words considerable impact.

Rob looked again towards the distant clouds, his eyes fading out of focus. Beyond the present he instantly visualised a traditional ceremony in dry, vast Aranda country:

Three mature men are painted and decorated with feather down stuck on with their own blood. Strong, thin legs create energetic rhythms as their feet pound and pound into the dusty earth. Practised voices repeat the sacred chants accompanied by the clack-clack, clack-clack of boomerang clapsticks beating time. They were performing a rain-making sequence and each man wore a very tall head-dress with a tassell on the top.

As quickly as he had left for a moment, Rob popped back into the present. Was his 'vision' based on photographs he had seen in the library? The images were so clear, so real, it was as if the dancers had visited him personally. Perhaps he had 'flashed back' to his previous traditional life again! A little surprised by his sudden 'vision', he described it to the Elder who knew exactly what had happened.

"You're more in tune with other levels, and getting closer to moving in spirit between dimensions. More people now speak of psychic events in daily life and they're widely accepted. That's because the vibrations of the Cosmos and our Earth Mother are increasing. Everyone's affected and personal awareness is growing. It's a gift to receive visions. Give thanks whenever you can."

* * *

Rob was still holding the returning root boomerang and wondered if vivid 'flashes,' like the rain-making ceremony, would help him make the big discovery. By the sound of what the Elder had said, intuitive messages would definitely accompany him on the journey. They would have to, Australia is too vast otherwise. Rob's thoughts had jumped to the boomerang quest, so this was the moment to tell the Elder about it.

"I've got a three-part action plan to find *The First Boomerang*. First, I'll keep reading legends and work out which ones to follow-up. Second, I'll go to the legend's locations, look for clues and meet local Aboriginal people. That'll take me around Australia and I'll record my findings. Third is learning to throw and catch a boomerang properly, which sounds like great fun. Then the big question. Will this plan guide me to the place where *The First Boomerang* landed in the Dreamtime?"

Rob inhaled then exhaled, pushing the air through his lips and shaking his head slowly from side to side, in awe already of a possible momentous discovery. He became quiet for a few seconds.

"If the Ancestors smile and the miracle happens I'll be in touch straight away. Then we can decide how to tell the world."

"And the world will be ready," the Elder smiled knowingly.

He knew Rob was the right man to undertake this huge challenging quest, even though he had only recently arrived in Alice Springs. He also knew the boomerang was a symbol for all Humanity and hoped its real significance would finally be revealed.

The sun was sliding behind the orange MacDonnell Ranges as beautiful yellow beams illuminated small white clouds, gilding them with golden auras. Still providing enough light for both men as they stood up together, each pondered the afternoon's words and feelings. Quietly, in a tone of reverence and appreciation the Elder acknowledged the sun.

"The magnificent Sun woman came in the Dreamtime, lighting up the land as she moved from east to west. Here and now we're experiencing sacred light and breathing sun-drenched air thousands of generations since those first days."

9

On a quest like the one about to start, Rob felt it was crucial to travel solo. He felt experiences would unfold differently, more doors would open, and his insights and interpretations would be more personal. The Elder had mentioned aspects to learn about and an ultimate goal, implying it was the journey rather than the destination that would be of most spiritual benefit. Rob agreed in principle, however he was highly motivated by the possibility of making a Dreamtime discovery. And why not? It would be unprecedented.

There was also a very important personal aspect for Rob to consider. In just over a week his lady friend Clara Beaumont would be arriving from New York City. She knew he had not left Alice Springs on the Rock Art expedition, but did not know anything about his secret quest to find *The First Boomerang.*

* * *

Rob thought the Elder agreed with his American girlfriend coming to visit, but he wondered why, now he knew his boomerang journey must soon begin. These thoughts accompanied him as he locked his room, walked along the timber-floored verandah and left the key at Reception.

Stepping into a beautiful sunny morning Rob set off from the Resort to take the short walk into town to have a late breakfast in the

Todd Mall. On the previous day he had discovered "The Boomerang Café" and wanted to try its food. What he found extremely interesting was that he had not seen it before. Not until after the Elder announced his quest! Could it have opened in the last couple of days? Was it a sign from the Universe confirming he was on the correct spiritual path?

While crossing the bridge a battered-looking blue car drove towards him and he immediately recognised the Elder in the front passenger seat. They both waved and the older man made a circling motion with his hand, signalling that they would turn around and meet him on the other side. It was not lost on Rob how the Elder had unexpectedly appeared, very soon after he had been thinking about him.

After climbing in Rob told the Elder he was going into town to have breakfast, but the Elder said he had an extra bottle of water and a few apples that he hoped would be okay for now. Then the car accelerated and surprisingly went right around the roundabout and back over the bridge.

"We were coming over to find you. I'm going to a hill very close to town named after a well-known author and anthropologist. He first came into our country over a hundred years ago. I'll explain more when we get there."

A few minutes and a few kilometres later the Elder asked the driver, a young Aranda cousin whose shoulder-length black hair hugged his head because of a tight red sweat-band, to let them off on the corner of Gosse Street and Lindsay Avenue. As they approached, Rob could see a rocky, grassy hill beyond the corner. They pulled up near a children's playground with fresh green lawn, playing apparatus and landscaped areas, created and nurtured by local residents. From there it was a short walk to concrete steps and down across a wide, grassless overflow channel then up the other side on to a good dirt track made by the Northern Territory Parks and Wildlife Commission. The smooth track had several flat rocky sections and ran along the western side of the hill, continuing beyond a closed gate to the Alice Springs Telegraph Station. They were not going that far, but veered off the track and walked straight towards a medium-sized tree whose white trunk contrasted perfectly with the rusty-brown boulders on the slopes of the hill. Rob was carrying a water bottle and apples thanks to the Elder, so they would be okay for a couple of hours. In fact Rob was not hungry now, his plan to eat in town evaporating once the Elder invited him to come along.

They walked past the tree and sat on a large tan-brown rock. Rob knew this must be a special place otherwise the Elder would not have brought him to it. The sunlight was as bright as usual, adding depth and contrast to the plants and boulders on the hillside. As they sat and quietly absorbed the energy, a large fork-tailed kite gracefully circled above them before lifting over the hill on an updraft of warming air. According to measured time it was close to 11.00am, the sun was almost overhead, morning shadows had nearly disappeared, and the Elder looked towards the hill.

"That author and anthropologist was Baldwin Spencer and he was genuinely interested in Aranda culture, and used the spelling Arunta. With Frank Gillen, Stationmaster and Post Master in the late 1890s and early 1900s he recorded aspects of traditional life such as stone and wooden artefacts, body decoration and important ceremonies. Some of my mob aren't happy about that, mainly because Gillen 'collected' a lot of sacred objects and both men filmed and photographed secret rituals. But, we're extremely fortunate to have their archive. Today we can see rare pictures and descriptions of the old days, learn about the advanced skills and high social standards of traditional culture. Spencer and Gillen did us a great service and still do whenever someone discovers their books, and they've both been honoured. The European name of this place is Spencer Hill, and there's a residential area as well as the mountain named after Gillen."

"Yeah, I certainly know the names and I was fascinated by a couple of their thick scholarly books I browsed in the library," Rob said, looking at the distinctive hill.

"It's a wonderful legacy," added the Elder, then changed the subject. "Now, this beautiful ghost gum is connected to me, but it's not my totem. It's connected to you too, because we all have the same energy of life. I learned this old knowledge through dances and stories, and reading about other cultures but you seem to have a natural understanding."

Concepts like this were not strange to Rob, especially after being with the Elder in the hidden gorge, researching traditional culture and reading spiritual books for years. However, he realised how vital it was for the world to hear this knowledge, yet right now he also recalled he wanted to ask the Elder about Clara's visit.

"Remember me saying Clara's coming out from New York? I asked myself if it was the right thing: I got a positive 'flash' and sent her an email. But things have moved along. My *First Boomerang* quest suddenly came up and I need to do that by myself. I'm puzzled because I can't see how I'll spend much time with her. Plus, we're going to a special place on the Full Moon and that's about the same day she arrives!"

The Elder, nodding slowly, allowed Rob's words to linger for a moment in the comfortable sunshine.

"No one can live the future before it arrives. You acted out of truth when you invited her. Now the picture's bigger. Keep acting out of truth. Don't give energy to what you think *might* happen. No one knows that, including Clara. But look forward to a bit of fun with her," winked the Elder.

"Yeah, for sure," Rob winked back.

"And the Full Moon's coming and there's important information to hear before setting out on your quest. Naturally, it can't be received until the right moment, in the right place."

After Rob heard the Elder's last sentence he stood up and acknowledged within that *Time* was *Now* and it contained the future and therefore the answers to his questions. Letting his thoughts ponder the concept he lifted his water bottle, savouring a mouthful of its cool contents. The Elder also drank from his water bottle and asked Rob an unexpected question.

"Can you see any light around the tree?"

Rob was surprised because he was just staring unconsciously at nothing in particular and thinking about *Time*. But as he had found during earlier meetings with the Elder, he should be prepared at any time to respond, interpret, and decide his next thought, word and action. Here was such a moment, so he confidently responded.

"If there was no light I couldn't see the tree at all, but I know you mean something else."

The Elder did not respond because he knew Rob would explore his own thoughts and go deeper.

"In Rock Art photos you see human figures with lines radiating from them, others with semi-circular lines around the head like a halo. That 'light' is the aura, and plants give off energy that can be seen and recorded. So that's probably what you're asking. I know the concept intellectually, but I can't see any light or energy coming from the tree: its trunk, its branches, or its leaves!"

Rob had nothing to add, so the Elder continued on the same theme.

"Energy radiates from everything at different frequencies all the time. There's energy coming from that gum tree right now - it's yellow in colour - but most people can't see it. Every plant, animal and mineral across the earth radiates energy. Everything's inter-connected. We all embody the same Universal Love Energy."

The Elder kept confirming this truth, day after day, so Rob would fully grasp its importance and magnitude. No doubt, Rob felt, so he would be thoroughly confident about it when giving public talks and interviews later.

The day was becoming warmer and there were few trees in the area so they moved closer to the ghost gum, finding a shaded rock. While sitting down the Elder gestured toward Spencer Hill, made of soil and grasses and dominated by neatly piled boulders.

"The hill was created by Caterpillar Ancestors who walked all over this country in the Dreamtime. Some journeys started in Mbantua and prominent natural features were formed. One type of caterpillar, *Yepe-renye* or *Yipirinya*, is honoured in town with an Aboriginal school and shopping centre named after it. Ancestors, animals and people have come together here since time began. That's why it's a *'meeting place'."*

"Yeah. It was our 'meeting place' too," Rob responded with a chuckle.

"The hill," continued the Elder, "is home to a colony of rock wallaby or *arrwe*. There's good protection up there. We've been quiet, but they know we're here and we're not hunters! Most are asleep because it's the middle of the day. That's part of their pattern. They rest during the warmer hours then come out before sunset. If we climbed up now we mightn't see any, even though dozens live there. But later when the shadows are long and the air's cooler they'll come out. They'd look down at us, especially the curious young ones, then hop away and get on with eating."

Rob was interested in the Caterpillar Dreamings and rock walla-bies, but suddenly he received a 'flash' that he had to go back to town. It was so quick and so definite. Now familiar with his intuition he knew it should be followed. The Elder, sensing a change and without a word, nodded up and down as if he had heard Rob's inner message. They both stood up and the Elder said.

"When we get back to town you'll know what to do. We'll talk about the Caterpillars later because they're always here. The Ancestors are still close, and the rock wallabies aren't going anywhere."

Rob was amazed because the Elder had apparently realised he wanted to go back to town before he said anything! But he should not be surprised. The Elder's knack for 'knowing' was often readily evident.

"How did you know?"

"Intuition's my constant mate," replied the Elder.

"How exciting, how exciting to be tuned-in so highly," Rob acknowledged with respect.

"We've all got it. It just takes trust."

It didn't take them long to walk back along the track to the street, and no sooner had they crossed to the other side than an empty taxi came along. Rob waved it down, inwardly thanking Cosmic Timing, and asked the driver to take them to the Elder's home before dropping him at the Resort. The Resort was closer than the Elder's place, but Rob regarded it as simple courtesy to see his artist-mentor home first. While en route they both relaxed without speaking, then as the Elder prepared to get out he said:

"Come back here about an hour before sunset, after you've finished everything."

* * *

The taxi pulled away and Rob was soon back at the Heart of Australia Resort. This was as much as he had 'seen' in his intuitive 'flash' at Spencer Hill. Now it was logical to ask at Reception for any messages. After quoting his room number to the smartly dressed young lady he was handed two sheets of paper neatly folded together. They were faxes and Rob began reading as he walked along the verandah, the first on the letter-head of the South Australian Museum.

Dear Rob,

Thank you for your recent enquiry about Legends and Boomerang references and materials of the Flinders Ranges. The Museum's collections are not usually categorised by region, subject or traditional group in the case of Indigenous archives, but rather in collections as they are donated or bequeathed to the Museum. For example, we hold the entire archive of Norman B. Tindale who spent several decades undertaking expeditions and researching Aboriginal culture throughout Australia. This is a vast collection containing many bound journals, papers, wax cylinders, slides and photographs, and would be invaluable for your research.

Another prominent anthropologist was Charles P. Mountford who also spent many years collecting Aboriginal materials, including numerous legends, some from the Flinders Ranges. However, the Mortlock Library holds the Mountford/Sheard Collection and you would have to approach it directly. Unfortunately, we cannot arrange to send any of our materials to the Alice Springs Library. Therefore, any part of the archive will have to be viewed in person, including boomerang artefacts and films, which I believe would be of particular interest to you.

On the following page I have enclosed details of the Museum's web site as well as that of the State Library, of which the Mortlock Library is part. Tindale's work was meticulously written up and often illustrated, and I have listed several suggestions for you to follow up on the web site. There is so much material so please be as specific as possible regarding your enquiries.

I have enclosed the Museum's guidelines regarding copying of material, publication fees, copyright, acknowledgements, etc. I trust that this outline is helpful and I would be happy to arrange an appointment for you.

Yours sincerely,

P. J. Frederickson, PhD., Director of Archives, South Australian Museum.

The second fax had familar, artistic handwriting and simply said,

Be seeing you soon honey, read your email, Love Clara XXX.

Rob closed the room door behind him, walked to the table and opened his laptop. It quickly sprang into virtual life and after clicking onto his internet provider he found three new emails, one of course from Clara. She again started her message with the joint, international greeting she had created.

Hi-G'day Rob, How's my wonderful Outback man? I can't wait to see you very soon... Time has been dragging and I'm just hanging in! My flights are now confirmed so I'll be arriving next week on July 16.

I've packed most things already and I figured two pieces of luggage plus my carry-on bag would be enough for the trip. On the family scene, my mother has not been too well and her doctor doesn't seem able to work out why she's so tired so often. He prescribed a mild stimulant and she's happy with that, but she has very little energy even during the day. I wish she would talk to a Naturopathic doctor. Work has been extra rewarding because I've really had to focus and work late each day to finish everything before flying out. New York's been hot and that's how I like it, know what I mean?

You must have heard a lot of 'men's business' from your Elder by now. It's something I want to share, but I can't ... as you said before. Will I get to meet any women elders, or do they live in the bush? I guess I'm open to whatever happens Down Under, but meaningful contact with the Aborigines would be special.

I'll fly into Alice Springs on Qantas domestic from Sydney after the long leg from L.A. So, Outback buddy, I touch down at 12 noon and I know you'll be there. All the hugs you will ever need are coming your way. Until very, very soon sweet love ... Clara XXX.

Rob read the message a few times, clicked it closed then clicked again, dragging it into "Clara's" folder. There were still two emails to read, but Rob wanted to have a shower then order a fresh salad lunch through room service. He did both and just before he finished eating, a Resort staff member phoned and said that another fax had come in. Rob walked down to Reception straight away and was surprised to see it was from the South Australian Museum, but curiously marked "URGENT"! Immediately, he read it to himself.

Dear Rob,

Since writing to you this morning we have received unexpected but welcome news from the South Australian Government. In its new financial year budget it has allocated funding for the refurbishment of our building and this work will impact directly on the availability of space for archival research. Unfortunately this means that all public access will have to cease on 25th July at close of business because building work can now commence during August.

In a similar but much larger undertaking several years ago, the large galleries of the Museum were redesigned and refitted, and now both staff and the public are reaping the benefits. That of course is what will flow from this building's refurbishment, but it will affect researchers like yourself for some time.

Most importantly however, the Museum Board said today that any appointments made for dates before and including the 25th will be honoured, and we hope that this sudden deadline will suit your timetable. This is specifically why I have written again.

Obviously, there is not much time before late July, so please let me know if and when you would like to view the materials at the Museum. I should add that both the Museum's Director, and I, do not know precisely when the building will re-open. Sincerely, P. J. Frederickson.

Rob was impressed by the conscientious approach of Museum management and knew he must act quickly and book his appointments. Delighting mentally in the research prospects, other thoughts suspended for a moment, Rob suddenly remembered that Clara would soon be arriving and their time together would be directly affected by this latest news.

However, he knew that in the next couple of weeks he must research the artefacts, recorded materials and other treasures of the Tindale and Mountford/Sheard Collections. This would be the first in-depth part of his *First Boomerang* journey so it had to happen. The quest was established and Rob needed to respond to its signs, knowing the time to act was now. Nothing else, personal or professional could stand in the way.

With his thoughts already racing and imagining new research trails, Rob had almost forgotten there were two other emails to read, so he quickly walked back to his room and re-opened the laptop. Since the quiet time with the Elder at Spencer Hill, Rob's afternoon had gained pace mentally and emotionally, and the next email would not slow things down.

Dear Lindsay Williams via Rob Noble,

You will recall your request on the Aboriginal Artefact Archive web site seeking information about specific objects (Tjurunga) removed from Central Australia late in the nineteenth century and early twentieth. In short, I believe I have found some. Information has come to me that a family whose forebears were directly involved at Hermannsburg Mission still have several objects because they were passed down through the family. My source, a relative and friend, says she remembers the objects were wrapped and kept in an old hessian sugar bag. She also said her older cousins always emphasised that none of the objects should be unwrapped or seen by anyone, particularly girls and women. It seemed to her that her cousins understood how special, even sacred these items were to the Aborigines who lived at the Mission.

This appears to be a genuine 'sighting' and I would be quite happy to connect you with my friend and arrange an exchange of details. It was amazing how this arose because I was simply surfing Aboriginal Artefacts on the net and came across your site. But what was really coincidental was that my friend was visiting from Sydney and literally looking over my shoulder when your request came on the screen! The subject matter sparked her memory, hence my note today. Further, I've seen over the years that coincidence is the coming together of people and events when they're supposed to, as if there's a life-script at work, so the whole episode was rather exciting.

Finally, and so you have a geographical perspective, these artefacts are in the spare room of a house in the Adelaide Hills! Please let me know if you would like to follow this up, and I do trust you're having success in your search.

Cheers, Peter Rockworthy.

Talk about Cosmic Timing, Rob said under his breath. Sounds like Adelaide's the place to be, then adding aloud. "Two vital destinations in the same city in under an hour. Fantastic. Proves I had to get back to the Resort! I'll forward this to the Elder straight away." Rob would now urgently make appointments to explore both opportunities during the same visit, knowing that's what the Elder would also want.

Rob's unfolding research played in his thoughts and signals were coming to mind about things the Elder had said. Not just words, but about understanding the flow of life. Since he had written *The First Boomerang* action plan important leads and information had appeared. The Universe supported the quest because his intention was clear, precise and empowered by enthusiasm. Now this flow was being confirmed with results. In thinking of the Elder, Rob remembered he had to meet him about an hour before sunset, and that time was fast approaching.

Rob closed Peter Rockworthy's email and clicked on his third Inbox message. It was from an address he immediately recognised. During the past week Rob had emailed institutions including the Museum and Art Gallery of the Northern Territory in Darwin and the Western Australian Museum in Perth. He had requested information about legends, boomerangs, and boomerang art in the lore of regional traditional groups, and was delighted one had responded so soon. The lengthy message was from Darwin.

Dear Rob,

Your email was passed on from the Museum because of my many years recording Rock Art in the Victoria River District (VRD) of the Northern Territory. This research enables me to develop close associations with Aboriginal custodians, a privilege I greatly value.

Remarkably, I've even taken custodians to see paintings because they did not know about them. In most cases I recorded art that had never been seen by non-Aboriginals, usually because the sites are remote, unmarked and barely accessible by vehicle or even on foot. Amongst them I'm sure there are several that would interest you. For example one site features an Ancestral Being, a large snake and two hook boomerangs or number sevens. They're painted on the ceiling of a large sandstone overhang and the art is outstanding and hasn't deteri-

orated over the years. You may be able to link these paintings with their stories, although much of the oral history has been lost for obvious reasons. However, clues and remnants can still be found.

I'm also writing to tell you I'll be visiting several sites in the VRD, three of which have excellent paintings of boomerangs, including the one above with the hooks, and you're welcome to join me and my field assistant. The arrangement would be that I'd provide transport and camping gear, (bring your own swag if you prefer), as well as food and other supplies. I would simply ask that you chip in one third of the food and fuel costs and agree not to disclose the location of any of the sites, although you may photograph them, but once again, without identifying where they are to anyone.

I've just been given the go-ahead by the N. T. Museum, so the notice is very short, in fact I'll be leaving Darwin on 28th July for approximately ten days. Let me know as soon as possible if you're able to come, so I can plan accordingly. Before the trip you may want to read Taboo *by Bill Harney and* Songs of the Songmen *by Bill Harney and Professor A. P. Elkin. Both would be excellent background. I look forward to hearing from you. Regards, Geoffrey Seekman.*

As Rob read the email his excitement grew and grew. How wonderful to receive an invitation like this. He had started library research to help find *The First Boomerang*, but did not have a pre-conceived plan about where to go. Yet in less than an hour the first two to three weeks had become perfectly clear. The surprising, even ironical aspect was that the Victoria River District had been part of the original Rock Art expedition. Apparently, he was destined to go there.

Rob opened his diary and wrote in dates for Adelaide and Darwin, realising there were only two full days between the Museum's closing date in Adelaide and the start of Geoffrey Seekman's trip to the VRD. But he was confident the details would flow smoothly because he felt sure this was how the journey was meant to unfold. In a word it was perfect, and Rob began repeating the word aloud as he walked around his room.

"Perfect.... perfect.... perfect."

Real inner excitement always got Rob moving, his muscles wanting to express his personality through action. Then he heard the Elder's voice within, reminding him they were soon to meet. Rob clicked and dragged both emails into the "Contacts" folder before closing his laptop.

Then, grabbing his red and green waist-length jacket, two apples and a large bottle of spring water, Rob put the room key in his pocket, left his room and walked down to the 4WD and climbed in. After driving for only five minutes he pulled up outside the Elder's house. Before he could get out the Elder came out of the front door, waved to Rob, and started walking towards the Toyota.

"Hey there, listen to this," called out Rob raising his voice. "An email came in to the Artefacts website about old tjurunga from Hermannsburg. Says there's some in a house in Adelaide..."

"Really? So soon. That's great Rob," the Elder smiled broadly. "That's a wonderful start, and I've got a good feeling."

"Yeah, me too. It was fantastic to read, and I forwarded it to you about ten minutes ago. I'll follow it up in Adelaide if you like."

"The Universe is smiling Rob. Let's work out details for Adelaide later," the Elder said, as he got into the car, and changed the subject.

"Have you been to Olive Pink?" The Elder did not need an answer because he knew what they were going to do next. "Let's go over and have a look."

Rob had not been to the *Olive Pink Botanic Garden* and it was a real eye-opener, especially the story of Olive Pink, its founder. After only reading the colourfully illustrated information boards, viewing photographic displays and collections of seeds and dried flowers, Rob realised the Garden was a significant legacy. A special area set aside and preserved to honour the vision of one caring, passionate and determined woman. But was there another reason the Elder had brought him here?

Outside the Visitor Centre the Elder pointed to the nearby rocky hill that looked more like an outcrop, beckoning Rob to follow him over to a narrow track at its base. Using the protocol to which Rob had become familiar, the Elder spoke in old Aranda, alerting the spirits of the hill that they were going to climb on it. Rob followed his lead, silently speaking in English to convey similar meaning.

From there they moved briskly up the hill for a surprisingly short and relatively easy walk. At the top there was a finely framed, antique-looking garden chair just wide enough and strong enough to hold them both. Spread out below, a panorama of the eastern side of Alice Springs faded into low ridge lines and far-off hills. And then, as they both carefully sat down, Rob asked a question.

"What's the significance of this place?"

The Elder adjusted his seating position slightly and looked wistfully at the horizon before answering.

"Caterpillar Ancestors were also responsible for this unique hill. Look how it rises abruptly above the Todd River and surrounding plain. It's been called Annie Meyer Hill for years, but was named *Tharrarltneme* in the Dreamtime.

For local Aranda it's a sacred site, but it's not honoured fully very often. If the real story was told and retold it could be, yet like all sites the full story's only available to the initiated. But we don't need the complete story to respect it. We only need the public story. Strangely, it's only when people have full knowledge of a sacred site that it can affect them. If we don't know the full story we won't be affected. But it's good to know some of the story and respect the site more."

Rob took in the Elder's words, reflecting seriously on them, then positively vocalised his thoughts.

"This hill is sacred, you know some of the story, and we're both walking on it, how does that affect its sacredness?"

There was no break in the flow of conversation, the Elder continuing:

"Sacredness has various levels, each related to an individual's level of understanding. An initiated Aboriginal has the deepest understanding and a person who only sees this as a hill has the least. But the public part of the Aranda story can be told. And it will add dimension to everyone's appreciation of it, as you know already. Yet whatever our level of understanding, this sacred hill respects us too."

"That's very interesting," Rob confirmed. "That means the Dreamtime legends we read are the public stories. But there's usually more levels to them, and we're connected to the hill by Universal Love Energy."

"Exactly. Although I'm not a senior custodian of this Mbantua country, I know some of the sacred places and the protocols for visiting them. I've talked about this 'business' with local men, and our visit wouldn't have happened today if things weren't right. The Ancestors know I brought you here to share enough knowledge to respect this place.

Some of my mob don't agree that our knowledge should be shared. But I'm being guided psychically by the Universe and the Ancestors, and that's my authority. People call this 'channelling,' but the description's not important. Content and timing are. Your girlfriend arrives next Full Moon, the biggest moon of the year."

The Elder often jumped to another topic while discussing something else, because that was how information flowed to him.

"Last week I said I'd take you to a place on the Full Moon and talk about the 'timelessness of time'. That moment's almost here, but you'll still be able to see Clara for about two hours before we go bush for the night."

Rob was not surprised by the Elder's words, even though he had not told him what time she was flying in. But he immediately wondered what Clara would think! She was literally travelling half way around the planet and they would barely have time to say hello before he would be leaving her for the night. But that is how it was, and how it had to be.

The Elder was confident that her visit would work out well, but as they walked back down the hill he had something else on his mind. "When I get home I'll read that email straight away," he said, thinking of the lost tjurunga in Adelaide."

1 0

Alice Springs Airport - 16th July, 2000.

The Arrivals screen showed that Qantas Flight 282 from Sydney would arrive in fifteen minutes at 12 noon, precisely on time. Rob was outside eagerly looking skyward for his first glimpse of the aircraft. Out beyond the bar and restaurant where he was standing, friends and passengers were taking advantage of a patio area, sitting in the shade or the sunshine and enjoying farewell drinks. Some talking. Some not. Adjoining this area, landscaped lawns and gum trees enclosed by a high mesh fence made the surroundings green and inviting, but blocked views of the runway.

Rob did not see the Boeing 737 jet touch down but it appeared suddenly and loudly, its roaring engines subsiding before it taxied toward its allotted parking position. He walked quickly back through the busy bar to the Arrivals and Departure Area, found a good position, then stared expectantly at the aircraft for the first sign of Clara.

Purpose-built vehicles incorporating stairways were driven up to the front and rear doors of the jet with its famous kangaroo livery. Once positioned, the stairways were raised hydraulically, and passengers walked down them and across the tarmac to a tiled, open-sided walkway leading to the Terminal.

It was a beautiful warm day, just 26 degrees Celsius, a Winter temperature some cities around the world would be happy with in Summer. Several passengers were descending the steps when Clara, in a flash of tropical turquoise came into view. She walked down the steps, a sea-green carry bag in her left hand, reaching the bottom then striding towards the Terminal. For a few moments Rob lost her behind the trees, but she reappeared under the covered walkway almost at the door.

Delighted and smiling Rob strode forward, his familiar feelings of affection suddenly rising from a dormant level within. She spotted him and rushed over, dropping her bag as they smiled, hugged and kissed. It was a beautiful moment and they felt it fully, squeezing tightly before easing back and looking lovingly at each other.

"Glad you made it Outback buddy. I missed you." Clara smiled.

Unspoken thoughts and feelings lingered behind every word, and Rob understood what Clara meant.

"Great to see you *mate*. Welcome, you look fantastic."

Rob emphasised *mate* because Clara enjoyed him calling her *mate*. Their excited reconnection was just a start, and in a short while they would talk and talk and share so much. That was the expectation of one of them anyway. Clara hooked her arm inside Rob's and he turned and began to walk, guiding them out to the Baggage Claim area. While they waited Clara could not contain herself and asked in a loud whisper directly into Rob's right ear.

"When are we going into the *bush*?"

Clara confidently exaggerated *bush* with her North American accent. She had picked up many Australian words from Rob in Manhattan and loved using them.

"Really soon sweetheart, but glad you asked." Rob offered with mixed feelings. "I know this'll be a surprise, but I've got to go bush with the Elder in a couple of hours. We'll be out overnight because it's the biggest Full Moon this year and there's information I have to hear."

"But I want to be with you tonight honey. It feels like a long, long time Outback man. Why does the Full Moon have to be today?"

Clara responded tongue-in-cheek with unspoken resignation because she sensed the arrangements would not change. She knew why Rob was in Central Australia and that his work was his priority. But a woman in love sometimes thinks her influence can change a man's priorities, and his direction can be refocused with subtle encouragement.

"Don't know who arranged the Full Moon this week, but I've got to go and see it."

"Are you sure? I'm longing for a cuddle."

"Me too," replied Rob. "And I want to show you how much, but..."

There was no need for Rob to finish the sentence because his face reflected his disappointment. For the moment Clara would have to accept the situation and spend only two hours with Rob.

This was Clara's first trip Down Under and she was ready to start exploring. She had learned about Australia from movies and tourism advertising, and also from Rob's entertaining travel anecdotes. Her interest in Aboriginal culture was developing because of Rob's knowledge, but as yet she had no personal experience. Nor would this be remedied soon because Rob had to go with the Elder, and Clara unfortunately would have to spend her first night in Alice Springs alone. As unexpected as this was, movement-free rest in a comfortable hotel bed without background jet engine noise would be most welcome.

Clara's two bags came around on the carousel and she and Rob trolleyed them out through the automatic terminal doors towards the car park. After loading them onto the back seat of the 4WD they headed into town along a very good two lane, bitumen road.

"You *do* drive on the left side!" Clara exclaimed with a surprised tone in her voice.

"Yeah. Remember I told you in New York?"

"But actually seeing it is weird. You can do all the driving." Clara confirmed as she started to appreciate a new and different landscape.

"I thought it would be drier with lots of red sand, but there's more trees than I imagined. It's beautiful." Clara smiled, looking toward the horizon.

"What's that low line of hills with the gap in the middle way across there?" She asked, pointing to the right. "Is that the Mac-Donnell Ranges?"

In answering, Rob began introducing local Aboriginal history.

"Yes, that's right. Isn't it amazing that Alice Springs sits behind them? The town's fairly close but we go through another gap in the MacDonnell's to get there. We're coming in from the south and the range runs about six hundred and fifty kilometres - four hundred miles to you - across the heart of Australia. The Caterpillar and Wild Dog Ancestors of the local Aranda mob created it."

"In the Dreamtime, right?" Ventured Clara, knowing she was correct. "And *mob* sounds familiar, you mentioned it in the States."

"Yeah, it just means family or people, big groups and small," Rob answered. "They have a story for every hill, rocky outcrop, water hole, bird and animal in their country, even stars and constellations. Traditional culture has layer upon layer of knowledge. I'm barely scratching the surface. But tell me, how was the flight?"

"I've been up and on the go for over 30 hours but the time passed in a blurr – it's like a dream now. But it was fine - the food, flight attendants, too many movies - everything was good. I read one of the books you gave me, so my knowledge of traditional culture is improving. And the stories Rob. Where did they come from? I know from the Dreamtime, but they're so simple and graphic and explain everything. Can I talk to someone about them?"

Rob knew exactly how Clara felt because years earlier he had a similar desire to make contact with Aboriginal people. Now after much book research and personal experience with the Elder he was learning a lot very quickly because he was invited to do so. But he also knew it was a rare experience for a stranger to speak to local Aborigines about their stories, and it had to be earned. How one earned that privilege was usually unspoken.

"We'll just have to see how things unfold. I hope you can speak to someone, but there's no set way to make it happen. It's really up to the Universe and Ancestors. I mean that sincerely, although it sounds a bit *different.* Contact will flow if it's meant to. That may sound passive, but it's not. You'll have to send out a clear intention, then be ready when the time is right: yours and Cosmic Timing. Now let's focus on *country.* We're getting close to *Ntaripe* in Aranda language, or the Gap, Heavitree Gap." Rob pronounced *Ntaripe* again, then said to Clara.

"Have a go at saying it..."

Without hesitation Clara attempted her first word in an original Australian language.

"Nahripay?"

"That's great. Are you ready to meet the Alice?"

Clara smiled warmly and acknowledged Rob's question by reaching over and softly caressing the back of his neck.

"I want to be close to you, share whatever we can, and I want to start, but tonight you're away! The Outback's always had tantalising mystique and been a must-see place, so I'm ready to explore as soon as we can, so please hurry back."

Rob responded with softly spoken affection as he drove through the Gap, pointing out its red-brown rock strata angled at forty-five degrees. He turned fourth left off a very wide roundabout and cruised alongside the dry, sandy river bed with islands of couch grass and gum trees.

"This is the Todd River or *Lhere Mparntwe*, famous because it's dry! But seriously, I'm glad you understand I have to go with the Elder. This whole experience is a once-in-a-lifetime chance. I don't know when I'll get back tomorrow but it'll be as early as possible. In the last couple of days things started happening very quickly and opportunities suddenly opened up, so I hope you really do understand."

Clara felt herself becoming slightly uneasy within. She could sense Rob had more to tell her and by the sound of his voice it wasn't about their time together! In fact, Rob was about to explain what he meant as they passed white-trunked gums in the river bed, when Clara perked up, saying,

"Aren't they beautiful. I've never seen trees like that. I'd love to touch them later."

"They're river red gums, Aussie eucalypts, and they've got a thousand stories to tell. But I'd better finish what I was saying. Out of the blue I received a fax from the South Australian Museum saying the building used by researchers will be renovated and there'll be no access for months. That means I have to view materials in the next week! Also, I've been invited on a field trip way up north in the Victoria River District. There's rare Aboriginal Rock Art which would be impossible to find by myself. And that trip departs in twelve day's time! This all happened just before you arrived."

The ensuing silence in the vehicle brought them to a smaller roundabout where Rob first flicked on the right indicator, then the left at exit three, and drove onto a bridge over the Todd River. They were seconds away from the Heart of Australia Resort and Clara's inner world was a mixture of nervous energy and scrambled thoughts.

"I think I must be jet-lagged! That's a lot to take in Rob. What about our time together?"

Rob eased the 4WD under the high roof linking two main buildings, sliding into a parking spot close to the Reception area. He was already feeling the vibrations of Clara's anxiety, but he had also been waiting to see her again. His loving feelings for her may have been in the back of his mind recently, but now he was experiencing them acutely. He leaned close, kissed her on the lips and whispered gently:

"We've got about an hour and a half. Let's catch up inside for a cuddle and see if you're jet-lagged at all."

1 1

After another full-body hug and a last, long goodbye kiss Rob left Clara at the Resort and drove off to meet the Elder. The afternoon had settled into familiar and dependable July sunshine, the temperature was about 25 degrees Celsius and for the first time in several days the breeze had dropped to a slight breath that barely flickered the leaves of the river gums.

Rob's contribution to the Full Moon trip was to bring medium-weight swags, a bag of food with apples and bananas, cans of fish and vegetables, a billy and loose black tea leaves and two large bottles of spring water. He was due to pick up the Elder at 2.30pm at his place, and then they would drive to a special location to watch the big moon rise.

He had wondered about this trip ever since the Elder mentioned it. His words now felt like a long time ago, but it had been less than a couple of weeks. Again, Rob was placing something in perspective by relating it to *time*. This word, this concept, popped up so regularly, probably a dozen times a day.

What would the Elder tell him on this perfect Alice Springs day? What did traditional people know about the concept with which most cultures manage society? To some extent Rob knew how sophisticated a clan member's knowledge of country was. But how could Aboriginal groups with basic material possessions, no alphabet for writing, and no mechanical devices for measuring, know about a complicated concept like *Time*?

These questions, as well as intimate thoughts of Clara occupied his mind as he drove the white 4WD towards the Elder's house. The Elder was standing outside and as soon as Rob stopped the vehicle he opened the front passenger door and climbed in.

"Afternoon," smiled Rob. "What a beautiful day."

"Afternoon. You look happy. How's Clara?" The Elder asked with a knowing smile.

"She's happy too. We made up for lost time." He answered, still smiling.

"Now you're right for the evening," the Elder chuckled. Let's hit the road."

The Elder asked Rob to drive out of town to the west along Larapinta Drive. Although this road is heavily used by locals and tourists, few know the meaning of the name, so the Elder explained.

"Larapinta sounds good, listen: "La-ra-pin-ta." He said slowly, emphasising its syllables. "Hear that rhythm? Isn't that a sweet sound?" The Elder enthused. "It comes from two Western Aranda language words: *"Lhere"* for 'creek' or 'river,' and *"apirnte"* which means 'salty'. They form the traditional name for the river we now call Finke. From *'Lhere'* comes *'Lara'*; from *'apirnte'* comes *'pinta';* which together make "Larapinta" now used on maps and road signs.

Larapinta Drive links the Todd in Alice with the Finke at Hermannsburg, and when good rains fall they both flow through gaps in the MacDonnells. Farther out, Namatjira Drive runs parallel to the old Caterpillar at varying distances, so you could say the Ancestors influenced its route across country."

"That's remarkable. People have to hear these stories. They'd love to know Larapinta's real origin." Rob said, thanking the Elder as they drove westward, the afternoon sun's glare impacting on the windscreen.

Although it was Winter there were still two hours before sunlight would disappear and bring on darkness for moonrise. Rob was only driving at 100kmph and the Elder did not say how far they were going or where to turn off, so he kept the Toyota cruising, adjusting the sun visor as the sun sank lower in the immeasurably wide sky. Quietness settled over the two men, both heading for a destination only one of them knew.

* * *

Soon after, Rob was hearing his inner voice stirring his physical voice, so despite the comfortable silence he encouraged the words to flow.

"When water's solid in a block of ice, it's like *Time* standing still. You know the feeling. Other days it seems to go fast, especially when we're enjoying ourselves, hence the proverbial, "Time goes faster when you're having fun". So, does *Time* have various speeds? Experiments prove that *Time* is slower at altitude than on earth. The human body's affected in space and over a long period a person's height will reduce! Imagine that!"

After gazing out of the passenger window at the ancient Caterpillar, the Elder gently wiped the back of his right hand across his lips.

"Good to hear your mind seeking answers, but mind leads into more of the same until thought after thought causes confusion. Clarity doesn't come from over-thinking. Most answers are found in stillness. Or when silently communicating with the Universe. There's always special feelings when the moon's full, so with clear minds and undisturbed landscapes, messages flow into our consciousness. We just have to be ready to receive."

"I want to be ready." Rob said with purpose.

The Elder nodded in agreement. "Water's a good analogy to use with *Time*, and it's measurable. But, *Time* is intangible like *Thought*. Unheard and unseen thoughts fly all over earth and the Universe constantly, influencing us and our environments! Not enough people accept these ideas yet, but when more do, and they change within, the world will change and become harmonious."

"It's great how you cup's always half full." Rob responded warmly.

* * *

Just ahead of the vehicle on the right side of the road a large brown sign announcing Simpsons Gap (*Rwengetyirrpe*) in white letters loomed up. The Elder told Rob to go just past it and turn left into Bullen Road, driving slowly through Honeymoon Gap (*Irreyarle*) a small yet beautiful break in the ranges. This sandy area is occasionally visited by Alice Spring's locals, some having family barbecues, others simply enjoying the peaceful location. The bitumen road continues on and joins Ilparpa Road, which, after crossing the railway line and connecting with the Stuart Highway forms a complete loop back into Alice Springs. It is a road from which the rounder, southern side of the Western MacDonnells can be seen for several kilometres.

Rob did not ask the Elder how far they were going, but by the time they passed the Ilparpa Clay Pans, various houses and horses on large residential blocks and stopped at the railway line, he realised they may be going right back to town! And that is exactly what happened. The Elder gestured 'left' when they reached the Stuart Highway. Then, without any explanation Rob found himself driving through Heavitree Gap and almost immediately into the big roundabout.

"Take the 2nd exit," the Elder said, only the third time he had given instructions. They exited onto Bradshaw Drive, cruising for several blocks to a major intersection where the Elder nodded 'left' and they turned onto a familiar road. He did not suggest stopping so Rob drove on to the outskirts of town, heading west again to his surprise along Larapinta Drive! By this stage he was totally puzzled and could not hold back any longer.

"What exactly are we doing?"

The Elder knew Rob would be puzzled, anyone would be, but he wondered whether Rob might come up with his own theory or explanation.

"There's a reason for doing this, but what do you think? Why are we travelling along the same road, in the same vehicle, on the same afternoon?"

Rob was happy to put his mind to the question. The Elder rarely worked like this, so it was intriguing.

"Well, we're travelling through the same space, but at *another* time. It's later because we've just done it! This second journey *seems* the same, but the sun's lower in the sky, so we could measure how much *time* has elapsed. But beyond that, no flashes of brilliance!"

The Elder did not give a direct answer, but simply said: "There is a real reason, but it won't emerge until much later in your *First Boomerang* quest."

This time along Larapinta Drive they passed the turn-off to Honeymoon Gap and continued, not speaking until the Elder began to outline where they were going. This was welcome news to Rob although he felt everything was under control when the Elder was present, even if some events puzzled him.

"There's very good vantage points outside Alice to watch the moon rise. Seems strange I suppose to be driving towards sunset rather than the east. But what's our aim? Just to see the Full Moon rise? Or to help us understand the *timelessness of time*?"

The Elder was not expecting Rob to answer and changed the subject, introducing the most widely used word in books, articles and TV programs about Aboriginal art and culture.

"The Dreamtime is regarded as the creation era of Aboriginal culture, but it's not an Aboriginal word. Baldwin Spencer was first to express it in English when he wrote "dream-time" in the 1890s. It was his attempt to describe the spiritual worlds or universe that gave law and meaning to traditional Aranda. Yet it doesn't explain the full cultural meaning. How could it? We also use 'Dreaming' which includes a person's stories and ongoing connection to spirit. Our word for Dreamtime is *Altyerre*. The Warlpiri say *Jukurrpa* and Anangu use *Tjukurpa* as I said on Anzac Hill one day, and language groups across Australia have their own word."

"So there's dozens of language words for it." Rob concluded.

"Many dozens, but Dreamtime and Dreaming are well known now." The Elder confirmed, adding. "It's not right to say the Dreamtime's finished. Just because it's about creation and contains 'time,' people think it's old and passed. But no, spirit is timeless, spirit creates and is in everything, flowing through all forms and levels. If it wasn't, none of us would be here!"

As they drove passed the road sign and turn-off to Standley Chasm (*Angkerle*) the Elder added local knowledge: "That's a Woman's Dreaming site, another Western Aranda story." "Can men go there?" Rob asked. "Oh yes, and maybe on another trip we'll go in and talk to the local mob about it." The Elder said, then pointed. "Just a bit further along we'll come to the road that honours Uncle Albert, our great artist."

Soon after, they turned right at the large brown sign with Namatjira Drive in white letters on it and continued west towards the sinking sun.

Along this road the West MacDonnells are comfortable companions, their caterpillar-like contortions exuding an ancient presence. As the sun moves on its daily cosmic path the colours of the rocks change and their beauty evokes a deeper appreciation of nature. Sometimes on Full Moon nights the rocky outcrops glow with silver faces, and a human voice or night bird's call can carry to the other side of the world. That is the feeling of uninhibited space out here, the feeling also of time being timeless. A place where although normal, everyday life purports to simply go along like anywhere else, other deeper and higher levels of meaning are present. It is as if the rocks themselves are voicing the planet's most ancient sound, providing a foundation of creative rhythm for all other life.

Both men were conscious of this profound knowledge and knew it was totally unimagined by the majority. Yet for now it simply underscored their empathy and the individual paths they were travelling together, and remained unspoken.

After several kilometres, the Elder asked Rob to slow down so they could find an unsign-posted track. It would take them into the ranges and the Elder suddenly spotted it.

"Here we are." He said, feeling very pleased. Rob followed the dirt track slowly, winding along for about fifteen minutes before parking the 4WD near a couple of slender ghost gums.

"Let's take the swags and tucker. The best place is up here, it's not far." The Elder suggested.

"Okay, let's go." Rob agreed with growing enthusiasm.

The track was barely formed but good enough to follow and they began to climb a little as the gradient increased. As Rob walked he wondered about Time and the Full Moon and stories the Elder might share, letting his thoughts play as he watched where he was putting his feet. There was still enough light when they reached the camping spot, so they placed their swags ready to be unrolled later. Rob unloaded river red gum branches from the back of the vehicle, collected when they stopped at a dry watercourse en route, setting enough in place for their camp fire.

"We're perfectly on time," the Elder said, signalling for Rob to follow. They walked for about fifty metres from the new camp to where large, rounded boulders rose above the skyline. Once at the top they had a clear and extensive view of the MacDonnells in both directions. Rob imagined he was sitting astride the rocky vertebrae of a gigantic, fossilised dinosaur that dominated the landscape. The blinding sun was almost setting at eye level and they watched in awe as the countryside transformed. Beams of sunlight speared into the sky, tinting individual clouds the orange-pink of last daylight.

"How long have you known about this place?"

Rob asked his question thoughtfully, as if thinking aloud, suddenly feeling he could have suggested an answer. The Elder replied softly so the vibrations of place and moment would not be lost.

"How old is the Dreamtime."

Rob knew the Elder was not asking a question, so he continued sitting quietly, filled with anticipation. The Full Moon was about to rise and he looked east. Both men were absorbed by inner thoughts and feelings, and then a feint creamy glow brightened the horizon. The moon had risen countless times over the millennia, and even hundreds of times in Rob's life, yet today he would witness something different.

To his amazement the egg-yolk orange Full Moon rose *exactly* on the range precisely as the golden sun was setting millions of kilometres away. Simultaneously, the moon had risen and the sun had set on the eastern and western extremities of the MacDonnell Ranges, and the intermingling light illuminated the legendary backbone of Central Australia.

All-pervading quietness seeped into Rob and the Elder as the huge, round moon rose slowly and silently into the evening. Other worlds may have existed across the planet or even in Alice Springs, but for the two men consciously at One with the moment, this was their whole world, their whole being. This was the first time Rob had seen a rising moon-setting sun alignment and he shook his head from side-to-side in awe. He was acknowledging the wonder of the natural world, and realising that traditional clans had known this phenomenon for generations.

The Elder stood up, stretched his legs, and became fully present.

"This incredible event happens about once every fifty years. It's so significant because the sun, moon and stars have always been important in our stories. Some clans tell about their Ancestors in the skies and sometimes call them "Sky Heroes." Through history, all cultures have been fascinated by the stars and constellations."

"And they still are." Rob confirmed knowingly.

"Here too, but our main story is Caterpillar Dreaming because they created our beautiful, rugged ranges. Scientists can't date these stories, can't place them in a *'time frame'*. In nature *time* isn't 'framed' or contained by anything. But it has rhythms. The sun, moon and planets move in accurate orbits, and suggest divisions of *time*."

There was always something to think about when the Elder spoke, but in this profound atmosphere there was no need for Rob to respond.

The Elder sat down again and immersed himself in the calm atmosphere. The big moon became slightly smaller as it lifted higher, its reflected sunlight brightening the range and the vast country on either side. Rob was alert in a semi-dreamy way because Full Moons always affected him, the Elder's words hovering in his consciousness for longer than usual, giving him more time to appreciate them.

Silhouetted on the translucent sky both men appeared to be part of the sculptured rocks they were sitting on. Rob's awareness reached a deeper level as he assimilated the vibrations of the sun-moon alignment, while the Elder connected profoundly to his inner self and the Source. In their minds and hearts 'physical' and 'metaphysical' became One, and the silence was deafening. Was the original sound of the Universe within range of their senses?

Rob's ever-growing sensitivity confirmed that this was not the time to ask a question. The energies being received were much more powerful than words. Even thoughts had to be guided so they did not disturb the cosmic connection.

Totally absorbed, both men were experiencing the Oneness of life that mystics, spiritual teachers and Aboriginal elders across the planet have spoken about for thousands of years. Their peacefulness and expanded awareness radiated into the moonlit landscape, serving these moments perfectly. Any words in any language would have been inadequate.

* * *

Soon after, Rob had a deeper understanding of the word *Full* when it described the moon. It was he who had become *'Full'*. He had become filled with Universal Love Energy, more accessible when one's heart is open, seemingly more available in natural places.

Then, as if from another dimension, two unexpected, yet often inviting words broke the solid silence.

"Feeling hungry?"

The Elder's voice suddenly brought the atmosphere back to earth. Before speaking he sensed that Rob like himself, was ready, inwardly and outwardly. It was time to feed the body after feeding the spirit. Later they would return to the spiritual dimensions within because there was more to experience on top of the legendary range.

The flickering flames of the campfire soon burnt the dry branches down to coals, and by the moon's bright light they enjoyed canned fish and vegetables and drank black tea poured from the hot billy. Rob sensed that the Elder would speak about *Time* after their food so he held back his questions, content to be *in the now*. Next they repositioned their swags on either side of the fire, put on thick jackets as cold air descended, and started walking back to their vantage point on the rocks.

After taking up similar positions, but this time on cooler boulders, the Elder briskly rubbed his hands together.

Suddenly a streak of white light as bright as the stars flashed across the southern sky. Rob half-inhaled, half-whistled at this cosmic magic, and the Elder's eyes opened wider with wonder.

"That's a meteorite burning up. It answers questions you asked in the hidden gorge." The Elder confirmed, introducing traditional knowledge. "Shooting stars mean different things across the continent. They can be someone's spirit coming back to find a new body, or their old one. Landscapes are alive with spirits. In some areas baby spirits are waiting to be selected to enter a mother's womb to be born. But other clans see them as signs that someone has died. The Warlpiri mob north-west of Alice say that sacred places came out of the sky as shooting stars. My Western Aranda grandfather said shooting stars were venomous snakes with big, fiery eyes flying through the air then dropping into waterholes. I used to lie on the ground as a boy and look for them in the sky."

"Yeah, I would've too." Rob said, delighted that the Elder's people had their own unique explanation. But he wasn't surprised because traditional clans had their own stories about all aspects of life, including the Sky-World.

The evening air felt cold and heavy, and the stars that were discernible beyond the Full Moon's light sparkled millions of kilometres away. Both men stood up with full hearts and inspired minds to return to camp, leaving their lookout to the spirits of the night.

* * *

Only a few coals glowed in the ashes so Rob placed a handful of small branches on them and they ignited in seconds. Meanwhile the Elder sat on his swag, positioning his legs as if preparing to meditate.

"Tomorrow, four journeys begin. Yours, Mine, Clara's, and Yours with Clara. You'll start searching for *The First Boomerang*. Clara goes with you to Adelaide. I'll put my energy into bringing the lost tjurunga home to country. You can start preparing tonight. Start *thinking Boomerang*. Create possibilities as you go to sleep. Dream about its magical flights through the Cosmos."

"Yeah, I'll start for sure. The mind's racing. I'm really keen to get going," Rob said, feeling enlivened by the Elder's words. "I'm seeing fantastic times ahead."

The Elder smiled happily at Rob, nodding in agreement. There was nothing more to say as sleep beckoned.

* * *

As first light met crisp July morning air, Rob and the Elder were already driving back to Alice Springs. They were both ready to get on with their quests and would not waste any time. The MacDonnell

Ranges looked magnificent, yet so different from their mystical quality of the night before. Now they were being coloured by the rising sun.

Rob dropped the Elder off at his cousin's house and drove across to the Resort where a tour group was boarding a coach painted with Outback scenes. He parked the 4WD and walked briskly along the verandah with a special friend on his mind. He knocked gently on the room door thinking Clara may be asleep, but she bounced to the door, opened it, and grabbed him with a hungry hug.

"You're early. Great! I haven't had much sleep, but I'm going to flow with local time, that's what they say." She said, still holding him.

"You feel very ... um ...warm and lively." Rob replied, giving her another squeeze. "How about we go for breakfast, after I've had a shower?"

"I was just thinking of showering, love to join you." Clara giggled.

* * *

By mid-morning they had dressed in fresh clothes and packed their gear for Adelaide. Their Qantas flight was due to depart at 3.00pm and they expected to arrive just before sunset. Rob was very pleased that Clara was accompanying him to South Australia's capital, but she could not go on the Victoria River District trip because there was not enough room for an extra passenger!

Rob knew that he must research the legends, Rock Art and other information by himself while searching for *The First Boomerang*. In Adelaide he could work alongside Clara without revealing the big picture. He was loving her company, so with mixed feelings he reluctantly restated what he had said the day before while driving in from the airport.

"This is still hard to say, but we can only do the Adelaide trip together - there's no space on the 4WD trip in the Top End. The Elder gave me a secret quest, that's why I can't even tell you about it, and it'll take weeks, maybe months. It's incredible how all this suddenly came out of the blue. There wasn't even time to change things or let you know! But that's the way things happened, and we have to go with the flow."

"Let's get going and enjoy Adelaide." Clara responded brightly, despite what Rob had said. "I'm here to be with you, let's have fun and do everything we can. I can't change the circumstances so let's get out there honey."

"Thanks. You're wonderful. We'll have a good time.... it'll just be shorter."

Rob was relieved that Clara understood the situation, and it took the pressure off him. But would the unexpected developments affect their relationship? Everything had happened so quickly and there had been no time to think about it. But now, most of his thoughts were buzzing with the exciting possibilities of the quest.

With over three hours remaining before the flight they decided to walk into town across the road bridge to buy an extra battery for Rob's still camera, stock up on colour slide film and have a good meal. They chose the "Mulga Tree Cafe" on Gregory Terrace and after a tasty roast chicken and Greek salad lunch they headed back to the Resort. They re-checked their gear for the short flight south and Rob telephoned to reconfirm the "Wildflower Bed & Breakfast" reservation, and his appointments at the Mortlock Library and South Australian Museum.

With their luggage ready and all arrangements confirmed, Rob booked a Private Hire car to take them to the airport.

PART TWO

Dreamtime Quest

Part Two — Dreamtime Quest

1 2

The Elder's mission was to find three specific tjurunga that had disappeared from Western Aranda country. His quest was daunting because the sacred objects could be anywhere in the world. He believed they had been missing for at least seventy but probably ninety years, or between about 1910 and 1930, a period when the Hermannsburg Mission was operating. Even so, the likelihood of finding them was close to impossible.

Large numbers of artefacts were taken from traditional owners and clan storehouses to many places beyond Central Australia. Collecting or trading them was not restricted to that period or region, but it was that time which interested the Elder. His grandfather told him they could not chant and dance at particular sites because the sacred objects had gone.

For the past four years the Elder had occupied the senior Art & Culture lecturer's position at FAD in Alice Springs. He developed a course for Aboriginal tourism operators and improved his computer skills for internet research, emails and word-processing. One major find had been the website of the Aboriginal and Torres Strait Islander Research Centre (ATSIRC) in Canberra. This was the nation's main archive of Aboriginal materials and it housed an enormous range and number of precious items and records. The size of this resource and its ease of online access surprised the Elder, and he made valuable progress.

He discovered that during the previous thirty years various researchers had identified large collections of Aboriginal artefacts in overseas museums and universities. This information did not surprise the Elder, but it certainly excited him. The researchers' detailed reports were lodged at ATSIRC and also made accessible through the Australian Federation University's Aboriginal and Torres Strait Islander Culture Library. The Elder applied to ATSIRC for copies of all data on Central Australian materials located in Germany. His logical focus was on German institutions because the Lutheran Church originated there and it established the Hermannsburg Mission on Western Aranda country, which joined the traditional country of the Luritja clans. He also knew only too well that many sacred objects and other artefacts had been taken from both groups. The Elder and Rob talked extensively about their loss and Rob totally supported his desire to bring them home to country.

Rob contributed by contracting a designer who created a simple website dedicated to Australian Aboriginal Artefacts. The Home Page mentioned Western Aranda tjurunga as traditional items of specific interest and introduced the Elder as custodian.

Surprisingly, after only a few days online the website had received a promising response about *several objects* in Adelaide. Rob sent the exciting information to the Elder who felt very positive about the story and agreed that Rob should follow it up in person. Exactly what he might find in a suburban house was not certain, but the information was credible and had to be investigated.

The story concerned objects given to a teacher at the Hermannsburg Mission School in the 1920s. In those frontier days life was difficult for the mission staff, but disruptive and life-changing for the Aboriginal clans who had foreign values imposed on them. The Mission staff discouraged traditional men and women from telling their age-old stories and performing ceremonies. Any artefacts associated with ceremonies were usually confiscated outright or traded for food rations. As a consequence many were either destroyed at the time or taken from Central Australia. The Mission staff also sold sacred objects and other artefacts to the South Australian Museum as a source of income.

The Elder had shared this historical snapshot with Rob in Alice Springs, and now, decades later, he was passionately determined to find the "three lost tjurunga," as he called them, wherever in the world they were. He was committed to bringing them safely home for his people and their descendants.

Also during the early days of their association, the Elder told Rob why these tjurunga were so important. He said they belong to a particular Songline that journeys throughout Aranda country. Made of stone, each tjurunga was oval-shaped, about 20cm long and 15cm wide at the centre, carefully incised with a unique pattern of lines and circles, and represented a significant totem. He emphasised that all details could not be revealed, but if people knew the public stories they would understand why it was so vital to find them.

"A Songline," the Elder explained, "is the path of an Ancestor that has to be honoured in special ways at special times because it's a path of creation. But," he stressed, "it's just as important these days to sing the songs and dance the dances because the earth needs it urgently. Earth Mother has suffered too much because people have mistreated her. She has to be regularly re-empowered through chanting and dance, and the associated tjurunga are needed to complete the ceremonies. Without these tjurunga we cannot honour this Songline properly. That's the tragedy. No-one has performed the ceremonies for years because the tjurunga were stolen long ago."

It was refreshing and rare to hear an explanation like this. Without such insights and perspective how could outsiders, whether non-Aboriginal Australians or people from across the world, know how significant these tjurunga and ceremonies were? Then the Elder revealed something else.

"There's another level to this story. Each of the tjurunga represents a totem that's significant in today's world. Is that surprising? It might be, but the public stories of the totems are very important and the knowledge will be communicated when the time is right."

* * *

The Elder was given an encouraging lead at the Faculty by a student who came from Beagle Bay north of Broome. He was boarding in Alice Springs while completing a three year Diploma of Aboriginal Tourism Management, and his older brother worked at Roebuck Bay Beach Resort, one of Broome's leading hotels. A feature of the property was a Cultural Museum that housed a large collection of old Aboriginal artefacts.

At about this time Lord McAndrew, the Scottish owner, was selling his extensive Australian property interests including the Beach Resort, and also the Museum's collections. Among bidders at the auction was an Australian Government representative, and according to the student's brother he purchased two collections. One was catalogued *Central Australian Stones* and the other *Central Australian Wooden Implements*, and after making the winning bids he had them air-freighted to Canberra.

The Elder knew intuitively that he must follow-up this information because "*Stones*" could possibly include tjurunga, as well as axe heads and quartz flakes, and the "*Wooden Implements*" could also include tjurunga plus hunting boomerangs and woomeras. Both collections could be in a number of locations in Canberra, but he believed he would be able to track them down with the help of an old friend.

The Elder now had clear indicators for his quest and would focus his energies on Germany, Canberra and Adelaide. His sources of public and personal information were dependable and verifiable, so he was ready to act. The target destinations had challenges, especially Germany because of distance, but the Elder felt confident that the tjurunga would be found in them. They had to be returned to country and there was no time to waste. Deep within he knew the entire Songline must soon reverberate again with the vigorous dance steps and chanted song-poems of its ceremonies.

To find tjurunga in Germany the Elder first contacted the Lutheran Archives in North Adelaide. The staff were very helpful during his telephone enquiries, providing an outline of materials the archives contained as well as making research suggestions. Most early reports from the Hermannsburg Mission were written in German, however some had been translated and could possibly provide clues. Another potentially good source were issues of *Church and Mission News* dated 1918 to 1921 and *The Lutheran Herald* from 1921, both of which had been published in English.

The Elder was hoping to find lists of artefacts that had 'gone south' from Hermannsburg, but after a while it was obvious these would be difficult to locate, even if they still existed. However, during one telephone conversation a staff member at the Lutheran Archives told the Elder there had been real controversy about artefacts taken from Central Australia to Germany in 1910!

This revelation was tremendously exciting. For the Elder it was proof that artefacts had definitely been taken overseas from his traditional country. Privately he had always felt that one of the lost tjurunga was overseas, and the logical place to look was Germany.

The archivist provided the Elder with postal details for the Hermannsburg Mission Society in Germany, but to expedite his search he telephoned again and confirmed the email address. Even without concrete evidence of any list of artefacts from Lutheran Archives he would still be able to ask detailed questions because of his knowledge and acute memory. In his enquiries the Elder did not intend to use the word "tjurunga'' specifically, but instead the general terms "artefact" and "sacred artefact."

He next turned his attention to Canberra and the sources that could provide vital information. One was a former colleague who emailed him a list of public buildings and foreign embassies that displayed Aboriginal art and artefacts. ATSIRC was another and its prompt response included a list of Museums and Galleries in the Australian Capital Territory that housed Aboriginal materials. This major Research Centre had significant artefact collections and a policy to repatriate items to Aboriginal Cultural Centres in the State or Territory of their origin. Therefore staff could provide documentation of returned artefacts, and also the categories of artefacts still held. ATSIRC's record keeping was the most thorough the Elder had encountered, and because lists of materials were available on a website, accessibility was excellent.

Knowing that a government representative had flown from Canberra to Broome and purchased artefacts from a Resort's Cultural Museum suggested two lines of enquiry to the Elder. He would research Parliament House, making it a priority to ask the Department of Prime Minister and Cabinet about its gift-giving policies to ambassadors and foreign embassies. He now had a list of embassies featuring "art and artefacts" and would cross-reference this information with that received from the PM's department, effectively double-checking what he was 'officially' provided with. Secondly, he would also research the records of artefact purchasing by the Australian Government for museums throughout Australia, because it partially funded some of them.

In the 1980s and 1990s the Australian Government often decorated its overseas embassies with Aboriginal Art such as bark paintings from Arnhem Land and dot-style paintings from Central Australia. It was also typical of the government to give gifts of Aboriginal Art to visiting diplomats as a gesture of welcome. However, it was not usual for artefacts to be given and taken overseas. In fact, any artefact classified as 'sacred', such as stone and wooden tjurunga could not leave the country without government clearance.

This background information was very helpful to the Elder and he focused on two possibilities. Did the government man who flew to Broome buy the artefacts so they could be presented as gifts? Did he buy them for a government-funded project, or even Parliament House? To find the correct answers the Elder needed key pieces of information. What was the date of the auction? Did any Museums set up new Aboriginal artefact displays near that date? Were any new foreign embassies opened at that time? Were diplomatic relations re-established with any country around the same period?

The Elder was positive that when all of the answers were known and the possibilities narrowed down, he would be very close to having the first of the lost tjurunga in his hands!

He attributed the excellent start of his quest to the Universe and Ancestors, a highly developed intuition and personal contacts. There was no doubt about his purpose. His intention was clear. His commitment total.

In a remarkably short space of time the Elder had commenced searching two of the target locations with practical strategies. Very soon also the investigation in Adelaide would unfold because Rob was going to pursue the whereabouts of another lost tjurunga in person, while he was there on *First Boomerang* business.

13

After a sandwich and fruit snack on board their Qantas flight to Adelaide, Rob and Clara held hands, closed eyes and snoozed. They were so comfortable together and relaxed very easily. Straight after their restful moments Rob wrote a plan in his notebook for the week ahead because their visit to the city of churches was going to be very busy.

His appointment at the South Australian Museum involved three and a half days to explore some of the extensive archive of anthropologist Norman B. Tindale, examine historical photographs of Aboriginal people, and view artefacts collected in the early days of first contact between European settlers and Aboriginal clans.

For the Mortlock Library he had arranged three full days with the possibility of an extension. His priority was anthropologist Charles P. Mountford's works including bound volumes of field excursion notes, selected manuscripts of published books, as well as films and photographs taken on his Outback bush trips.

According to Dr Frederickson from the museum and Ms Penny Fairsight at the library there was a huge amount of material to look through, so Rob would have to be totally focused in the historic rooms of the grand old buildings. Fortunately, staff of both institutions would prepare the resources he had requested. Some were archived off-site and would be brought into the main buildings so he could get straight to work. Clara had offered to do anything she could, and Rob asked her to work alongside him, reading, taking notes, etc.

The other vital task was to find the family who had a hessian sugar bag containing old artefacts. These pieces had been given to a teacher and relative for safe-keeping decades earlier at Hermannsburg Mission, and had been handed down through the family. Rob had Peter Rockworthy's email which introduced the story in his laptop, and if it was true, sacred treasure was lying undisturbed in the spare room of a home in the Adelaide Hills.

The Elder had told Rob in Alice Springs that he sensed the 'Adelaide' story was accurate, then discussed precisely what he had to look for. After vividly describing the tjurunga, he picked up a pencil and drew the totemic designs that were incised into their surfaces. This was difficult from a cultural point of view because it was sensitive 'business,' but he knew it was the best way for Rob to recognise the lost sacred objects and to search independently. The sketched patterns were unlike those Rob had seen in England on tjurunga and bullroarers, but they may have been from different traditional country.

Like the hand-drawn details, all other information the Elder shared was confidential and must never be mentioned to anyone. The protocol was clear and so was Rob's task. Only specific tjurunga belonged to the Western Aranda Songline. Finding these correct artefacts was the unchangeable priority.

* * *

Descending in flight over the Flinders Ranges was exhilarating as the soft afternoon sunlight of a cool Winter's day bathed the ranges in brown and purple patterns. Green dots became bushes, as pockets of eucalyptus trees brushed blue-green hues across large grazing areas. The ranges run 400kms north south, commence approximately 200kms north of Adelaide, and were named after seafaring explorer Captain Matthew Flinders. He saw the distant ranges from the top of a hill, later named Mount Brown after one of his crew, while onshore during a survey of the Great South Land's southern coast aboard the *HMS Investigator*. The year was 1802, very early in the continent's European story but only recent history compared with thousands of generations of Aboriginal people. These ancient ranges, specifically the northern Flinders, are the traditional country of the *Adnyamathanha*, or "rocky hill people", and like every Aboriginal country it is alive with stories and sacred places.

Rob had gathered some information about this area, knowing it was a rich, legendary landscape full of spirits and ancient traditions. And he wanted to find out more. There was little relevant information in the Alice Springs Collection because it holds predominantly Northern Territory materials, but Rob had located two books written by Charles P. Mountford and Ainslie Roberts. During field trips in the 1930s and 40s Mountford made hand-written notes about local legends shared by Aboriginal informants in Central and South Australia, some from the Flinders Ranges. This invaluable recording of stories, including compilations from different areas, gave Rob several leads to follow.

Combined with Dr Frederickson's very helpful email reply about archives and collections in the Mortlock Library and South Australian Museum, they had given him the framework within which to start his *First Boomerang* quest. Rob felt that searching for boomerang legends respectfully, whether he made a major discovery or not, would be rewarding in itself. He hoped that this approach would mirror the attitudes and demeanour of traditional men and women in tune with their timeless beliefs.

* * *

Adelaide airport was buzzing as Rob and Clara collected their luggage and joined a queue at the taxi rank. Hotel courtesy buses, the

Glenelg & Beaches shuttle, and a line of taxis dispersed the waiting passengers efficiently. In a little over thirty-five minutes and just a few kilometres east of the city centre, they arrived at the "Wildflower Bed & Breakfast."

Rob instantly liked the homely atmosphere of the brick and timber building with its lights on for evening, a place to relax with Clara after long days of research.

"This is sweet, honey. Thank you. I love it." Clara said joyfully.

"Yeah, it's great. Be cosy when we come back each day." Rob said mischievously.

They had walked into a delightful double room with ensuite, featuring native timbers, discreet lighting, vases of colourful flowers, and a beautiful aroma of freshness. Outside the curtained window two weeping willow trees watched over a quiet, shallow creek, enhanced by well-placed lights as it flowed slowly through the gardens.

According to Rob's schedule they were due at the South Australian Museum at 10.00 the next morning. After checking a local bus timetable kindly provided by the owner/manager they decided to leave at 8.30 so they could have a look around the lawns and gardens near the Museum before the appointment.

Opened in 1856 the South Australian Museum is a grand three-storey building standing between the Art Gallery and State Library of South Australia. All three buildings are made from light-coloured limestone, and their entrances are from leafy North Terrace.

The largest collections of Australian Aboriginal artefacts in the world are held by the South Australian Museum. Most are not displayed, yet dozens of traditional pieces and associated materials are on permanent exhibition in the Aboriginal Cultures Gallery. About six hundred thousand people visit the museum each year, and they enjoy inter-active tours, educational programs and special exhibitions. Vibrant, appealing presentations welcome everyone, including many visitors from overseas.

It was into this stimulating atmosphere that Rob and Clara walked right on opening time on a sunny, yet cool Adelaide morning. At the Visitor Information desk a female staff member took their request, inviting them to "take a seat". She paged Dr. P.J. Frederickson immediately, adding that she had seen him come in earlier. Within minutes he was at the desk.

"Good Morning. Peter Frederickson, glad to meet you," he said, enthusiastically thrusting his right hand forward. If there is a typical PhD museum executive then Dr Frederickson was not it. There was no white laboratory coat, no black-rimmed glasses, and no aloof, intellectual welcome.

Rob responded warmly, shaking hands energetically.

"I'm Rob and this is Clara." He sincerely yet casually replied, continuing the usual tradition in Australia of using first names, even in most business situations.

"Hi Peter." Clara smiled.

"Welcome." The tall museum man replied, nodding his greeting. "How was the trip?"

"Good, thanks. We came down on Qantas. The captain even mentioned Wilpena Pound and the Flinders Ranges, and told us Woomera Rocket Range closed years ago. They're good, I use them as often as I can."

"I'm glad you had a good flight. Come this way please and I'll show you where we've set up some of the material for viewing."

Rob and Clara followed Dr Frederickson through to the rear of the Museum into the Natural Science Building where anthropological collections are housed. Approaching one of several doors, the Director of Archives continued his introduction.

"There's a medium-sized room adjacent to my office and we've placed journals, files, and other records on the desks. In case you didn't bring the fees and copyright information, I've put a copy in this folder, "Museum Protocol". There's also a plan of the buildings with directions to our multi-media studio and the requested artefacts. They're set up in two rooms in another part of this floor. Unfortunately we don't have a spare PC but I'm sure you're well prepared. Naturally, researchers only use pencil to write with, and no food or drink is allowed near archival materials. You'll find tea, coffee and good food in the cafe when you need a break, and there's a water cooler just around the corner. Here we are. Make yourselves comfortable, and if you need anything let me know. I'll be working next door all morning, so please don't hesitate."

Rob could not have hoped for a better welcome and introduction. Museum staff had selected and made the material readily accessible, and he and Clara would be able to commence immediately. He only wanted to know one thing to help his planning for the next three and a half days.

"Thanks so much. Just one question. How much material is there?"

"We've issued twenty seven bound volumes of Tindale's expedition field notes, nine acid free archive boxes of supplementary papers, three videos converted from old 16mm black and white film, and five audio cassettes. Our count of the artefacts came to fifty seven, mainly boomerangs. I've also included one box that holds an important nineteenth century book, and another with notes and sketches by George French Angas. It's a lot to cover in the time you have, so I won't interrupt at all. Oh, and please use the white gloves when handling the material, but by all means lift the boxes with bare hands before opening them. We prefer that."

"Okay, we will. Many thanks again." Rob replied warmly, his mind already building a mountain with the quantity of material he imagined.

The bound volumes, labelled with Series, Item and Unique Identifier numbers, the latter running one to twenty seven, were neatly stacked on one desk. The question was where to start. While thinking about the approach to pursue, Rob said to Clara.

"Can you believe one man wrote so much, it just amazes me." It was more statement than question and Clara nodded in agreement. Even so, twenty-seven volumes only represented about one third of the bound volumes. Tindale also produced an enormous amount of supplementary papers, slides, maps and photographs. However, the reality was that part of this irreplaceable resource was available to research, and research right now.

"Let's look at volumes one, two, three, and take it from there." As he heard his own voice Rob became conscious of his logical brain wanting to dominate the selection. But then he suddenly felt this was a time for intuition, adding without hesitation.

"Sixteen is important, and so is twenty seven."

"I'll find those two if you want to start with number one." Clara offered. She had been surprisingly quiet, enabling Rob to get things moving in his own way.

What lay on the desks in front of them was a feast, a banquet for any researcher. They had struck gold before even opening one box or one volume. Expectation filled the office as they positioned chairs to begin reading. Book and paper research is usually quiet work, but there was nothing quiet about Rob's feelings bubbling within. With a pencil lying ready on the second page of a new notebook, the first page left for a contents list, he was poised to begin. Clara did not know Rob's secret quest but she could certainly feel his positive energy.

She was very keen to assist and had already located volumes sixteen and twenty seven amongst the neat piles and placed them near the corner of another desk, allowing enough space for Rob or herself to sit and explore.

"Actually," Rob said thoughtfully, "before we start with Tindale's work let's look at that old nineteenth century book, and try to gain some understanding of the early days in South Australia."

"This is the one." Clara said, gesturing to a specific box, and adding with emphasis: "Are you ready Outback man? This is a big moment."

"Yes, definitely yes, and I'm glad you're here. Let's go."

Rob carefully and expectantly opened the acid free archive box especially mentioned by Dr Frederickson, then put on a pair of fresh white gloves. Inside it he found a treasure, a slim booklet entitled *Aborigines of South Australia*. This rare 1841 publication of thirteen pages by C.G.Teichelmann, *"German Missionary to the Aborigines"* was an overview of *The Manners, Customs, Habits, and Superstitions of the Natives of South Australia*. Rob curiously perused each small page, soon finding fascinating comments and observations. Then suddenly he was stunned. According to the author, local natives believed the white-skinned strangers were spirits coming back to their old country!

"Listen to this, you won't believe it!" Rob eagerly said to Clara, quickly lowering his voice because Dr Frederickson was working next door.

".... they considered the Europeans as their ancestors, which after they had become white and had attained all the knowledge, were returned once more to see their native country and would then go back again..."

He read Teichelmann's amazing sentence to Clara in a loud whisper, emphasising almost every word as clearly as he could, adding, before she could respond.

"Can you believe they regarded Europeans as *THEIR* ancestors?"

"Sure sounds strange to me, but I have no idea how they thought. From what you told me their spiritual life is advanced and sophisticated, but that idea sounds incredible."

"It *IS* incredible. I wonder does it explain why many groups were so trusting of the white settlers at first? That would be very hard to find out, but it really makes me wonder."

Rob kept thinking as he replaced the slim booklet, published almost one hundred and sixty years previously. Yet, because its pages had not revealed anything relevant to *The First Boomerang* quest, he closed the box, satisfied enough because it gave valuable insights into first contact between the cultures. Looking up, he caught Clara's eye.

"Found anything?"

"Yes. Sure have."

"Great. Let's hear about it," Rob said, his face lighting up, his exhuberance tangible.

"I'm like a kid in a candy store, everything's inviting." Clara said happily. "There's a long list of articles written by Tindale over many years, and a thick two volume book set with tribal maps protected in a slipcase. There's a note in brackets saying they can be found in the Museum Library. And I had a quick look in volumes sixteen and twenty seven and page after page comes to life with words and sketches."

"Fantastic." Rob said eagerly. "Looks like we're being guided to start on his material straight away. I'd like to read everything at once! What about the book set? Would you mind getting it a little later? But now, let's change places. Keep looking through this material, I'm up to the George French Angas box." Rob said, gesturing to it.

"Okay *mate*." Clara said with good-natured emphasis on mate. "I'd love to," answering both suggestions.

Rob's intuition had compelled him to say volumes sixteen and twenty seven earlier, and now he was extra keen to see their contents because of what Clara had just said. Quickly changing chairs with her, Rob opened volume sixteen and instantly found an article: *"Central Australian Expedition including Legends and Artefacts of the Aranda, 1930."* What a discovery! Here were observations and data recorded seventy years ago. It was the type of material Rob was expecting, but actually seeing the original hand-written notes was unbelievably exciting. Reading them would be like going back in time and being in the presence of the Aboriginal people Tindale had spoken to.

Rob apparently wanted to put off feeling real excitement for a little longer.

"Before I start reading this closely, let's have a break and a quick coffee at the cafe. I just want to be totally ready."

Clara was surprised and wondered if Rob was putting off receiving the fruits of his research, just like people put off success.

"It's all laid out for you honey, and ready to roll."

"I'm ready, but some sort of inner voice said '*slow down*', that's all."

There is always something to learn about a friend, and Clara knew she had just learned a little more about her Outback man.

After checking their museum map they set off for the cafe, and as they were walking along a corridor Peter Frederickson suddenly caught up to them.

"Excuse me Rob. I've just marked another museum map with the location of our library which may come in handy. Also, I just re-read my notes about your original requests. You'll find various references to boomerangs in Tindale's volume number sixteen."

"That's great." Rob replied. "Clara has to find the library and I'm just about to start exploring that exact volume. What a coincidence! It's fantastic how you and the staff have prepared so much material for us."

"Our pleasure. We just want people to get the most out of their research time and perhaps as a bonus, acknowledge us in the fine print somewhere."

"Sounds reasonable to me. We're just off for a quick cuppa, like to join us?"

"Thanks, but no thanks. I'm off to an unexpected meeting about more corporate sponsorship. Talk to you later."

Rob and Clara did not spend very long having their coffee, just long enough for Rob to say that he loved sharing with her, greatly appreciated her assistance and hoped the research was interesting enough. Clara touched Rob's hand and responded warmly.

"It's a pleasure honey. I'm fascinated already, so let's not waste a minute."

14

Natural light poured into the Mortlock Library as Rob and Clara looked up at the glass-domed roof, their eyes then focusing on the beautiful wrought iron balustrading along the upper balconies. An atmosphere of reverence for learning was tangible. Housed in this heritage building for posterity were the cultural and historical collections of South Australia. The Mortlock Library is part of the State Library of South Australia and stands conveniently next door to the South Australian Museum.

Rob and Clara arrived early for their appointment and curiously scanned the historic Reading Room before being greeted by Ms Penny Fairsight who was instrumental in locating materials and bringing them from off-site storage to the library. She was also archivist of the Mountford-Sheard Collection and was very willing to share her knowledge.

"Welcome." She said warmly. "I'm so glad you're here, good to meet you both. I've got most of Mountford's bound journals of field notes out because a researcher from Canada and two from Germany have been reading his work. So there's more to look through than you requested and you can use the same small room we set up for them."

"That's great timing." Rob said, actually thinking Cosmic Timing. "It's really wonderful to be here."

"Nice to meet you too." Clara chimed in with a broad smile.

"How much material is there now?" Rob asked.

"There are 51 of the 64 volumes of field notes, conveniently numbered chronologically, typescripts of five of his field trips, six archive boxes of typed and hand-written legends in acid free sleeves, all of the Dreamtime book series, a list of films beginning in 1935, and even 3 sets of galley proofs. You're going to be very busy."

"That's great. Thanks so much for organising everything. Sounds like we'd better get started straight away."

They then spoke briefly about Rob's original requests, Penny confirming the details before finally saying:

"Welcome again. Here's my mobile number if you need anything. Good luck."

Rob and Clara sat down in beautifully carved wooden chairs at a superb and solid timber desk, taking a minute to contemplate the adventure ahead. But that was all the time they could take because there was a mountain of material to search through and not very long to complete the climb.

* * *

Rob was bursting with anticipation and wanted to have a quick look at one of the volumes before deciding what to read first. He put on a pair of supplied white gloves and carefully began turning pages by the top right hand corner. Mountford's field notes were written in a small, cursive script and over the years the original blue ink had faded, but it was still clear enough to read easily.

Clara also put on her supplied gloves, selected a volume at random and began leafing through its historical pages, marvelling at the large archive in front of them, but feeling daunted at the same time.

Rob's natural tendency was to put himself in the picture, travel the journey with the writer and feel close to the action. His imagination could create pictures all day, but they only had three days to look at everything so he would have to be totally focused. Having seen two of Mountford's books in the Alice Springs Library Rob knew precisely what he was looking for. He wanted to find Kudnu the Dreamtime Lizard Man who was a great boomerang thrower in the Flinders Ranges.

"My intuition's saying explore the archive boxes first, so why don't you start with the published books or the bound volumes of his journals. What's your preference?"

"Maybe some of both so I get an overview." Clara replied, adding with her growing enthusiasm: "Let's go for it honey."

Rob was eager to find hand-written notes of the published stories and therefore be as close as possible to the original spoken versions. Feeling that the field notes would form the basis of the typed pages in the archive boxes, he methodically began to compare them, intent on finding the common content in each story. At the same time he would also be on constant lookout for any references to boomerangs.

Mountford had shaped information given by traditional men and created vivid and realistic pictures of their life and legends. He seemed to have deep empathy for the people and this connection was evident in his writings. Suddenly, without warning Rob heard the Elder's voice in his mind saying… *"Follow Mountford, Follow Mountford"*.

Rob had no idea how the Elder arranged it, but had been around him long enough to expect the unexpected. He took it as confirmation that he was on the right track. Then he remembered he had not checked his mobile phone all morning. Switching it on he heard the musical signal for messages. The sender did not leave his or her name, there was no need to. The message read: "Follow Mountford, Follow Mountford." What? What's happening? Rob thought to himself. Had he somehow heard the Elder's message coming in to his switched-off phone? Or had the Elder reached him telepathically again?

Rob made a quick decision not to analyse, instead he simply acknowledged that another level of communication had occurred. A level he would discuss with the Elder one day.

Soon after Rob's 'telepathic' moment, Clara held up several books and looked very pleased with herself.

"These look good, but you're in the middle of that, so let's look later, okay." Clara said, more than asked, as she put down the illustrated books and turned her attention to bound volume number one. She found reports of Mountford's first field trips, not surprising because the volumes were arranged chronologically from the earliest date onwards.

"Okay." Rob replied belatedly, barely lifting his head for a second. Then he turned another of Mountford's pages and found a very enticing title, *Kudnu and the Boomerang*, the story beginning...

"Informant showed me his totem was the lizard and his name was Kudnu. This Ancestor walked on the earth as a lizard-man. He was very strong AND he made the first boomerang. (The people were amazed when he threw it.) He threw it into the sky (informant waved both hands in a circular motion) and it was running like that - meaning, like his circling hands. His brother's totem, a tree, was looking and his branches started running...(he gesticulated again, demonstrating circling movements with both his hands and arms)."

"I've found *Kudnu*." Rob exclaimed, looking over at Clara with an excited smile. "He's here in flesh and blood almost."

Clara had no idea who or what Rob was referring to, but she smiled in response. "Is that what you've been looking for?"

"I've known this old character for a while, and wanted to catch up with him one day. He's in legends where boomerangs are very important objects that do incredible things. This bloke threw a boomerang that brought sunlight back to the world!" Clara's face lit up as she took in Rob's words. "Finding these original notes is fantastic. *Kudnu and the Boomerang* is most likely the first ever written version of this Dreamtime story. Mountford was only able to write it down because traditional storytelling preserved it over hundreds of generations. It's fantastic, can you believe it?"

Rob did not need an answer. He was thoroughly immersed. He was in the Flinders Ranges brushing flies from his face, listening to a traditional man and writing notes with pen and ink alongside Mountford. At the same time he was in a room at the Mortlock Library also writing notes, but with a modern pencil, gathering evidence about the boomerang's first legendary flights.

"Have a look through his books and find that legend about Kudnu and the Boomerang, and I'll search for the typed version of these field notes." Rob suggested to Clara without lifting his head.

It took Clara less than a minute to peruse the contents page of Mountford and Robert's book *The First Sunrise* and discover a title *The First Returning Boomerang* on page 42. This must be the one she thought, quickly turning the pages.

"Here it is. There's pen and ink sketches of different shaped boomerangs. And, and, he includes information about boomerangs first." Clara said while quickly scanning the page. "But the story's only one paragraph at the end. Want me to read it to you?"

"Yes, absolutely." Rob replied. "Sounds great, let's see how different the story part is from the original."

The painting is based on a myth about the creation of the Flinders Ranges of South Australia, and relates how the lizard-man, Kudnu, made the first returning boomerang. When he first threw it into the air, the peculiar action of the boomerang so attracted the attention of the small mallee trees at Waraminta that, in trying to follow its curious flight, their upper branches became much twisted and distorted.

What Clara read and Rob heard was a polished gem, an event from the Dreamtime interpreted and preserved by the articulate voice of a caring writer.

"That's superb, the word pictures are wonderful. But I'd like to know more about the boomerang and exactly where *Waraminta* is. What exactly did he say about boomerangs?"

"There are three paragraphs. Here we go:"

The Australian boomerang is a specialised sharp-edged throwing stick which, when thrown at considerable speed and with a vertical spin, can inflict a serious or even fatal wound. A skilful boomerang thrower is often remarkably accurate, and is able to hit and disable a kangaroo at distances of up to fifty yards. However, this weapon is only effective in comparatively open country, for low trees or high grass will divert its flight and destroy its accuracy.

Contrary to a general belief, the boomerang is not in use in all parts of Australia. It is seldom used in the central Australian deserts, because the spear and spear-thrower is a much lighter and more effective combination. Nor is it used in large areas along the northern coasts, where the country is heavily wooded.

As a weapon, the returning boomerang has many limitations. It is effective only when thrown at right angles to the wind, and even the slightest obstruction will interfere with its spin, and cause the weapon to fall harmlessly to the ground. It is likely that, before the arrival of the Europeans, this type of boomerang was restricted to the southern coasts. But the interest of the white man in the flight of this strange weapon, and the fantastic stories told of its capabilities, undoubtedly increased the area of its distribution.

"That's great reference material. He says a lot in a few words, but nothing more about *Waraminta*. I'm intrigued by that name for some reason."

"Maybe he made more notes about it." Clara suggested.

"Hopefully. I'd really like to find out."

Rob was digging for detail, very determined to find the typed version of the original notes, hoping it would provide the location of

Waraminta and a description of the physical characteristics of Kudnu's "first" returning boomerang.

Clara continued reading the same illustrated book, looking for any mention of boomerangs. The stories were short. They comprised text and line drawings on one page and an interpretive painting by Ainslie Roberts on the opposite page. Each one vividly described dramatic events and characters in realistic detail on the broadest canvasses. In one act a Dreamtime Ancestor would escape dire circumstances on earth, and in the next be a star in the sky. Another would win a raging battle, his decisive actions creating a steep-sided gorge where he disappeared into the earth.

"Here's another one with boomerangs." Clara said, her voice rising. It's called *The Origin of Day and Night*, and it's on page 68 in the same book".

"Let's read it." Rob said straight away.

In the days when the world was young, light was provided by the great fire on which the cannibalistic sun-woman, Bila, cooked her human victims. At that time the lizard-man Kudnu, who was a famous boomerang-thrower, and the gecko-man Muda, paid a visit to their neighbours, the euro-people. They found that all the euro-people had been killed by the dogs of the sun-woman and dragged to her camp. Angered by this bloodthirsty deed, the lizard-men decided to kill Bila in revenge.

When the sun-woman saw Kudnu approaching she howled with rage. She snatched a boomerang from her belt to throw at him, but she was too slow. Before she could throw her weapon, Kudnu's boomerang had wounded her so badly that she, transforming herself into a ball of fire, disappeared over the horizon, leaving the world in complete darkness.

The lizards were terrified by the calamity they had caused, but Kudnu decided to use his remaining boomerangs to try to bring the light back again. He threw one of them to the north, but the darkness still remained; he then threw two more, one to the south and one to the west, but still there was no change. But when he threw a boomerang to the east, the lizards saw a great ball of fire rise, travel slowly across the sky, and disappear below the western horizon, thereby creating day and night.

After this, no Aboriginal in the Flinders Ranges would kill a goanna or a gecko. They said that these creatures not only saved mankind from destruction, but created day and night; the day in which to gather food, and the night for rest and sleep.

"Yes!" Rob said in a triumphant tone. "That's one I heard about years ago. Isn't it the most incredible story you've ever heard." What sounded like a question was another of Rob's confident statements. He knew exactly how he felt about the old stories. He felt part of them. Connected somehow to their essence, and this feeling motivated his steps.

Clara was nowhere near as familiar with Aboriginal legends as Rob, and she expressed real surprise after reading the story.

"Why is it so violent and gruesome? Kudnu's 'light-bringing' boomerang throwing is awesome, but for me it's overshadowed by the revenge and cannibalism."

"Part of the storytelling," Rob responded a little defensively, "...is to teach children the rules and values of their clan. Sometimes fear gets the message across, or kids may appreciate sunshine more when they hear what Kudnu did to get it back. But I'm only interpreting the story as an interested 'whitefella'. The Elder could tell you a lot more."

After a short pause Rob added. "I want to have lunch soon, but before we go I'd love to find the type-written, pre-publication version of *Kudnu and the Boomerang.* Let's give it another fifteen minutes, can you hang on?"

"Sure, honey." Clara replied. "I've got plenty of legends still to read in the other books, so I'll keep going until you're ready."

"Didn't Penny say that she or her staff found *Waraminta?*"

Clara looked up from Mountford's book..

"I'm positive she said notes about the lizard totem and *Waraminta* are in one of the archive boxes, so you must be getting real close."

"Yeah, I must be. There's only a few more articles to look through, perhaps it'll be the last one!" He added with a sense of irony. Then, after only two or three minutes he almost shouted.

"Got it. It's here. There's just one page, that's why it's been so elusive. He's typed it as *Kudnu's First Returning Boomerang*, and there's a few paragraphs."

Rob read quickly but carefully, comparing the hand-written version he had placed to one side with the typed story, totally alert for any reference to *Waraminta*. The versions of Kudnu's story were similar, the typed one polished, punctuated and obviously written later, but there was no mention of *Waraminta!*

Then Rob saw the feint outline of hand-writing through the paper, so he quickly turned the page over and there it was: *Waraminta - place of mallee trees.*

"That's it?" Rob asked, his words edged with disappointment. "That's a shame. I want to know *where* it is!" Clara caught his eye and nodded understandingly.

Nothing else was written on the back of the page. Rob had been hoping to find a description of the area so he could go there one day and study the landscape. He wanted to see first-hand where the "first returning boomerang" had spun through the air, and see if the mallee tree branches were still "twisted and distorted". Traditional stories describe real places and events, so why was *Waraminta's* location not included, Rob thought to himself. Had he missed a clue somewhere? Perhaps he was not yet ready to know. Whatever the reason, he definitely wanted to keep searching for this legendary place.

Rob was always mindful of the main reason for his research, and now it was particularly pertinent. The Elder had given him the task of finding *The First Boomerang*, literally the *original physical object*. Yet, although this legend was about Kudnu and the "first returning boomerang," Rob intuitively and intellectually did not believe the two were connected. It was an important legend from one area, but as far as finding the physical *First Boomerang* was concerned, he still needed to acquire more knowledge.

"I'm ready for lunch after all that." Rob said with a mixture of relief and resignation. "I'll change focus after our meal, but I'll stay with the notes and I'd love you to stay with the books."

Clara nodded to agree before saying, "I'm hungry too, let's work it out over our tucker." There she was again, using a real Aussie word although she had not done so for a couple of hours.

* * *

After bowls of hot vegetable soup and buttered multigrain rolls at the cafe they returned to the research room, more eager than ever. Rob was intent on finding out where legendary *Waraminta* was, but because of such a large amount of research to complete in just the next two and a half days he could not afford to be obsessive about a single topic. Nevertheless, his detective senses would be alert for even the slightest clue.

"Here's a legend that gives real importance to boomerangs and their connection with certain women." Clara remarked with surprise, her enthusiasm for the subject growing by the minute. "It's called *The Fighting Cloud-Women* and is in Mountford & Robert's book *The Dawn of Time.* Want to hear it?"

"Yep. I'm ready." Rob said, hearing the eagerness in Clara's voice. "Go ahead."

The Wibalu women were angry over the loss of their boomerangs. The exclusive possession of this weapon had given them a position of much power, and they were ashamed at the ease with which they had been tricked, turning them from people of importance to objects of ridicule.

The women could well imagine the roars of derisive laughter in the camp that would follow the account of their stupidity, and were fully conscious of the damage they had done to their boasted claims of superior intelligence.

Tempers were short and sharp in the camp of the Wibalus. Each woman was quick to accuse the other of rushing to see the white swans, and of forgetting that the men were always waiting for an opportunity to steal their boomerangs.

Storms of recrimination soon turned the whole camp into a melee of fighting women. At the height of the turmoil, the Wibalu were taken into the sky, where the blood from their many wounds stained the clouds a brilliant scarlet.

Today, when the Aboriginal men see a vivid sunset they say to each other - "The Wibalu women are fighting again. Surely it's time they forgot their foolishness and their silly quarrelling."

"Great story. So much action. Do we know where it comes from? Is *Wibalu* their clan name?" Rob asked. "That's what I'd really like to know. And it's remarkable how owning the boomerangs gave the women so much power. Do you like that part?"

"Yes. But I want to know more too." Clara answered. "Why did they think possessing boomerangs gave them superior intelligence? That's a big concept when you think about it."

"It's a big story because boomerangs are usually *men's* business. We'll have to track down Mountford's notes if there are any, otherwise try to locate *Wibalu* in word lists or other books. But it's very difficult without knowing the area the story comes from." Rob explained.

"Okay honey. How about I keep looking through the other books for now and see what else I can find."

"Yeah. And by the way. Thanks again for your willingness." Rob said in a gentle and appreciative way as he looked at Clara with caring, happy eyes. He had not been paying much attention to her as a woman for most of the day, because of their search amongst the archives. But at that moment deep affection touched his heart, and suddenly the word 'balance' came to mind.

"Let's go out tonight. I want to see you properly again."

"Love to Rob. We haven't got all that much time. Let's do it."

"We need another discovery this afternoon, something to really top off this morning's good work. I'd also like to start on the old black and white 16mm films. At least see one, maybe two before we finish today. So let's keep going here until about four o'clock."

Amongst the other books Clara picked up was one that seemed to belong to the Mountford-Roberts series. The format was the same and it contained legends, paintings and drawings but the text was by Melva Jean Roberts, not Charles P. Mountford. Titled *Dreamtime Heritage* her writing echoed his respectful and celebratory introductions. In the list of contents no titles included 'boomerang' so Clara began reading from the beginning. Rewarded almost immediately, she found a legend called *The Fighting Brothers* on page 16. Unable to hold back her excitement, Clara asked in a tantalising way...

"How do you think the shark got its big fin?"

"Well, um, um........ can I guess?"

"Yes, sure".

"On second thoughts, I've got no idea."

"Okay, let me introduce the story. It's about two brothers called Gerdang and Pupadi, wife stealing, rage, anger, jealousy, and what happens when they fight to the death. It's called *The Fighting Brothers* and here's part of it:

Pupadi climbed a large rock to gain a better view, but Gerdang circled behind him and threw a boomerang with such force that it buried itself deep between his brother's shoulder-blades and knocked him into the bushes at the cliff's edge.

Reckless with triumph, and expecting to find his brother dead, Gerdang leapt into the bushes. But Pupadi, calling on the last of his strength, lay on his stomach with his spear held upwards. Gerdang jumped straight on to it, to die with the barbed point sticking out of his back.

The impact carried them over the cliff, and Pupadi fell into the sea and became the shark. The big fin on his back is his brother's boomerang, still deeply embedded. Gerdang hit a shelf of rock with such force that his body was flattened, and in this form the tide carried it away as the stingray, with Pupadi's spear changed into the barbed sting at the base of the tail.

"Wow. How original is that. I'll look at those sea creatures differently now. Amazing." Rob said with real appreciation.

"It's so amazing." Clara nodded enthusiastically, as Rob continued.

"Isn't it marvellous how these stories are so real, yet the western mind criticizes them as impossible. Even if this was just a simple, creative story it would be outstanding. But for the clansmen and women of that area it's an episode of history. It is real. It is truth. Could you even imagine thinking of a storyline where a boomerang becomes a shark's dorsal fin?"

Clara knew Rob was not asking her a question. He was asking people everywhere. But she was still holding the book, was moved by the story, and said...

"What a way to link humans and creatures. That's why it's so remarkable. I don't know many traditional stories of our Native Americans, but that's the first time I've read about connections like this. Are there more stories in Australia with these themes?"

"For sure. There's thousands of Dreamtime stories and we've got a very long coastline. Maybe there's more in that book. Maybe there's even one about how the boomerang was made. Perhaps you came Down Under to discover Aboriginal legends. Perhaps you'll follow it up back in the States. I don't know. I'm only thinking out loud."

"Well Rob, I'm not thinking that far ahead. But I do want us to keep seeing each other, that's what I'm sure of."

"Yeah, of course." Rob answered dreamily, without fully responding to Clara's sincere words. "There's a lot to do here, I know that for sure."

This was the first time Clara had consciously tried to penetrate Rob's focused mind and express her feelings. She had travelled a long way and wanted to let him know how much she cared. Yet even with this knowing in her heart, it was obvious Rob needed to keep working so she pushed her thoughts aside.

"Let's see what else I can find here." Clara offered, gesturing to the book. "Have we got time?"

"Yeah. That should just about do it." Rob replied. "Then we'll go for a cuppa."

Barely three minutes later and just six pages further into *Dreamtime Heritage*, Clara made a discovery.

"Rob look. You've got to see this…"

Clara quickly stepped towards Rob and handed him the book opened at the story *Linga of Ayers Rock*. Rob saw the painting and was momentarily speechless. It featured a lizard in the foreground and Uluru with a large boomerang inside it! He had never seen anything like it before. Yes, he repeated in his mind, Uluru with a boomerang inside it!

"Unbelievable. What a picture. I'm amazed. Delighted. Let me read this one, do you mind? I'll read it to you, to the world, to anyone who's listening."

This myth, handed down by the Pitjandjara tribe, relates how Linga, a little lizard-man, lived by himself near the place where Ayers Rock (Uluru) now stands. Linga had spent many days making a boomerang, and when it was finished he threw it to test its balance. The boomerang flew higher and higher into the air and spun across the desert until it buried itself in the soft sand of the great red sand hill from which Ayers Rock was later created.

Greatly distressed at the loss of such a fine weapon, Linga hurried to the spot and dug everywhere with his bare hands to find it. Today, many of the spectacular features of Ayers Rock are the result of Linga's frantic digging. The deep holes and gutters, which he made in the sand, have since been transformed into large potholes and vertical chasms in the steep face of the huge monolith.

Linga, forever associated with the sand in which he lost his boomerang, became the little sand-lizard. And, if you are quiet enough, and quick enough, you may surprise him alongside a small hole in some red sand hill.

"Wow. What a story! It's fantastic. And look at the boomerang. It looks like the one the Elder gave me in Alice. I've got to find out why Roberts drew that shape of boomerang. Thanks a million Clara. This really makes my day. How about you?"

"It's incredible and beautiful! How many people know Uluru was created in the red sands of Central Australia because the lizard-man lost his new boomerang? Is this taught in your schools? How many people have seen this painting? I really want to know more. Let's have that coffee break now, and let the story sink in."

"Great idea. Let's go." Rob smiled with delight in his eyes and voice, adding quickly, "I wonder how the Elder's going?"

15

After arriving at his office and turning on the computer the Elder found an email from the Evangelical-Lutheran Mission (ELM) in Hermannsburg, Germany. His heart leapt because during the previous week he had sent out messages to several institutions, and this was the first reply. With a quick click he opened the attachment.

The short and to-the-point message stated that the Mission had a strict policy regarding researchers: they must visit personally to look at all materials. However, the next paragraph was less direct informing him that an Executive Board meeting was going to be held in three weeks, when guidelines for researchers would be reviewed. The writer invited the Elder to send a letter supporting his case for "access-in-absence", a strange-sounding phrase in English, but exactly what he needed.

The Elder did not hesitate. He re-read the message, clicked off the internet and clicked open a window to start his message. Credibility was vital so he would print on the Faculty of Aboriginal Development's letterhead with its distinctive red and yellow ochre logo, confirming him as senior Art & Culture lecturer. The Elder also knew how important it was to paint a word-picture for the far away Germans so they would gain a basic appreciation of culture, and an understanding of why the lost tjurunga were so important.

He first thanked the office in Hermannsburg for its email and the opportunity to write to the Executive Board. Then he considered how to tell the story of the lost artefacts. He sensed that a two-level approach expressing his knowledge with both head and heart would favourably influence members of the Board. Drawing on his wisdom, experience and poetic nature, the Elder began.

"Have you seen the red rocky ranges of the Outback become beautifully mauve at sunset, or the incandescent white of a ghost gum highlighting the deep blue of an afternoon storm, or the miniature white and yellow flowers hugging green stems freshened by rare rainfall, or the uncountable, sparkling diamonds of the ancient night sky? If you haven't, you do not know my country and its rich diversity of life.

In the beginning, a period now called 'Dreamtime' in English, all of our people, our country, our laws, the landforms and seascapes, and all other beings, were created by our Ancestors. Our Ancestors took various forms, including human, as they travelled over the landscape, creating its features and stories that have been handed down from generation to generation. As in any good school classroom our elders or teachers related these stories on several levels. Each story was danced as well as recited so the children could learn it properly. The classroom extended to the north, south, east and west horizons, linking earth and sky and all the seen and unseen dimensions. There were no walls, for our school was nature. You also, sitting in an office or walking in the forest, are part of this natural world, our shared Earth Mother.

As our Ancestors travelled they created recognisable pathways called Dreaming Tracks or Songlines, and we still honour them by singing songs and chanting poems at sacred places along them. For some songs, dances and places, sacred objects were also needed. Without these objects, made from either wood or stone, the ceremonies cannot be completed. Some of the ceremonies have secret levels for senior initiated people, but most levels are for teaching our children, reinforcing the values of life and honouring the earth and our heritage.

Even I, an older man, have not had enough experience of these ceremonies because as a young boy I left my country. This was the country of the Western Aranda people which adjoined the country of the Luritja people, and where your Lutheran Mission was set up. But even though our cultural life was badly impacted, those days have passed, and I have been fortunate to reclaim and learn some of the stories of my people. This privilege has been like a second life for me, a transfusion of heritage that brought the sparkle of the Ancestor stars back into my eyes.

Now, across the planet, we see increasing respect for many Aboriginal peoples and their cultures. This attitude comes from greater awareness because of various events. One was the return of a skull from England to a West Australian group a few years ago, and others include official apologies to Aboriginal peoples by some governments for past injustices. As appreciation of these oldest of world peoples grows, the process of reconciliation in the hearts of ordinary people is gathering momentum. That's why my letter is arriving at your office today. One step begins every journey and it is time to commence a new chapter.

I am now custodian of some stories or Dreamings and sacred objects, so it is my responsibility to my people and descendants to protect and preserve our cultural heritage. This is an ongoing challenge because so much material was 'collected' and taken from traditional Aboriginal country to Museums in Australia and to Museums and Institutions beyond our shores. Artefacts that sit in glass cases on display, or in storage drawers in basements, are more than material objects to us. They embody the energy of the Ancestor they are associated with. A level of my heart is embodied in the artefacts that were taken away, and I cannot, nor can my people, interconnected as we are with story, country and objects, be complete spiritually without their return.

The sacred tjurunga (pronounced churunga or churinga) that I believe you have belongs to one of our major Songlines. Without it we cannot tell the full multi-layered story, complete the special ceremonies, or achieve the spiritual sustenance that our hearts and souls yearn for. Our well-being will improve when everything is together again, and it is the birthright of our children to share this rich heritage.

Imagine a growing baby almost ready to walk. Imagine red soil and white-trunked eucalyptus trees under the biggest, bluest sky you have ever seen. Shouldn't this baby have the opportunity to learn the stories of its society so it can learn its values? Shouldn't it feel the resonance of its family's Outback homeland in its heart? Shouldn't its first steps be the beginning of a journey toward dignity, self-respect and spiritual fulfilment? Aren't these the rights of all babies everywhere, not only a baby of the oldest living culture in the world?

In our traditional days, boys passed through several stages as they grew towards adulthood. Every young man, during a particular initiation ceremony was given a sacred tjurunga that embodied his spiritual Ancestor, his connection with the Source of life. There is no equivalent in western society. Can you imagine the significance these objects have to our people? Can you imagine the pain caused by their disappearance after the settlers and missionaries came? My grandfather told me it was like losing real people, and the men and women of his Western Aranda clan wailed for days because of the tragic loss."

The Elder paused in a mood of deep reflection, his eyes glazed over with emotion, his message ebbing naturally to an emphatic end. This window to the culture and explanation of the spiritual significance of tjurunga concluded the first part of his letter. He now needed to add precise details of what he was searching for so the Evangelical-Lutheran Mission could locate which artefacts it held from Central Australia. In the second part he wrote:

The sacred tjurunga I am looking for are distinctive in shape, mostly small, and could easily have been mislaid in your archives for decades. I'll sketch various shapes including oval and circular stone examples about 1cm thick and 15cm across, wooden ones about 30cm long with rounded ends and 5cm wide, and enclose them. I don't know if any long sacred boards, from one metre to two metres in length and about 10-20cm wide would have been taken to Germany, but they possibly were!

Each tjurunga has either a pattern on one side or both, and these designs interest me the most. Do you have existing photographs of some pieces, or copies (even photocopies) that could be sent? If you take new photographs please keep them confidential out of respect for our traditional Aboriginal law.

As I said in the earlier part of my letter, I believe many tjurunga went to Germany, but now we are ready for their return and look forward to your understanding and co-operation. Please email any photographs or photocopies in an attachment to me at the Faculty where I have been senior Art & Culture lecturer for four years.

Sincere Regards,

Lindsay Williams

Lecturer & Custodian - Faculty of Aboriginal Development

Alice Springs - Northern Territory - Australia

The Elder's letter spread over three pages and he carefully folded them together and placed them in a Faculty envelope. This letter was extremely important so he decided to go to the Post Office before it closed at five o'clock and post it himself. Driving along South Terrace he admired the white trunks of the old river red gums in the Todd River bed, and reflected upon the changes they had witnessed. Many were standing in traditional times when the only man-made lights were campfires. Now those mature, spirit-filled trees had seen the white man change the landscape and bring electric light, but it had not been a light of real understanding.

He parked the Faculty's vehicle opposite the Yeperenye Centre and walked back to the Post Office. The precious sealed envelope was weighed, stamps and Airmail stickers were attached, and it was ready to fly. Posting it outside in the "Overseas and Bulk Packages" box, the Elder was very pleased with what he had written, and felt positive it would arrive in Germany on time. He patted the curved top of the tall red post box several times and sent it off with strong thoughts for success. Freshly motivated, he drove back to his office deeply satisfied that the lost tjurunga quest was right on track.

* * *

Momentum was building because a response had also come from Canberra. One of the Elder's former colleagues had pursued the suggestion of gifts for visiting dignitaries and embassies with the Department of Prime Minister and Cabinet. In response to his enquiry staff had been surprisingly helpful due to a new policy of openness. To an outsider familiar with the corporate world, similar assistance was a normal public relations expectation. However, the Department had opened its books, responded quickly, and revealed valuable information.

At a higher level of understanding the way was being opened because of Cosmic Timing, and clues about another lost tjurunga were coming through. In his enthusiastic email the Elder's former colleague remarked:

Good news from busy Canberra. The Department of Prime Minister and Cabinet maintains a Gift Register that keeps a record of all gifts presented by Ministers of the Australian Government. A database lists the gifts, the name of who presented them and the name of recipients. The Register is maintained by the bureaucracy and is ongoing, whichever party is in government.

I believe the key entry is one that appeared in October 1999. This is a gift of Aboriginal artefacts to the Ambassador of the Republic of Iraq! Why he would be given artefacts is puzzling, but I doubt whether there is an official reason despite the new openness. However, the fact remains that according to the Register the Ambassador was presented with several pieces. The really good news is that the same man is still here in Canberra, despite world events of the past few years.

I suggest that your next step is a direct approach to him, explaining the reasons why you are searching, etc. There are no specific protocols to follow, simply write to the following address in Canberra:

The Ambassador,
Embassy of the Republic of Iraq,
Roundabout Garden Way,
Barrayumla ACT 2602

Good luck with this avenue ... I'll be in touch if any other significant leads come up and I'll drop you a personal note in a week or two. And remember, you're always welcome down here.

Warm Regards,
John K. Mixwell

This was more great news for the Elder. The next step was obvious so he sat at his computer to write two more very important letters. One would be to the Ambassador of Iraq and the other would be to the Prime Minister of Australia, a female for the first time in the country's history.

16

Day three dawned in Adelaide and Rob and Clara arrived at the Museum precisely on opening time for their second visit. On the previous night they spoiled each other at a Japanese restaurant in O'Connell Street, North Adelaide, a well-known location for good restaurants. Their togetherness was gentler and more intimate than during their daytime hours of focused research, and they felt as close as they ever had. They enjoyed every special moment, but it was not all romance. Rob and Clara also discussed their exciting and rewarding work at the Library and the Museum, and wondered what else was waiting to be discovered.

Filled with anticipation and knowing their way to the research room, they walked confidently through the Museum into the Natural Science Building behind it, and almost immediately heard a familiar voice.

"Good morning. I thought you'd be in early," beamed Peter Frederickson as Rob and Clara neared his office door. "I have the title of a book which may be of real interest."

"That's much appreciated Peter, you've been so helpful already." Rob said with genuine feeling, adding with curiosity, "What is it?"

"It's called *Flinders Ranges Dreaming* by Dorothy Tunbridge and was published in 1988, but you may not have seen it because it's out of print. This is one of the best books of legends I've ever seen, so I hope you can track it down," he said, handing a note with full details to Rob. "There's a copy in our library but I know your time's limited."

"Thanks so much Peter. I'll make sure I find it if you say it's that good." In Rob's mind there was an instant knowing that this book would be very significant.

"Well, we'd better get started. So thanks again, we'll catch up later." Rob said, smiling his appreciation.

Once inside the room where all the archival materials were still laid out from the previous session, Rob and Clara sat for a moment to plan the day ahead. Clara wanted to get an idea of how much Rob was trying to achieve.

"Are we going to go through everything?"

"Yeah. I think we should because look what happened yesterday. We made terrific discoveries at the Mortlock, and there's got to be more hidden treasures here."

"Okay. Let's go for it," added Clara, her voice rising with enthusiasm. "How about I look at Tindale's books from the library and you keep on with his bound volumes..."

"Sounds good. Let's really get into the mood and attract what we're looking for. I want another big boomerang discovery before lunch," announced Rob, both heart and head full of determination.

* * *

By early afternoon Rob and Clara had researched a considerable amount of the remaining material including a set of historical photographs. Amongst the old black and white and sepia images were studio portraits of Aboriginal people holding boomerangs and nulla nullas. There were also others featuring boomerangs only. The practice of taking such portraits also occurred at Kerry Studio, Sydney circa mid

1880s to 1917, but usually the provenance of the artefacts and names of people in the photos were not provided. And most artefacts were merely props for supposed authenticity. However, the shape and dimensions of boomerangs, and hence their potential to be returners or not could sometimes be estimated with confidence.

Rob was looking for returners similar to the traditional root returner presented to him by the Elder. He carried a photograph of it and believed he could make accurate decisions about boomerangs in the archival photographs. After examining each one, carefully protected in an acid-free sleeve, he found that none compared favourably to his special returner. The old photographs were interesting records, but they would not help him advance his quest, so he moved on.

Rob and Clara were both now reading Tindale's bound journals of field notes of his South and Central Australian expeditions when they heard a knock on the door. Rob stood up, opened it, and saw Peter Frederickson holding an archive box.

"Hope I'm not interrupting but I wanted to present this personally because it's unique in the history of Australian archaeology. We regard it as one of the Museum's premier exhibits. This file will introduce it, but I won't say anything else in case I spoil your surprise."

"Thank you, thank you." Rob uttered eagerly as he accepted the archive box and Peter Frederickson stepped back from the door. "I'll let you know what we think."

Rob placed the box on the desk straight away, and then with Clara at his shoulder, carefully opened it.

"*WOW*, look at this, look at this!" I've never heard anything about this before." Gasped Rob, glancing straight at Clara and shaking his head from side to side in amazement.

Inside the box were colour and black and white photographs of the oldest wooden boomerangs ever found! Rob and Clara's faces immediately brightened like Venus in the Outback morning sky. Clara was amazed by their incredible age and Rob knew they were a direct link to very old traditional culture. They were looking at an archaeological jackpot, a one in a multi-million discovery.

In terms of the preservation of wooden objects this 1973 find was miraculous. Three complete boomerangs and pieces of others had lain undisturbed in a peat bog in south-eastern South Australia for close to 10,000 years! Their age was impossible to comprehend, but the momentous nature of the discovery was not.

"I never even imagined anything like this." Clara said with a tone of awe and wonder.

"This is unbelievable! There must be legends from that area." Rob remarked hopefully, his busy mind instantly wanting to find the ancient stories. "I'll bet this was big news around the world, it would have to be...." He added, although with a question mark because he was only three years old when reports of the discovery were published! That's why he would not have known about it!

But instantaneously his brain began flowing with questions. Would boomerangs be included in local legends? Would this area reveal the whereabouts of *The First Boomerang*? Who collected the stories from that part of the state? Where is the material now?

"Peter Frederickson will know a lot more, or he'll point us in the right direction." Rob winked to Clara.

"Sure beats me this boomerang story," said Clara, her mind opening to possibilities.

Rob's mind was still full of ideas, but he gathered his thoughts.

"We'd better finish what we're doing here first. What do you think?"

"I'm with you," replied Clara, her eyes bright with excitement.

They agreed to complete the material they were reviewing, knowing they would later be able to concentrate fully on finding legends and more details about the incredible 10,000 year old boomerangs.

* * *

Later, Rob and Clara walked purposefully to another research room where superb traditional boomerangs were laid out on three tables. Staff had selected them from the Museum's vast collection of Australian Aboriginal artefacts. After putting on white gloves Rob picked up a boomerang and rested it on his open palms, trying to imagine it being used by a traditional man hundreds of years ago. According to accompanying notes the basic shapes of boomerangs had remained the same since they were first made. This occurred because traditional knowledge was handed down, and therefore outline shape, wood types, cross-sections and hand-making techniques with stone tools did not change. Consequently, even though a particular boomerang had been 'collected' during first contact in the late eighteenth or early nineteenth century, its design features were thousands of years older.

The boomerangs on the tables were longer and much more open-angled than Rob's traditional returner, most only curved gently near one end. They were like the hunting boomerangs carried by the Elder to the hidden gorge. However, it was crucial to find returning boomerangs because if they were labelled properly they would lead him to their area of origin. And those locations Rob believed would be likely places to find *The First Boomerang*.

Amongst the typical hunting boomerangs were several distinctive hooks or number sevens, used traditionally in hand-to-hand fighting by a few clans only, but these were also non-returners. Even by examining them all closely he may not gain extra information for his quest. However, there may be other things to learn. Clara had also put on a pair of white gloves and Rob handed her a boomerang.

"What do you think? Any impressions?"

Clara took a moment before responding, and whether it was a woman's experience with cosmetics or not, she first asked...

"What's this brown powder all over it?"

"That's red ochre. It was applied wet and used to preserve shields, coolamons and boomerangs, especially in Central Australia. It was also used for ceremonial purposes and I once read about it being applied to a body in a burial ceremony at Lake Mungo in south-west New South Wales. That event was about 40,000 years ago, which is about the earliest recorded date of its use in the world. It was highly sought after and Aboriginal clans who had deposits in their country traded it to other groups for objects they needed, like stone implements or finished wooden artefacts."

"Very good. You sound like a professor." Clara said with a chuckle.

"Thank you. Is there anything else I can clarify for you?" Rob replied, tongue in cheek.

"It's not as heavy as it looks, but I wouldn't want to be hit by one!"

"No, me either. It's not heavy but Australian hardwoods are very dense. Hunting boomerangs were thrown hard and fast with a lot of spin and packed a real punch."

Clara placed the boomerang back on the table and ran her gloved hands over a few others, as Rob imagined...

"I'm visualising a hunter stalking his prey from downwind, he's creeping as quietly as possible. Getting closer and closer, he balances himself for the throw. Then whoosh, his boomerang flies, spinning fast towards an unsuspecting 'roo or emu."

"Wow." Clara exclaimed. She could also *see* the hunting scene as Rob's convincing words created vivid pictures. Yes of course, Clara thought. We may be looking at static boomerangs on a Museum table, but these were dynamic implements, crucial technology in the daily lives of native people. And, as if confirming her thoughts, Rob outlined their multiple uses.

"This type of boomerang was so versatile. It was used for hunting, fighting, cutting meat, scraping campfire coals, and pairs were clapped together to beat time for dancing and chanting. Specialist craftsmen knew the proper trees and made them with practised skill, and very good makers were highly regarded. When traded into other traditional countries, especially far from their source, some boomerangs became sacred objects and were used in ceremony. And the story goes on. But we'll have to keep moving. It's getting on towards four o'clock and I want to start looking at the films, so we'll have to go." Rob suggested hurriedly as he took off the white gloves.

Clara also took off her gloves and placed them neatly near the large selection of traditional, hand-carved boomerangs, some of them collected by Tindale. They then walked out into the corridor to find the multi-media viewing studio.

* * *

The first tape they watched was filmed on celluloid in 1931 and transferred to VHS video in 1994. The notes placed it at Cockatoo Creek which was in Warlpiri country in Central Australia, a few hundred kilometres north-west of Alice Springs. The black and white classic featured various traditional practices including footage of one Aboriginal craftsman smoothing a boomerang with a quartz flake hafted to a handle, and several others throwing boomerangs.

Rob found the throwing technique of one or more throwers very puzzling. They were throwing long, open-angled hunting boomerangs, called *karli* by the Warlpiri, very high into the air. Rob replayed the video several times.

"I think the camera operator must have asked one man to throw high so it was easier to film. Sounds strange, but I can't think of any other reason. Some might suggest he was throwing at a bird in flight, but that doesn't make sense. If a Warlpiri hunter was hunting birds like galahs or white cockatoos he'd throw into a flock on the ground, or the moment they took off. He'd give himself the best chance to hit one or more, and he'd hunt with other men to increase the chances of getting fresh tucker. But despite all that, how fantastic to have the footage."

"I like hearing you talk about these things." Clara said with genuine appreciation. "It brings them to life."

Rob simply smiled acknowledgement without speaking. He was still out in the bush throwing his imaginary hunting boomerangs at imaginary, emus, 'roos and cockatoos.

"You might have been there once." Clara suddenly said, surprising herself.

Without mentioning his past life as an Aboriginal man, Rob responded.

"Well, *I was* just then...that's for sure."

They both found the next film just as fascinating. Made in 1936 it featured ceremony, ground painting and body decorations and had also been filmed in Warlpiri country. However, what pleasantly surprised Rob and Clara was that one contributor was Charles P. Mountford, author of the Dreamtime books they had researched at the Mortlock Library. Suddenly a quick flash reminded Rob of the Elder's telepathic words: *"Follow Mountford, Follow Mountford."* Now his work was in front of them again.

"What a contribution he's made." Clara said admiringly.

Rob amplified her words, saying purposefully, "Good work lasts a long time doesn't it."

This valuable anthropological film did not contribute directly to Rob's quest, yet it provided him and Clara with rare insights into traditional life as events actually happened. However, he always had to keep his quest in mind and despite his passion for it, not disclose it to Clara.

They still had one and a half days booked, but there was a lot of material to look through. However, that was for tomorrow, or even the following day, because other thoughts were building in Rob's mind.

While in Adelaide he also had to become a detective and track down the hessian bag of sacred objects. This needed focussed attention very soon, and his thoughts had already jumped to achieving this goal.

"I want a day away from the Museum to find those sacred objects for the Elder, and a bit of space to think about what else we may find here."

"We've done real well so far. Just these few days have taught me so much." Clara said, feeling proud and grateful for the experiences. "I love the ideas in the traditional culture, even though I'm a visitor. It feels like a heart culture to me."

"Yeah. I think you're right. It's a privilege learning about it. But let's change pace and have tomorrow concentrating on the Elder's quest."

Rob certainly had to watch his priorities, especially time, because he and Clara only had a few more days to complete their research in Adelaide before they were booked to return to Alice Springs.

17

Mrs Heidrich who lived in the Adelaide Hills picked up Rob and Clara from the "Wildflower Bed & Breakfast" and continued driving toward the home of her friend. This was the home, according to an email Rob had received from Peter Rockworthy and confirmed by Mrs Heidrich, where a bag of objects from the Hermannsburg Mission had been kept for many years. As they cruised along on a partly cloudy, partly sunny day she said...

"She's a dear lady Mrs Braxton. Very young at heart, in her eighties, and she's made a batch of date scones for morning tea, bless her. She also lives in the Hills just a few kilometres from our place. Do you know Adelaide?"

When Rob phoned on the previous night to introduce himself and his artefact search, he and Mrs Heidrich only had time to agree on the details for getting together.

"No unfortunately." Rob answered, "I've only been through the airport before."

"And I haven't been here either." Clara added, her North American accent suggesting the probable reason why. Then Mrs Heidrich, who was a warm and welcoming type of woman, commenced a brief introduction to local history and family connections.

"Adelaide has a wide variety of suburbs, probably more than a lot of places. It stretches from the seaside to the hills, and it's been called the city of churches for a long time. We're related to Mrs Braxton. She's my aunt but I call her Mrs B. Her family's been in the Hills for about a hundred years. One of her late husband's relatives worked at Hermannsburg Mission in the days before the train went through to Alice Springs from Oodnadatta, so it was very isolated. That was before 1929 when their mail and supplies arrived by camel train only about twice a year. Imagine that. I don't know how the Germans coped because you know how hot it gets up there. They were so keen to do God's work and help the Aborigines that daily hardships were just part of the sacrifice."

Rob was sitting in the front passenger seat and quietly nodding his acknowledgement until he asked, "Were your forebears German missionaries too?"

"Well no, but on my husband's side they were strong Lutherans and taught in the Lutheran schools here. I married into it and now I fly the flag too. We're almost there."

They got out of the car, Rob carrying expectations and a daypack, and walked towards a very tidy white cottage with olive green trimming under the gutters and around the windows. Light blue smoke curled out of a brick chimney and floated away on a cool breeze. A timber verandah seemed to surround the house, but it was impossible to determine because smooth-trunked eucalypts of varying sizes crowded the sides of the property. Neatly pruned rose bushes stood behind the white picket fence adjacent to freshly mown lawns, and a straight concrete path took them towards the front door, also painted olive green.

"Come in, come in, it's warm inside," said Mrs Braxton, greeting them all happily.

"Thank you dear." Mrs Heidrich said, and introduced the visitors.

"Nice to meet you." Clara smiled.

"Thanks for inviting us Mrs Braxton, we're very pleased to be here." Rob added.

"That's quite all right. I'm very pleased to meet you, and I hope you find what you're looking for. Would you like a cuppa now or later?

"I'd like to see the objects first." Rob replied, glancing at Clara. "But let me tell you how we came to be here."

Mrs Braxton gestured to chairs and everyone sat down as Rob continued.

"I've been living and travelling overseas and came out to Alice Springs to join a group that was driving up to the Kimberley to look at Aboriginal Rock Art. But I didn't get there because I met an Aboriginal elder and artist. He was born in the Hermannsburg area and told me that his people lost their sacred objects many years ago. He emphasised how vitally important it was to find them and bring them home, because they want to dance and sing special ceremonies to help the earth."

"And you found me through Mrs Heidrich because we've got that old bag of things," said Mrs Braxton concluding Rob's story, then continuing with her own.

"I never knew what they were," she explained. "My husband used to say women *must not* look at them under any circumstances. I didn't know the ways of the old Aborigines. Their traditions were beyond me. My generation didn't take much interest in the native culture, it just wasn't done."

"Yes, I understand that," replied Rob, careful not to offend her in any way.

"But if you'd like to see them now I'll get the step-ladder. They're on top of the wardrobe in the spare room. Come through this way, just take the first right." Mrs Braxton directed.

She walked out of the dining room to the back of the house and returned with the aluminium step-ladder, meeting Rob, Clara and Mrs Heidrich in the room she had directed them to.

"Oh thanks," said Rob, referring to the step-ladder, "I could have…."

"No, no dear," Mrs Braxton cut in as she placed it near the wardrobe. "It's very light."

The spare room had a single bed, a small chest of drawers, and a fluffy rug on the floor but its main feature was the wardrobe. Made from solid tan brown oak probably in the 1930s or 40s, its full-length mirror gave the impression that the room was bigger than it really was.

"They've been on top of the wardrobe for years, can't remember when we put them there... my husband was alive but he's been gone fifteen years...so it was before that, a long time before that. I don't even dust around them now, don't take any notice..."

"It's wonderful you've got them. Thanks again for letting us visit today."

"Oh no, my pleasure, I'm very glad you're here." Mrs Braxton said warmly, the tone of her voice changing. "Your visit's a relief. Those things never belonged to us. But we didn't know what to do with them." She continued, clasping her hands together. "They're from the old days when the wild natives were coming into the Mission. They came down with my husband's cousin, that's why they're here. The family and I wondered about that bag from time to time, but you know how it is, life goes along and priorities take over."

Rob responded understandingly.

"Hardly any sacred objects are ever taken back to where they came from. People don't know what to do. My elder friend in Alice asked me to look at the ones you have and hopefully identify one he is looking for. It's very important and he'll be able to retell a traditional story near Hermannsburg for the first time in decades. So thank you for keeping them safe."

"Oh, I hope it's here. You've come a long way. We never looked at them. No one ever unwrapped them," she said proudly.

Rob smiled with gratitude.

"I'll just look at the designs now to see if the exact object the Elder described is here. So please excuse me, I won't be long. Then I'll take you up on that cuppa with pleasure."

After the others left the room Rob took the drawing of the sacred tjurunga out of his shirt's top pocket, unfolding it carefully. He had not looked at it since the Elder sketched it in Alice Springs, but now clear, straight lines and concentric circles reminded him of what he was looking for. He climbed up the step-ladder with accelerating excitement.

* * *

"*YES, YES*...it's here." Rob could not contain himself. "I've *FOUND IT!*"

Everyone in the house heard him shout, but they didn't rush into the spare room. They would not because they knew the objects were taboo for women.

He had looked briefly but respectfully at each object, ultimately finding the pattern that matched the Elder's drawing exactly. His heart filled with joy as he held it in his hands. The other tjurunga also had lines and circles but this was the one. Instantly he imagined the Elder's happy face. Only he understood its full significance and the broken journey of his people since these sacred objects had been taken from country. But after so many years there was now cause for celebration.

Rob carefully re-wrapped the tjurunga in the old Lutheran Herald newspaper pages and put them back into the hessian sugar bag, inwardly thanking the Ancestors, God and the Universe. Then he stepped down the step-ladder, sacred treasure in hand, and joined the others in the lounge room where Mrs Braxton had laid out morning tea.

"I've got it. It's definitely the one. The Elder will be absolutely delighted. You can't imagine. There are actually five pieces in the bag, so they must have all come down from Hermannsburg."

"You must be so pleased," Mrs Braxton said. "How do you like your tea?"

"White with no sugar thanks." Rob responded, feeling over the moon.

"With a fresh date scone perhaps?" Smiled Mrs Braxton, holding a plate full of them out for him.

"I'm very happy for you." Mrs Braxton continued. "As I said it's quite a relief that you've come over today. You should take them *all* back, if they can be of use to your friend."

"Thank you very much. I will." Rob added, as he spread butter onto the scone.

"My husband's cousin used to say the natives had religious beliefs and he tried to explain, but it was like another world. I didn't understand it, do you?"

"Only a little Mrs Braxton. Aboriginal spirituality is very complex. It mainly relates to land or country, and is associated with the Ancestor's journeys in the Dreamtime when the world was created. In the old culture all of the knowledge was handed down through storytelling and ceremony."

Rob stopped because he sensed his general description was enough for Mrs Braxton who had picked up the plate of date scones half way through his answer.

"Have another scone." She said to Rob, adding...

"I'm very pleased that bag of objects is going. That finishes a chapter here."

"And starts one for my friend in Alice." Rob replied buoyantly, spreading butter on his second scone.

The morning tea with home-made date scones was a delicious conclusion to a wonderful visit. And soon after, Rob, Clara and Mrs Heidrich stood up to say their good byes. Outside the front door, with the small bag of precious objects safely in his daypack, Rob reached for Mrs Braxton's right hand.

"Thank *you*." He said sincerely with warm appreciation. Her hand was small, but her grip was strong. "Thank *you*. Thank you so much again for everything."

"It's been my pleasure Rob," said Mrs Braxton, shaking his hand firmly.

Then Mrs Heidrich hugged Mrs Braxton. "Lovely to see you Mrs B. I'll ring soon."

"My pleasure dear." Mrs Braxton responded. "Come again anytime. It's been such a wonderful morning. Good bye dear."

* * *

After the wonderful discovery in Mrs Braxton's home, Mrs Heidrich drove Rob and Clara back to their Bed & Breakfast.

"Thanks *so* much." Rob said to Mrs Heidrich, offering his hand.

"Didn't it work out well. Mrs Braxton was so pleased," replied Mrs Heidrich shaking Rob's hand.

"It sure did. My friend in Alice will be so, so happy. Big thanks again, and all the best."

"So nice meeting you." Clara added warmly.

"You're welcome. Enjoy your stay. Bye now." Mrs Heidrich replied.

Rob and Clara got out of the car with the sacred objects now secure in Rob's possession. They waved to Mrs Heidrich and then arm-in-arm strolled into the building and their welcoming room.

"Wasn't that great, and so easy." Rob said to Clara. "These objects have been sitting there for all that time, just waiting. How about that for Cosmic Timing?"

"You mean serendipity?" Clara responded.

"No. I mean when circumstances are appropriate things happen, but not by chance. There's a right time for everything and it's easiest to see with hindsight. So if we accept this approach and trust it, we recognise it happens most, if not all the time!"

"I'd rather step out and make things happen," Clara responded. "I need to get things moving."

"Yeah, that's what we do. We don't stop, we keep living life, but we're part of a bigger picture. We take action and get results, but because we're part of the Universe in spirit we're connected to everything. Am I making sense?"

"I understand the words but you jumped from personal to Universal very quickly."

"Well, because we're connected to everything in spirit we're affected by everything. So our actions are also linked to the timing of the big picture."

"Interesting. Keep going."

"Most of us think *WE* do everything, but we only do *OUR* part. We're all ripples in the universal ocean of spirit. That's how we're connected to the big picture. But it's difficult to understand because like feelings, we can't see spirit."

"That's a philosophy, but how do you see it day by day?"

"I try and see every person as a spiritual being first and a physical being next. It's very difficult because I can't see spirit. That's my approach and I'm only gradually getting better at it."

"Maybe I'll get it sometime," added Clara. "But at the moment I think serendipity or coincidence is still a mystery."

"Like women." Rob cheekily suggested, changing the subject by pulling Clara close, hugging her tightly and whispering...

"We're in the right place at the right time, how about sharing a bit of Cosmic Timing?" he teased. "But after I've sent an email to the Elder," he quickly added.

"Love to try your theory." Clara whispered back, kissing Rob's cheek.

"Yeah, let's try a few. I'll be back shortly." Rob chuckled as he reluctantly unwrapped his arms from around Clara. He took a few steps to the table, opened his laptop and in the subject heading typed:

Lindsay: Tjurunga Found!

Fantastic news! I've found the one you wanted!

Everything fell into place. The tjurunga was still in the original hessian sugar bag with four others. They were definitely collected at Hermannsburg in the mid 1920s according to the kind lady here, and they've been with the family ever since. No one ever looked at them she assured me, and they've been wrapped up the whole time. She's so relieved they've gone after so many years.

Hope you're getting good news about the other tjurunga too.

Best Regards, Rob

* * *

The next morning was their last scheduled visit to the Museum and they needed to use the time as productively as possible. Peter Frederickson was standing at the Visitor Information Desk when they walked in and he greeted them with a generous offer.

"Morning again. You can work right through until closing if you need to. No-one else has booked the material so the space is yours."

"Thanks very much Peter. We're actually going really well but a little extra time could come in handy. We'll pop in before we go. You and the staff have been great."

"It's a pleasure, that's our role. The associations we develop with researchers are very important to the Museum so I'm glad you feel satisfied with everything."

"The whole experience opened my eyes." Clara offered. "There's so much in the traditional Aboriginal culture and your facilities are first class. Thanks from me too."

"Anytime. Come again soon." Peter said, making friendly eye contact.

Rob and Clara then strode directly to the room, Rob saying as they neared the door, "We've got to finish the Tindale material, that's the strong feeling I've got."

They were both excited by the prospect of their last day, especially because they were delving into such a fascinating archive.

The material was laid out exactly as they had left it, and as they stood at the desk Clara said enthusiastically...

"I've still got his *Aboriginal Tribes of Australia* to look through. That's these two books and four large maps of tribal areas in the slip case, so there's plenty to work on. What are you going to start with?"

"I want to go Outback with him, so I'll get into the bound expedition journals, and there's a couple of file boxes that are calling me too. How's that sound."

It was not a question as usual, but Clara replied anyway...

"That's okay mate, you're the professor!"

With heads down they began immediately, pouring over some of the life's work of a dedicated and meticulous man, a pioneer collector and recorder of valuable Aboriginal lore. Clara had begun to unfold one of Tindale's maps on her desk when Rob suddenly said...

"Look at this. Look at this."

Rob had discovered a slim cardboard folder containing a neatly typed manuscript and he was thrilled instantly. Entitled *A gathering of Australian Aboriginal words for boomerang by Norman B. Tindale,"* it was a rare treasure of continent-wide words gathered over many years.

"Can you believe it!" He exclaimed, holding up the folder with both hands. "There are hundreds of words for boomerang. It's fantastic. What ever else we find this morning, this list has already made my day!"

"How wonderful." Clara said, sliding behind Rob and placing her hands on his shoulders.

"I've got to see *what* makes your day!"

Rob loved her mischievous response and put his hands back on top of hers.

"Sure sweetheart. Let's find the words for boomerang in Aranda, Warlpiri and Luritja mobs up in the Centre to start with...."

18

Back in Alice Springs Rob and Clara's first priority was to deliver the tjurunga to the Elder. The 4WD Rob had used before the Adelaide trip was still being serviced, so he phoned a Private Hire company to pick Clara and him up from the Resort. Rob thought that the most logical way to find the Elder was to visit the home he shared with his extended family.

The young cousin who had driven Rob and the Elder to Spencer Hill a couple of weeks earlier in the old battered blue car came to the front door.

"Howya goin', uncle's out bush." The young man said, naturally knowing why Rob had come. "I dunno when he's comin' back."

"Ah, that's disappointing. But thanks Nathan. Just tell him I'm back at the Resort, if you don't mind." Rob replied. "We'll catch you later".

"Okay, seeya." The young man responded.

Rob did not leave the hessian sugar bag containing the tjurunga. He was absolutely clear that he must hand them to the Elder personally. So for now he would keep them safely locked up at the Resort.

"I wonder where he is..." Rob thought out loud.

"He loves his country so much, he'll be there again." Clara said confidently.

Rob admired Clara's insight as he nodded in agreement, knowing that Cosmic Timing would bring them together again at exactly the right time.

Rob and Clara's second priority was each other. They only had two full days to share before they had to go their separate ways. Unfortunately it had to be like this. There was no seat for Clara on the Rock Art field trip into the Victoria River District, nor did she have enough time, and Rob wanted to continue his secret *First Boomerang* quest alone.

Clara was deeply disappointed because she had another full week available and wanted to spend more time with her man. She had dreamed of trips with him into the Outback. For her it was the fabled landscape of mystique, endless distance and timeless space. She had travelled half way around the world to experience the land called "Down Under" with the man she loved. Clara wanted to walk on the ancient red soil by day, and by night gaze into the enormous sparkling skies while holding Rob's hand. She craved these simple pleasures, as well as more intimate ones, and was frustrated.

"I'm sorry but I'm feeling bothered by how things have turned out. I accepted it last week and really enjoyed Adelaide, but we're running out of time. I know that's how the cookie crumbles sometimes, but I wanted more bites. I don't know if I'll go straight back or take a side trip, it's a long way to come for just a week…"

"I know, I know. Everything happened at once. I'm disappointed too." Rob said quietly.

Rob understood her feelings but could not change his travel plans. According to his growing awareness they were flowing as they were meant to, and his quest was unfolding exactly on time. Rob loved Clara and also his work, but it was not a matter of choosing between them. Rob's life was evolving, especially after meeting the Elder. Living in the *now* was vital to him, and right *now* he had to pursue *his* journey. That was the big picture.

In practical terms, and almost immediately, he had to fly to Darwin so he could link with Dr Geoffrey Seekman and explore rock paintings of boomerangs in the VRD.

He had of course apologised to Clara on the day she arrived, and they both knew the timing of events had not been in his hands. But that did not change the fact that they were both disappointed, Clara more so because of her romantic priorities and tiring trip from New York. However, Clara was resilient and professional during the Adelaide trip and quickly decided to stay for several more days in Central Australia. She planned to store some of her gear at the Resort and take an Aboriginal-guided 4WD tour to Uluru via the West MacDonnells and Kings Canyon (*Watarrka*). She especially wanted to see the big Rock that Rob had told her so much about in Manhattan.

"That's *great*." Rob said as his spirits lifted. "You *have* to see it and feel the energy. Stay three nights and catch the changing moods and colours. I love Uluru. I've been privileged to see rain cascading from its ancient shoulders. It was magnificent, awe-inspiring, even though I got wet! Then go to Kata Tjuta. There's thirty-six massive domes, some higher than the Rock. Go when it's quiet. You might sense the Dreamtime on the winds that whistle around them. God's out there too. I get carried away and touch deep levels of spirituality out there, so when I talk about it, whoever is close hears my heart."

"I love hearing it too." Clara said warmly. "I want to be there right now, you paint such an inviting picture. But I'll go after you go because I want to see you off at the airport first. Bit ironic eh, Aussie mate." Clara said, mimicking the Australian accent. "I've come to visit with you but *you're* the one leaving town!"

Clara did not mention her disappointment again, even though her heart had not fully reconciled the flow of events. She did not blame Rob's quest, or the Aboriginal worlds he was profoundly linked to.

The concept of living in the *now* resonated with her, but its practical implications were harder to get used to. Perhaps if she lived in Central Australia and came to know Aboriginal characters, her understanding would grow. Not that living in the *now* is confined to any place or group of people. However, on this trip there was no time for relationships to grow with locals. There was not even enough time with Rob. Sadly, Clara had only shared a week with the man she had come to see. But that was how it was, and her feelings could not change it.

* * *

In the time remaining before Rob's flight they agreed to have as much fun and do as much as possible. Clara's 'get up and do it' attitude came to the fore and Rob admired her once again. She was ready to enjoy the time they had, confirming her attitude with a big New York smile.

Alice Spring's abundance of cultural activities, historical venues and surrounding scenic landscapes could easily occupy two weeks, but Rob and Clara only had two days. Some quick tour planning was required. From the Resort's Reception area they collected a handful of brochures and took them back to their room.

"We'll need wheels so I'll sort that out with the Rent-a-Car mob – they're still servicing the 4WD." Rob explained. "We won't go off-road so a car will do. But if you're going to see me off, how will you get back to town?"

"Guess what Outback man? I'd now like to try driving Down Under! Surprise eh? It still looks weird on the wrong side, but I can do it." Clara said convincingly.

"Good for you sweetheart. After the airport, you can drop it off at Outback Oz, then go on your Uluru tour the next day. Perfect."

"It's going to work out real well." Clara responded confidently.

Rob called the company and booked a medium-sized car. As a good public relations exercise the manager offered to deliver it that afternoon, a business gesture Rob and Clara greatly appreciated.

"This 'Didgeridoo Experience' looks pretty good." Rob suggested as he browsed the brochure. "It says, *'A master didgeridoo performer and players on keyboards and international percussion instruments introduce audiences to the incredible Outback. With evocative, ever-changing photographs of Central Australia the journey is a blend of musical skills, Aboriginal culture, history and natural beauty.'* What do you think?"

"Yes, definitely. I'd love it honey. There aren't many didgeridoo shows in the States you know. Book it right away." Clara directed. But the show was the next night, so they still had one night and one full day to plan.

Clara held up a brochure. "What about Alice Springs Desert Park? I'd love to see the emus and kangaroos, and the bird show especially."

"Yeah, why not. I've heard you need about four hours there, but it's close to town, only a few minutes along Larapinta Drive."

Rob knew Clara really wanted to see the magical night sky, so he looked though the brochures and found "Outback Astronomy Tours" which offered hotel pick-ups and the opportunity to *"See the Sky come to Life."* After booking by phone Rob realised they would just have enough time before the Astronomy Tour to see sunset from Anzac Hill. He wanted to take Clara because he had spent so many memorable moments there with the Elder, but also because it was the best vantage point in town for viewing sunset and sunrise.

With both nights and half the first day planned they agreed to decide other activities in the moment. This was more Rob's suggestion than Clara's who wanted to fill every minute because of limited time. Their ways of thinking seemed completely opposite, but they knew each other well enough to appreciate each other's approach.

As they folded up the tour brochures Rob answered a phone call from a Reception staff member advising him that the rental car had arrived. He happily hurried down to the front desk, signed the paper work, paid by credit card and thanked the Outback Oz's manager.

Anzac Hill was not far from the Resort and Rob wanted to take Clara for a drive in the new car. From the familiar lookout he and Clara watched the fiery golden ball slide below the horizon as mauve-tinged twilight calmly settled on Alice Springs. They were feeling peaceful, but nevertheless concerned about the increasing cloud. Would it affect the Astronomy Tour? Was it too early to know? After only a five minute drive they were back at the Resort and the room phone's flashing light indicated a message. Rob pressed a button and listened. The tour company had phoned to say that the weather would not be good enough for star gazing so tonight's tour was cancelled.

"Oh no, that's a shame." Rob said.

"And really disappointing, but let's look forward to the morning." Clara suggested.

* * *

An action highlight at the Desert Park is the feeding of Central Australian native raptors or birds of prey. Free flying kites and falcons electrify audiences, swooping in at speed to catch airborne food thrown by handlers. Clara was absolutely thrilled when a falcon whooshed under the shade-cloth canopy only a metre above her head. Whether this was part of the show or not did not matter.

"How terrific honey." I've never seen that in the States. How long has the Desert Park been here?"

"The N.T. Government funded it, the gates opened in 1997 and it's been developing each year. There's research into endangered desert animals, Aboriginal artefacts displays and seed growing projects for bush tucker. Its sister property is Territory Wildlife Park near Darwin, and I think it opened in 1989. And up there you get tropical zone flora and fauna. Around the Territory there's lots of National Parks and Conservation Reserves, and there's thousands of visitors every year."

"Impressive, what's next?" Quizzed Clara, looking down at the Desert Park's map and day's program.

Rob and Clara entered the desert creatures' Nocturnal House, feeling they should tip toe through the darkness until they saw how active the bilbies and echidnas were. After exploring the exhibit they returned to daylight and proceeded along the red soil walking track, seeing big red kangaroos lying flat out in the sun, and later, curious emus in another area of the Woodland habitat. Then superb, artistic signs directed them to Dingo Territory where they enjoyed watching Australia's native dogs, before reaching the main Exit.

"Like a cuppa before we head back to town?'' Rob asked, gesturing towards the cafe.

"No need honey, I've got my water bottle. Maybe later, let's keep moving.''

They drove back on Larapinta Drive, the same road that Rob had driven the Elder along to the Full Moon site, when suddenly a subject came to his mind.

"When I was out bush with the Elder we talked about the *'timelessness of time'* that no-one has been able to measure. But how do we interpret that concept with logical thinking, conventional formulae or existing scientific instruments when its reality is in several dimensions? It's at the ends of our fingertips but not touchable. It's at the ends of our eyelashes but not visible. That's how close it is."

"You amaze me Professor! Time might be timeless, but *we* haven't got enough!" Clara said, her usually animated voice slowing as her words concluded.

"I know. I agree. But can you see the big picture?"

"I'm more down to earth. I just want to enjoy the time we do have."

Rob could have kept talking about the topic, but he knew it would be wiser to give his attention to the lovely lady sitting next to him.

"We're doing okay, we're enjoying the moments. Let's have a look at the Royal Flying Doctor Service. We'll be there in a couple of minutes."

After watching a contemporary video about the Service and viewing historical displays housed in a classic Central Australian building, Rob suggested they visit another unique local attraction, but he wanted it to be a surprise.

Panorama Guth was one artist's interpretation of Central Australia's landscapes that stood two storeys high in a purpose-built circular building. Before they entered Rob did not tell Clara about the wide, painted vistas or the impressive traditional Aboriginal artefacts that decorated walls and filled display cases.

Clara loved it. The panorama gave her a perspective of Central Australia she had not expected, and the realistic 3D elements of red dirt, preserved goannas and clumps of spinifex the artist included were surprising. In its simplicity it was a highlight of her day.

They walked back to the car holding hands.

"Thanks Rob. Somehow it brought the Outback closer, and I don't mean physically. His painting draws you in to the essence of the landscape. You can feel his love and respect for it."

They had just enough time to drive back to the Resort and shower, change, and have a bite to eat then make it to the "Didgeridoo Experience" at a private theatre in Todd Mall.

Outback lore and landscape came to life as haunting, mysterious melodies enthralled the packed theatre. Unique sounds in various musical keys reverberated from long, hollow sections of native Australian trees. The audience was spellbound. A virtuoso was entertaining them with the world's oldest woodwind instrument, the traditional *yidaki* of eastern Arnhem Land known to millions as the *didgeridoo.*

Angus Longman and his band blended ancient rhythms, Outback images and humorous anecdotes and the audience clapped for more. Rob and Clara joined in, tapping their feet and loving every moment. After the show audience members were invited on stage to blow a sound on the didgeridoo, and to try circular breathing. Some made reasonable notes, most found the breathing technique difficult, but at the end of the night the music ringing in everyone's ears was the fun of a great performance.

* * *

Waking on their last full day, Clara propped herself up on one elbow as Rob asked...

"Do you want to see Corroboree Rock, it's a special place in the Eastern Mac....."

Clara quickly but gently placed her index finger over his lips, saying softly...

"Let's stay in bed and make love all day. I'd rather *rock* with you."

"Yeah." Rob agreed as he nibbled her finger. "How does Clarita wanna play?"

"Mmm. I'm very happy down under." She whispered, sliding her hand down his stomach. "And then we....."

Rob kissed Clara's next words away, pressing his lips hard into hers. For the next hour they gave and received, moment by moment.

Timelessness took them in its arms and they felt the nurturing of love that connects individual hearts with the universal heart. Robust and passionate, their lovemaking was blessed by the lightness of angel wings, its rhythms deeper than any previous moments in Manhattan. Underscored by the vibrations of an ancient landscape, life with a capital 'L' pulsated through them.

Later, Rob and Clara emerged from their love-filled bliss and awoke fully to the day. They had not planned anything but suddenly thoughts of the next day's flight jumped into Rob's mind. He had to prepare his gear, but that would not take long, so they still had time to explore more of the landscape together.

After a snack lunch delivered by room service, they decided to drive out along the Ross Highway that runs close in sections to the Eastern MacDonnell Ranges. Stopping briefly at Emily Gap (*Anthwerkke*) and Jessie Gap (*Atherrke*), both Caterpillar Dreaming places, they rolled on to another Eastern Aranda site. It was Corroboree Rock (*Antanan-*

gantana) that Rob had briefly mentioned earlier. Under the information shelter built by the Northern Territory Parks and Wildlife Commission, Rob and Clara read on a printed sign that it was a men's sacred site. And its traditional name was one Clara could try to pronounce. Rob could not speak the language and there were no native speakers of Aranda around to help, but she made two brave beginnings before saying...

"An-tanan-gantana, is that it?"

"Sounds good mate. It's all very complex. Don't forget that all Aboriginal languages were oral and never written down. We try the best we can, but it's hard. Linguists do a great job interpreting and translating into English, but their interpretations change over the years and so do their spellings!"

They walked slowly on the public dirt track around the impressive landmark, noticing how shapes changed abruptly from different angles. This was a surprising feature of the sacred place. Rob did not know its story but Corroborree Rock's profound presence touched them deeply before they returned to the car to drive back into Alice Springs.

On this quiet afternoon with Clara, Rob had no idea that in a few weeks time he would again drive along the Ross Highway under totally different circumstances.

As they drove along Rob described a project obviously close to his heart.

"There's going to be a Boomerang Museum in Australia one day. I wish I could show it to you. The plans and partners are coming together and the ground will be blessed before building begins. It will be visually striking and environmentally impressive, and will house boomerangs from every traditional group in Australia, from the oldest to contemporary pieces. It will be computer interactive, artefact makers and artists will share their techniques, forgotten archives will come to life, and cultural displays will add more authenticity. The Museum will entice people from all over the world for years and years."

"That sounds great Rob. I know you're into boomerangs, but how do you know?"

"It came to me. The vision just popped into my mind. It's going to be THE place for Boomerangology, the home for multi-media information about our world famous symbol. People of all ages and nationalities will come. It's a perfectly clear vision."

"That's real passion. We're having a lot today honey." Clara said with a suggestive, satisfied chuckle, caressing the back of Rob's neck with her outstretched right hand.

* * *

Their final morning together was flat emotionally because the main thing on their minds was the 11.45am flight. Nevertheless, they playfully cuddled in bed for as long as they could before Rob had to get up, finish packing and load his gear. Even though he was going out bush for over a week up north, he travelled lightly taking just the basics in clothing, but taking extra care with his cameras and laptop.

As they were about to get into the car Clara asked a question.

"Do you mind me driving out to the airport?" Rob was pleasantly surprised and agreed without a second thought.

"Thanks Outback man, I thought you'd never offer!"

It was their private joke because previously she had not been interested in driving at all.

Clara's natural inclination to host and manage was pushing through the sense of separation she was experiencing. By leading the way emotionally, she could balance her feelings plus farewell Rob personally, and that would be good for her.

With Clara at the wheel they began the drive to the airport.

"This gap's such a beautiful gateway to Alice Springs. I hope I see it again soon." Clara said, as they passed the distinctive, angled rock strata of Heavitree Gap.

"Sounds good to me sweetheart." Rob responded.

A short while later they pulled into the airport car park, Clara saying confidently, "Well, *it is okay* driving on the wrong side. We got here safely Outback man!"

* * *

After Rob checked-in they stood together and wrapped their arms around each other. Tears filled Clara's eyes, and Rob could not hold back his tears either, as they hugged closer. These were not moments for many words. Instead, their kisses carried feelings of love, hope, sadness and a hundred more.

As the final boarding call for the flight was announced Rob squeezed Clara for the last time, whispering...

"See you later sweetheart. Enjoy Uluru."

"Yes honey. See you at home. Come back real soon."

19

"The Rainbow Serpent is everywhere" flashed into Rob's mind as he took off from Alice Springs airport bound for Darwin, 1500kms north in the tropical Top End. The Qantas Boeing 737 lifted off smoothly into the bright sunshine of a clear Winter's day. Rob was sitting in a window seat and his attention was immediately drawn to the Mac-Donnell Ranges, perennial caterpillars of the Aranda Dreamtime. The traditional stories describing country were often more meaningful to him now than towns and man-made roads that marked the landscape.

Rob was puzzled by the momentous Rainbow Serpent statement, and wondered how it could be "everywhere". What does this mean, he wondered. He had become increasingly familiar with the way messages *'arrived'* when it was appropriate, so he was not surprised by the new information. However, he did wonder how the Rainbow Serpent connected to his quest.

The Rainbow Serpent is represented in legends throughout Australia, its form changing from area to area, its powers retaining potency in the everyday lives of traditional clans. But why had it suddenly flashed in today, just as Rob was heading to Darwin?

In the zippered side section of his carry-on bag he had placed books, pens and pencils, and as the jet cruised high above the virtually unpopulated Northern Territory he selected a book. It was the one he found in the Museum Shop in Adelaide. Titled *Lardil - Keepers of the Dreamtime* it was an intuitive purchase, but so far there had been no time to read it. He knew the Lardil people lived on Mornington Island in the Gulf of Carpentaria, the huge sweep of ocean between the west coast of Cape York Peninsular and the east coast of Arnhem Land. He also knew they used boomerangs. But he knew nothing of their story-telling. Now he was eager to explore this small, illustrated book that fitted snugly into his hands.

Rob was impressed by the book's elegant layout that included a number of key named sections. After seeing a photo of a tribesman painting himself for ceremony he turned the page and discovered the section titled *The Rainbow Serpent*. Rob was shocked because it had just flashed into his mind during take-off. What would he find out about this well-known Dreamtime character? He did not have long to wait. On the next page was a traditional Lardil story about it.

Would the ancient tale meaningfully contribute to his search for *The First Boomerang?* Pleasantly surprised, Rob marvelled at how the Universe illuminated his research path. He was being guided by what many still regard as 'co-incidence', but Rob knew it was Cosmic Timing manifesting in everyday life.

A flight attendant served a complimentary snack with tea, coffee or juice. Rob thanked her and pondered what he had just discovered, his thoughts stretching across the continent like mental Songlines, recon-necting with boomerang legends he had read.

Ancient boomerangs in flight had great creative powers. They formed landmarks, cleared plains and carved mountain features as they touched down in the Dreamtime. Rob knew that these places can be seen today as examples of the Ancestors' presence on earth, and this traditional knowledge brings a fascinating dimension to the land around us. It was now natural for him to view the Outback and other regions of Australia as legendary landscapes.

With this background in mind Rob excitedly started reading *The Rainbow Serpent*.

The Lardil story was as graphic and memorable as any he had read. It tells, surprisingly, of selfish *Thuwathu*, the Rainbow Serpent who will not share with his sister and her baby, the rainproof shelter he has built. When the rain comes he continually claims, despite her pleading, that there is only enough space for himself, his two heads, two arms, etc. Tragically, the baby girl, his niece, dies of cold and exposure, so the mother sets fire to the shelter in revenge. Writhing in agony and trying to escape... the Rainbow Serpent creates the Dugong River, locally known as *Minyindagarr* or *"suffering man"*, and *"the stones are said to be his blood, reefs his backbone, and messmate trees his ribs."*

The Rainbow Serpent remains embodied in that landscape, but it was the next sentence that grabbed Rob's already heightened attention.

The power of boomerangs are said to derive from the fact that they are made from messmate trees, and are therefore Rainbow Serpent's ribs.

"That's amazing," Rob said under his breath. He had never heard anything like it before. The boomerang was a 'living' part of one of the most important and powerful Ancestors in Aboriginal culture.

Always on the lookout for signs, Rob wondered if there was anything in what he had just read, any geographical reference or other clue that might take him closer to fulfilling his quest. To be straight to the point, as his thoughts usually were, could *The First Boomerang* be found on Mornington Island? As quick as this thought was, he was instantly confronted with pictorial evidence of his discovery.

He had skipped over a photograph on the previous page which captures three dancers decorated with earth pigments, leaf tassels and feather down, one with a tall head-dress and outstretched arms, one playing a didgeridoo, and the other holding a white-painted boomerang

... *"which represents a rib of the Rainbow Serpent"*, according to the caption. Here was a traditional ceremony associated with the *'boomerang ribs'* of the Rainbow Serpent!

"Fantastic. Absolutely fantastic." Rob shouted within.

He had to speak to a Lardil elder or storyteller as soon as possible. The Rainbow Serpent was such a significant and Australia-wide story that he had to follow its trail for as far as he could because of this incredible boomerang connection. It was astounding. But he could not do any more while still in flight, so he placed the book back in his carry-on bag positioned between his feet and started enjoying his orange juice and sandwich snack.

* * *

Darwin was about two thirds through the Dry season, its irrigated gardens still flush with green lawns, hibiscus and frangipani, its monsoon rains on hold until approximately November, when the flight from Alice Springs touched down. Rob had sent Geoffrey Seekman an email with his arrival details, and had not expected to be met, so he was pleasantly surprised to see someone holding a printed sign with his name on it when he walked into the Arrivals area. Rob's plan had been to use a hotel free-phone at the airport, travel to the accommodation by taxi or shuttle bus and then make contact. But now there was no need to do that.

Offering his hand to the sign holder Rob said: "You must be Dr Seekman, I'm Rob Noble, thanks very much for coming, I wasn't expecting...."

"Yes, g'day Rob, but I know what it's like in a new place," interrupted Geoffrey Seekman, "It's good to be shown around until you get your bearings, and if you don't mind the sofa bed you can stay at my place until we leave. It's only one night. My assistant's already here but there's enough room. We'll have to get to know each other anyway, so why not start straight away. And call me Geoff."

"Well, you've convinced me." Rob replied, his accent mimicking the friendly tone of his new host and soon-to-be guide to the VRD. "I've only got one bag to collect, and then I'm ready."

With Rob's bag retrieved from the baggage carousel, Geoff drove them out of the airport for an extended trip around the city as a brief introduction to Australia's northern most capital, stopping at several locations to walk around. Rob said nothing about the humidity, but after he wiped his forehead with a folded handkerchief as they stretched their legs along the Esplanade, Geoff explained.

"You get used to it... believe it or not. It took me a while though."

"That's good to hear. I've sampled it overseas but never been in it for long. Isn't this the Dry season?"

"Yes, so you won't want to be here in the 'build-up' if you feel it now."

Geoffrey Seekman lived in a semi-rural area of Darwin and its southern location would give them a flying start to the field trip because they initially had to travel south to Katherine on the Stuart Highway.

They arrived at his home as late afternoon patterns of sunlight and shadow lay across the timber front verandah. Lipstick palms, tropical flowers and a freshly cut lawn led them into the house, as delicious cooking aromas wafted through the air. The anticipation of sharing a home-cooked meal gave Rob a warm feeling of being welcomed to the Top End and the next stage of his quest.

Rob always had to remember one vital thing. The Elder insisted that he must never tell anyone he was looking for *The First Boomerang*. He could say he was researching various forms of boomerangs, their representations in art and appearances in legend. But he had to keep his ultimate quest confidential. He was being reminded mentally now because Geoff and his assistant would soon be asking about what he was doing.

They were inevitably drawn into the kitchen by the tantalising aromas and Geoff Seekman introduced the chef.

"Meet my assistant Sally from Sydney."

A bright, teethy smile lit up a tanned face fringed with sunny blonde hair. It fell straight to about 30cm below her shoulders, and her warm blue eyes invited Rob to smile also.

"Hello Sally, smells fantastic in here."

"Hello Rob. Nice to meet you. Glad you've made it."

The inviting aromas were intensifying.

"Sorry I can't shake hands, but I'm doing the meats. Would you prefer chicken, crocodile, barramundi, or the lot?" Her words flowed like miniature smile bubbles, engaging everyone around. Then she added quickly, "And I've got tasty stir fried veges to go with it."

"Sounds superb, I'll go for the barra thanks." Rob replied, already feeling at home in a new place.

"And what about vino?" Geoff offered with the flourish of a fine host. This field trip leader was a man of many parts, as he continued. "I don't drink when I'm in the field so I like to have a glass or two before going bush. I've got a few reds and a few whites, dry and sweet, so what do you fancy?"

"I've got friends and relatives in the Hunter Valley in New South Wales so if you have a crisp, fruity Chardonnay I'd love it."

Over dinner the conversation flowed from topic to topic. Geoff suggested at one point that the Northern Territory and Federal Governments had a lot to answer for because of the shocking state of Aboriginal health and education facilities in remote communities. However, he partially balanced this by saying that some Aboriginal Land Councils and Aboriginal Agencies were not always pure conduits of available financial assistance either, and the Aboriginal peoples who needed it most were still missing out.

"It really makes you wonder." Geoff said with a long exhalation of breath. "If pollies and bureaucrats don't start understanding the culture, they'll never know enough to help the next generation before it misses out too. I've been here twelve years, and that doesn't make me a local, but I've got a good idea of what's going on. I work with blackfellas, whitefellas and many others up here. Darwin's been a multi-racial community since day one. And generally we all get along well. We get a bit tense when the Wet's approaching. The atmosphere can be stifling. And that affects everyone. It doesn't depend on colour or heritage. But the lack of real understanding's an ongoing issue. What do you reckon?"

He looked at Rob in search of his opinion, as he started to fill everyone's glass from a jug of fresh, chilled rain water.

"This is only my second trip to the Territory in ten years, but I research the culture and I've trekked in South America where Indigenous peoples also had their land taken over. It always gets back to respect and understanding. Governments of all types have stuffed it up for decades. They've used our money, large amounts of resources, and they've had time. One huge issue is that we're a mind culture and Aboriginals are a heart culture. So we have to bring our hearts to the table too." Rob paused to have a refreshing mouthful of water. It was the Dry season in the Top End but still over twenty degrees Celsius around the early evening table.

"I understand what you're saying. The culture's so interesting." Sally said.

Sally had a bright and enthusiastic personality, which Rob knew would be ideal for the trip. She became interested in Rock Art after seeing rock engravings of Ancestral Beings in the Kuring-gai National Park in northern Sydney. She was surprised there was a spiritual dimension to the culture, because there was no mention of it at school. She gained a Bachelors Degree in Science and a Diploma of Education at the University of Sydney, and was having a year off to see Australia. On a notice board at university she read Geoff's message seeking a graduate to do fieldwork. Although not an anthropologist she was accepted, and by long distance train and even longer overnight coach rides made the journey to Darwin. This trip to the VRD would be her second with Geoff. The first had been into World Heritage-listed Kakadu National Park with its vast landscapes and rich Aboriginal heritage.

"Geoff told me you're into boomerangs and I read your email last week. How did you get into boomerangs?" Sally asked.

"Well, strangely enough I was inspired by friends from the USA who asked a lot of questions I couldn't answer. That was years ago. They were intrigued after throwing a boomerang on a tour, said they loved it and wondered how many Aussies could do it. And being Americans they had to ask, "What's a boomerang that doesn't come back?" Before I could answer they shouted, "A stick," but added that it was an incredible invention and a lot better than a stick any day! After that I wanted to know more too. I was living in Sydney in those days so I started spending hours in the Mitchell Library." Rob explained.

"I'll bet throwing is fun," Sally smiled with genuine interest. "Americans are so curious aren't they? I've never thought of boomerangs as a research topic. I remember painting cardboard ones at Primary School. They've always been in tourist shops. And oh, that's right. Grandad had an old Aboriginal one." Sally suddenly remembered. "He kept it in his favourite glass-doored cedar book case, but that's the only contact I've had."

"That's about normal for Aussies." Rob replied knowingly. But for me it opened up the whole world of Aboriginal culture from material objects to Dreamtime legends. The connections keep expanding, that's why I want to see boomerangs in Rock Art."

"I didn't know there was so much to it." Sally pondered, her voice rising with interest, and then adding. "You must really like it. Are you going to publish something?"

"I've got a camcorder, a still camera, a laptop plus my notebooks. The video will be a good record of the Rock Art, and I'll write descriptions based on the footage. And yeah, I'd like to publish later."

"It's hard getting papers on Rock Art published, or any grants for field work, so it may be hard to get a grant for your boomerang work," broke in Geoff. "But let's hope you can. Things change sometimes with new heads of departments, and neglected subjects can suddenly be more fashionable."

Rob looked confidently at Geoff and Sally, saying: "It's funny, although I'm backing myself on this trip, I don't feel I'm doing it for me. It feels like a project for others. The boomerang's known all over the world, so that's probably why. In any case it's terrific to travel around seeing different places, meeting people and hearing their stories. I love it." A sudden thought flashed into Rob's mind as he remembered the legend of the Rainbow Serpent.

"Do you know much about the Lardil mob on Mornington Island? Have you met any of the old storytellers in your travels Geoff?" Rob asked purposefully.

"I met one of the greatest. Years ago I was in Cairns and his paintings were in an Exhibition. His name was Dick Roughsey or *Goobalathaldin* and he was a genuine, sensitive character. His barks and canvasses became very collectable. He's gone now, but he wrote his life story in *Moon and Rainbow*. It's a beauty and I've got two paperback copies, one in my collection as good as new, the other for people to borrow. You'd better take it. You asked about a great Lardil storyteller, so it's yours. But it's a *boomerang*." Geoff emphasised as he chuckled. "Just send it back later."

"Thank you." Rob smiled broadly, marvelling at the instant and positive answer to his question. "Thanks Geoff, that's great. The timing couldn't be better."

"It's my pleasure. Now we know a little about each other and we've solved the world's problems, let's tuck into Sally's fantastic meal and raise a glass. Later we'll check the gear list, see if we've missed anything and discuss what we're aiming to do in the VRD. Then tomorrow morning we're off..."

20

Geoff Seekman slowed his modified Toyota Troop Carrier or Troopy as he passed the first buildings on the northern outskirts of Katherine. After an uneventful three hour drive from Darwin they stopped to stretch their legs and have a cup of tea, the hot water poured from a large thermos which Sally had packed. The morning was fresh and sunny and had just reached a comfortable 20 degrees Celsius.

Their destination was Timber Creek and after the relaxing stop they turned right off the Stuart Highway and headed south-west, looking forward to an easy cross country drive. Boab trees loomed up occasionally, their bulbous trunks squatting on the landscape like they do in Africa at similar latitudes where they are called baobabs. Geoff, Rob and Sally drove into Gregory National Park before crossing the Victoria River, the 230km long waterway that gave its name to the district they were heading for to research the Rock Art. They continued along the Victoria Highway through a variety of landscapes and arrived in the one pub town about mid-morning.

First priority was to use the afternoon to follow-up preparations made in Darwin, then to stay overnight. They had plenty of time and started by double-checking all gear, also setting up the tents and cooking equipment. As an experienced bushman Geoff Seekman knew that it was much better to be sure than sorry when driving beyond mapped roads in remote areas.

With Timber Creek as the starting point proper he had planned a trip into the escarpments along dirt roads that led part-way to the various Rock Art sites. From the vehicle, usually parked well off the tracks, they'd walk, sometimes very steeply, up the escarpments to the sandstone overhangs that 'housed' the precious art. Their routine would be driving, camping, walking and recording for a solid eight days.

After their lunch of take-away roast chicken, sliced tomatos and green salad with fresh bread rolls and butter, Geoff was about to reiterate the plan and goals for the trip when Sally suddenly beamed.

"We've got carrot cake!" As she presented three portions wrapped in aluminium foil.

"Thank *YOU*." Rob said happily, holding a can of lemon squash.

"That's great Sal, that's why I'm paying you so much!" Geoff added, at once joking about the small amount of his research grant, and also hinting at how much he appreciated Sally's thoughtfulness.

"I thought you'd love it." She winked and smiled again, both men realising she had made the cake.

"Basically we're going to three locations for two days each." Geoff explained. "There's reasonable distances between them and we'll get as much time as possible in front of the art. This trip's vital because I'm following-up last year's work, it's relatively short, and you'll see a couple of big boomerangs."

"That's what I'm here for." Rob said with half a mouth full of cake. "How old's the art?"

"It varies a lot throughout the Territory, but where we're going the dates range between three and ten thousand years BP, or Before Present. There are recorded dates a lot older in the Top End. Have you come across George Chaloupka's work? He rediscovered acres of art, more than 3,000 sites in Arnhem Land over several decades."

"No, I haven't unfortunately." Rob replied.

"His magnificent Rock Art book came out in '93. You'd definitely enjoy it."

After lunch there were only a few jobs to complete. Geoff drove off to refuel the 4WD and fill the jerry cans with diesel, Rob topped up two large plastic containers with drinking water and Sally stocked up on fresh foods, their last supply for a week. As dusk settled on a productive day they chatted about the trip and Geoff's aims, getting to know each other better by the hour. The next morning they rose early and packed away all the gear, making time for a cooked cafe breakfast and real coffee. Then at 8.30 on a sunny Winter morning the trio left town with Geoff Seekman at the wheel.

* * *

Station owners in the VRD knew Geoff well because of his Dry season visits over the previous five years. He had earned their trust, they were confident he would never reveal the location of any sites, and had permission to come and go when he needed to.

The Rock Art seekers travelled for about an hour before turning off onto their first dirt track, its usually dusty surface still settled after an unseasonal shower of rain the night before. They headed deeper into country that was rarely travelled, a fact reinforced as the reasonable track deteriorated into a shallow vehicle-wide channel intermittently overrun with grass.

"It's pretty clear through here." Geoff began. It looked okay to Rob too, having driven the Elder on dirt roads beyond Alice Springs. "We're cutting across country to get to the station's access road which should be in good condition."

Geoff's mind was on his work as he drove. His personal quest was to record more sites, and before coming to the VRD spent a few seasons exploring the Pilbara and Kimberley regions of Western Australia. Many sites he found were not even known to Aboriginal custodians, such was the fracturing of local traditional cultures. But although many had missed learning about important aspects of culture, Geoff Seekman felt sure his re-discoveries would contribute positively. Ultimately, he hoped that clan members would proudly celebrate their Rock Art heritage, the oldest in the world.

For several years he had alerted Aboriginal and non-Aboriginal institutions about his discoveries, but it was only recently that he had been offered support. Fortunately ATSIRC provided Geoff with a travel grant and the facilities to archive his field notes, slides and videos. This welcome outcome also opened the prospect for publication of his findings in peer-reviewed journals, a pathway that had so far eluded him.

Few people would understand what it was like for Geoff to walk this rugged landscape. With a bushman's instinct he paced himself through dry gullies and broad timbered flats to reach the sparsely grassed slopes of the escarpments. Equipped with a couple of water bottles in hand-held plastic bags, and canned foods, cameras and notebooks secured in a daypack, he continued for weeks at a time, using his 4WD as his base.

He was a tall, friendly and chatty man who also liked his space. The Rock Art lifestyle provided it perfectly, taking him away from home and friends for half the year. Sitting around a nightly camp fire or lying in a swag he often tuned in to the vibrations of the Cosmos and speculated about ancient man and ancient art.

Dr Geoff Seekman was a pioneer, a man who was blazing a trail like other Europeans had before him. However, his was a quiet journey. He was not droving stock, building factories or adversely affecting people or the environment. He was rediscovering the artistic treasures of the continent's first inhabitants. He regarded it as crucial work, but there were no airs and graces about this twelve year Territorian. He had the walk and talk of a rural man sure of his ground.

* * *

"We're almost at "Moonrise Downs." Geoff announced, gesturing with a nod of the head. "They know I'll be coming through about now, but not the exact day. There's a site on this place you won't believe. Only found it last season, so I'm extra keen to work on it. The family will be very happy we're camping for a few days. This is like coming home. I love it more and more. Who's ready for a close-up look at the ancient past!"

It wasn't a question, but the statement of a passionate man on his proper path. He was in *his* country ready to share its surprises. Rob caught Geoff's excitement as it instantly mingled with his own.

"I'm ready. Just lead the way."

"If it's as good as Kakadu, I'm happy already." Sally responded, also feeling the anticipation in the vehicle.

"It's better!" Proclaimed Geoff, the seasoned campaigner still at the wheel. "Just wait and see. But first we'll pop in to the homestead and say g'day to the family. They need to know if someone's on the property."

"That's good. I'd like to say hello too." Rob added.

The visit was much longer than expected. Owners Peter and Liz insisted on showing Rob, Geoff and Sally around the homestead. They chatted about the family's time in the Territory, extra challenges when the Dry season lasted too long, even mentioning the flavour of local politics. And of course they would not let the visitors leave without a little Outback hospitality. Soon they were all tucking into cups of tea and coffee and home-baked scones, jam and cream served on the best fine china usually only brought out for special occasions.

Sometime later and after warm, sincere goodbyes the trio was off again. Geoff continued driving through the property for a further ten kilometres to reach an area that hardly anyone in the world knew about. Not even the owners had seen all the Rock Art sites on their extensive cattle station.

"We've arrived." Geoff exclaimed with immense satisfaction.

On the grassy area where he had parked they began setting up camp. The tents, one for each person, were up in minutes. Simple to erect, they were quickly secured by one internal centre pole and a steel peg through an outside flap on each of the four corners. While Sally and Rob were getting these and their personal gear organised, Geoff unpacked the barbecue and gas bottle like an experienced tour boss. As they worked Sally and Rob wondered how close the first art site was. As if hearing their thoughts Geoff surprised them.

"We've got time before sunset. Let's get up there. Who's coming?"

Geoff's enthusiasm affected the others immediately.

"The atmosphere changes as the light softens and all sounds diminish. The art feels different. But before we go let's put swags in tents, zip them up, and collect firewood because it'll be almost dark when we get back." Geoff added, as he positioned three fold-up canvas seats near where the camp fire would be set later.

"It'll be well worth the climb. It's so inspiring to experience this art in different light, even for a few minutes."

* * *

One main challenge was the spinifex grass. Its long needle-like spikes could easily puncture unprotected skin. Clumps of it dotted the slope and Geoff wore ex-army gaiters to cover his lower legs from mid-calves to boot tops, so he was protected. Sally and Rob had blue denim jeans on which they tucked into thick woollen socks, and with accurate stepping could also avoid the problem. Leaving flat ground behind they began to push toward the top. The gradient increased and Rob soon called their uphill efforts "steep walking." He and Sally followed Geoff on a partly zigzag route toward the sandstone overhangs, the silent, geologically ancient rocks looming larger as they moved closer.

"How's it going?" Geoff called out after turning around.

"I'm okay, it's fabulous." Sally called back. She was a go-getter, up in the north for adventure, to do her share and more.

"Great for me too." Rob said, adding his progress report.

"About fifteen minutes, and we're there."

The sunlight was fading but as they walked higher the beauty and vastness of the property spread out below them. Slim, straight-trunked gum trees threw long shadows and Rob and Sally saw flights of birds and flying foxes winging their way home for the night. There was still adequate light and they were closing in on the art.

Geoff was first to reach the top, with Rob and Sally not far behind. Without a word he pointed at large smooth rocks, signalling Rob and Sally to go ahead. Neither of them had been in this country before and did not know what to expect. Rob walked forward between rocks nearly as tall as himself and saw an image with multiple concentric circles and short straight lines radiating from it, painted white on a tan brown surface. He gasped, staring at his first image of VRD Aboriginal Rock Art. His mind filled with thoughts but he moved on as Sally followed, and stepped under the overhang.

On the ceiling outlined in white was a very long snake or serpent… as well as the white outline of an elongated human-like figure with a large head.

"They're so awesome." Sally whispered.

"Yeah, aren't they." Rob agreed, now completely focussed.

Moving further under the figures by bending low he could just discern a narrow shape well over a metre long in-filled with a dark colour. What was it? Could it be a boomerang, the first he had ever seen depicted in Rock Art? He took another step, raised his head and could just make out a definite shaft and hook. Yes it was. What a fantastic start to the trip. The limited light prevented Rob from seeing real detail, but in his mind he was already rushing back the next day.

"Isn't this wonderful," said Geoff who had been standing nearby. "Let's sit quietly on the rocks and feel the energies." He added in a reverent tone of voice.

Rob found a suitable place, closed his eyes, and flashed back to the paintings in the hidden gorge in Central Australia, instantly reconnecting with feelings of immense spiritual empowerment. But here in the VRD the energies were calm, as if the spirits were relaxing in the twilight. Then Rob suddenly remembered that the Elder always alerted the Ancestors when approaching a site, reminding himself to tell Geoff later.

Sally sat a few metres away and created her own space. She brought her hands together as if in prayer or to say "Namaste," closing her eyes as the last rays of sunshine beamed through the eucalyptus leaves, highlighting her blonde hair.

A few timeless minutes later Geoff stood up and gently interrupted the quietness.

"Aah." He exhaled. "Isn't this the place. There's always something more around Rock Art. Something you can feel, but can't quite touch."

Rob and Sally nodded, agreeing inwardly, relaxed after their own meditative moments.

Soon after, Geoff led the way from the cave gallery back down the slope, walking the same route taken on the way up. Mental images of Dreamtime paintings and echoes of ancient storytelling accompanied them as they returned to the camp. They would rest happily overnight, knowing that tomorrow they would see Rock Art in all its well-lit splendour.

* * *

Few things are as magical as a campfire in the bush. It provides warmth and a focus that brings people together. Rob had found enough soccer ball-sized rocks to make a small circle for it, lighting the scrunched-up newspaper, twigs and small branches arranged in the middle. Sally got the gas cooker going instantly and soon the fresh aromas of sliced red onion and cut root ginger greeted the hungry team.

"I don't bother with meat when I'm out here." Geoff said. "I feel lighter inside without it which is good because I do so much walking to places people wouldn't believe."

Like Rob, Geoff could not help smelling the cooking aromas.

Sally's an expert with the wok. It helped her through Uni she reckons."

"Sure did. We had great parties at Uni. Scrumptious smorgasbords of Thai, Chinese, Indian, Italiano, Vietnamese and Singaporean food every week. Met most of my friends over international dinners. And oh boy we used to pig out sometimes. You know what it's like! I've brought lots of herbs and spices, so just tell me your favourites as we go along. I want you to really enjoy my tucker."

Rob loved the idea and said, "Couldn't be better. It's doing me good already."

"We're thoroughly spoilt and love it," added Geoff as he got up to lend Sally a hand. From the red plastic container of utensils he selected three bowls, three forks, three spoons and three cups. Everything had come in threes.

"How long will we be up at the site tomorrow?" asked Rob.

"I'll need three quarters of the day, probably more, so we'll get up there for first light. I'm following-up last season, so I've got field notes but I need to make a thorough review of the whole site. With video too. I've learned over the years that it's vital to complete a site survey, because there's hundreds of others to record. Some can be re-visited, and later finds may have bearing on earlier interpretations, but you *have to complete the work* before moving on, in case you never get back!"

"I'm ready to go as early as you like."

"Same here," said Sally, putting the finishing touches to her latest stir-fried creation.

"You'll see that I don't talk much at the sites." Geoff confided.

"The silence of the landscape gets into my veins, plus I'm focussed on the work. I usually save my thoughts until nightfall when the campfire's cracklin'."

"Okay gentleman, dinner is served." Sally declared, only twenty minutes after starting. Steam was rising from the full bowls as she passed them around.

"Hope you like it. There's chopsticks too Rob, if you'd prefer."

No one spoke for several minutes, a positive sign that confirmed just how good the food was. Then Geoff, apparently in an expansive mood, began to share his thoughts.

"I've heard that Rock Art researchers in the Kimberley have publicly questioned the origins of some Aboriginal art. Maybe that's understandable if there's no living custodians to explain the traditional meanings. But some stuck their neck out and said that a certain style of painted figures was not Aboriginal! Now that type of theory raises interesting ideas...."

Rob was not sure if Geoff was inviting comments, but he wanted to respond.

"I can see it being offensive to local Aboriginals, but you can't stop people speculating. I'm not up with Rock Art, but in Aboriginal cosmology there's mysteries I'd love to work out. It's hard to find all the traditional stories, but the prospect of discovery keeps me going."

"Even if this culture is 60,000 years old who says there haven't been others before it."

Sally's challenging remark from the opposite side of the campfire hung in the warm evening air for a long moment.

"Well," she added, "we were encouraged to think laterally at Uni, and I've learned to think outside the square. But it doesn't diminish my respect for Aboriginal culture one bit."

Geoff continued in his same expansive mood.

"Those controversial researchers used latest dating techniques, spoke to Aboriginal men, even compared their findings to explorer's journals, to support their opinions. I like reading explorers' reports too, especially where *I've* recorded art. They wrote with the honesty of children seeing something for the first time, which is precisely what was happening. Those early descriptions provide valuable perspective when modern theories are compared with them. But without making this a long story, the conjecture about who painted some of the art flares up like a bush fire from time to time. We've all got ideas, but until real evidence comes up or God speaks about it, I'm on the side of Aboriginal people being the original artists. If I thought space men painted it, I'd give up right now!"

Geoff's considered opinions did not exhaust the topic, but they did bring the campfire conversation to a close.

"What time are we up?" Rob asked.

"About an hour before first light. I don't need an alarm, but Sally's got the official camp clock which sounds like Big Ben out here." Geoff responded.

"You *won't* sleep through it." Sally confidently said. "We'll have a cuppa and high energy health bars before we climb the slope, and we'll carry fruit as well as a surprise lunch and water bottles of course. There's spring water for drinking in that strong plastic yellow container with a built-in tap if you need some tonight."

"Thanks a lot." Rob said. "It's been a great day. See you both in the morning."

"Night, night." Sally said brightly.

"Sleep well. Seeya before the sun." Geoff said, confirming their early rising time.

* * *

The bright, clear light of sunrise poured into the cave gallery and the figures appeared to be much larger than the evening before. Underneath the thick white-outlined snake was another figure, a long and spindly spirit character with extended arms and large hands painted in red ochre. But most prominent was the human-like being with two eyes and surprisingly no mouth, white stripes across the face continuing into a halo-like band around the head. Was this an Ancestor? The tall yet solid body, legs and short arms were fully painted with white pipe clay, and there was a straight, horizontal line across the figure, just below the waist.

They were magnificent but Rob only had one thing on his mind. He took two strides forward as best he could while bending over, and looked up. There they were. Two large hook boomerangs revealed completely by the reflected sunlight.

"Wow. Fantastic. They're fantastic Sally, come and have a look."

Sally was sitting and sketching into her blank-paged pad, but got up straight away.

Rob was jumping inside. These were the first Rock Art boomerangs he had ever seen, and they were rare hooks or number sevens only made in a few areas of Australia. "Wow." He repeated excitedly.

"You've struck gold Rob. I'm thrilled for you." Sally beamed, now looking closely at the boomerangs. Then she backed away, sensing Rob needed his own space.

To fully feel the energies he sat down on the dry sandy earth and looked up at the painted artefacts. Outlined with white pipe clay, the shafts and hooks were in-filled with deep red ochre. Both were over a metre or nearly four feet in length. They were outstanding. After a while he took a series of photographs with slide film. With his camcorder he filmed various angles of the boomerangs plus the impressive spirit and Ancestor figures, then moved outside taking wide-angle shots of the entire gallery for context and perspective.

The overhang was much wider and deeper than either Rob or Sally had realised and it contained many smaller figures staring out at the world. Some looked like quick ochre sketches compared with the major figures of the gallery. Yet they still communicated a tangible presence that had been painted and chanted into the rock surfaces several thousand years ago. From observation alone the age and meaning of the figures could not be determined conclusively, but this did not detract from their stunning impact.

Sally walked over and commented in her thoughtful, bubbly way.

"I'd like to know the stories. They'd bring it all to life. There might even be similar ideas and figures in Kakadu, or possibly in overseas Aboriginal art."

"Yeah, maybe. But if there's no traditional custodians alive how do we really know?"

"There must be a way." Sally said, smiling hopefully.

Rob nodded, placed the cameras in his daypack and walked across to a tree, sat down with his back against the trunk and began writing in his notebook.

Sally walked back out to the comfortable smooth rock she had been sitting on and resumed sketching into her pad. Geoff had been poking around since they arrived, writing more details and observations about the site and the art. And also capturing quick ideas by speaking into a mini cassette recorder as he moved around.

Rob looked up as Geoff walked closer, catching his eye.

"The two hooks are fantastic. What can you tell me about them?"

"Oh yes, aren't they great. I heard your reaction earlier. They would've been traded into this area, most likely from the south of the Territory." Geoff said confidently. "They're a rare type of boomerang anyway, but here they would have been treated as sacred objects and used for ceremony. And that was over hundreds of years at least." He emphasised.

"Yeah. It's incredible. Thanks so much Geoff. And for the trip." Rob said gratefully. "This is so enjoyable, and really excellent for research."

"A pleasure Rob. I love sharing this heritage. Glad it's good for your work."

Rob jotted down Geoff's points, adding them to his own observations and numbered list of photographs. It was fascinating being in the field and coming face to face with the hook boomerangs. The unique shape of this artefact set it apart from all other boomerangs. But even though Rob sensed it would not contribute specifically to his ultimate goal, the entire experience was highly motivating.

* * *

The Rock Art seeker's field trip continued harmoniously and productively, and the days of exploration at the other two sites, bush camping, delicious food and lively conversation passed far too quickly.

On their last evening around the campfire they shared feelings of real satisfaction and achievement, and all would have happily continued for many more days. Geoff Seekman had made it all possible because of his passion and commitment. He was a bushman through and through who embraced the discovery of Aboriginal Rock Art to inspire his life. And as if to echo Rob's feelings, expressed weeks earlier to the Elder about his love for the Outback, Geoff spoke about the past week together amongst the sandstone escarpments.

"God seems a lot bigger out here. There are so few distractions and the natural world breathes like it always has. Aboriginal groups know this in their own ways. Rock Art often celebrates spiritual life and maintains a link to their origins. It's a privilege to walk in the footsteps of the Dreamtime artists and feel connected to culture. And it's been a pleasure to share my discoveries. Thanks for enriching the experience. We can be so far removed from all of this in the city. But out here I feel a lot bigger too."

* * *

The team rolled back into Timber Creek a little tired, but more than satisfied with their week's work. They stayed in the hotel overnight and enjoyed real beds, then in the morning set out to reach Katherine for lunch, aiming to arrive in Darwin by mid to late afternoon. Reliable, Dry season sunshine and happy spirits guided them along the Victoria and Stuart Highways and they pulled up at Geoff's house just before five o'clock.

A couple of hours after the Troopy was unpacked and all cooking and camping equipment had been cleaned, they showered, changed into fresh clothes, and drove into Darwin's CBD for a farewell dinner. Rob brought all of his gear because Geoff and Sally would drop him off at his accommodation in the city after their meal. They selected "The Asian Lotus" restaurant where diners choose from a menu of camel, crocodile, barramundi, beef, chicken, emu or kangaroo plus various vegetables, and watch them being stir-fried.

What an experience it was. Flames leapt above the gas stoves as chefs wrestled artfully with large, perfectly heated woks, expertly taming and stirring the contents into fine, tasty meals. After seeing Rob's smiling reaction to the flamboyant cooking performance, Geoff and Sally knew they had selected the best restaurant for their last night together.

Conversation was easy because of the meaningful bonds the trio had developed in the VRD. And it was helped along by fine Australian wines and a guitarist playing acoustic versions of popular movie soundtracks which massaged their words and laughter.

After the wonderful dinner together Geoff and Sally drove Rob to Hibiscus Lodge, his accommodation only a couple of kilometres from the restaurant, their parting words confirming real friendship.

"Good to have you along. I've really enjoyed your contribution. I hope you soon get a sponsor for your work. I've never heard the full boomerang story, so it needs to be told."

Coming from a man with Geoff Seekman's credentials and experience Rob felt uplifted by his supportive comments.

"If the boomerang's a torch, someone passed it to me, so it's a responsibility as well as a privilege. Look at the fun I'm having digging up the story. Thanks again, it's been fantastic." Rob said, emphasising 'fantastic' as he shook Geoff's hand with both of his. Then he met Sally's eyes, drawing her close for a very friendly hug.

"Love your lateral thinking. Thanks for sharing so much."

"A real pleasure for me too. Keep smiling and keep in touch." Sally said, kissing Rob on both cheeks.

* * *

Comfortably settled into his first floor room after a great night out Rob's priority was something other than sleep. He was going to immediately concentrate on *Moon and Rainbow* which Geoff Seekman had kindly loaned him. At Geoff's place before the Rock Art trip he had flicked through it briefly, but now he was ready to explore its pages properly.

Sitting up in bed with the book already open under the white glow of a vintage reading lamp, Rob marvelled at the combination of events that led him to it. From *Lardil,* purchased intuitively in Adelaide, to the discovery while flying to Darwin that the Rainbow Serpent and boomerangs were linked, to wanting more information and a Lardil storyteller, then finally meeting Geoff Seekman who provided the answer. That is how the appropriate book had found him. In his hands was the autobiography of a traditional Lardil artist and storyteller. The Universe had again heard and answered Rob's requests!

Almost immediately the words and phrases were captivating as descriptions of traditional ceremonies and characters commenced. Then Rob's attention was quickly focused by the first mention of *Thuwathu* the Rainbow Serpent. Author Dick Roughsey appeared to be retelling the same legend as the one in the little *Lardil* book Rob had read on the plane, but this personal version leapt off the pages, alive with authenticity.

The story unfolded in epic fashion, and Rob found it familiar yet just as compelling. The action and characters were almost identical to the version he had read previously, and at the end *Thuwathu* also created major features of the landscape.

Then, after almost two pages of vivid description came the 'boomerang connection' that Rob had been hoping for.

His body was burnt and blistered and some of his ribs fell out. These grew into gidyea trees for boomerangs.

After re-reading the legend closely, there was no doubt in Rob's mind that both stories had the same source. They were so similar, except for one thing. The type of wood used to make boomerangs was different, a detail he would pursue later. Nevertheless, Rob knew this was an important Dreamtime legend for the Lardil of Mornington Island, and also a very valuable one for his quest.

* * *

Rob stayed an extra night at Hibiscus Lodge, giving himself a full day to survey the boomerangs for sale in Darwin city, walk part of the Esplanade, and take a government bus to the Museum and Art Gallery of the Northern Territory. The building overlooks Fannie Bay and the water views provided a perfect backdrop for Rob to reflect on his superb week in the VRD. At the Museum Shop he picked up a display copy of *Journey in Time* by George Chaloupka, the Rock Art book highly recommended by Geoff Seekman, and was instantly impressed. The sites Rob had seen did not prepare him for the amazing scope and scholarship of this large format volume. He asked about the author and found that he was a Museum staff member, but currently out in Arnhem Land recording more of the innumerable galleries engraved and ochred across the sandstone escarpments.

Back at Hibiscus Lodge after a wonderful day Rob picked up *Moon and Rainbow* and re-read the Rainbow Serpent story. This time the traditional significance of the legend became readily apparent.

At initiation time we danced and sang the whole story of Thuwathu, and the young men were told all the laws and responsibilities, especially that they must look after their sister's children.

Rob confirmed it was like a parable, as many legends are, handed down through the generations to teach traditional values to young initiates. What it revealed was inspiring, but he did not feel he had to go to Mornington Island and seek *The First Boomerang.* Underlying all of Rob's experiences, however illuminating, was his ever-present quest. But now it was clear why *"The Rainbow Serpent is everywhere"* originally flashed into his mind. And the reason was extraordinary. This great Ancestor is linked traditionally to the boomerang. Both are found throughout the continent in various forms, and both are very important in Aboriginal life.

Rob also wanted to find information about the uses and types of boomerangs in Lardil culture, but that research would have to wait. The wonderful autobiography of a traditional artist had opened his eyes and heart. Fortunately he still had more chapters to read. But they would also have to wait because in that moment in the tropical Top End of Australia, his mind had already taken off for Alice Springs.

2 1

Rob's first glimpse of the distinctive dark brown ridgeline across the horizon welcomed him back to the Centre. Minutes later, the ancient caterpillar-created MacDonnell Ranges were readily visible on descent into Alice Springs. Welcome rain had nourished the region while Rob had been away and native and introduced grasses were already green and flourishing. Vegetation may have grown faster in the heat of Summer, but on this sunny, Winter afternoon the landscape looked fresh and abundant.

This impression echoed Rob's positive outlook after his eye-opening trip. He had uncovered fascinating information in significant books and by teaming up with good people who shared their knowledge. These first-hand experiences had crossed his path at precisely the right time, and at every step he knew he was on the right track.

Rob learned that the Elder was out bush for a few days, giving him the opportunity to review his collected information from the VRD expedition. This included the *Lardil* and *Moon and Rainbow* books and his notes on the boomerang Rock Art. He also wanted to send rolls of slide film to Melbourne to be developed and read all other notes made so far, especially those made with Clara in Adelaide at the South Australian Museum and Mortlock Library.

* * *

The Araluen Arts Centre in Alice Springs is a five hundred seat theatre and gallery complex which hosts many of the town's arts activities. Rob noticed in *The Alice Springs News* that an exhibition entitled *The Yuendumu Doors* was currently showing, and it featured original school doors painted at the Yuendumu community on the Tanami Track in 1983. It was the culmination of the efforts of a school principal who encouraged senior Warlpiri men to record their Dreamtime stories, and of the South Australian Museum that conserved and stored them. Rob had a strong feeling that he must see this unique-sounding art.

Enthusiastic, but without expectations, he walked into a small gallery that housed the exhibits. They were standing up like doors usually do, yet were neatly secured by a circular steel base and frame which were painted rich tan brown. These decorated installations were the first attempts by local traditional men to use acrylic paints on modern materials, transferring their stories from ground designs in soil and sand to manufactured wooden doors.

One fully painted door had a section of bare metal where paint had flaked off, apparently caused by exposure to sun glare and desert winds at Yuendumu, and a few remnants of texta pen graffiti. This door immediately interested Rob. As well as being covered with large white and pale lemon dots over bluish background in the upper half, and orange in the lower, it included numerous boomerangs of many sizes and shapes. Rob stepped closer, his excitement building. Needing an explanation he opened the small, slim catalogue he had purchased with his ticket.

The photographs of the doors were much brighter than the real ones in the exhibition. The story of each painted door was printed in English, but not Warlpiri, main language of the artists. Rob quickly read the first few sentences about the door in front of him and was astonished. Entitled *Old Men Dreaming* the legend tells of old *"Dreamtime Men"* carving and testing boomerangs in preparation for battle, and described them vividly.

After chopping down a tree and bringing roughly hewn wood back home, they made a great number of splendid boomerangs. The first boomerang flew through the air, turned around and came back to them. They threw another small one and it also spun around and came back to its owner.

"WHAT!" The word reverberated loudly inside Rob's head, as his whole being stalled in disbelief and amazement. "What are they talking about!" Then he spoke quickly and quietly to himself.

"There are no recordings of returning boomerangs in Central Australia. But the story says old Dreamtime Men carved *"splendid boomerangs"* that came back! What's this all about? Did comeback boomerangs ever exist in Warlpiri country? Is this real? Is it symbolic?"

Rob did not know the answers, but this information was as mind-boggling as the *'boomerang ribs'* of the Rainbow Serpent! How could he verify this latest revelation? For the moment it was simply unbelievable. He had never heard anything like it, and according to his research to date, neither had anyone else. Why would the storyteller include returning boomerangs when they are not part of his culture? Were there any clues in the story itself? How did it conclude? He read another paragraph from the catalogue.

When the Old Men struck each other with boomerangs, they turned into birds and flew away. They turned into all sorts of birds, like falcons, kites and hawks, which still fly in our skies today. This is a true story of what happened in the Dreamtime. It belongs to me and I have painted it.

There was no doubt about the truth of the legend according to these quotes by the traditional author! Rob was still puzzled, yet excited, and his thoughts began to sprint. Maybe the Warlpiri once had 'come-backs' or returners, but lost them! A very strange thought, but who could he ask about this? Unfortunately, he was still in the small gallery room that was just big enough to hold the displayed doors. The atmosphere was pin-drop quiet. He put his inner questions aside and looked even harder at the door, and another question popped in. Were there any boomerangs shaped like returners on it? His mind would not stop!

The story of each painted door was printed on an accompanying panel, set to one side. Included were some Warlpiri language words linked by straight lines to corresponding figures in the painting, enabling viewers to see English translations of Aboriginal words.

Of immediate interest to Rob were two boomerang types on the *Old Men Dreaming* door that had Warlpiri word equivalents. One, called *"kurrupurda"* was long and gently curved, the other was *"wirlki,"* of hook boomerang shape, like he had seen in the VRD. Rob was initially attracted to the many small curved boomerangs, but none had a Warlpiri name on the panel. He believed some had enough bend to return! But would he ever know? How could he ever see if they had adequate airfoils to fly out and come back? As more questions arose in his mind, he continued to walk thoughtfully around the small gallery.

Rob came to the last door that seemed taller than the others. Called *Two Men Dreaming* it presented the legend of two young, handsome and fully initiated men who go hunting, their country, their weapons and ceremonial objects. Close to the top, on a background of yellow dots, a large, surprisingly curved boomerang was featured. Rob's eyes were instantly drawn to it. Near the bottom of the door, a big, distinctive hook boomerang with a very curved shaft appeared ready for action. Both of them and three other large, curved boomerangs were painted black and outlined with small white dots. Within the middle of each wing or arm were simple patterns, either small circles or crosses of white dots. But to Rob the most captivating aspect was the rare acuteness of the top boomerang's curve.

In Warlpiri country, according to his research, traditional hunting boomerangs were not made like this, nor were they now. They range from about 60cm to 90cm, even to one metre in length and are only slightly curved toward one end. This is cultural fact, but Rob was immediately faced with another puzzle.

On the accompanying panel that included a line drawing of the *Two Men Dreaming* door's art, a straight line connected the top acutely curved boomerang to its Warlpiri name. Rob stared in disbelief. The word he read was *"Karli!"*

How could this be? A *"Karli"* is the traditional long, slightly curved boomerang. It is not acutely curved. This multi-purpose implement is the universal shape of all Central Australian hunting boomerangs. Had there been a mistake in the writing-up of the panel? Could different-ly-shaped boomerangs have the same name? Did traditional storytellers use poetic licence?

Again Rob had no answers. Yet if knowing them was important, he knew he would be guided to find out at the appropriate time. But he also reasoned that someone, somewhere, perhaps in Alice Springs must know the answers. However, for the moment he would keep looking closely at the artwork.

He focused his attention on the curved boomerang near the top of the *Two Men Dreaming* door. A boomerang with a curve like this definitely had the potential to be a returner! The cross sections of the wings must be shaped properly... But in mid-sentence Rob's thoughts stopped him: his over-working mind repeating loudly that there were *NO* returning boomerangs in Warlpiri country, or in any other part of Central Australia. But there was still an overriding question. Why had the artist painted such curved boomerangs?

The Dreamtime is a mystery to most non-Aboriginal people but Rob had a feeling he was about to learn something very significant. Suddenly, another thought coming from far beyond his mind, guided him instantly to an immense and exciting possibility.

Was the painting on this last door a link to the old Dreamtime men on the *Old Men Dreaming* door, who carved boomerangs that came back?

Rob consciously gave this idea time to hover and settle, before asking himself two vital questions. Was this a mystery he could solve? Were any of the stories on the painted doors linked to *The First Boomerang*?

Rob walked out of the gallery and the Araluen Arts Centre. With catalogue in hand he strolled to a nearby children's playground to ponder his discovery and the puzzles it created. He had come to see a unique exhibition and was leaving with a head full of questions.

He took in the peaceful surroundings then angled his tall frame onto the seat of a swing, hoping that answers would come in on the breeze as he pushed off the ground.

2 2

Flight, powered flight, man's dream, man's quest for so long was finally achieved in the early years of the 20th century. For inspiration man observed the gracefulness of birds on the wing .... gliding, hovering, diving, soaring on breezy updrafts, seemingly unimpeded by the gravity that kept him earthbound.

However, another version of man-propelled flight had already existed for thousands of years in a far away corner of the world. This was the flight of the 'come-back' or returning boomerang: spinning and circling in the sky, apparently not attached to anything, yet under the skilful control of an Australian Aboriginal thrower. Those flights occurred in different areas of the island continent but not all were connected by trade and ceremonial routes. Instead, they were connected by an idea whose origin was in the Dreamtime, and which was transferred from generation to generation.

After its "discovery" by European explorers this boomerang became world famous, capturing people's imagination because of its extraordinary, and Rob thought, magical capacity to come back to the thrower. But the returning boomerang is not an artefact lost in the mists of antiquity, it is a readily-made recreational object available across the world.

Rob's knowledge was growing by the day, and he already knew that the boomerang story embodied several levels of expression. One of them was the practical, throwing level and he wanted to experience it very soon.

* * *

Rob felt instinctively that learning how to throw would be great fun, a feeling he first experienced when the Elder announced *The First Boomerang* quest. Now he was ready to try. But where would he find someone to teach him? The boomerang may have originated from the oldest culture on the planet, and be famous world-wide, but did professional instructors exist in Australia? Here was a challenge, but Rob's secret quest had been given by the Elder and was being guided by the Ancestors and the Universe, so he knew the appropriate circumstances would happen at the right time.

Rob was still in Alice Springs and had been invited to a sunset barbecue on the Old Eastside part of town. As the enticing aromas of cooking onions, steaks and sausages filled guests' nostrils, he got talking to coach driver Bill Jackson. They chatted about local tourism, Australian Rules football, and the Alice Springs to Darwin railway, and Rob casually mentioned that he wanted to learn how to throw a boomerang.

"Maybe I can help?" Bill said.

"Well, I need an instructor and a boomerang," Rob replied.

"I keep a boomerang on the coach to throw for passengers. I've got a day off tomorrow before the next tour. So if you're up for it?"

"Yeah. For sure," Rob responded, knowing Cosmic Timing was at play again.

On the following morning uninterrupted sunshine poured from the widest blue sky. They met at Ross Park on the Old Eastside, a grassy sporting area kept green and growing all year round by a computerised system using recycled water. Although the sun had been up for a few hours the wind had not yet fully woken, and only a light breeze was coming in from the north-east. The coach driver's first words were very positive.

"It's a perfect day for a throw!" Bill said happily.

"Yeah, hope so. G'day Bill, thanks for coming," replied Rob.

"Do you throw right-handed or left?"

"Right."

"That's good, I haven't got a lefty"

"I know there's a difference," said Rob a little chuffed, "because I had to explain it to American friends a few years ago."

"Okay. Hold it firmly, flat side against your palm, index finger curled around the tip. Hold tight enough to control it, just like you would with a bat or racquet. Hold it vertical, lean it over to the right to about one o'clock." Bill explained, gesturing with his hand.

"Like this?" Rob asked.

"Good. Okay. Now, feel the breeze coming straight onto your face from that direction. Turn your body forty five degrees to the right of it. Aim straight out just above eye level, and give it a good forward spin with your wrist as you let it go. Good luck and go for it."

Rob stood ready, holding the boomerang firmly, the light breeze now on his left cheek.

"Oh, before you do, I bought this one in Sydney years ago. I've forgotten the bloke's name but his Boomerang Shop was in The Rocks. He told me a good boomerang should be at least five ply, 6mm thick marine grade so it's strong and flexible. This one's 16 inches in old money or 40cm, wing tip to wing tip. It's got a few nicks and marks here and there, but it still flies true and gives the tourists a thrill every time. Righto, go for it."

Rob had never thrown a boomerang before. He did not know how hard to throw, or how much spin to impart. But "go for it" he did, taking one step forward on his left foot and throwing it like a baseball or cricket ball. Out it went lifting to about three or four times his height but flying horizontally, smoothly turning left into a circular trajectory. Heading back and still spinning fast, it stalled in mid air above his head and hovered momentarily, reversing direction and descending to the grass about two metres away from his feet! All this, in less than ten seconds!

Rob was amazed. What had he just done!

Just before the boomerang hit the ground Bill yelled in awe.

"Bewdy mate. That's one of *the best* I've seen!" Adding quickly after it landed. "Did you say you've never had a throw before?"

"Yeah. Never. Not one."

"Your father wasn't a blackfella by any chance." The coach driver joked. "It looks as though you've had one in your hand all your life. I dunno where you go with boomerang throwing talent, but you've really got the knack."

The coach driver paused for a few moments. Rob was exhilarated and took only a couple of strides to pick up the boomerang. He was thrilled by his first throw and the energy that rushed through him during the incredible flight and the following minute or two.

"Have another go. This time try and catch it." Bill said, upping the challenge.

"How?"

"Do the same throw, even a touch softer. Then clap your hands together, like this, with the boomerang between them. And keep your eyes on it the whole time."

Rob positioned himself again, visualising the mental footage of the previous throw. His energy had a slight edge to it because he had been so successful, but he gripped the boomerang firmly, stepped onto his left foot and threw. Flying at a similar height, yet spinning a fraction slower, the boomerang banked to the left and circled around, heading back towards him. Holding its line it came in at shoulder height, slowing into a short hover, giving Rob just enough time to quickly sandwich it between his hands.

"OH YES!" He shouted.

"You really know what you're doin' mate. That's better than beginner's luck." The coach driver said, obviously impressed. "You can't buy this type in Alice, but there's pretty good plywood ones in a shop in the Mall. It's the Coolibah Gift Gallery, you can't miss it."

"That's good Bill. I love this. I'll check it out later."

Rob handed the boomerang back to Bill and he stepped forward. Spinning his familiar boomerang out easily, it returned to within a couple of metres of where they were standing. He was a solid man with thick, strong wrists and only had to give the returner a quick flick and away it went. It flew an elliptical flight path and a shorter range than Rob's throws because he tilted it over to the right more than one o'clock. His modified technique gave consistent results and was practical at campsites on tour when there was not much space.

"There we are," Bill said, feeling satisfied. "It's a great thing to show people. Have a few more throws before we go."

"Thanks so much Bill. It's bloody fantastic," Rob said, about to focus on his next launch. He had been introduced to something ancient yet modern, a unique activity from the Dreamtime which came to him naturally.

* * *

The session had been excellent for Rob, but he needed to learn more. Part of his quest was to discover as much as possible about this simple-looking implement and its sophisticated flight characteristics. He had made a successful start and suddenly the Elder's original words flashed into his mind.

You have a very important task to undertake. You are going to search for the First Boomerang, the one that came in the Dreamtime! The boomerang that just materialised is similar in shape to the one you're looking for. The original one could be anywhere in Australia.

Rob knew the five-ply boomerang he had amazingly caught was not the same as the boomerang that materialised on Anzac Hill. They were from very different worlds. The traditional returner given to him by the Elder was made of *one* piece of naturally curved wood. It was cut from the bend formed by a root and the trunk, was also heavier and had a very different feel, a quality derived from its inner energy as much as its smooth hand-finish.

Rob was keen to find the gift shop and "pretty good" plywood boomerangs Bill had suggested. He left the park, drove over to the main shopping area and parked on Gregory Terrace, soon finding the Coolibah Gift Gallery around the corner in Todd Mall. Colourfully filled with quality merchandise including leather bush hats and painted didgeridoos, Rob spotted boomerangs displayed on the back wall. More angled at the elbow than Bill's model, and about 35cm or 14" from tip to tip, he selected and purchased two returners, one with sprayed red and yellow tips, the other black and yellow. Each one had a folded piece of paper with instructions attached to one wing with a rubber band.

Rob strode happily out the door, walked back to the 4WD and drove across the Todd River causeway from Leichardt Terrace, continuing for a couple of long blocks to Ross Park. Carrying both boomerangs he jogged to the middle of the ground, confirmed the printed instructions were similar to coach driver Bill's directions, and faced the breeze. Rob then gripped one of the boomerangs and turned forty five degrees to the right.

The boomerangs were very good, flying out to about 25 metres before circling back. They were lighter than Bill's favourite model, so Rob imparted more spin, strongly snapping his wrist forward. He threw eight times and made five catches as he fine-tuned his technique. It was obvious that the timing of throwing and catching was vital. Was the millisecond before release the most critical contributor to success? Rob thought it was.

With consistently good results he recognised that other levels had come into play. He definitely sensed more than the remarkable physical level. Throwing relaxed his spirit and enabled him to feel acutely in touch with the present. Time seemed to stand still as the boomerang circled and captured space for a moment, and for Rob it felt like a moving meditation, one he could experience throw after throw.

During the next morning Rob visited several souvenir shops and galleries in the Mall and asked for returning boomerangs. In the "Aboriginal Outback Art Gallery" a female assistant showed him solid wooden pieces with figures and motifs burnt into the upper surface, saying they *"definitely come back"*. So he bought one, keen to see how it compared to his new recreational plywood models. It looked similar in general outline shape to Rob's special traditional hand-carved returner, but did not have the same "feel" or "presence."

Later that day Rob went back to Ross Park as shadows lengthened in the cool twilight. After a few throws with a plywood model to warm up his arm, he picked up the solid, heavier boomerang. Holding it with the usual grip and angle off vertical to the right, he adjusted to the breeze and threw. *Whuuush*, it rocketed straight ahead and kept going: no curve, no circle, absolutely no hint of returning!

Rob jogged up the park and picked it up, came back to where he'd thrown from and re-positioned himself for another attempt. This time he threw harder. Off it flew, straight ahead again and another ten metres farther, landing on the grass with a dull thud. It was a bit more aerodynamic than a brick, but not much! What was going wrong?

It was heavier, thicker and its wings were much wider than Rob's plywood returners. These factors must be influencing its performance, he thought. However, he tried again, tilting the boomerang over more to the right. In this position he released it hard: it zoomed forwards, rising for a couple of seconds but then it dived, crashing onto short grass about thirty five metres away and breaking!

"Oh no!" Rob uttered loudly. He had seen it but could not believe it! After only three throws the boomerang had broken. What a disaster. The plywood returners were performing beautifully so the problem was obviously the solid, decorated boomerang.

He hurried to the spot and found three pieces. The boomerang had split precisely along the grain that ran straight across each wing. Rob had not seen the straight grain earlier because burnt designs covered most of the wood and oil had darkened it. In total contrast, the one the Elder gave him was made with the grain running around the curve, which is why it had a special "feel" and "presence." But the solid, broken one was made completely differently. It had been cut from a straight piece of manufactured board with straight grain, causing it to break very easily.

But why had it been made like this? Were tree roots too difficult to get in sufficient quantity for commercial production? Was it because current makers did not know how to craft a natural root boomerang properly? Or was it simply to produce large quantities for quicker profits? Then Rob's thoughts leapt to a more poignant matter.

Did staff at the Aboriginal Outback Art Gallery realise it was made with straight-grained wood and did not return? Rob wanted to know. He felt uneasy about the whole issue and was determined to take the broken pieces back to the gallery. Maybe he had purchased one with a weakness? Bill the coach driver said he really had "the knack," so unskilled throwing did not cause it to break.

Rob calmed down about the episode that had just occurred and enjoyed the rich, changing, cloud colours as the sun was setting behind Mt Gillen. Then to round off the session in a positive mood he enjoyed his colourfully-tipped plywood returners, catching about half of his throws before leaving the park.

Next morning and with no sign of the Elder who was probably still out bush, Rob knew he must keep moving and continue his search for *The First Boomerang* beyond Alice Springs. He planned to fly to tropical North Queensland and pursue the interesting clues he had found in Dick Roughsey's autobiography, *Moon and Rainbow.*

However, before leaving town he had something very important to do.

* * *

Rob walked along Todd Mall and into the Aboriginal Outback Art Gallery. He said "G'day" to the assistant, the same young woman who served him the previous day. Unwrapping the package on the counter, he carefully placed three boomerang pieces in front of her.

"You might remember I bought this here yesterday? Well, it broke while I was throwing. I was just throwing in the normal way, and crunch, it broke after just three throws. I'm hoping you'll be able to replace it."

"That's a shame, but you might have thrown it the wrong way. These do come back." The assistant replied over-confidently. "The Aborigines who sell them to us say they come back."

"Have you seen them throw one?" Rob responded, already sensing the answer.

"No. I haven't met them. I only work here part-time."

"Well the boomerang didn't return and I know how to throw. You told me yesterday that this would come back, but it didn't. These heavy, solid wooden types don't come back, so how can you help me?

"I can't sorry."

"May I speak to the owner?"

"They're down south, but they'll be back in a couple of days..."

"That's no help. What about a refund?"

"I'm sorry, perhaps you can stick it together. Most people just hang them on the wall."

Rob instantly knew where he would like to stick it, but chose not to express that thought as he re-wrapped the three pieces of broken boomerang.

"Are you sure you can't help? What do you normally do when you guarantee something and it doesn't work?

"Sorry, it hasn't happened before."

"I'll bet it has. Seeya later," Rob said abruptly, ending the conversation.

His response was the ambiguous way many Australians say good-bye. It can mean see you later that day, that week, that year, or possibly *never*, which is exactly what Rob was thinking!

Rob had no idea when he embarked on his quest that he would feel any anger or frustration. His original perceptions of a smooth, fascinating journey in search of an ancient artefact may have to be modified. But he knew why this episode bothered him: a false claim had been made for a product that was inferior in the first place. And the fact that the gallery could not deal with a bonafide complaint properly, also left a bad taste in his mouth.

* * *

Taking off from Alice Springs airport Rob's thoughts were crowded with memorable impressions. His three-day stopover had been vitally important. Problems with the broken boomerang and the gallery were memorable for the wrong reasons, but his other major experiences were highlights of the quest so far.

One was the thrill of learning to throw and catch a boomerang for the very first time! Only a few experiences in Rob's life could better the fun of that moment. And without feeling embarrassed at all, Rob knew that his heart had been touched and his spirit uplifted.

The other significant event would definitely test his research skills. *The Yuendumu Doors* travelling exhibition embodied an intriguing mystery. This rare collection of hand-painted Warlpiri Dreamings included the biggest boomerang puzzle to cross Rob's path. Did returning boomerangs ever exist in Central Australia? No material evidence has ever been found to support this idea, but his discovery of ancient legendary clues had motivated him to find the truth.

What Rob was confident about however, as the Qantas jet reached cruising altitude bound for Cairns near the Great Barrier Reef, was that the answers would come effortlessly at the perfect time, on the wings of intuition.

23

The emerald green rainforests of North Queensland are possibly the oldest on the planet, and confirm that visitors have arrived on Australia's north-east coast, even before they step out into the tropical air. Rainfall and temperatures vary seasonally and Rob was arriving in sunny August when the humidity was low. During the mild Winter months the city hosts thousands of visitors from across the world.

Approximately 100km north of Cairns lies the Daintree National Park, and farther north is Cooktown, named after Captain James Cook. One hundred and twenty kilometres west of this historic place as the crow flies is Laura, but on the bitumen road which goes the long way, it is still only about one hundred and fifty kilometres to drive. The township is surrounded by ironwood, bloodwood and eucalyptus forests in extensive sandstone country. And amongst these landscapes, hundreds of galleries preserve a vast and surprising treasure of outstanding Aboriginal Rock Art that was only rediscovered around 1960.

Rob had been reading about it in *Moon and Rainbow* while in-flight, and he was most excited by the fact that boomerangs were represented in many of the galleries. Not only that, the art was of a unique style. In the St. George area about 100kms west of Laura, traditional men had engraved multiple figures of boomerangs into rock surfaces. The curved indentations had then been outlined with ochre pigments, usually deep red in colour. According to fieldwork reports that Rob had seen, this was the only area in Australia where that style of boomerang depiction occurred.

Rob had finished reading the fascinating personal story of traditional Mornington Island life that includes numerous anecdotes about the warm, brotherly relationship between its late author Dick Roughsey O.B.E. and the late Percy Trezise O.A., former Ansett Airlines pilot, artist and writer. They were the greatest of mates and worked closely together. Percy guided Dick's successful career as an artist, and over many years Dick shared his Dreamtime stories. Their collaboration reached the public through the many books they wrote and illustrated, as well as in Art Exhibitions.

Rob discovered that it was Percy, called *"Warrenby"* by his old Lardil mate, who began the mammoth task in the 1960s of recording Rock Art in the Laura area, now referred to as Quinkan Country, because of the Quinkan spirits in the galleries. The joint creative and determined efforts of these two men brought this art to world attention.

In the last chapter of the autobiography, called a "classic" by Dr Geoff Seekman in Darwin, Rob came across a surprising and original idea. Dick Roughsey had speculated on a fascinating possibility.

The boomerang must have been an important clan totem in those far-off days, as there were dozens of them. (engraved into the sandstone) The red paint around them seemed to be very old when compared with the paintings lower on the wall. I tried to imagine what it was like thousands of years ago when the Tomahawk - or was it then Boomerang? - language people came to camp in the rock shelters during the wet season.

"That's incredible." Rob said under his breath. "That's even more amazing than the Rainbow Serpent's boomerang ribs!" He had to come to terms with it so he paraphrased mentally. The author stated that there may have been a "Boomerang Language" people in the Hann River area, north-west of Laura. This was a sensational idea, far beyond any possibility Rob had thought of. But how would it contribute to finding *The First Boomerang?*

Two aspects of traditional culture had crossed Rob's path. One was the unique Rock Art style depicting boomerangs, the other was the suggestion of a Boomerang Language people. Both were connected, but each could be studied separately – one anchored solidly in the earth, the other, speculation about the past. Both fascinated Rob, but would greater knowledge about them contribute to his quest? This was always the underlying consideration. His curiosity was deeply aroused, but would a trip to Quinkan Country answer the big question?

Even though Rob was not sure of the answer, he did not feel compelled to seek *The First Boomerang* up north. No inner voice was saying *'go and see for yourself.'* This was the clarity he could now rely on for decision making. His intellect was operating well, but his intuition was better and faster.

Everything contributed to his quest at its own level, but for now at least, it was enough to have discovered the boomerang information. What a privilege it would be to see galleries that had been 'lost' in the bush for millennia. Nevertheless, he had to follow his inner guidance.

* * *

Travelling to new locations was a highlight of Rob's journey, but he always had to be true to the messages he received. Sometimes they came via his inner voice, sometimes via physical signs in the environment. As yet they had never been grand visions complete with music and flashing lights! Usually an object, a person, or a few words would provide a clue to the next place and experience, thus revealing the next step. The fact that he was now in Cairns was a perfect example. Rob did not find clues in any local Aboriginal legends from the coast or tablelands to guide him to this north Queensland city.

However, he had flown in because of a series of events. He had set up a website. Geoff in Darwin had responded, inviting him on a field trip into the VRD. Geoff had loaned him a special autobiography with many links to Cairns. Rob's positive feeling about specific subjects in the book confirmed that he should make the trip. In the grand scheme of things, the role of each event was best seen in hindsight, but that was the logical way.

The other way was Rob's inner view of his quest, already developed to the extent that he could usually *see* how things were flowing. Sometimes even seeing snippets before they occurred. But he was not the kind of man to make any claims about it. Many people trust their hunches or gut feelings, the instant inner knowing which guides them to outcomes. His insights were no greater or no less than that. However, unlike most, he was completely aware of them and completely trusted them.

* * *

Rob's decision not to go north in search of *The First Boomerang* in the galleries of Quinkan Country enabled time for sightseeing. He grabbed the opportunity and after leaving his hotel headed straight for the Esplanade. The tide was in and morning sunlight sparkled on the tropical waters which stretched beyond the bay into the Coral Sea and Great Barrier Reef. After an easy, mind-clearing jog Rob received an intuitive message to change pace and make his way to Shields Street. He briskly walked along, not knowing why, but on a corner he saw an old two storey wooden building. Painted on the upstairs outside wall was "Cairns Historical Society Museum" and he knew this was where he was meant to be.

At the top of the stairs books, furniture, photographs, gadgets, artefacts and display cases surrounded him. He stepped past hand-made wooden boxes and saw a display about local Aboriginal clans and their rainforest shields. Then he moved past it, and around some vintage leather suitcases saw a large, coloured poster on the wall. It's surprising title was *The Boomerang and Double Island Story!*

Basking quietly off Palm Cove the island was the scene of a major Dreamtime event. An Ancestor's boomerang had landed there. "That's incredible!" Rob exclaimed under his breath, "Is that why I'm in Cairns?" He read that this legend belonged to the two clans who are traditional owners of the country the city is built on, as well as surrounding areas. What was so good about the legend was its location very close to Cairns. Rob paused and thought about making the 30 minute drive to Palm Cove and seeing for himself, but for the moment finished taking notes and photographing the rare poster.

Feeling delighted with his discovery Rob walked out of the museum and back onto the business streets of Cairns to look at boomerangs in gift galleries and souvenir shops.

Among displays of Aboriginal paintings, dot-painted didgeridoos and casual tee shirts featuring koala and kangaroo designs, were racks of boomerangs. The quality of art and finishes varied greatly. Some were decorated with finely painted dot art, others with burnt designs covered with heavy lacquer, and some were painted with unappealing stick-figure kangaroos. Rob had a closer look and found they all had something in common. All were cut from straight timber with the grain of the wood running straight across the wings. Rob's feeling of dejavu was acute! These were the same boomerangs with the same decorations he had seen in Darwin and Alice Springs. Without doubt the same type that had broken after three throws!

Rob was always seeking authenticity, so he asked an Aboriginal shop manager about local traditional boomerang makers.

"There used to be an old fella up at Kuranda but I think he moved down south, eh. I haven't seen him for months. There's not many good makers around these days, eh."

Rob thanked him, mentally filed the helpful information, then continued his walk around town.

Later, while enjoying a cappuccino and delicious cheese cake al fresco style at a cafe near the Night Markets, he reflected on recent events. He thought he would definitely come back one day and travel to Laura to see the Quinkan Rock Art galleries, and locals told him he would have to hire a boat to get to Double Island because there was no ferry service from Palm Cove jetty. This was disappointing, but a sign that *The First Boomerang* would not be found there, Rob knew intuitively.

Suddenly his thoughts flashed back to the brief conversation with the Aboriginal shop manager. "Down south" could be anywhere. It could be a hundred kilometres, or a thousand, or more! Although the information was basic to say the least, it was also a sign.

Rob picked up his cup and had another sip of frothy coffee, just as a car reversed into a parking spot in front of his table. On its back window was a large sticker with the words: *"Brisbane or Bust!"* complete with a photo of a busty blonde in a bikini! Now *there* was a sign, Rob stared and chuckled.

* * *

Rob's taxi cut through the centre of Brisbane on the way to his hotel. He had followed signs to the capital of Queensland and suddenly saw an Aboriginal Art & Artefacts shop through the passenger window. Rob instantly knew this was his next sign. He asked the driver the name of the street so he could find it as first priority after checking-in. Rob had taken the 7.00am Qantas flight from Cairns and arrived in Brisbane soon after 9.00am, and this sector plus the taxi ride from the airport meant the shop was probably open. He left most of his gear in his new room then hurried back and found it in twenty minutes.

Rob walked in and boldly designed paintings, a wall of artefacts and a corner display of Aboriginal music CDs greeted his eyes. This was a vibrant place filled with creative and abundant energies. But before he looked around the premises, he approached the counter.

"Good morning, nice looking shop..."

"Yeah, we try. It's a family business, eh." The middle-aged Aboriginal man replied with some pride.

"I need a bit of help," Rob said. "I'm looking for a good traditional boomerang maker."

"Do ya mean a man who cuts roots and knows what he's talkin' about?"

"Yeah. That's the kinda bloke," Rob confirmed.

"Leave it to me, eh." Without hesitation the Aboriginal owner picked up the phone, tapped in a number and waited for the response.

"G'day Uncle. What have you got going on today?"

Rob could not hear the answer but the man nodded happily, and asked Rob...

"Would you like to meet one of the best?"

"Well, yes, uh… Yes, please."

"What time Jack? Thanks old mate, I'll tell him, eh."

"It's all set, but before you go have a look around. Over there you'll see Uncle Jack's black wattle pieces. They're classics, eh." The helpful owner said, pointing to a section of the artefact display. "And here's his address in Caboolture, it's not far up the line, eh."

It had all happened so quickly and effortlessly. Rob was on his way to talk about traditional boomerang making with one of the best men around. Inside his head and heart he knew Cosmic Timing was again happening on earth!

* * *

The train ride took just under one hour from Roma Street Station and Rob arrived at his destination filled with positive feelings, then walked for ten minutes with a bounce in his step to 21 Greenup Street. He knocked enthusiastically on Jack's door at about 2.30pm and was greeted by the man himself: broad smile, black face and grey hair.

"G'day Uncle Jack, thanks for inviting....."

242

"That's all right young fella, call me Jack, come in and I'll show ya round," Jack responded, his eyes opening wider, as if he was looking straight into Rob's soul.

There was no need for Rob to ask much at all. Jack had been alone, except for visits from family since his wife died several years earlier. He loved company, especially someone interested in his life's work.

"How about a tea or coffee," Jack said, not really asking, he was naturally hospitable.

"Yeah…..please…. Tea with milk and no sugar thanks," said Rob.

"Add your own milk. I like it black, tea or coffee, with a bit of brown sugar. Yeah. Black tea for a blackfella, eh," Jack added with a happy chuckle.

Then he presented a plate of sweet biscuits as they settled onto chairs around the kitchen table which was covered with a red and white checked plastic tablecloth.

After his first sip of tea Rob outlined briefly that he was researching boomerangs in different parts of Australia and expected to publish articles and photographs, some on the internet when he was finished. Jack took it all in as he enjoyed his black tea, not even blinking at the word 'internet'. By Rob's estimate Jack would be in his seventies, or about the same age as the Elder, so he wondered how much boomerang making he did.

"Do you still make a few these days?"

"I don't make too many now… just some for that shop in Brisbane…. it's too hard… you've got to go bush and find the elbows… cut the big pieces… then slab 'em into workable thicknesses… then soak 'em for days or weeks… before cutting the outline shape with the band saw. It's tricky work on the sanding belt at my age because ya can really rip ya fingers! I lost two finger tips on the saw about fifteen years ago...yer have to learn to be bloody careful."

Rob knew he had at last found a man who was a fair dinkum boomerang maker, a man with years of practical experience and the heritage to go with it.

"Do you still throw?" Rob asked.

"I used to teach all the young fellas, both makin' and throwin.' But they lost interest or couldn't run a business. People always want boomerangs but the boys get into other things, and I'm too old now. I used to make a lot, but people never paid a fair price."

"Did they know how much work went into them?" Rob asked.

"Nobody does. Can ya imagine the old traditional fellas with stone tools? Crikey. I don't think I can either," he stated, answering the question for both of them. "At least we've got metal tools and sanding belts. But up here it's a dying art. There's still a lot of boomerangs being made but they're all straight grain."

"I think I know what you mean," Rob said, in a slightly questioning way, even though Jack's last phrase sounded so familiar.

"Well, the grain of the wood doesn't run around the curve, it goes straight across. They cut 'em outa straight timber boards and they're not strong like the proper bends I cut from roots."

Rob immediately confirmed why "straight grain" sounded so familiar.

"That's the same as I bought in Alice Springs. I tried to get it to come back but it lifted a bit, crashed into the ground, and broke into three pieces! It was bloody disappointing. It broke right along the grain which went straight across both wings, like you said."

Traditional boomerang maker Jack was really warming to the topic and was far from finished.

"People don't see the real thing now. Even my people are making that straight rubbish. But I tell ya what, I'll tell ya what gets on my goat, there's something even worse. Blackfellas are stickin' labels on those straight-grained ones and callin' 'em come-backs! It says: *Aboriginal Returning Boomerang - Authentic Product.* It's bullshit, they wouldn't come back in a month a Sundays! They're bloody liars and they expect people to respect 'em. I wouldn't pay 'em two bob. And there's plenty of whitefellas who make boomerangs that'll never come back either. Queensland's full of 'em, black and white. They're all ripping off the real boomerang, and the people who buy 'em. My grandfather would turn in his grave! He was a boomerang maker from the Dalla mob near Kilcoy and he respected and maintained the tradition. But who's doin' that today? Who cares about it now?"

There was a mixture of emotions in Jack's eyes. Like a lot of people of his generation he lamented the passing of familiar things, but obviously the boomerang meant much more to him than just that.

"Let me tell you another thing. Down in Sydney there's a computer machine that churns out thousands of so-called boomerangs every week. They used to use interior three ply, which is rubbish anyway, but now they use particle board made from sawdust! There's no bevelling to make a trailing edge on the arms, it's like a big router. I dunno how they get away with it."

Rob did not quite get the connection.

"Get away with what?"

"Callin' 'em 'come-backs,'" answered Jack, emphasising his words. "Yeah, on the package it says *"Guaranteed Returning Boomerang"*. I reckon the overseas people who buy 'em don't believe boomerangs come back at all. It's atrocious. And ya know, they have that little green kangaroo thing - Australian Made - what a bloody disgrace, fancy that fake rubbish representing Australia! But whataya do. I've been at this game over half my life. Now the tourist shops are full of rubbish boomerangs," he concluded despairingly.

"I don't know if this is my fight," Rob responded, "but I get the picture. Even the shops in Alice, Darwin and Cairns are full of straight-grain stuff. I'll bet most of the shopkeepers and gallery owners don't know the difference."

"Too right. But the makers are still lyin' about come-backs," replied Jack who was as tough as the black wattle roots he had been cutting and shaping for forty years. "They shouldn't be allowed to get away with it. A lie is a bloody lie, whoever tells it."

Jack's voice lowered in pitch momentarily, before he raised it again to give a final burst on the subject.

"And another thing. And this one takes the bloody cake. There's a family down south who've been gettin' boomerangs made in Asia, in Asia for God's sake, for umpteen years. Then they import 'em and get *Kooris* to decorate 'em up. Talk about a bloody rip-off....." Jack's voice trailed off in utter frustration.

"What if I finish my research," Rob suggested, feeling Jack's emotion. "Then see what we can do about it. How does that sound?"

"It'd better be soon brother... The old Ancestors up there might wanna see me before too long!"

Rob allowed Jack's last remark to float away before speaking. "Will you tell me about the real root boomerangs?"

"Sure. I wanna talk about it. Up here we give 'em a few names, depending on their size and weight. Let's take a few outside. There's still plenty of time before sunset..."

The two men got up from the kitchen table, leaving their empty mugs and walked through the house to Jack's workshop. They stood on a floor of sawdust, noticed cobwebs high in the corners and smelt the aroma of the Australian bush, the acacia bush of south-east Queensland. After so many years of cutting and sanding acacia roots, which Jack called "black wattle," the aromas had seeped into the walls, work bench and timber framework. Uncle Jack loved the "bush smell," as he called it, because it reminded him of so many good times out there.

There was a grassy, freshly mown park on one side of the house and they walked about a third of the way across it. Jack was in his element. Placing two root boomerangs on the ground he held the other one up and began to explain.

"The tips we call "toes" and each side has its own name. The front or top is the "belly" because it's rounded. And the flat side's called the "back." Have yer heard that before?

"No. I've never even thought about it. Which end do *you* hold when you're throwing?" Asked Rob, as the question popped into mind.

"There's only one end to hold.. Yer hold it here and point the toe forward...so yer can aim properly. Yer really have to aim properly, even when ya aim at blue sky!

"So you've got the belly facing inward..." Rob's question trailing off because he knew the answer.

"Yeah. The flat back always has to be against the palm of yer hand, otherwise it won't fly. You'd better have a go..."

Rob had been hoping to throw, so he said confidently, "I'm ready Jack, I want to be good at this."

"You're a right-hander." Jack stated rather than asked and Rob agreed with a nod. "Hold it tight on the toe and face the breeze. Wrap two fingers around it, or one if you're strong enough, with your thumb straight across, now turn forty five degrees to the right of the breeze on yer face." Jack said, gesturing toward the forty five degree position with his right arm while standing behind Rob.

"I had a pretty good lesson in Alice Springs less than a week ago. There was a coach driver who...."

"But did you throw one of these?" Jack quickly interrupted.

"No. I've never thrown a black wattle root boomerang."

"They're a different breed. They still have spirit because they're made from real wood the real way."

Jack's words resonated with Rob, his thoughts dashing back to the time in the hidden gorge when the Elder told him that boomerangs were "living beings". It was really good to hear words on this wavelength again. It gave the throwing experience deeper significance.

Jack continued the instructions.

"Aim at the sky just above yer eye level...just above those trees... and pick a good spot to aim at. Now lean it over to the right about 20 to 30 degrees..."

The 20 to 30 degree tilt was new to Rob but he did not question it.

"Use plenty of spin. Here, want me to show yer? I haven't had a throw for a while, but this smaller one's a real bewdy."

"Mind if I take some video?"

"No." Jack nodded straight away.

It flew like a bird. Jack whipped his arm through, spinning the boomerang out very fast. It climbed to a surprising height, circling anti-clockwise on a horizontal plane. Flying around once, the 'come-back' started to circle around again. Then beginning to descend, its spin and momentum carried it towards Jack. Stalling in mid-air, and hovering a couple of metres above and behind him, it finally ran out of spin and landed on the grass only five metres away.

"Wow. Poetry in motion. That was fantastic. Do you ever catch them?"

"I've caught a few, but I don't bother now. The old people never caught 'em. It just wasn't part of the culture."

"Okay, I'm ready. Oh, just one thing. How did you throw so hard without warming up your arm?"

"I used my head. Threw with my mind. The technique's been grooved into my muscles and tendons for years, so I only have to channel energy by focusing my thoughts on the job. Are yer with me?"

Jack had jumped to a new level of meaning and discussion, and Rob picked up on it immediately.

"Seems natural to me. Makes more sense than just a physical approach. Now let's get this real one into the air... "

Rob stepped forward and threw. Stable in flight because of plenty of spin, the boomerang achieved an outward range of about thirty five metres, completed a full circle, then landed flat on the grass about six metres away. His first throw was a success.

"Good one," Jack said buoyantly. "You've got a good arm. You might have some blackfella blood." He chuckled, as they both stepped forward to pick up their boomerangs.

The two men took turns to throw and stayed until dusk, sending the beautiful handmade root returners out and back with poetic rhythms as timeless as the culture they came from.

After their throwing session Jack insisted that Rob stay for a beer, which he did, and they continued to talk boomerangs until they got hungry. At that point Rob offered to buy a meal and they agreed on Thai food. It was Jack's favourite and he called it "Thai tucker." He had been a meat and potatoes man before his wife died, but now he found the taste and convenience of take-away Thai perfect, at least a couple of times a week.

They enjoyed a delicious and memorable meal, but soon after finishing Rob had to leave to catch the train because the suburban line services were not very frequent after a certain time each night. As they stood up Jack's parting words touched on the deeper dimensions of the boomerang in a very down to earth way.

"There's nothin' like a boomerang yer know. I haven't got the best words to say it properly, but anyone anywhere can use one. You can make 'em and paint 'em; yer can look at science and learn why they fly; yer can get to know the old culture; and yer get to know yourself. Do yer know what I mean?"

Rob did not have to answer in words. He only had to raise his eyebrows and nod knowingly as Jack continued.

"Yeah," Jack said with the confidence of seventy five years life experience. "Yeah. The boomerang let's yer know instantly if you've done the right thing. You only get back what you put in..." Jack's voice faded, his eyes full of contentment like any mature man speaking his truth.

Rob was touched deeply by the sentiments.

"Yeah Jack, I know what you mean. I took to throwing like a duck to water and I feel great inside when I throw a good one. And somehow there's a connection to the Cosmos."

"Yeah, that's it.... and you throw like a natural.... so keep at it. Thanks for comin' over today....it's been one of my best afternoons for years."

Rob grasped Jack's hand between both of his. "Thanks Jack..... thank you.... thank you for everything."

They finished their farewells, Rob assuring the master boomerang maker that he would let him know how his journey unfolded once he was back in Alice Springs.

* * *

In his hotel room late that night Rob typed notes about the day straight into his laptop, capturing the essence of Jack's philosophy and the rare experience of throwing a traditional root returner. He was due to fly to Sydney the next day about mid-afternoon so he had plenty of time to finish writing up his activities. He had also taken good footage of Jack throwing his black wattle boomerangs and knew this was very valuable material.

* * *

Brisbane opened its wide, sunny arms the following morning and Rob went out early for breakfast. He had wondered about the Elder as he woke up, so he knew that the Elder was probably think-ing about him. The two good mates had not been in touch since Rob flew to Darwin almost two weeks earlier. Perhaps they were about to connect, Rob thought, as he tucked into a fresh croissant filled with tomato and avocado, a healthy follow-up to his bowl of cereal, yoghurt and fruit salad.

After breakfast he looked around the shops and found an arcade running off the Queen Street Mall. A small souvenir kiosk beckoned and inside several attractively packaged five ply boomerangs caught his eye. He purchased them straight away because they were models he had not seen before, and because they had a colour photo of their Aboriginal maker.

Rob arrived back at the hotel and a lady at Reception handed him a message. Rob's face ignited into a broad smile as he read it to himself: "Ring me in Canberra on this number. Have you found it yet? The Elder."

"Aah. There he is." Rob smiled again, a smile that acknowledged their higher communication. How reliable their telepathy had become. "I wonder how he's going down there?" Rob added to himself.

The Receptionist pointed to a commercial pay phone and Rob made sure he had enough $1 and $2 coins before tapping in the number.

"Hello.... how are you?" Rob chuckled into the phone, still amused by their extrasensory connection working again. "Got your message."

"I found the collection with the tjurunga but the Iraqi Embassy people won't give it back. They said it would be "diplomatically insensitive," but they're a bit ignorant. This search has a higher purpose than just the return of physical artefacts. They need to appreciate that the items are spiritually significant and very important to my mob. I wrote a letter to them, but they either didn't read it properly or don't want to know the truth."

"What are you going to do?"

"I was talking to the Prime Minister yesterday...."

"Really. That's surprising. How did that happen?"

"She came in while I was having a meeting with her department, and was obviously on a mission. I know she's a wily politician but she's also been thinking about a big issue. For small talk she told me that she and her husband really like the Outback, but I can't tell you what else she said. She asked me not to and I gave my word ..."

"Are you sure?"

"Yes Rob."

"Do you like Canberra?" Rob asked, quickly changing the subject.

"There's mixed energies because politicians are strongly ego-driven, but the lake, the mountain and abundant open space within the city soften and balance some of that. But there's Central Australian spirit here too." The Elder said proudly. "The big ground mosaic outside Parliament House is based on a canvas by a Warlpiri man, and it speaks to everyone. Visitors don't know all the levels, but they interpret the design for themselves. That's better than not seeing it at all. Are you coming down here?"

"I'm in Brisbane now…. flying to Sydney tomorrow for about a week. How long will you be there?"

"I want to hear what the PM announces, but I don't know her timing, and I can't be away from country and the Faculty for too long. Her words will be big news if she says what she told me. You'll be extremely surprised, and so will everyone else!" The Elder emphasised.

"I can't wait," Rob replied, his mind galloping through fields of possibilities. "Timing's been working beautifully for me, and I reckon the PM will pop up at the right moment. And you'll get that tjurunga back when everything's right. There's just a little education needed down there, eh?"

"Yeah. That's right. But the Ancestors are guiding it all. Did you get to Mornington Island?" Asked the Elder as Rob pushed another $2 coin into the phone. Rob was only slightly surprised that the Elder knew he had been researching Mornington Island. He was now used to him having *inside* knowledge.

"There's a big boomerang story with the Rainbow Serpent over there, and I read a Lardil elder's autobiography, but I wasn't guided to go. Same with the Quinkan Rock Art around Laura up north of Cairns. There's also a fascinating boomerang legend near Palm Cove, but I didn't receive a sign to follow it up either. But my knowledge is expanding and I'm fulfilling parts of the quest.

And yesterday was fantastic. I met Jack, a master boomerang maker at Caboolture just outside Brisbane. It was full-on boomerangs from the moment we met, but I'm running out of coins, this is the last one. Why don't I phone from Sydney?"

"Okay," agreed the Elder, adding, "You're getting closer to it."

24

Rob loved flying into Sydney over the ocean from the north as bright sunshine illuminated the Opera House and Harbour Bridge. Although not born in the harbour city, just seeing those landmarks engendered a feeling of coming home. And sometimes the Opera House inspired thoughts of Uluru because both magnetically attracted people, both were culturally significant, and each was a distinctive signature of the Dreamtime continent.

Rob had to undertake important projects in Australia's largest city. During the past couple of weeks he had gathered information in the field, but now needed to explore historical writings on Aboriginal culture like he had done in Alice Springs and Adelaide. He planned to research in the Mitchell Library and progress his quest amongst its valuable collections.

Another aspect of increasing importance was the quality of boomerangs available in souvenir shops. Rob was highly motivated after his time with Jack in Caboolture and wanted to informally survey products for sale in Sydney. Would the discoveries confirm his new mate's passionate criticisms? Would he find more straight-grained, decorated pieces of wood claiming to be returning boomerangs?

Rob had more than enough to occupy him in Sydney and first priority was to examine precious books and other archives in a grand, historic building.

* * *

Eight giant columns at least five metres tall and reminiscent of an ancient Greek edifice towered over Rob as he walked up thirteen sandstone steps. He was excited about the day as he reached the three metre high metal doors. The middle pair was closed while the other two were open, each door faced with a bronze panel of relief figures and portraits. European explorers and Aborigines, most based on historical photographs greeted every visitor. To Rob's delight boomerangs were featured, one panel including a pair as clapsticks. Another held by a *"boomerang thrower"*, and the third brandished by a *"Boomerang thrower Central Australia"* in a fighting stance. Rob quickly noted that the boomerang held by this warrior was too small to be an effective striking weapon, a detail he found puzzling.

Rob now had more knowledge under his belt and planned to focus on specific subjects. One priority was to find first-hand accounts, particularly of Aboriginal throwers. It was also important to locate the areas where returning boomerangs were used, and find legends from those areas. Rob also wanted to investigate misconceptions about the boomerang and do his best to correct and explain them.

He secured his daypack in a numbered locker and walked into the huge reading room where light poured in through high skylights, creating a sunny glow. He selected a table and chair, laid out his laptop, notebook and pencils, ready to focus.

Rob was keen to review Charles P. Mountford's description of returning boomerangs included with *The First Returning Boomerang* legend that he and Clara had explored. Since improving as a thrower because of his time with Jack, some of Mountford's published words did not ring true. Rob had saved a copy of the story featuring Kudnu the

Lizard Man in his laptop. He clicked Mountford's words onto the screen to refresh his memory...

As a weapon, the returning boomerang has many limitations. It is effective only when thrown at right angles to the wind, and even the slightest obstruction will interfere with its spin, and cause the weapon to fall harmlessly to the ground. It is likely that, before the arrival of the Europeans, this type of boomerang was restricted to the southern coasts. But the interest of the white man in the flight of this strange weapon, and the fantastic stories told of its capabilities, undoubtedly increased the area of its distribution.

After re-reading this excerpt Rob was clear that Mountford had made several mistakes. When he first read the legend and associated boomerang information in Alice Springs he did not have the knowledge to analyse it. Now he was much better informed.

Rob had not seen any evidence that the returner was a weapon. Mountford may have been referring to its use as a decoy when hunting ducks over water - an ingenious method used traditionally along the Murray River and other water ways - but Rob did not think so. Apparently Mountford was not because he mentions throwing at *"right-angles"*. When throwing returners Rob knew that an angle of forty five degrees - *off* the oncoming breeze - was the optimum for returning throws. He was positive that boomerangs do not return to the thrower if they are thrown at ninety degrees off the breeze. Imagine how difficult it would be he thought, to hit a fast, wary emu or kangaroo if a thrower had to aim *away* from it, and hope to hit it, as the boomerang circled?

For Rob, speculation was unnecessary because he was sure returners were not used for hunting. They differ in size, shape and weight from non-return hunting boomerangs, but these vital contrasts are not mentioned by Mountford. The longer hunting boomerang which flies straight is a bigger, heavier implement and is designed to inflict damage, unlike lighter, more acutely-angled returners used traditionally for fun and games.

Rob did not agree with the main points of Mountford's last two sentences either. Returning boomerangs were definitely not *".... restricted to the southern coasts"*. They were used in many areas including the north coast and north-west rivers of New South Wales, around Brisbane and the south central-west of Queensland, on the west Kimberley coast and south-west corner of Western Australia, as well as in regional parts of Victoria and South Australia. Apparently Mountford did not know they were used in these extensive areas. Therefore his claim that the white man's interest and *"...the fantastic stories..." "...increased the area of its distribution"* was not plausible. Even so, Rob did know that when European explorers reached new districts they asked Aboriginals if they could make returning boomerangs, however, in traditional times this amazing implement was widely used.

Mountford's description surprised Rob. How could a leading writer and anthropologist with such a huge body of magnificent work make these mistakes? Especially, Rob wondered, when this legend and information were published years after other authors had correctly written about the returning boomerang, including its distribution. Rob also knew that the earliest European reports referred to the returning boomerang as a *"weapon."* But why had Mountford not sourced up-to-date and accurate information for his Dreamtime book?

Notwithstanding Rob's criticisms of Mountford's text, a bigger question came to mind in the focussed atmosphere of the Mitchell Library. It concerned the study of the boomerang. Has research ever been conducted on the construction and performance of traditional returning and hunting boomerangs? Even as Rob asked the question within and wrote it down, another equally poignant one arose: To whom or to what Institution would he direct his enquiry?

* * *

There were many references to *Boomerang* in the catalogues and Rob had flashes of his previous visits to the library, enjoyable days spent a decade earlier. He would not have time to peruse every article or book but he wanted to have another look at Thomas Mitchell's explorations, volumes by Howitt and Brough Smyth, articles by Frederick D. McCarthy, as well as the maritime journals of Philip Parker King, 19th century seafarer and hydrographer. He vaguely remembered treasures from each publication that might assist in his search for *The First Boomerang*.

Over the following few days Rob located the fascinating texts he was looking for. He read personal accounts and travelled *with* explorers through unmapped areas of land and sea, looking over the shoulders of some of the first Europeans to contact Aboriginal people. He was *there* in his imagination seeing first-hand how history had unfolded. To balance his energies during the book research he spent time on Sydney's busy streets doing his informal survey of boomerangs on the market.

* * *

Rob soon found out that there were thousands of boomerangs in Sydney's souvenir shops in The Rocks, Darling Harbour and Circular Quay. When first walking around he saw the same 'straight-grained' so-called 'boomerangs' he had seen everywhere, the solid wooden ones Jack said were made in Queensland. He was also seeing more types for sale than anywhere else. With so many different boomerangs available, Rob wondered how international visitors especially, or even local first-time buyers would know which model to select. How would they know what to look for?

Confronted by different sizes, colours, shapes and packaging, potential customers who were seeing boomerangs for the first time would be very challenged. Rob had no doubts about it. But even worse, the same claim was made for all boomerangs: *"Our boomerangs come back"!* Staff members of all shops guaranteed this legendary characteristic. Some models even had basic throwing instructions printed on a label glued to the back. Similar labels appeared on some 'straight-grained' pieces, none of which would ever return. One brand even claimed a 30cm or 12 inch long piece was traditionally used for hunting! Jack's strong words were all being confirmed. Many other boomerangs also claimed to be authentic in some way, or that they were *"Aboriginal-Made."*

But it was the claim that most boomerangs *"come back"*, whatever their shape, size or weight that really bothered Rob. He had seen and heard the same misleading information far too many times. His informal survey suggested that at least 90% of boomerangs in souvenir shops were not returners! The unique characteristic that made the boomerang world famous had been reduced to a shamelessly exploited promotional ploy.

* * *

In one souvenir shop near Circular Quay an assistant yelled "15% off, 15% off" as soon as Rob walked in the door. Like most people Rob was interested in a bargain, but he found this sales technique off-putting. However, after selecting a particular boomerang he asked the shop assistant the key question: "Does this one return?"

"Yes, yes they're all coming back. I've thrown one myself."

"Have you? It must be fun," Rob replied with a knowing smile, adding: "I've thrown some too but I'm sure this one wouldn't come back. It's too dense, too thick, not shaped properly and out of balance."

"Oh no, it comes back, we sell a lot of those and there's 15% off."

Without throwing the boomerang and showing the assistant that it would not come back Rob knew there was no point in debating the issue, but he did ask one other question.

"Could I please speak with the manager?"

"I'll go and find him. One moment please."

After seeing false claims about the returning capabilities of boomerangs in every place he had visited, Rob was becoming increasingly uncomfortable with the blatant, widespread misrepresentation. As this thought occupied his mind a short Asian man, who looked a little bothered, walked up.

"I'm the manager can I help you with something?"

"Hello, my name's Rob. I've been looking through your boomerangs. Most of them are decorative and nicely painted but your assistant tells me they *all* "come back." But that's wrong. What if I want to throw one, or an overseas visitor wants to throw one?"

The manager, apparently not disturbed by the question took the offensive.

"It does not matter. They never throw them."

"But is that the point? You're making false claims about a product."

"No...no. We just sell them. I don't know anything about them. I've never thrown one. Go and talk to the people who make them. Tell them, if you think there's a problem."

"It's your problem too. Would you sell boomerangs that did work?"

"They all work for me. Now please excuse me. I'm very busy."

Rob had not known what to expect, but standing in someone's shop and claiming that a staff member was not telling the truth could have received a shorter, sharper response! But under the circumstances he felt that the owner was not too unreasonable, even though he obviously didn't care. Why would a shop owner not be protective of his business? No one likes to be shown up as ignorant, especially about something they are selling.

Rob found the whole issue, which had begun when he unknowingly purchased the non-returning piece of straight-grained wood called a *boomerang* in Alice Springs, very, very annoying. That was the major issue. The shop assistant told him he was buying a returning boomerang!

He walked out of the Circular Quay souvenir shop saddened and frustrated that people misrepresented boomerangs. Since beginning his quest he had grown to deeply respect them. The boomerang was linked via legend to Uluru and the Rainbow Serpent, was represented in ancient Rock Art, and was originally made by craftsmen with stone tools and finely honed skills empowered by tradition. Throwing it added a dimension of fun. Catching it completed a meditative moment in time.

With this knowledge how could anyone abuse the boomerang's heritage? How could they sell ordinary pieces of wood or particle board and even use the word *boomerang?* Rob knew the answer of course. They were interested in making money, not heritage or authenticity, and deceived the public every day to do so. But this dishonest activity had continued for far too long.

* * *

After six very full days of research in the beautiful harbour city, Rob had one last afternoon and evening to catch up with a couple of old friends for a ferry ride and dinner. Before arriving in Sydney he did not know where he would be guided to next, but during the week he received a message about the destination in an effortless way.

It came in a dream. One morning he woke up as it was ending, but what he had 'seen' and could remember was very real. He was flying over the Flinders Ranges in South Australia. Glimpses of the landscape, a helicopter, and a local area name confirmed for Rob that this was his next sign.

Later on the same day he purchased a Qantas ticket to Adelaide at a travel agency on George Street opposite Wynard Station. His journey was now more about trust and belief than making plans. He was in tune with his inner universe and its connection to the broader Universe and Cosmic Timing, and knew they consistently affected daily life. To Rob it was obvious that spiritual awareness helped achieve tangible outcomes.

One evening he phoned the Elder in Canberra and asked about his progress with the lost tjurunga search.

"How's it going down there?

"It's not in the bag yet Rob," The Elder responded. "But I want to fly home soon. I don't know when the Prime Minister's going to make her announcement. She didn't say."

"You might just have to go with the flow," Rob suggested.

"Yes, no doubt. I've got a strong feeling she'll announce it somewhere beyond Canberra anyway. That's my take on it. So I'll let you know later," The Elder concluded.

"Okay. All the best."

* * *

A good friend dropped Rob off at Sydney's Kingsford-Smith Airport for his flight to Adelaide via Melbourne and the next stage of his quest. As soon as the Boeing jet was cruising above the clouds Rob took a well-used notebook out of his carry-on bag, eager to review information gathered in the Mitchell Library.

He knew that traditional Aboriginal men enjoyed throwing and watching their hand-carved boomerangs lifting into the breeze and hovering above them, noting they competed in games of skill to test accuracy of return in Victoria, Queensland and New South Wales. While discovering these facts he unearthed a fascinating piece of Australia's colonial history.

The story unfolded in the published journals of Major Thomas Mitchell. As Surveyor-General of the colony he led four government-sponsored expeditions in the 1830s and 1840s that departed from Sydney, or Port Jackson as it was then called. During one overland journey he met local Aborigines in the north-west of New South Wales and observed them using *"bomerangs"*, as he spelled the word. He specifically recorded how these missiles soared into the air while spinning very fast, describing this action as *"...their rotary motion upon the air."* He also saw the *"natives"* twisting or bending the arms of boomerangs after heating them in a campfire, apparently to influence their flights.

However, what Rob found most intriguing was that Mitchell kept his discoveries secret when he returned to the colony! Then, years later in 1850, he announced an invention called *"The Bomerang Propeller"*, a remarkable device for ships. But it was not surprising that its curves and airfoils were derived from the aerodynamic shapes of boomerangs that came back!

While reading notes and photocopies of Mitchell's discoveries on board his flight Rob had a flash-back to his time with Jack. He told him something crucial about returning boomerang design, and Rob remembered the words and images clearly.

"If anybody ever tells yer the arms *have to be twisted* for boomerangs to come back, tell 'em they're wrong. Tell 'em an old *Murri* boomerang maker in Caboolture said it's wrong, and it's always been bloody wrong!"

"I'm sure I read something about the "classic twist" of the returner," Rob responded.

"Yeah, I'd say yer have," continued Jack. "But it's a lie and people have been tellin' it for years. Look at this." Jack placed the boomerangs they had been throwing onto the kitchen table. "Look at this," He repeated. "Flat, completely flat, with just a little bit of undercut on the wing. They're completely flat, that's it, that's the real story."

Rob believed Jack, but was still puzzled. So he closely re-read the explorer's journal account. Then it became clear. Mitchell mentioned that the arms of the boomerang were twisted so it would rise into the air. Nowhere had he written that twisting the arms made boomerangs come back! Rob was now sure that Mitchell's description had started the 'twisting' misconception, so often mistakenly quoted since as the reason boomerangs return!

Suddenly a fleeting thought crossed Rob's mind as he flew south. He was researching probably the oldest man-made flying implement embodying complex aerodynamics, while flying in a modern aircraft that relied on similar aerodynamics!

As Rob read through the historical information an important fact became clear. Aboriginal clans in the Port Jackson area when the First Fleet arrived in 1788 did not have or use the returning boomerang. He estimated that it was brought to Sydney in the 1830s, a theory he could examine later. As he continued reviewing his research material he found the hunt for facts and explanations totally absorbing.

The late Frederick D. McCarthy, former Curator of the Australian Museum in Sydney wrote books and many articles about Aboriginal culture. Rob had tracked several down, recalling that McCarthy observed there are more figures of boomerangs than spears in Rock Art throughout Australia. A remarkable finding in Rob's opinion. McCarthy's articles often appeared in the Museum's magazine, one being *The Boomerang,* a comprehensive account published in September 1961.

Rob also located an impressive article by D.S. Davidson entitled *Australian Throwing-Sticks, Throwing-Clubs and Boomerangs.* Published in the *American Anthropologist* in 1936 it illustrates the distribution of wooden throwing implements on the Australian map, and he regarded this pioneering work as excellent reference material.

The Qantas Boeing 737 began descent into Melbourne, Australia's cosmopolitan second largest city that hugs the shores of Port Phillip Bay and spreads into the hinterlands, barely an hour after leaving Sydney. Rob would be in transit for an hour and a half before boarding his connecting flight to Adelaide. His thoughts zoomed to the Gippsland region of Victoria and the vivid descriptions he read in an article by A.W. Howitt entitled *Boomerang.* The author had written a valuable first-hand account of Aboriginal clansmen who gathered in Bairnsdale about 100km east of Melbourne.

When Rob first read the article in the Mitchell Library he paused, glanced up from the 1876 edition of *Nature* magazine and 'looked' into the historical distance. Howitt had written about traditional men from different areas congregating to throw boomerangs, describing flights, estimating distances thrown and heights achieved, as well as playful antics the throwers participated in. Seemingly knowledgeable about the subject he painted a word-picture of a fun-filled, entertaining time. But there was something that puzzled Rob. One key word in particular flew off the one hundred and twenty four year old page.

The word was *"downwind."* Howitt had written that on a bright and breezy afternoon the Aboriginal men were throwing *"downwind!"* Rob could not believe it!

Questions rushed to mind. Did Howitt report what he actually saw? Did he know how returning boomerangs fly? Had he ever thrown a boomerang? Did he make an error because of language difficulties? Rob did not have the answers, but knew that this throwing technique was not feasible. As a competent thrower himself he was aware that boomerangs do not and will not come back if thrown *with the wind.* If throwing *"downwind"* was the correct technique Jack would have demonstrated it in Caboolture and coach driver Bill would have shown him in Alice Springs!

However, maybe Howitt reported a variation of the usual throw, Rob thought, trying to explain his puzzling description. Perhaps while they were enjoying the high, circling flights of their root boomerangs, some men may have thrown a few "downwind" just to watch them carry forward on the breeze in ever-diminishing circles! But if so, they would have done a lot of chasing!

Rob still had forty five minutes transit time remaining in Melbourne, enabling him to look over more research notes, gathered so productively at the Mitchell Library. He also made good use of the time by typing information into his laptop. The boomerang story had taken many pathways, and also provided rare insights into 19th century thinking.

After initial reactions of amazement to the returning boomerang by European explorers in the new colony, and readers of their reports back in London, observers wondered how such a remarkable implement came to be in the hands of Aborigines! How did these *"primitive natives"* know about this unique *"weapon?"* In various London societies in the mid to late 1800s the subject was debated, and the major conjecture was whether the returning boomerang was a *"deliberate invention"* or an *"accidental discovery"*. Rob had not read much about the lively discussions, but it seemed that no consensus was ever reached. However, he felt sure that the British people voicing their opinions had no knowledge of Dreamtime legends. Not surprising in that era, but consequently they did not know the Aboriginal history of the boomerang.

Rob had made notes about many other historical events, and since his first day of research in the Alice Springs Collection the journey had been fascinating and revealing. From the South Australian Museum and Mortlock Library, the sandstone escarpments of the Victoria River District, and two Aboriginal books set on Mornington Island, to throwing "real" returners with Jack in Caboolture, and making discoveries at the Mitchell Library, all had provided crucial material and experiences.

Rob felt more than satisfied after reviewing his hand-written pages. His knowledge of the boomerang kept on increasing in depth and scope as he travelled. Now with a clear mind and abundant energy he was ready for the next important part of his quest, somewhere in South Australia's Flinders Ranges.

As Rob was about to board the aircraft his thoughts instantly flashed back to the just-completed flight from Sydney. He had flown in an air corridor close to Canberra where the Elder was pursuing his own challenging quest.

25

Spread across the forecourt of Parliament House in Canberra is a surprising mosaic of Aboriginal art created in the dot style of Central Australia. On cold Winter days it massages one's eyes like the first blossoms of spring, its thousands of coloured granite discs illustrating a timeless Dreamtime legend. When days are hot in Australia's national capital it tells the same story and burns with the clarity and presence of its Outback origin.

Based on a painting by Michael Nelson Jagamara the impressive art installation was completed before 1988, the year of the massive building's official opening. The story it illustrates is symbolic. Called *Possum and Wallaby Dreaming* the original 1984 canvas features a meeting place in the centre, and the tracks of many animals coming to that place.

Parliament House was built for the Bicentenary of modern European Australia, its highest point a giant flagpole that supports a twelve metre by six metre Australian flag. As well as the Aboriginal mosaic there are two other outstanding aspects inspired by Aboriginal culture.

Architecturally created, they are huge, solid and integral to the building's design. When seen from the air, the long, symmetrically curved features stand out prominently and unmistakably. These boomerang-shaped walls 'landed' back-to-back perfectly and define the enormous building. They are partially buried by the landscaped hill and the remainder of the structure, but readily acknowledge that the mystique of the boomerang is deeply embedded in Australia's consciousness.

* * *

The Elder was not well-travelled in terms of towns and cities, but highly evolved on the journey of spirit, intimately knowing his inner self. Rob had learned many things from him in Central Australia, including the fact that the Elder knew about some places he had never been to! However, he did know something about Canberra, but had not been back for ten years. To prepare for the visit he contacted John Mixwell, an old friend and former colleague. They had worked together in the Department of Aboriginal Affairs and kept in touch over the years. John would definitely be very pleased to help the Elder, or Lindsay as he knew him, in any way he could.

Before departing Alice Springs the Elder had written to the Prime Minister, and a representative of the Department of Prime Minister and Cabinet had replied, setting up a meeting to discuss the repatriation of artefacts. In his important letter the Elder stated:

These tjurunga are sacred to my people because they represent our connection to the spiritual source of life. In any western religion such objects would be highly respected and acknowledged as irreplaceable. Can you deny that we have the same level of reverence for our sacred objects?

In the climate of potentially greater Reconciliation between Aboriginal and non-Aboriginal Australians in the preceding decade, no government could ignore the Elder's request. Partly because it recognised the issue, but mainly because its private polling was recording increasing positivity towards Reconciliation. On behalf of Western Aranda people the Elder wanted the sacred objects returned and the Australian Government should offer its support, he believed, if politicians were smart enough to see the big picture!

* * *

The Elder was not thinking of the boomerang-shaped walls of Parliament House when he flew into Canberra. He was totally focussed on the increasingly hot trail of the lost tjurunga taken from his country about ninety years earlier.

John Mixwell, the Elder's contact in Canberra had discreetly searched for the Central Australian stone and wooden artefact collections, and made a major discovery. A selection of the artefacts purchased in Broome by an Australian Government agent, and probably including one of the lost tjurunga, had been presented to the Ambassador of Iraq!

According to John, who kept a low profile while verifying the facts, the precious traditional objects were displayed in two glass-topped cedar cases in the main reception area of the Embassy of the Republic of Iraq!

Delighted with the information yet not over-excited, the Elder believed he now knew where one of the lost tjurunga and other artefacts were, and therefore whom to approach. But the next steps would have to be diplomatic ones, both personally and officially. This was likely to be challenging, but fortunately John would advise him on strategy.

Before travelling to Canberra the Elder had also written to the Ambassador of Iraq stating his credentials as a senior custodian and his desire to have the *"stone and wooden objects"* returned to his people in Central Australia. The Ambassador, who may have been incorrectly advised, responded by saying:

The collection of Aboriginal artifacts was presented to our Embassy as a gesture of goodwill by the Australian Government. We believe its representatives would have sourced these materials properly, and it would be diplomatically insensitive of us to give them to someone else, regardless of their claims.

The Elder was surprised by this reply because it lacked sensitivity and ignored his words about the sacred nature, spiritual importance and of course, real ownership of the objects. Why would the Iraqis want to keep them, now that they knew their significance to the Elder and his people?

Unfortunately, the Elder had heard too many ignorant and disrespectful comments about Aboriginal culture during his life. But he had not come this far to be denied. He would have to find ways, probably face-saving ways for the Iraqis, so they would hand back the lost tjurunga. In fact, returning any tjurunga to its traditional country was of national importance, although few people realised it.

* * *

After a happy reunion at Canberra Airport John Mixwell started to drive Lindsay across the spacious, planned city towards his home. They were old friends and work mates and neither was actually sure when they had last seen each other, but the detail did not matter now they were catching up in person.

John recognised his old friend's face and voice, but was not expecting the hat. The well-worn fawn Akubra with dot-painted band and silver heart pinned to the left side, gave him an Outback presence, John thought, for want of a better description. But there was also a feeling about him he did not recognise. He seemed bigger and brighter, possibly John guessed, because he lived in his own country near the MacDonnell Ranges. Picking up on John's thoughts the Elder said...

"I'm home on every level when I'm out there."

"You look really good for an old bugger, Lindsay," John laughed as they drove across Kings Avenue Bridge over Lake Burley Griffin.

"Aren't we the same age?" Lindsay retorted, also laughing because he knew John was sending himself up too, then adding...

"Well, I talk to the Ancestors. They keep me young."

"I can't beat that old brother. It's a privilege to have you here. The place has changed a lot, so we'll have a good look around. I'm at your service."

''Thanks so much. What a special lake, I miss it from time to time.''

''Yes, Lindsay, I know what you mean.''

John Mixwell knew Lindsay had important 'business' to do, but for the following morning he had arranged a guided tour of Parliament House, knowing he would enjoy seeing the *Possum and Wallaby Dreaming* mosaic. It would be an Aboriginal introduction to the capital, a good start to the day before Lindsay's meeting.

Canberra usually has colder Winters than Central Australia and the morning of their visit to Parliament House started with a very frosty bite. The outside temperature was five degrees below freezing so they dressed in layers, John loaning Lindsay an extra large suede and merino wool coat and a pair of lined leather gloves. Now warm and comfortable, Lindsay sensed a very significant day ahead.

After their guided tour of Parliament House, a building Lindsay found totally overwhelming in size, he commented to John:

"Even the columns in the foyer are much bigger than our mulga trees and desert oaks. But it wasn't here in the early Department days when we started."

"No, that's right. It was a big idea which was ultimately designed and constructed. But forgetting what the pollies spent on it, it's a magnificent building."

"It's big and beautiful, no doubt about that. But are the political decisions made here big enough and good enough for our Dreamtime continent?"

"You always had deep questions back in the old days."

Lindsay was not looking for answers from his long-time friend and associate. They were just reacquainting themselves with each other.

"We need that tjurunga back John. Do you think the government will help?"

"Well, they're all strategists so if they see political mileage in it you're on a winner. And there's always a bit of power play between the government and other countries, so we've opened up possibilities. The parties concerned know the score, so if it fits their positions, you're a happy man."

"The timing's right old friend. I have a good feeling."

"Let's hope it happens soon Lindsay. You've waited too long."

At about noon they stood outside on the forecourt close to Michael Nelson Jagamara's mosaic. They had seen it briefly on the way in but waited until now to fully appreciate it. Lindsay wanted to see the art without any shadows, even though he knew the midday sun would reduce the depth and strength of the colours.

In traditional culture an artist has both personal and shared Dreamings that he or she can paint. Personal Dreamings belong to an artist exclusively and no one else can paint them. The mosaic artist was a Warlpiri man and Lindsay was a Western Aranda man, and they belonged to different countries with different stories. Lindsay knew he could tell the public story of the artwork, but instead offered a philosophical interpretation to his friend.

"The mosaic's presence recognises Aboriginal people and contributes to a vision of one Australia that walks together. Overseas visitors see it and wonder what the art work means. They think of the artist and culture that produced it. For some a whole new window opens. It's very positive. Just seeing traditional art here makes me happy too."

"Yes indeed. I make a point of showing all my visitors," John acknowledged.

That night they had dinner in a Vietnamese restaurant and talked about the old days when they worked as bureaucrats in the 1970s and 1980s in the Department of Aboriginal Affairs. So much water had passed under their respective bridges. John was married with three adult children and had left the public service years ago because he finally wanted to *"make real decisions"*, as he put it. Lindsay had inevitably returned to country where he worked in Aboriginal organisations that administered health and education services in remote communities, and currently held his senior lecturer's position at FAD.

"Well. Here's to old black and white mates, and many more great days." John said, raising his glass of Barossa Valley shiraz to toast their reunion.

Lindsay clinked John's glass with his glass of sparkling mineral water.

"Thanks so much for all your help with this. The whole country will benefit spiritually because at deeper levels we're all connected."

"You always used to talk like that," John remarked warmly.

"That's me. I'm even closer to the old energies than I used to be. But just between us, spiritual energies are timeless and still work today," Lindsay said, pausing for a few seconds.

"Come up sometime John. You've *got* to see my country."

"I'll get there old brother. But first. Make it happen tomorrow."

* * *

The Elder arrived at the Department of Prime Minister and Cabinet with the quiet enthusiasm of an experienced man. Knowing the ways of Aboriginal and non-Aboriginal leaders, he was prepared to speak and negotiate in whichever way was required. After introducing himself at Reception, the attendant offered to place his jacket in the cloak room, which he accepted, taking off his leather gloves and pocketing them. An aide then ushered him along a carpeted corridor where framed portraits of previous Prime Ministers were hanging. The aide guided him into a timber-panelled office and started to explain how the Department functioned. The introduction had only been under way for a couple of minutes when a loud and urgent knock on the door interrupted them. A young woman with dark pulled-back hair and yellow-framed glasses walked in briskly and handed a folded note to the surprised aide. He read it silently to himself and suddenly exclaimed,

"The Prime Minister wants to meet you. She'll be arriving in ten minutes!"

The Elder was stunned and did not say anything. Within a minute he felt pleased at the prospect of meeting the Prime Minister, whatever her reasons. It was very unusual for the PM to have time for spontaneity, but she obviously knew about the Elder's visit to Canberra.

"What do you think she wants?" The Elder said in a seemingly innocent tone which belied his natural wisdom.

"She was aware of our meeting and was told where you came from, but she often has her own reasons." The Department representative replied, looking puzzled, because he really had no idea at all.

As a result of this surprise development the Elder inwardly confirmed his resolve. He knew precisely why he had come. His mission was clear and his commitment total. He would not allow whatever the PM might say distract his unchangeable purpose. He knew the ways of politicians. They tried to link with people and projects to gain kudos. But although it initially stunned the Elder to be told that the PM was coming to see him, what he was about to hear in their private meeting would amaze the wise Western Aranda man.

Soon after, the Prime Minister of Australia was ushered in and the Elder stood up. The PM walked over to where he was standing and offered her hand. They shook hands firmly, as the PM spoke.

"Pleased to meet you Lindsay, you don't mind if I call you Lindsay," The PM said as a matter of course, not as a question. "I've asked my staff member to leave for the moment because what I have to say is private. Just take a seat, make yourself comfortable and we'll commence."

The PM commented on the distance the Elder had travelled, and that she was becoming more interested in Aboriginal Art. She also expressed her fascination with the Outback and the "famous" town of Alice Springs, explaining that Australians love the mystique of the vast red centre of the country. Adding apologetically that she and her husband had only been there once a long time ago, and only for two days.

Politicians sometimes decide and implement plans without consulting those directly involved. Unfortunately, history records many interactions like this between non-Aboriginal and Aboriginal Australians. But this PM wanted to do better.

"I feel proud working here knowing there's an Aboriginal mosaic on the forecourt. Many visitors comment favourably then ask about your culture. Most of us don't know enough Lindsay, but we've seen Aboriginal Art and share what limited knowledge we have. But there is so much more. I know you are here for a special reason and I want to offer my support." The PM paused…

"I would be extremely grateful for your assistance. Our stories, sacred objects, country and Ancestors are our culture. We have lost so much over the years, but I'm here to find a sacred object and take it back to country," The Elder gently explained.

"My Department will help with that, but I have another matter to discuss."

Impressed with the PM's sincerity the Elder listened intently.

The Prime Minister began to describe her idea. She drew on her basic understanding of Aboriginal issues and history, her words genuine and well thought through. The Elder nodded knowingly several times and then she announced her complete vision. The Elder could not believe his ears: her vision would be history-making.

However, nothing would be revealed publicly until the PM was ready, and definitely not before the most opportune political moment. The Elder was sworn to secrecy in their brief, closed meeting. He agreed wholeheartedly because his life would also be enriched by the PM's future announcement.

Lindsay was uncharacteristically overwhelmed by the meeting because thoughts of what may eventuate had touched him deeply. His intuition earlier that morning of this being *"a very significant day"* was an understatement. What the Prime Minister had just told him was the best news he could hear any day.

26

The stony hills of the northern Flinders Ranges burned ochre-orange as the sun sent its last, long kisses of light for the day. Rob arrived in the area after a 500km plus trip from Adelaide in a rented 4WD to pursue the crucial signs received in a dream in Sydney. During the trip north he had hoped to see the Aboriginal petroglyphs engraved into the ancient rock of spectacular Wilpena Pound, but he had to miss them. The call of his quest was so strong.

Rob set up camp not far from the big, old gum trees and dramatic tan-brown dolomite cliffs of Chambers Gorge about 60km north-east of tiny Blinman, South Australia's highest town. He was in the traditional country of the Adnyamathanha people. Here he wanted to move closer to finding *The First Boomerang*, experience the spiritual vibrations, and film a Dreamtime story. He also hoped to locate *Waraminta*, a mysterious place somewhere in the Flinders Ranges. Not long after arriving he went for a walk to familiarize himself with the surroundings. As well as breathing the pure invigorating air he found a variety of simple petroglyphs on the vertical and sloping rock surfaces, an unexpected surprise.

While in Sydney he remembered a book that Peter Frederickson mentioned at the South Australian Museum entitled *Flinders Ranges Dreaming,* and he finally discovered a copy in a second-hand book-shop in George Street. Its evocative stories and artistic photographs inspired Rob and brought legendary and topographical features to life, but there was also something magical about finding it. This appealing book appeared on the morning, in fact only hours after, his dream about flying over the Flinders Ranges! Obviously, Cosmic Timing could happen anywhere!

The Dreamtime stories were not only captivating and entertaining, two of them mentioned boomerangs and the exploits of Ancestral boo-merang throwers. Why else would he have been guided to it? Rob could not have found a better published companion to guide him.

There was no reference to *Waraminta* in the book, and Rob began to wonder if it really was in this area. He had read about the north, but maybe it was in the south because the Flinders Ranges was definitely the location of the legend featuring Kudnu and the first returning boo-merang! However, it now appeared that this elusive place, although still of interest, was not a key to finding *The First Boomerang.*

* * *

The land speaks its stories if we know how to see and hear, and Rob wanted to rediscover this principle. He wanted to tune in and listen, walk gently amongst the living landforms at dawn and sit high on a ridge at night, just like he and the Elder had done near Alice Springs. The Flinders Ranges and MacDonnell Ranges have at least one aspect in common: the same immeasurable sweep of stars and planets above. He knew the stories may differ, but at their heart were Ancestors of the clans who recognised the Sky-World as an integral part of their lives.

Suddenly two white shooting stars hurtled across the dark mystery of the night sky. Rob instantly wondered whether they were Aboriginal spirits returning to earth, or a sign that Aboriginal babies would be conceived. For how many millennia had Humanity explored the Sky-World he pondered, as he scanned the Cosmos and blinked back at the stars.

In contrast to the clarity of the sparkling diamonds above, Rob was not yet clear on how to solve his biggest challenge. Where was *The First Boomerang* that came in the Dreamtime? This quest was his focus, his passion, his nearly every waking moment. Without being able to ask anyone this question of questions, he had often asked the Universe and although a definite answer had not come, Rob believed all his steps were guided and timed perfectly. The search enthused his heart, intrigued his intellect and enlivened his spirit. Life was great.

Rob's odyssey was inspired by real Aussie characters who profoundly respected the boomerang. He had never met any of them before, but all seemed to have been waiting for someone to come, someone to show genuine interest in the boomerang. These were men who had carved boomerangs from the remnants of their culture, men who held the boomerang in their heart. They wanted it to be given the recognition it deserved. They wanted Aboriginal peoples to be honoured properly because they gave this unique object and symbol to the world.

* * *

Rob had carried the plywood boomerangs since purchasing them in Alice Springs and was ready to spin them through the energy of the northern Flinders Ranges. In every place he visited he made time to practise, the highlight being his time with Jack in Caboolture when throwing the black wattle root returners.

As late afternoon dissolved into twilight he positioned himself relative to the breeze and threw, launching the lightweight boomerang against the backdrop of sky and earth with a forward snap of the wrist. Spinning from his right hand it circled perfectly on the air, as if embodying the spirit of an eagle, returning within two metres of where he was standing. Now that he was consistently good at throwing he found it relaxing and satisfying, ideal for the gentle conditions and softening colours. Like he had experienced with his first throws in Alice Springs, he sensed other levels, unseen yet tangible vibrations that enriched him.

Several levels became obvious when he experienced the rhythm of throwing and catching. First, the better his focus the better the result. Second, the world around him disappeared for the few seconds it took for the boomerang to fly out and back. And third, he was thrilled after catching the boomerang without even moving one foot. That experience was perfect. Rob was tapping into the energy of the Universe, the entire natural world which has run on perfect cosmic clockwork since the Dreamtime when the boomerang came into being.

Later, while sitting by his campfire Rob mentally flashed back to the Full Moon night near Alice Springs and the *'timelessness of time'* concept because something incredible happened in Adelaide. Before driving north he purchased the *Advertiser* to read some local news. On page seven an article headed *Moon and Sun Show Ten Years Ago* instantly grabbed his attention. It contained a surprisingly familiar story.

According to the article a rare astronomical event had occurred in Central Australia a decade earlier. Described as an alignment of the sun and the moon, the article explained that the moon had risen precisely as the sun was setting on the MacDonnell Ranges. An expert astronomer was quoted as saying *".... that variations in the earth's orbit were the principal contributing factors to this impressive act of Nature, which occurs only once every fifty years."*

"What?" Rob asked loudly within. He could not believe what he was reading. But the most astonishing fact was the date of the event. This alignment occurred on the 16th July, precisely the night on which Rob and the Elder had witnessed it! But something did not make sense! They had seen the phenomenon about four weeks earlier, *not* ten years ago!

Rob was stunned. Somehow he and the Elder had experienced an event that occurred ten, or fifty, or even five hundred years ago! But how could this be?

Then a flash of insight rocketed into his mind like a meteor across a blackened sky.

"Aah," Rob gasped audibly in the quiet, cool evening air in rocky hill country, as realisation dawned: "The *'timelessness of time'*, that's it! What happened to us in the MacDonnells was *'timeless'*. We slipped into a dimension where all time is simultaneous: where past, present and future occur together! No wonder the Elder did not explain more that night. He knew the answer would cross my path!"

Rob initially found the incredible discovery in the Adelaide newspaper too mind-boggling to digest. But he knew it was correct. He *had been* in the MacDonnells that night and here was a published description for all to see. Therefore, he reasoned that the Elder and the Ancestors had guided him there on the Full Moon because they knew he was ready for the *timeless* experience and knowledge.

For Rob, this wonderful astronomical event reconfirmed how information is received. It comes when *WE* are ready, because that's *WHEN* the time is right. This was the concept of "Cosmic Timing" he mentioned to the Elder early in their association. Greater intuition guided him as he moved closer to finding *The First Boomerang*, and daily experiences and so-called 'coincidences' consistently confirmed it. Now he had evidence from an independent source that supported his understanding of this Universal Law.

* * *

While in Adelaide Rob arranged to hire a two-seater Bell 47 helicopter so he could be flown over the Chambers Gorge area. Because of a previous contract, one of the company's aircraft was still at Leigh Creek about 550km north of Adelaide and within easy range of Rob's camp. This small helicopter looks like a bubble with rotor blades on top and is often used for mustering on huge Outback cattle stations. It was also perfect for Rob's plans. He wanted to simulate an eagle's-eye view of the ranges and find the distinctive geological features created by Dreamtime boomerangs described in *Flinders Ranges Dreaming*. Rob knew that Central Australia's dot paintings depicted figures and landscapes in plan view. Why not discover ancient boomerang stories looking down from above also? He felt sure that few researchers had ever tried to see legends in this way.

The hired helicopter was due early next morning. Rob cleaned his camera lenses, checked maps and planned several routes and flight paths. As he prepared he was tremendously motivated by the project's original and exciting content. He was about to attempt something that may never have been attempted before. His airborne strategy to record boomerang legends in the landscape had fallen perfectly into place.

Rob realised there were hundreds more Aboriginal legends he could explore, but in this moment he was meant to be in the northern Flinders Ranges. He also knew he could not explore all legends Australia-wide, nor research all regions, unless his quest was going to take years! For now he would continue to be guided by signs and intuitive messages, knowing he was always on track.

The Elder had presented this surprising challenge because it was an important part of Rob's destiny. What would the world make of *The First Boomerang's* discovery? Rob did not know with certainty. But he was positive that a lot of people would be totally amazed, while others would protest that it was impossible! However, he had to find it first!

* * *

About an hour after first light Rob heard the distinctive engine of the helicopter and was instantly excited because it promised exhilarating adventure. The air was fresh yet completely still and he guessed it may be about 5kms away, allowing him just a few minutes to pick up his gear, all prepared the night before, and walk over to the graded dirt area where he had arranged for the pilot to land. On his way he realised the Bell 47's down draft would stir up a lot of dust, so he ducked behind a couple of trees until it touched down.

"Morning mate. I'm Peter. It's fantastic flying in this country.... the landscape jumps out and says '*look...*'"

"G'day. Great to see you, glad it was a good flight. I've been awake nearly all night." Rob said. "I'm really looking forward to this, can't wait."

"I've brought water and a few bags of nuts and raisins, and I should have enough fuel, depending on what you've got planned. If we have to fly longer than you expect I've got a mate on a property pretty close who keeps a bit of Avgas, and he won't mind us dropping in. Other than that I'll just stretch my legs for five minutes."

"Sounds good Peter. Then let's compare notes."

Rob and the pilot spent fifteen minutes before take-off looking at each other's maps and working out a comprehensive flight plan, estimating and noting the approximate kilometres to travel and probable duration in the air. Peter also explained how the intercom worked and made sure Rob's seatbelt harness was secure.

Then they literally climbed on air, the Bell 47 lifting loudly beyond the trees, catching horizontal rays of sunshine that added colour and definition to the rocky ridges.

Rob was keen to investigate two legends, one he felt more strongly about. This was intuition again, his trusted and comfortable companion. The legend Rob most wanted to fly over was from *Flinders Ranges Dreaming* and featured *Yuduyudulya* the Ancestral blue wren who threw comeback boomerangs and changed the landscape. This story was one of the most extraordinary Rob had seen. To remind himself of the magnitude of the events, he re-read the final two paragraphs and visualised the blue wren in action.

Standing on the ridge and facing the mountain, with his left hand Yuduyudulya threw a comeback boomerang at the eastern end of the rock wall. There is a heap of white quartz at the spot from which he threw the boomerang. The boomerang broke into pieces. It is now rock spilling down the mountain under the cut it made.

Yuduyudulya then ran further along the ridge (towards the west) and threw another comeback boomerang towards the rock face. The boomerang went right through the mountain making a big gap in it. It went on southward, and Yuduyudulya waited for it to turn around and come back to him. It spun around towards the west, but on the way back it hit the top of the western end of the mountain and stopped there. The boomerang is still there. You can see it sitting up there on top of Wadna Yaldha Vambata.

The photographs accompanying the legend clearly showed the gap in Mount Chambers and also the summit where the second boomerang hit and crash-landed. Rob had excellent indicators to look for during the helicopter flight.

Clear blue skies went on forever as they gained altitude, their perspective moving rapidly as the forms of the ranges changed. The Dreamtime story of *Yuduyudulya* filled Rob's mind as the pilot set his course for Mount Chambers. They would fly to the place on the ridge where the left-handed Ancestral blue wren threw his first comeback boomerang. Rob was going to personally experience flying along its trajectory, see the gap in the mountain, and also see where the second boomerang landed. Rob had wondered about the originality of his method earlier, and suddenly an intriguing question popped up. Was he the first person to deliberately fly the flight path of a Dreamtime boomerang? He did not know, and may never know, but in a few minutes he would be airborne in that space.

Rob was totally amazed by the scale of this ancient feat. As a boomerang thrower he could not even imagine a performance anything like it. Obviously, no human being could throw such distances. The immensely powerful Ancestor blue wren had thrown his first comeback boomerang about one kilometre before it hit the mountain! And his second went even farther! It went spinning out and partially back for a total flight of almost four kilometres! There was no point in trying to compare these Dreamtime acts with anything else...

Aboriginal Ancestors had created the world, so naturally their physical feats were spectacular and incredible.

Peter flew directly towards the mountain, following the Dreamtime flight path, lifting above it precisely where the boomerang had created the huge gap, levelling off then turning back towards the original throwing point.

"That's exactly how it's described in the written legend," yelled Rob into his mouthpiece, more from excitement than necessity. He had only told Peter the basics of his research, not the fact that he was in pursuit of *The First Boomerang*, yet his enthusiasm was overflowing.

"I meet a lot of people in this business mate, but I've never run into anyone looking for Aboriginal legends before," Peter replied as he skilfully guided the helicopter. "There's always a first time eh? It sounds better than looking for iron ore deposits."

"Yeah," Rob shouted. "I've been up in the Top End, over in Cairns and down the east coast, and you start to look with fresh eyes. All the landscapes are so much more than trees, rocks and rivers. Everything comes to life if you know the Aboriginal stories. There's a completely different map of Australia!"

On the second sweep they flew again over Mount Chambers, continuing for about a kilometre and a half before turning right gradually, then heading back towards the mountain. Significantly, the reason why the helicopter had turned right on both sweeps was because legendary *Yuduyudulya* was a left-handed thrower, and left-handed boomerangs circle clock-wise or left to right. Reaching the summit where the Ancestor blue wren's second Dreamtime comeback boomerang landed, Peter hovered the helicopter so Rob could look closer and film precious seconds for his video journal.

"Amazing!" Rob exclaimed as the ancient mountain revealed its full story. "I wish more people knew about this," he shouted. Some knowledge of the multi-dimensional landscape was, he believed, one avenue that would help non-Aboriginal people appreciate and understand Aboriginal people better. In fact, Rob was absolutely positive about it.

"Do you want me to put her down?" Peter asked loudly, gesturing about landing on the summit. Rob was caught a bit off guard, but was instantly certain, even though his mind occupied other dimensions when thinking of legends and landscapes.

"No thanks Peter, I'd like to leave this place to the Ancestors.... for now anyway. Let's return to the starting point the other way, as if the boomerang is flying backwards. I'd like to get a feel for that perspective."

On the outward flight Rob had focused his camcorder straight ahead through the bubble, and recorded as if the helicopter was the actual boomerang on its Dreamtime trajectory. Later, his film would present an eagle's-eye view and provide mountain-sized evidence of this captivating legend.

* * *

Morning had become afternoon, and Rob was sitting down, his back leaning against a tree. The helicopter had flown away several hours earlier and he was still absorbing the thrilling fly-overs. For company he had a dancing campfire and a mind full of thoughts wanting to leap out. Seeing such huge landscape features created by the Dreamtime boomerangs impacted on him. He was in awe of the Aboriginal storyteller's beautiful ways of illustrating and interpreting the country they belonged to. So profound and fundamental were their connections and understanding. No wonder being separated from country was, and still is, such an emotional and spiritual wrench.

After this wonderful day Rob's thoughts quietly eased into a still, inner place, his mind slowing as he watched the yellows, oranges and occasional greens of the fire's flames. But soon after more thoughts started to crowd in, and although going to get his notebook he quickly changed course and picked up the micro-cassette, switching it on to "Record". Rob was being guided by an *'inner voice'*. He felt *'here but not here'* as words started flowing into his consciousness, compelling him to repeat them into the recorder:

The Boomerang is known by nearly all Australians and recognised as coming from Australia's Aboriginal culture by people throughout the world. But most do not know enough about it. However, it is a blessing to be born in, or live in the country of the Boomerang's origin. Why? Because it gave rise to the oldest peoples in the world, the longest living spiritual cultures on the planet.

Rob could not believe what was happening, and happening so suddenly, but there was no time to ponder or question because the information kept coming.

In the beginning Aboriginal peoples were directly linked to the Source or Universal Love Energy and given sacred, spiritual information, laws and artefacts. The Boomerang that 'landed' in the Dreamtime embodied spiritual messages. Like the people themselves who have survived, so too has the Boomerang for good reason. This artefact is now very important to modern Humanity, and readily accessible because individuals can still see and interact with actual boomerangs. More than surviving any so-called 'test of time', the Boomerang will keep on flying even beyond the third millennium because it is the symbol for Humanity's spiritual growth. There is more to tell you tomorrow night.

And the *'inner voice'* was gone.

"Incredible," Rob uttered excitedly, the recorder still running while he regained his composure. He had heard of people receiving information, but he had rarely experienced anything as obvious and as urgent as this. He knew ideas and thoughts popped in out of the blue and intuition was a reliable inner guide, but this was specific information given directly to him. "Incredible" was the inadequate word he expressed aloud again, as part-realisation of what had just occurred.

During the next morning Rob transcribed the 'given' words from the micro-cassette tape into his journal, and was even more awed by their significance in the light of day. For weeks he had sensed there were deeper levels to the boomerang, but had not yet tried to learn about them. He journeyed in the knowledge that the appropriate information, people and experiences, and finally the 'big' discovery would occur in perfect time if it was meant to. And this would be when he and the circumstances were ready. This 'knowing' he was confident of. Even so, to hear an inner *'universal voice'* say that the boomerang *"is the symbol for Humanity's spiritual growth"* was amazingly moving to say the least.

Rob was restless all afternoon because he wanted the night to come quickly so he could receive more information as promised. Don't clocks speed up sometimes, he thought, instantly remembering his theories on 'time' over four weeks earlier! He looked over his transcribed notes and re-lived the moments of receiving the information, feeling humbled by the whole experience. The expectation of another message excited him tremendously.

Rob collected wood for his campfire, set it at the same site as the night before and in no time friendly flames were dancing in the cool, twilight air. He prepared his notebook, pens and micro-cassette, felt nervous energy in the stomach, and was ready to record new information. But when would it come? He sat and tried to relax, then began breathing consciously and rhythmically. Suddenly, there it was, the *'inner voice'* as clear as the star-filled sky.

The Boomerang dislodged from the starry Cosmos, spinning effortlessly through space, landing on the island continent now called Australia. Currently at the physical level it is a tourist souvenir, a sophisticated yet little known sporting implement, and a famous Australian icon. As an art and leisure object it has survived through all chapters of Humanity's development. However, as a spiritual symbol and metaphor its meaning has hardly been explored at all. But now that Humanity needs to choose a spiritual path for its own survival and that of the Earth, the significance of the Boomerang's messages need to be heard, understood and embraced throughout the world. There is more to tell you near Alice Springs.

"What? Near Alice Springs!" Rob exclaimed, looking into the big, dark sky. "I'll have to go back straight away!"

He had expected to stay for another night in the Flinders Ranges near Chambers Gorge, but it was now crystal-clear that he must get back to Alice Springs as soon as possible. Even if he had not experienced the philosophy of "living in the moment" fully before, he had to now. The information just received compelled him to do so. A sense of urgency and a surge of adrenaline coursed through his being. Thoughts of how to reach Alice Springs in the quickest possible time flashed through his mind faster than the speed of light, and he suddenly knew what he had to do.

Rob was also off mentally, travelling way beyond practical considerations, wondering what the *'inner voice'* would say to him next.

27

Australia is one of the world's largest democracies geographically and a Federal Election was looming. All citizens aged eighteen years and over are eligible to vote and are obliged to do so because voting is compulsory. Politicians of the major political parties were visiting communities throughout the continent, flying everywhere because of vast distances to shake as many hands as possible. However, there was also something different about this election. Australia had a female Prime Minister for the first time in its history, and she was standing for re-election.

Alice Springs was not usually on the campaign trail for nation-wide voting. However, the media had revealed that the Prime Minister would be breaking her journey from Canberra to Perth to deliver a speech in the Outback town.

A fleet of Private Hire cars brought the PM and close aides into Alice Springs, the long line of bright, white vehicles rolling along like the caterpillars of local legend. Some security staff were obvious along the route into town from the airport, and no doubt undercover agents had scoured the roadside earlier. Traffic lights on the section of the Stuart Highway that passes through town had been turned off, and traffic was being directed by Northern Territory police officers in typical khaki-coloured uniforms, complete with broad brimmed hats and semi-automatic Glock pistols holstered at the hip.

The convoy turned right off the four-lane highway, then turned right again just after Territory Top Tucker, passing a signpost that displayed the long Aranda name of Anzac Hill. This was possibly the PM's first exposure to local language but unfortunately her car passed the sign quickly, changing down a gear soon after to reach the car park near the top. The media contingent had been driven ahead in a fleet of taxis and was already assembled.

Many of the political journalists enjoyed being on the road and away from their regular rounds in Canberra. Election time meant stop-over after stopover, filing their reports, eating in new restaurants and sleeping in strange beds for days at a time. This was also the time when politicians made grand promises so their stories were often colourful, not least because of some of the places they visited. All reporters had keen ears for slip-ups and contradictions on the campaign trail, and like other Australians knew how the major parties pitched themselves. When in Government they applauded their own party's recent achieve-ments and tried to convince voters that they should also applaud them for the future, which of course they had mapped out for everyone's good! On the other hand, Opposition politicians criticized the current government's performances, trumpeting how their policies would enable all Australians to see brighter horizons because the sun would shine every single day when they were in government!

Preparations had been made on Anzac Hill look-out and included a small marquee, several white cloth-covered tables, a lectern, side stands and vases with native flowers, microphone and speakers, as well as rows of chairs which were roped off for dignitaries. The lectern was positioned on the look-out facing north, so the media could photograph the PM with Heavitree Gap in the background on the southern edge of town. With this well-known break in the MacDonnell Ranges as backdrop the public would see that she was definitely in Alice Springs, heart of the Outback to most Australians.

Upon her arrival the PM was carrying a neat package about the size of a shoe box wrapped in material printed with Aboriginal designs. This was unusual because an aide would normally do it. She was welcomed by the Chief Minister and members of the Northern Territory Parliament, local Federal Member of the Senate, the Town Mayor and councillors. After a round of formal photographs the PM was guided to her seat, and everyone else went to their allocated chairs. Nearly one hundred local people, the usual Territory mix of young and old, white, black and brown faces had also gathered to view the proceedings from close range. All was in readiness, and as if to salute, a pair of white cockatoos screeched overhead, dipping away toward the town centre, and on rocks down the hill a wiley black crow raucously called to its mate.

The Prime Minister stood up and moved to the lectern with a flourish, no doubt hyped by the adrenaline of campaigning, but also with an air of relaxed confidence. Obvious questions hung in the air. Why was she in Alice Springs? What did she have up her sleeve?

With printed notes carefully placed and hands resting on either side of the lectern, she was about to deliver a speech that no one knew the contents of. Not one word had been leaked. Apparently the PM had written the speech herself. Political commentators could not work out why she was in the Northern Territory, vast landscape of natural beauty, contrast and legend, but hardly any people and even fewer voters! Approximately 200,000 lived in the Territory and only about 105,000 were eligible to vote. Nevertheless, the PM apparently had reasons for being in Alice Springs, but her opening words still surprised everyone.

"I acknowledge the traditional owners of Mbantua whose country we are in. This prominent hill we are standing on is a sacred place for both the Anzacs and the Aranda, and in local language it is called Atnelkentyarliweke."

The PM made a very good fist of pronouncing the traditional name of Anzac Hill, and if any journalists were not paying attention before, they certainly were now, their combined hush as noticeable as the screeching cockatoos earlier.

To locals, journalists and everyone else present, these words were a shock from a Prime Minister whose party and predecessor had a recent history of not being able to come to grips with Aboriginal issues. But today something special was in the air. Not one onlooker whispered, or even took a sideways glance as she continued:

"To the Chief Minister, members of parliament, the Mayor, councillors and ladies and gentlemen. It is a pleasure to be back in Alice Springs. Thank you for your warm welcome. My husband and I have only visited once before, but we do hope to remedy this in the future. There is a mystique about your town and the Outback that many Australians acknowledge, so it's very good to be back. Unfortunately, I won't be staying long today, but I've come to do two important things.

However, before I do I want to acknowledge some great women of Central Australia, women like Olive Pink and Ida Standley. They and others were pioneers in a very challenging environment, yet they created legacies that we can all admire. They overcame many hardships, their achievements still inspire us today, and they are honoured in your Pioneer Women's Hall of Fame. In the Territory you have a successful woman Chief Minister, but although Australian women were second in the world to win the right to vote, it took nearly one hundred years as you know, before the country elected its first female Prime Minister. Naturally I would like to build on our heritage of pioneering women in Australia in the coming election."

There was little noticeable reaction among journalists to the speech at this point. Maybe a nod or two about pioneering women, and a chuckle about the PM's self-promotion, but nothing stronger. They still wondered why she was speaking in Alice Springs.

"Now to those two other important things.

Firstly, I want to call up a local man whom I'm sure many of you know. He's from Western Aranda country out near Palm Valley and the Hermannsburg area, and he came to Canberra on a very special mission less than two weeks ago. We met briefly and I have some very good news for him."

The PM signalled to an aide to escort an older Aboriginal man to the lectern, then gestured for him to stand beside her. It was Lindsay Williams, the Elder, custodian, senior lecturer, watercolour artist and Rob's mentor. The PM picked up the colourful package she had arrived with and commenced a presentation to him:

"On behalf of my fellow Australians it gives me great pleasure to bring this special artefact back to you and the place it rightfully belongs. Ladies and gentleman this is one of many sacred objects taken from Lindsay's country decades ago, and he told me that it is of great importance to his people and his country. With some diplomatic manoeuvring between my government and a foreign government's officials in Canberra, I was able to retrieve this object without causing an international incident, and bring it today.

From today, my government will give greater assistance, both financial and technical, to Institutions, including many overseas, for the repatriation of any culturally sensitive items which traditional custodians want returned.

Thank you Lindsay for coming to Canberra and telling me your story. I trust the return of this sacred artefact will help your people and give others confidence to do the same."

Turning and leaning towards the Elder the PM extended her right hand. They shook hands firmly, and looked each other in the eye, warmly confirming their close connection.

A round of applause rippled through the crowd as the Elder walked back to his chair holding the wrapped package tightly. People looked at each other, notes were now being written, and most journalists were very surprised.

"The other reason I've come to the heart of Australia is to say..." and here the PM paused for effect, a pause noticed by all in attendance. Now they were straining their ears to hear what was coming next. *"..... I came here to say, on behalf of my Government and all previous Federal Governments, a public SORRY to the Aboriginal and Torres Strait Islander peoples of Australia for all Government policies of the past which so drastically changed their lives."*

The reaction was immediate. Some cheered, some cried, some hugged each other as instant applause erupted. Others fell silent in disbelief. A few grabbed mobile phones to spread the word. Journalists began shouting questions, but the PM, looking remarkably cool amidst the excitement, lifted her hand for silence.

"I'd like to tell you a little story which happened recently. I don't pretend to know a lot about Aboriginal culture. I'm like many older Australians, but I was in Canberra and I met Lindsay...." gesturing toward the Elder seated nearby.

"In just a few minutes he told me enough about the Dreamtime and his connection to 'country' and everything in Nature, to start me thinking about my own life. He told me passionately about three lost sacred objects that had to be returned to his country and that one of them was in Canberra. Then he made a surprise remark. Lindsay said there must be a reason that I lived in a Sydney electorate called Bennelong, named after an Aboriginal man well known in the early years of first European settlement! I hadn't thought about the irony of it before. It was this conversation that made me rethink many things, and brought me here today. Thank you Lindsay, and thank you ladies and gentleman. We are flying to Perth straight away and I'll be holding a press conference there tonight."

The PM had finished, but the gathered media wanted more. Eager to have their questions answered the journalists jostled forward, momentarily halting her progress. But the PM had completed what she had come to do and brushed aside the repeated pleas for further comment. A rope cordon gave her enough space to walk to the steps leading to the car park, and as journalists tripped over each other in their attempts to follow, she reached the white limousine. But just as the PM's aide was about to close the car door, a microphone-waving journalist shouted a question.

"Why do ya want the blackfellas on side?"

It was a pointed remark, especially given the history-making apology in the PM's speech and her gesture of returning the sacred object, and it received a quick response.

"Sometimes even a Prime Minister listens to her heart, why don't you try it sometime!"

The PM wanted the last word and she got it. Few would disagree that her brief "Sorry" speech and presentation to the Elder had been perfectly stage-managed. Even though the journalists had not discovered earlier why the PM had come to Alice Springs, they now had a massive, unexpected story to report as she departed to campaign in Perth.

The official cars eased down off Anzac Hill and back onto the Stuart Highway to begin the fifteen minute drive to the airport. The journalists accompanying the PM followed in taxis, hurriedly recording first drafts of their stories into dictaphones, or speaking direct with city offices. Left in their wake were local media staff and dignitaries, still feeling disbelief at how the events had unfolded.

Every paper, news broadcast on radio and television, and internet news site in the country would run this story first. They would all lead with one word. The word *"SORRY"* would be seen in very large and bold letters, heard with strong emphasis and be repeated many, many times. A Prime Minister had finally spoken the word and it was now beaming across the land. "Sorry" was the currency of the media, emotive word of the week, and a pivotal moment for the Prime Minister of Australia.

On a sacred hill in Alice Springs history had been made.

28

Rob arrived back in Alice Springs on the evening of the Prime Minister's visit but was not aware of it, nor of the extraordinary content of her speech. The print media had not yet delivered its stories and Rob was too involved with his own quest to switch on the television that night. The intensity of his journey was increasing as he followed the guidance of the *'inner voice'* he heard in the Flinders Ranges.

Checked-in again at the Heart of Australia Resort he carefully prepared the gear for his next vital trip. He packed a range of items which, as usual, included the traditional returning boomerang given to him by the Elder. He sensed that his mentor was in the area, or even in town, but Rob was totally focused. He was filled with the exciting realisation that *The First Boomerang* quest could soon reach its unprecedented climax.

Next morning in a rented 4WD Rob drove through Heavitree Gap onto the Stuart Highway, turned left into Palm Circuit and crossed the Todd River before heading out along the Ross Highway. The bitumen road runs roughly parallel in sections to the East MacDonnell Ranges that are part of the Caterpillar Dreaming. It was new territory for Rob, except for the quick trip he had made with Clara when they visited

Corroborree Rock. It is of major significance to Eastern Aranda clans, and tjurunga were once stored there safely. But tragically, as in too many other places, they had been stolen in the early days by unscrupulous people.

Rob's drive on this cool, sunny morning was edged with expectation as he enjoyed the beauty of the East MacDonnells, believing he was heading in the right direction to discover *The First Boomerang*. During the Qantas flight from Adelaide he had received crucial information. The *'inner voice,'* now his reliable guide, had described several significant signs which indicated that his goal was getting closer and closer.

Included were geographical and other clues about the area he must locate. But there was no final destination marked on a local map. He still had to find and interpret the signs correctly as he came across them. Even with those considerations Rob felt instinctively that *this* road was the right track. Furthermore, he was back in the heart of Australia, and this felt totally appropriate because he had travelled widely, but been guided back to his starting point.

The first of the 'given' signs guided Rob passed the turn-off to Corroborree Rock and on towards Ross River Homestead. He saw a few wild camels grazing along the side of the road, but they only looked up briefly at his passing vehicle. Rob turned left before the Homestead at the Trephina Gorge Nature Park & John Hayes Rockhole signpost, continuing to the red dirt parking area at the gorge. This was not Rob's destination but he had been guided to see a beautiful ghost gum, a proud sentinel that had been growing for three hundred years. This was an old tree to any human mind, but compared with *The First Boomerang's* Dreamtime origin, it was barely a blink on the cosmic clock. Apparently for Rob this comparison of relative age was a good reason for seeing it, but not the only one. He got out of the 4WD and approached the big tree.

He walked around the graceful eucalypt, placed his open palms on its white trunk and sensed its massive strength. After several reverent minutes, and now filled with the Universal Love Energy that connects us all, he ambled contentedly back to the vehicle.

Then Rob, with a red apple, Brazil nuts and sunflower seeds in hand, walked over to a timber shelter to read the information panels produced by the Northern Territory Parks and Wildlife Commission. One of the signs included the Eastern Aranda words for River Red Gum (*apere: uh-puh-ruh*) and Dreaming (*Altyerre: al-ch-ra*). Also described were walks of varying distances and duration near and through the gorge which appealed to Rob, but he did not have enough time. His quest was calling louder and louder and he was compelled to keep going. Climbing back into the 4WD he knew he only had to find a hidden dirt road and drive for about an hour to reach what could be his final destination.

* * *

The dirt road turned out to be a very rough track, parts of it gouged out by heavy rains and run-off, probably months earlier, with rocks and dead branches slowing Rob's progress. The track, as he abruptly found out, was rarely if ever graded because it was hidden and seldom used. But 4WD vehicles are made for rough conditions, so with careful, low-geared driving he bumped his way towards his destination, persevering for the best part of two hours. Surprisingly, the track ended in the middle of nowhere. But in this case 'nowhere' was a grassy and peaceful clearing dotted with bloodwood and eucalyptus trees, overlooked by a low ridge just a few hundred metres away. As Rob pulled up he noticed a willy wagtail flitting amongst the witchetty bushes just ahead of him. Was this black and white fan-tailed bird a messenger of some kind?

After returning from a walk to the ridge Rob gathered an arm full of gum tree branches near the end of the track that doubled as a watercourse. Dusk would soon give way to darkness so Rob lit his campfire and sat down. He was thinking consciously about the next sign, revealed to him on the flight from Adelaide, but which he did not understand. He relaxed for quite some time, fuelling the fire and reflecting on his journey, when a sudden urge compelled him to look up. Rob gasped with amazement, immediately springing to his feet and shouting, "Look at that. Look at that!"

Way above the ridge he saw a pattern of bright lights with a familiar shape. Rob stared and stared. It was a boomerang formed by stars! The enormous outlined boomerang was as clear as the night was quiet. An avalanche of questions tumbled through his mind. What is it? Is it real? Is it a constellation? How long has it been there? Other questions faded as Rob continued staring in awe at the unbelievable sight. A sense of wonder flashed through his mind as he glimpsed another sector of sky for perspective, but when he looked back the huge, starry boomerang had disappeared! Rob had only seen it for about a minute, but he suddenly realised what it was.

"That's the *Cosmic Boomerang!*" He said slowly, still feeling amazed. "I didn't even dream it would be like that. A boomerang of stars. How cosmic can you get!"

The *Cosmic Boomerang* was one of the major signs guiding the last part of his incredible quest. After its magnificent appearance Rob knew he was in the most likely location to achieve his goal. Astonished by what he had witnessed, he stood in the cool night air and consciously felt in his heart that tomorrow would be one of the most memorable days of his life.

* * *

It was the morning after experiencing the *"Cosmic Boomerang"* and Rob knew he was extremely close to completing his quest. The sun shone brightly and would burn any unprotected skin as it climbed through the day, yet the temperature would not rise above 27 degrees Celsius. It was ultra violet radiation (UV) that would do the damage. But with this challenging aspect of sunshine comes the benefit of sunlight, and how far and what one can see. On Rob's previous afternoon's walk to the ridge he rested quietly near a distinctive sandstone outcrop, but in shadow because it faced east. Now, however, the early sunlight was highlighting its features and he felt drawn towards it again.

Knowing that his quest was nearing its climax, Rob picked up his daypack containing a garden trowel and geological pick, a bottle of water, nuts, apples and bananas. Over his other shoulder he slung his camera bag and set off for the outcrop. He was no geologist, nor had he participated in archaeological digs, but throughout the entire quest he had been guided to whatever was necessary to meet the challenge at hand. Today would be no different. He headed off briskly, moving with the nervous energy of an experienced actor about to perform on stage, hand in hand with the excitement of a young boy looking for lost treasure.

Striding towards the same section of ridgeline he had walked the afternoon before, the world around Rob was fresh, clear and inviting. Those were the words that popped into his consciousness as tiny zebra finches darted nearby and green and yellow ring neck parrots cavorted in the beefwood trees. Amongst the grass, the pinkish petals of Sturt's Desert Rose and the old, wise corkwoods greeted his purposeful steps. High overhead a pair of wedge-tailed eagles circled on the warming air. What a morning, what a gift from the gods, Rob thought, effortlessly tuning in to nature's vibrations. As he slowed down he thoughtfully reviewed other days and moments in Central Australia and found they had all been positive, uplifting, and spiritually enlightening especially with the Elder, except for the brief episode of the broken boomerang. This was certainly his place. When he was within coo-ee of the Mac-Donnell Ranges, East and West, he felt content and at home.

He noticed that various colours characterised the soil. From typical Central Australian red-brown to deep charcoal, with small deposits of creamy beige, looking like they had been poured down the slopes of the low ridge. As well as a local legend that would explain the colours, Rob knew there would also be geological reasons for them. However, in the context of his quest, the colours were part of the puzzle because he had been guided to this landscape, and this exact area, on this specific morning.

Suddenly a wedge-tailed eagle with characteristic upswept wings skimmed across the ridge, gliding low then soaring above the distinctive outcrop that Rob was walking towards. The big and powerful bird was a captivating sight. These magnificent eagles are the flying kings of the Outback, the largest birds of prey in Australia having wingspans of up to two metres and more. They are a protected species and live as singles, pairs or in family groups, producing one to three offspring in a good year. In various cultures and traditions they stand at the pinnacle of meaning and symbolism. They are related to profound spiritual growth and their presence is sometimes interpreted as confirmation of divine blessings. In the Christian Bible the eagle is the symbol of St John.

Rob had heard of spiritual qualities embodied by eagles, but at first did not relate them to the eagle he had just seen. However, in this moment out along the East MacDonnells something beyond normal was unfolding. Without warning a wedge-tailed eagle, perhaps the one which had soared into the endless blue sky only a minute or two before, swooped across the top of the outcrop closely followed by another, probably its mate. Rob had never seen wedge-tails so close. Did they have a nest nearby? Was there a dead animal's carcass on the ground?

Suddenly *within* he got it. This strong, majestic creature was the final sign he needed to see and interpret before discovering *The First Boomerang*! What a moment! What a realisation!

Both eagles had landed at the base of the outcrop even though Rob was barely fifty metres away. As he stopped to observe these large, mostly black birds he noticed that the tan-brown of the outcrop's sandstone contrasted with the beige-coloured soil upon which they now stood.

"That's it. That's the spot!" Rob shouted, his heartbeat racing with excitement. The eagles were standing on the actual spot he had been guided to locate. His weeks, even lifetimes of searching had led him to this place at this moment. He had found it. Rob was only minutes away from fulfilling part of his destiny.

As he eased forward his thoughts flashed to constellation *Aquila the Eagle* and its main star *Altair*, perched in the sky seventeen light years away. How appropriate he thought that the final sign had a cosmic 'cousin' in the stars. Rob continued, steadily approaching the eagles and the site of certain discovery. He had advanced about twenty metres when they lifted off the ground, a high-pitched whistle clearly audible in the otherwise soundless space. Although Rob's feet were firmly on the ground he was experiencing a kind of altered state, but there was no doubt that two very real eagles had shown him the way.

Rob reached the spot and immediately saw a rounded object slightly above the surface. Squatting down he rubbed soil off it and was immediately startled. It was hard like stone and colours were visible. He kept rubbing and beautiful blues, greens and reds were revealed. Rob's imagination was flying. Could this rounded, colourful object possibly be one of the tips of *The First Boomerang?*

He set to work carefully with his small trowel and geological pick to release the beige-coloured soil around it. After digging carefully for at least fifteen minutes he exposed a straight, semi-rounded section as thick as his arm and nearly one metre long. As Rob kept digging and clearing away more soil he was not conscious of a world beyond his focused energies. Then he uncovered a bend in the smooth object.

"YES! This is it!" He shouted, his words bouncing off the outcrop. "YES!" he shouted to the world. "YES!" He shouted to God and the Universe. "I'VE FOUND IT!"

An image of the Elder's face suddenly popped into Rob's mind. Does that mean he knows I've found it? Rob wondered, looking up into the late morning blue sky.

He continued digging straight away and after another half an hour had almost exposed the entire object.

"Unbelievable!" Rob exclaimed. His insides were jumping up and down as he rubbed off the last areas of attached soil. Now he could confirm what he had increasingly suspected.

The First Boomerang was made of solid opal!

How this was geologically possible was beyond Rob's comprehension, but it was most definitely solid, multi-coloured opal. Fiery reds, greens and yellows leapt into life as sunlight illuminated the ancient object. Could it have been here since the Dreamtime?

Rob eased onto the ground next to the heavy boomerang. He had worked up a sweat during the excavation, but even after starting to cool down he was still throbbing with the excitement, almost disbelief of discovery. *The First Boomerang* was symmetrical in outline shape, almost two metres long from tip to tip and unbelievably beautiful. Rob had been on the trail for weeks, but actually having his hands on it was overwhelming.

The climax of his quest filled him with profound joy, and a growing sense of its significance. He consciously connected again with Oneness, just like in the hidden gorge with the sacred paintings, where all was energy, the energy of Universal Love. Rob was ecstatic, and felt even 'fuller' than on the Full Moon night in the West MacDonnells.

* * *

Sometimes after achieving a goal or fulfilling a dream an inner calmness descends. This feeling overtook Rob during the first couple of hours back at his camp after the momentous event. He had made the discovery of a lifetime. But even that was an understatement.

Rob had found *The First Boomerang*. A history-changing discovery that would resonate for decades. It was perfectly preserved, made from solid opal, shaped in outline like a returner and found in a limestone deposit far away from any opal fields. These were the never-imagined details that completed the story. Or did they?

Rob's present quietness contrasted totally to the excitement just hours earlier. He had been staring at the incredible, colourful Dream-time artefact for what may have been an eternity. The warm afternoon had flowed fast and the sun was sliding toward the horizon as Rob leaned back on his rolled-up swag and thought about making a camp-fire. Dusk began to settle silently over the landscape and Rob wanted to stay relaxed and be open to what may happen next. Challenging, because his busy thoughts were a mixture of euphoria, satisfaction, partial disbelief and absolute wonder.

Then as clearly and as suddenly as every other time, the *'inner voice'* started to speak and Rob quickly grabbed the micro-cassette from his nearby camera bag.

The Ancestors and Gods gave the Boomerang as the symbol of a soul's journey from the Universal Love Energy to planet Earth and back, back to the Universal Love Energy...

The *'inner voice'* paused.... then continued...

Do you hear this loudly and clearly? The symbolic Boomerang's out and back flight path through the timeless Cosmos, touching down on earth for a lifetime, represents the soul's journey of each individual.

Rob felt instant recognition as the message resonated with his deepest inner frequency. He knew the boomerang represented other meaningful levels, yet this message was a wonderful, illuminating sur-prise. A discovery as magnificent as the solid opal *First Boomerang* itself. Before he could try and consider the vastness of this spiritual *'Soul Boomerang'* concept, the *'inner voice'* spoke again.

This deeper message about the soul may not be recognized by many people yet, but the important, everyday message will be. Chil-dren and adults will relate to the personal message: What We Give Out Comes Back. They will realise that their words and actions, and even their thoughts are directly influenced by this timeless principle. Posi-tive human values will develop because people will apply the Boomer-

ang Metaphor personally in all areas of life, wherever on their journey they are up to, even if they do not know that life is a spiritual journey.

Then the *'inner voice'* was gone and Rob pressed the micro-cassette's off button, relaxing against his swag. The *'inner voice'* had become an amazing presence. This latest message confirming the Flinders Range's statement that more information would be given *"near Alice Springs"*. Filled with countless thoughts Rob got up, gathered food containers and the billy from his vehicle, and placed twigs and branches together for his campfire.

* * *

After the momentous experience of discovery and the equally significant spiritual messages, Rob did not know if further information would be given, or even if his quest was complete. He had found *The First Boomerang*, but was there more? Fortunately he did not have long to wait for an answer.

Under the clear and vibrant Central Australian sky around his campfire on the night of the discovery, Rob slipped into the space and time dimension in which he had received all other information. He was being guided by his inner knowing, rather than waiting for the *'inner voice'*. However, he connected with it immediately, as if it was always there.

This time the *'inner voice'* did not relate information as words and sentences. Instead, Rob heard a deep sound, a seemingly endless sound that was reasonably familiar. As it began, the word *'original'* flashed into his mind. Resonating through his whole being and flowing on and on repetitively, the low-pitched sound comprised only two letters of the English alphabet. At first the pulses were short, then they became progressively longer, with just a brief pause between each one:

oooooommm, oooooommm, oooooommm, oooooommm, oooooommm, oooooommm, oooooommm, oooooooooommm, oooooooooommm, oooooooooommm, oooooooooommm, ooooooooooooommm, ooooooooooommm, ooooooooooommm, ooooooooooommm

As the *oooooommm* sound kept flowing Rob lifted his eyes to the stars, the uncountable distant diamonds that reminded him of the immensity of the Universe. They also reminded him of the earth's unique place in the immeasurable Cosmos, and of legends that describe the ancient journeys of Dreamtime Ancestors. Some explained the formation of stars, some acknowledged clans whose campfires light up the Milky Way, while others present parables for daily living. But what was this profound sound that enlivened Rob's spirit? Was it linked to his quest?

Closing off his conscious thoughts still rising as *oooooommm* continued, Rob allowed the replenishing vibration to flow through him over and over again. He was reaching a state of complete inner harmony and openness, a rarity in his life up to this moment. The feeling was similar to the deep inner renewal he and the Elder experienced near the paintings of spiritual masters in the hidden gorge. He was experiencing an all-encompassing feeling of Oneness with both the Universe and all life on earth.

Then suddenly it stopped.

The *oooooommm* sound stopped reverberating through Rob's inner being and he was consciously back at his campfire, fulfilled and in awe, somewhere east of Alice Springs.

As he became completely present, Rob's first thought was that the *oooooommm* sound *must* be linked to his quest. Apparently, even after his successful search to find *The First Boomerang* there was still more to be revealed.

* * *

Rob had packed the traditional root returner with his gear, and on the morning after hearing the *oooooommm* sound he was nudged intuitively to take it out of his bag. Guided by his inner voice and holding the returning artefact in his hands, he slowly said the word aloud three times: *Boomerang, Boomerang, Boomerang,* and then again with emphasis on its syllables: ***Boomerang, Boomerang, Boomerang.*** Finally, and for fun Rob attempted to make the *oooooommm* sound as he visualised the letters in his mind.

The first attempt came out well, then a grab of memory from travel experiences in India flashed into his mind. He apparently needed another level of information. *Om is used in daily prayers and comes from Sanskrit, one of the world's oldest languages.*

"Oh yeah, of course." Rob happily acknowledged to himself and the silent, unseen stars, instantly clearing his memory. "I've seen it written as *Aum*, but just as often as *Om* in books of Hindu prayers and chants translated into English. But *LOOK.*" He exclaimed loudly and urgently while leaping to his feet: "*LOOK. Om* is *IN* the actual word. *Om* is *IN Boomerang!*"

Rob was stopped in his tracks as complete silence washed over him and hung in the still air. Words were unnecessary and he stood motionless, still holding the traditional root returning boomerang. Nothing within Rob had pre-empted this moment of discovery. Nor had there been any clues. He needed time for this extraordinary revelation to sink in, but he could not help himself repeating his own words: *"Om is in Boomerang, the sound Om is in Boomerang!"*

29

Rob's next step was to get moving and find the Elder. His purpose was as clear as the awakening Outback sky and there was no time to waste. At the start of his quest Rob said he would make contact as soon as he made the big discovery. Now the time had come. He did not know where his mentor was, but going back to town was the best way to find out.

But even though seeing the Elder was his priority there was no escaping the mental gymnastics filling his mind. They related to his unprecedented discoveries in the East MacDonnells, including the completely unimagined fact about the word.

What had been revealed was a link between the returning boomerang of Australian Aboriginal culture and the *Om* sound from another culture, in another part of the world. Unspoken questions hovered in the stillness around Rob's camp. Was this a real connection or just coincidence? If there was no coincidence, how could this be explained?

While recently in Sydney at the Mitchell Library Rob had uncovered very important historical facts about the boomerang. As he recalled them he realised how amazing this latest revelation really was, particularly because compared with ancient Sanskrit, the English word *'boomerang'* is not very old at all.

In 1820 Captain Philip Parker King, while on a government survey to chart Australian waters aboard the *Mermaid,* anchored off the coast of Bowen, Queensland. It was the 22nd of July and after a trip ashore he wrote in his journal: *"...one of the men carried a spear, another had a boomerang of a smaller size, but otherwise similar to that which the Port Jackson natives use..."* This was immensely exciting to read because according to his research it was the first time the word had appeared with its current, familiar spelling.

This casual entry in a mariner's journal in the nineteenth century created a little known piece of history. In those pre-telephone days news travelled by sailing ship across the world, and most books from the British colonies were published in London, so the current spelling of *'boomerang'* did not come into general use until the 1850s. The startling aspect, in the context of Rob's discoveries, was that the first writing of *'boomerang'* appears to be a random historical event, yet the existence of *Om* in the word may confirm the boomerang's spiritual importance!

Several years earlier in India Rob had seen explanations of *Om* while reading about the culture, yet he had forgotten all about them until this moment. He had not heard the chant *oooooommm* for a few years either. But what really amazed him was that *Om* was the original sound, the first creative sound on planet earth! It was the sound that gave rise to life and landscape, a concept so immense that trying to comprehend it is still beyond most human minds. Yet in contemporary life *Om* is used universally. It is the sound repeated three times to begin the pooja in Hindu temples, and also a chant used world-wide at prayer vigils, multi-faith gatherings and consciousness-raising events to inspire world peace.

While pondering these ideas Rob packed his gear for the drive back to town, already visualising telling the Elder his momentous news.

Even so, a huge, obvious question was demanding attention. How could there be a connection between the original sound of the Universe and a unique Aboriginal implement? On a superficial level there is none: one is a sound, the other a wooden artefact. Yet Rob had been given the boomerang's profound spiritual messages and he could see the link. It was as clear as crystal: within the word was the two-letter sound Om. It was that simple. Any distracting thoughts could wait, because right now he had to hurry back to town and find the Elder.

* * *

Rob quickly finished loading his gear into the 4WD to return to Alice Springs. He had driven over 150kms on his successful quest since leaving town and would travel back on the same roads. But first he had to carefully drive along the challenging hidden dirt track, more a bumpy creek bed than a graded gravel road, before he would be back on the black.

After a quick walk around the campsite to make sure he had left no rubbish, also checking that the campfire coals were black and cool, he slid into the driver's seat and slowly accelerated out of the clearing. Beyond the rough track after about an hour and a half, he turned onto the Ross Highway and picked up speed.

Rob was very happy and felt as free as the breeze whistling through the 4WD's partially open window. The East MacDonnells had released a Dreamtime secret, and he had been guided to discover it. It was an unbelievable privilege and a life-changing event.

The journey was surprisingly quick, not because Rob drove fast but because ideas were dashing in and out of his mind the whole trip. Therefore the drive appeared to take no time at all. Recent flights had been similar as his mind overflowed with imaginative scenarios and *The First Boomerang* quest. Time seemed non-existent. Another dimension took over his conscious thinking and the world became timeless. There it was again, the *'timelessness of time'* concept, even though time apparently does pass during a flight or a drive.

Suddenly he was close to town and approaching Heavitree Gap, thinking that this southern entrance to Alice Springs was where Aranda men received message sticks, danced for visitors, and stored sacred objects in the old days. But was he imagining this? Or was it a memory from his past life? Driving on towards the roundabout, his next message came in very clearly: *Go up Anzac Hill.* Rob always followed his intuition now because it guided him to the right place at the right time. He parked the 4WD in the top car park, beginning to suspect why he was there, then walked up the concrete steps to the large circular lookout area.

And there, as if on cosmic cue was the Elder, looking as though he had been sitting there forever. Just the man Rob needed to see.

"I FOUND IT!"

The words exploded from Rob's lips, his vibration emanating joy and accomplishment. The Elder's face instantly lit up with a broad smile as he stood up. Rob strode forward and they warmly shook hands and hugged, simultaneously patting each other on the back. Rob immediately sensed the Elder already knew, or at least expected a positive outcome as they sat down together.

"What a fantastic time. Just incredible." Rob said brightly.

"Welcome back. Congratulations. Remember I introduced the quest here? Just as a boomerang circles back to its starting point, so often does a journey. You've come back to the same spot also, but you're now a different person. Your mind, body and spirit have had a lot of exercise," said the Elder, winking knowingly and pausing. Then the wise Western Aranda artist and lecturer added more insight.

"The physical *First Boomerang* is the discovery of the century. You came for this quest and now you've fulfilled it. Is the world ready to hear about it?"

"Yes. Yes," enthused Rob with conscious emphasis. "Yes, because of what the boomerang represents. I found the unbelievable Dreamtime treasure, but it's the spiritual messages that the world needs to hear. But I'll talk about it in a minute. Wait till I show you *The First Boomerang*. It's amazing. It's carefully wrapped up on the back seat of the Toyota," said Rob, gesturing toward the car park. "Come on, let's go." They stood up and got going.

"It's bigger and a lot heavier than the traditional returner you gave me. The colours are spectacular, and radiate the light and hues of nebulae, galaxies and the burning sun, with fiery red and glacial green. Its physical beauty reflects the cosmic wonderland. But its spiritual messages are the real gold."

They reached the 4WD, Rob unlocked the doors, accessed the back seat which was lying flat and began to unwrap one of the most amazing archaeological discoveries ever made. The Elder leaned forward as one of the wings was uncovered.

"It's solid opal! How absolutely beautiful!" He was awestruck. "The colours vibrate with love, and people will feel connected to it. Even if they don't grasp the full story, they'll still be inspired and changed. They'll awaken to the Dreamtime boomerang's spiritual messages because they'll have a physical object to relate to."

Rob finished unwrapping *The First Boomerang* while taking in the Elder's words.

"My feet haven't touched the ground since I dug it up. So many thoughts flooding in. And a million ideas. It's been the journey of a lifetime. Have a really good look then I'll wrap it up. Isn't it abso-lutely incredible."

The Elder touched the solid opal. "This will be talked about for hundreds of years. What a privilege. Thank you," he added. Rob wrapped up the beautiful boomerang and locked the 4WD. He was very keen to tell the Elder more about his quest, so they walked back up the steps to their seat facing the blue-purple hills. As soon as they sat down Rob began.

"It's been so quiet in the bush, down in the Flinders, out in the East Macs. And so busy in Sydney. But what I call *"Universal Voice"* spoke to me and guided the whole quest. This *'inner voice'* was so clear, so concise, yet the spiritual messages seemed fresh and familiar at the same time. Both simple and profound for all kinds of people to understand. The simplest one says: *"What We Give Out Comes Back,"* and it's a very old concept in other cultures too. You'll find it in Hinduism and Christianity. The Bible says: *"As you sow, so shall you reap"*, and the Bhagavad Gita mentions *Karma*, which means action and the consequences of action.

Therefore, the out and back flight of the boomerang is a metaphor for our human life. Isn't that fantastic. The spiritual dimension is so meaningful. But there's another one too, and it's really great fun.

That's the art of throwing and catching. Wow. It's so satisfying. You throw the boomerang, watch it spin out, turn into a circular flight path and return close enough for a catch, sometimes without even moving. It's fantastic. It's poetry in motion. It's a moving meditation because time seems to stand still when the boomerang is flying. I'll have to show you one day..."

"I'd love to see you in action Rob," the Elder said keenly. "I've heard that Americans say *"What Goes Around Comes Around,"* so they know there's a meaningful metaphor."

"Yeah, I've seen that too." Rob quickly added.

"The next bit might surprise a few people." Rob continued. "Science also makes a contribution that aligns precisely with this spiritual message. Sir Isaac Newton's Third Law of Motion states: *"For every action there is an equal and opposite reaction."* To put it another way, the message of the boomerang's flight is *The Law of Cause and Effect* or Karma, and it applies to every person, every day. It's all so simple yet profound, ancient yet modern, for young and old."

"How remarkable. You've been given so much," the Elder said. "And you've accomplished all the suggestions I made at the beginning."

"Yeah. The trip gave me all that and more," Rob responded.

He did not realise he had so much to share until describing his findings to the Elder, the sentences flowing as if he knew the information from another place and time.

* * *

"Before we go I want to tell you about Mount Gillen," the Elder said, as Rob looked toward the distinctive ridge, eager to hear what he had to say.

"This is also a big story. Are you ready?"

"I'm ready for anything after the last couple of days," Rob replied.

The Elder chuckled, then gestured with his outstretched arm.

"The point of the ridge we see from here is also the elbow of a huge boomerang, an unbelievably huge boomerang."

"What? Really?" Rob said, instantly surprised, as the Elder continued.

"The boomerang can only be recognised from the sky, looking down from several thousand feet! One arm ends at Heavitree Gap and the other at Honeymoon Gap, that's how big it is."

"Unbelievable. I've never even imagined a landform like that. Have you seen it?"

"I've seen it. I know it. It's old knowledge that's never been revealed before. From a high enough altitude the boomerang shape is obvious."

"Incredible. You always have something more to tell. Is there an aerial photograph of it somewhere? I'd love to see it."

"There is. And it will find you when the timing's right, as you know by now."

"Yeah that's right." Rob agreed, adding, "Does it link with my discovery or the boomerang's messages?"

"You may receive more information from the *'inner voice'* when you're ready," replied the Elder, "but do you recall the Full Moon night when we drove out along Larapinta Drive and....."

"And turned left through Honeymoon Gap?" Rob asked, finishing the Elder's sentence.

"Yes, that's right," continued the Elder. "That afternoon we drove right around the gigantic boomerang formed by that section of the MacDonnells!"

"And that's why we did it?"

"Yes, so I could tell you at the right time, which is now. Remember I said during the drive that all information wouldn't be revealed until later in your quest?"

"I do, but...." Rob said, his voice trailing off. He was also surprised because he thought their drive along those roads twice was about time, not topography. But this fascinating news of a mountain-sized boomerang quickly became more important. As if picking up on Rob's thoughts the Elder confidently suggested...

"Because you discovered *The First Boomerang*, the 'mountain boomerang' as we'll call it, means much more to you. It really adds to the story."

"Does it affect the Caterpillar Dreaming?" Rob asked, with some concern.''

"No. Nothing affects it. It will always be," responded the Elder with sage-like words.

"This landscape becomes more incredible the longer I'm here. Now let me tell you what I saw in the East Macs. Something absolutely extraordinary. Something happened out there that will be etched on my memory for the rest of my life!"

"As memorable as *The First Boomerang?*" The Elder asked.

"Yeah, I'd say so, but much more mysterious!" Rob responded. The mid afternoon sunshine on Anzac Hill was still warm as Rob began to relive his unforgettable experience.

"I was sitting near my campfire on the first night and an inner urge compelled me to look up. Immediately I saw a huge curved shape made with lights! But the lights were stars. Yes. Stars defined the complete outline shape of a huge boomerang! Now I'm describing it I'm even more amazed. But what was it? It seemed to be moving slowly. Was it a constellation? How could it be moving? I don't know, it was only there for a minute or so. I glanced away for just a few seconds but when I looked back it was gone! This star boomerang had disappeared! I just sat down in awe and disbelief. I've never seen anything like it."

Before the Elder could comment, Rob kept speaking.

"Then a short time later I remembered it was one of the signs given by the *'inner voice'*, the second last one I had to see before finding *The First Boomerang*."

"I'm amazed too," the Elder said genuinely. "The Ancestors, the gods and the Universe have guided you profoundly."

Rob nodded happily in agreement.

"The *'inner voice'* called it *"Cosmic Boomerang,"* but it wasn't until I saw the star boomerang in the night sky that I knew what *"Cosmic Boomerang"* meant!

"Seeing that sign indicated I was very close to the big discovery. And that's what happened the next morning, just yesterday!" Rob exclaimed, pausing for a moment then adding: "What a journey. I've been half way around Australia, or maybe the Cosmos, I'm not sure. But I'm positive this is only the beginning."

"You've found an original symbol, probably *THE* original symbol of Humanity's spirituality. Yet even though many believe there's a spiritual dimension to life, having a symbol in solid form makes the connection accessible to so many more"

"Yeah. Definitely. I can see that. Revealing *The First Boomerang* story is going to be enormous."

The Elder agreed with his eyes and nodded in agreement.

"Now we must ask for guidance about how, when and where to tell the world."

"You still ask for guidance?"

"Oh definitely. I've gained insights and knowledge over time, but I'm a very small part, just an instrument of higher energies, like the Ancestors, like the gods, like the....."

"Like the *Universal Voice...*"

"Yes, exactly. It's all the same energy with different names and forms in various cultures across the world, throughout history."

"Yeah, agreed. Now I'm ready to ask."

"Well, before we do there's local news you should hear about."

"I'm all ears."

"Have you heard the Prime Minister was here?"

"No...No..."

"She said *'SORRY'.*"

"What!"

"She actually said a public *'SORRY'* to all Aboriginal and Torres Strait Islanders for the way we were treated by all governments of the past! In Canberra during our meeting she hinted that an apology was coming. She was convincing at the time, but I didn't know if she would carry it through. But she did. This is a great moment in Australia's history. And she delivered the tjurunga I couldn't retrieve from the Iraqi officials!"

"That is fantastic, really fantastic. There's been a lot of journeys going on around here," Rob suggested in a typically understated Australian way, by including several major achievements in a single sentence. "The Cosmic Timing must be right," he added.

There was also another important journey in progress overseas.

"How is your search going?" Rob asked. "What about the third tjurunga?"

"Everything's flowing. You brought the Water tjurunga back from Adelaide, the Prime Minister handed me the Eagle-hawk tjurunga and the final 'lost' one is coming from Germany, and it represents the Star Ancestor. I had an email yesterday saying its return has been expedited after the PM's words right here on Anzac Hill just three days ago. The staff at Lutheran Headquarters in Hermannsburg carefully packed it and Qantas will fly it from Frankfurt to Sydney, then home to Alice..."

"It's so close eh. That's wonderful. Your Songline's going to come to life again. I'll bet the Ancestors are ready to lead the singing."

"They're always singing Rob. They're just waiting for us to re-create the proper circumstances so we can join in."

The Elder tilted his head back and looked skyward as if he was seeing the stars before they came out. Perhaps he was looking at the Dreamtime trajectory of *The First Boomerang*. Maybe he was already holding the last of the three lost tjurunga. Or, was he with the Ancestors preparing for ceremony?

www.ingramcontent.com/pod-product-compliance
Lightning Source LLC
Chambersburg PA
CBHW031108030726
47496CB00002BA/433